THE STONE CANAL

Also from Legend by Ken MacLeod:

THE STAR FRACTION

THE STONE CANAL

Ken MacLeod

F/470218

LEGEND

To Sharon and Michael

Thanks to Carol, Sharon and Michael for love (and peace) while writing the book; to Iain Banks for reading the draft in good drinking time; to Mic Cheetham for believing in it; to John Jarrold for keeping his nerve; to the partisans of Libertaria, and of Nowhere (you know who you are); to Lara Byrne, for an inspiration (and a genotype).

– we have the certainty that matter remains eternally the same in all its transformations, that none of its attributes can ever be lost, and therefore, also, that with the same iron necessity that it will exterminate on the earth its highest creation, the thinking mind, it must somewhere else and at another time again produce it.

Frederick Engels *Dialectics of Nature*

Contents

The Machinery of Freedom

I

Human Equivalent

HE WOKE, AND remembered dying.

His eyes and mouth opened and he drew in a long harsh gasp of thin air. His legs kicked and his fingers rasped the sand. Then his limbs sprawled and he lay still. Each breath came quickly, as if he suspected that the next would be his last. His fingers hooked the soil as he stared upwards at a deep-blue, fathomless sky.

He rolled over and clambered to his feet and looked around. He was standing on the lower slope of a low knoll above a canal. The canal was about twenty metres wide. For a few hundred metres on either side of it, the ground was sparsely covered with grass and shrubs. Beyond that the ground was a reddish colour.

The man looked back and forth along the canal. It ran from horizon to horizon, a line of blue along the middle of a band of green, bisecting the great circle of red beneath a dome of blue. Near the top of the sky a sun shone bright and small; the man looked up at it, then raised his arm with his thumb up as if in a greeting. He moved his fist with the extended thumb back and forth, sighting along his arm with one eye. He smiled and nodded.

A few metres up-slope from where he stood, the hillside was broken, exposing the rock beneath the thin layer of soil and roots. Among the tumbled, jagged boulders lay an ellipsoid pod a metre long, half a metre across and twenty-five centimetres deep. Its upper and lower halves were identical, and reflective; between them was a sort of equatorial band where duller, hinged or jointed surfaces could be seen. The man stepped up and examined it with a wary look. Then he stooped closer, in an intent inspection, and abruptly turned away.

He ran down to the edge of the canal and stood gazing into it for some minutes. He took off his clothes – boots and socks, a padded

3

jacket and trousers, tee-shirt and shorts – and began moving his hands all over his body, as if washing himself without water. Then he put his clothes back on and walked up the slope to the pod.

He put his hands on his hips and frowned down at it. He opened his mouth, closed it, looked around and shrugged.

'My name is Jon Wilde,' he said. 'Who are you?' He didn't look or sound as if he expected an answer.

'I'm a human-equivalent machine,' said the pod, in an attempt at a pleasant, conversational voice. The man jumped slightly.

'I'm about to stand up,' the human-equivalent machine added. 'Please don't be alarmed.'

Jon Wilde took a couple of steps back, his boots dislodging grit and pebbles on the slope. Clicking, grating noises came from the machine as four metal limbs unfolded from its central portion. They looked identical, with clawed digits, wrists or ankles, elbows or knees. Two of the limbs swivelled and swung downwards, the jointed extensions at their ends clamping to the ground. The machine straightened its limbs and rocked to its feet – if such they could be called. It stood at about half the man's height, its posture and proportions vaguely suggestive of a man running in a combative crouch, head down.

Wilde gazed down at it.

'Where are we?' he asked.

'On New Mars,' the machine answered.

'How did I get here?'

There was a silence of perhaps a minute. Wilde frowned, looked around, leaned forward just as the machine spoke again:

'I made you.'

The machine turned and strode away.

Wilde scrambled after it.

'Where are you going?'

'Ship City,' said the machine. 'The nearest human habitation.' It paused for a moment. 'I'd come along, if I were you.'

The human-equivalent machine and the man it claimed to have made walked together along the bank of the canal. Every so often the man turned his head to look at the machine. Once or twice he got as far as opening his mouth, but he always turned away again as if the question or remark on his mind were too ridiculous for words.

After an hour and twenty minutes the man stopped. The machine stopped after another couple of strides and stood rocking slightly on its metal legs.

'I'm thirsty,' the man said. The water in the canal was sluggish, flecked with green algae. He eyed it dubiously. 'D'you know if that stuff's safe to drink?'

'It isn't,' said the machine. 'And I can't make it safe, without using up an amount of energy I'd rather keep. However, I can assure you that if you go on walking, with perhaps the occasional rest, you'll drink in a bar in Ship City tonight.'

'Mars bars?' Wilde said, and laughed. 'I always wanted to hang out in Mars bars.'

Another hour passed and Wilde said, 'Hey, I can see it!'

The machine didn't need to ask him. Without missing a step, it smoothly extended its legs until it was striding along with its pod almost on a level with the man's head, and it too saw what Wilde had seen: the jagged irregularities at the horizon.

'Ship City,' the machine said.

'Give me a break,' the man shouted, hurrying to keep up. 'No need to go like a Martian fighting-machine.'

The machine's steady pace didn't slacken.

'You're stronger than you think,' it said. The man caught up with it and marched alongside.

'I like that,' the machine added, after a while. '"Like a Martian fighting-machine". Heh-heh.'

Its laugh needed working on if it was going to sound at all human.

They walked on. Their shadows lengthened in front of them, and the city slowly appeared above a horizon that, for the man, was unfamiliarly but not unexpectedly close. The irregularities differentiated into tall, bristling towers connected by arches and slender, curved bridges; domes and blocks became apparent between the towers, among which a matted encrustation of smaller buildings spread out from the city, obscured by a low haze.

The small sun set behind them, and within fifteen minutes the night surrounded them. The man stopped walking, and the machine stopped too.

Jon Wilde turned around several times, scanning from the zenith to the horizon and back as if looking for something he might recognise. He found nothing, and faced at last the machine, dim in the starlight that reflected like frost from its hull and flanks.

'How far?' The words came from a dry mouth. He waved a hand at the blazing, freezing, crowded sky. 'How long?'

'Hey, Jon Wilde,' the machine said. It had got its conversational tone right. 'If I knew, I would tell you. Same spiral, different arm, that's all I know. We're talking memory numbers, man, we're talking *geological time*.'

The two beings contemplated each other for a moment, then hastened the last few miles towards the city's multiplying lights.

Stras Cobol, by the Stone Canal. Part of the human quarter. A good place to get lost. Surveillance systems integrate the view –

A three-kilometre strip of street, the canal-bank on one side, buildings on the other, their height a bar-chart of property values in a long swoop from the centre's tall towers to the low shacks and shanties at the edge of town where the red sand blows in off the desert and family-farm fusion plants glow in the dark. On the same trajectory the commerce spills increasingly out from behind the walls and windows, on to the pavement stalls and hawkers' trays. All along this street there's a brisk jostle of people and machines, some working, some relaxing as the light leaves the sky.

Among all the faces in that crowd, something focuses in on one face. A woman's face, tracked briefly as she threads her way between the other bodies on the street. The system's evaluation routines categorise her appearance swiftly: apparent age about twenty, height about one metre sixty – well below average – mass slightly above average. Her height is lifted within the normal range by high-heeled shoes, her figure accentuated by a long-sleeved, skinny-rib sweater and a long narrow skirt, skilfully slit so it doesn't impede her quick steps. Shoulder-length hair, black and thick, sways around a face pretty and memorable but not flipping any switches on the system's scalar aesthetic – wide cheekbones, full lips, large eyes with green irises and suddenly narrowing, zeroing-in pupils that look straight at the hidden lens that's giving her this going-over. One eye closes in what looks like a wink.

And she's gone. She's vanished from the system's sight, she's just a blurry anomaly, a floating speck in its vision and a passing unease in its mind as its attention is turned forcibly to a stall-holder wheeling his urn of hot oil across a nearby junction without due care and attention and the we-got-an-emerging-situation-on-our-hands program kicks in ...

But she's still there, still walking fast, and we're still with her, for reasons which will sometime become clear. We're in her space, in her time, in her head.

Her pretty little head contains and conceals a truly Neo-Martian mind, an intellect vast and cool and unsympathetic as the man said, and right now it's in combat consciousness. She's running Spy, not Soldier, but Soldier's there, ready to toggle in at the first sign of trouble. Body movement's being handled by Secretary, in leisure-time mode: her walk is late-for-a-date hurry and doing fine so far. Except she's walked farther and faster than any girl in such a circumstance normally would, and the skin over her Achilles tendons is rubbing raw. She sets a Surgeon sub-routine to work and – its warning heeded – the pain switches sensibly off.

She allows herself a diffuse glow of pleasure at having spotted and subverted the surveillance system. Her real danger, she knows, comes from human pursuit. She can't see behind her because she daren't switch on her sonar and radar, but she uses every other clue that catches her eye. Every echo, every reflection: in windows and bits of scrap metal and the shiny fenders of vehicles, even in the retinae of people walking in the opposite direction – all go to build an all-round visual field. Constantly updated, an asynchronous palimpsest where people and vehicles in full colour and 3D pass out of her cone of vision and into a wider sphere where they become jerky cartoon figures, wire outlines intermittently blocked in with colour as a scrap of detail flashes back from in front. (She could keep the colour rendering if she wanted to, let the visual and the virtual merge seamlessly, but she doesn't have the processing power to spare right now. Spy is a demanding mind-tool and it eats resources.)

It tags a warning, unsubtle red arrowheads jabbing at one face, then another, both far behind her. She throws enhancement at those distant dots, blowing them up into something recognisable, and recognises them. Two men, heavies employed by her owner. Their names aren't on file but she's glimpsed them at various times over the years.

7

Spy analyses their movements and reports that they haven't spotted her: they're searching, not tracking. Not yet.

She sees a bar sign coming up on her left, 'The Malley Mile' spelled out in fizzing rainbow neon. By good luck the nearest pedestrian coming her way is huge and walking close to the sides of the buildings. She lets the two-metre-thirty, two-hundred-kilo bulk of the giant pass her – the only noticeable thing about him is the inappropriately floral scent of the shampoo he's most recently used on his orangey pelt – and as he occludes any view of her from behind she nips smartly through the doorway.

It's a trashy, tacky place, this joint. Lots of wood and metal. The music is a thumping noise in the background, like machinery. The ventilation isn't coping well with the smoke, and somebody's already had a poppy-pipe. Freshwater fish are grilling somewhere in the back. Low ceiling, dim lights. Her vision adjusts without a blink and it's daylight, give or take the odd wavelength. Spy takes over fully for a staking-out, second-long sweep of the room. There's surveillance, of course, but it's just the hostelry's own system, exactly as smart and dangerous as a dog. She pings it anyway, leaving it with a low-wattage conviction that this *person* who's just walked in is *nice* and has just given it a pat on the head and can be safely ignored from now on.

There are a couple of dozen people in The Malley Mile: farmworkers and mechanics on bar stools, and office-workers – mostly young women – around the round tables. Looks like they've come in here for a drink on their way home from work, and stayed for a few more. Good. She sees a notice: no concealed weapons. She takes a pistol from the purse she's carrying and sticks it in the waistband of her skirt and walks up to the bar. The girls around the tables notice her, the men on the stools notice her, but that's just because she's pretty, not because she looks out of place.

The barman's another giant, some brain-boosted gigantopith or whatever (she's never had occasion to sort out the hominid genera) and he's slumped sadly on his elbows, wrists overhanging the near edge of the bar counter. He turns away from the gladiators on the television and smiles at her, or at any rate bares his yellow fangs.

'Yesh?'

'A Dark Star, please.'

Without getting up the barman reaches for bottles and mixes her a rum and cola.

'Eyshe?'

'Yes please.' She's careful with the sibilants; the urge to slide into mimicry (it's a bug in Spy, actually) is hard to resist. She lets Spy handle the process of paying, selecting the right grubby note from her filched collection of promissories. Gold values she can handle in any of her frames of mind, but crops and machine-parts, land and labour-time are foreign to most of them.

The ice clinks as she takes her drink to an unoccupied table nearest to the end wall. She sits down with her back to that wall. She lays her purse, and her pistol, casually on the table. She sips her drink, lights a cigarette, and keeps an eye on the door as if waiting for her friends or boyfriend to turn up.

The two photofit faces currently hovering in her pattern-recognition and target-acquisition software might come through the door any minute now. If she's lucky, they don't know she's armed. She's almost certain they don't know about Spy, and Soldier, and all the other routines she's loaded up. They're expecting Secretary, and Sex, and Self, who between them can't raise more than a kick or bite or scratch. They can handle that, and as for the others here ... once the heavies flash their cards the customers will watch her being dragged out of the place with all the empathy and solidarity and compassion and concern that they'd give to the recovery of a stolen vehicle.

But there are people in this district who don't see things that way, and if the repossession guys – the greps, as the slang goes – don't come in and find her, or if they do and she gets away, she'll be off into the back streets to seek human allies.

That's all as may be. Her owner might by now have discovered just what hardware and software she's packing, and he'll have someone and/or something more formidable on her tracks.

She keeps her eyes on the door and her fingers close to the pistol.

'English spoken here?'

Wilde scuffed the surface of the canal-bank path – it had changed from trodden dust to a strip of fused sand which broadened and merged with the street ahead, the permanent way made from the

9

same material as if the finger of a god had drawn the lines from space – and waited for the machine to reply.

The city had grown on the horizon as they got closer, eventually into a huge, vaguely organic-looking jumble of soaring spiky towers, their visible structure like the interiors of bones or the skeletons of sea creatures, their outlines picked out by lights. What had looked from a distance like some matted undergrowth was now resolved into a fringe of low buildings which – unlike all the other shanty-towns Wilde had seen – appeared to extend in through the main body of the city on whose edge they now stood. To their right and left were fields. The bulky moving presences of machines in those fields were the only traffic they had so far encountered. Lights had passed over, but it was difficult to tell whether they were natural or artificial. Once, something huge and silent and leaving a green after-image or trail had rushed above their heads, above the city and made a distant flash beyond.

'Waterfall,' the machine had explained, unhelpfully.

Now it shifted on its feet and answered Wilde's question. 'You'll be understood,' it said hesitantly. 'English is the predominant language. Your usage and accent – and mine, I might add – may seem a little quaint.'

'Before we go any farther,' Wilde said, his gaze flicking from the buildings under the first street-lights ahead to the machine, 'get me straight on a couple of things. First, is it normal to be seen talking to a machine? I mean, are – robots? – like you common around here?'

'You could say that,' said the machine dryly.

'OK. Next item on the agenda as far as I'm concerned is getting something to eat and a drink and a place to crash out. Am I right in thinking that I'll have to pay for it?'

'Oh yes,' said the machine.

'And you don't happen to have some money stashed away in that shell of yours?'

'No, but I can do better than that. See the second building along the road? It's a mutual bank.'

Wilde said nothing, although his mouth opened.

'You do remember what that is, don't you?'

Wilde laughed. 'So I get to raise some cash by mortgaging my property?' He gestured at the clothes he stood up in. 'That's not much help –'

The machine gave a creditable impersonation of a polite cough.

'Oh.' Wilde looked at it with a renewed, speculative interest. 'I see.'

He set off along the road, ahead of the machine for the first time since they'd met. The machine lurched into motion after him.

'Just don't get the wrong idea,' it said, its voice as stiff as its gait.

One of the girls at the nearest table is giving a rendering of the pub's signature song in an authentically dire accent, full of maudlin yearning.

> *'If Ayyyye could walk acraaawrse the ryyyinbow*
> *that shiiiines acraaawrse the Malley Mile ...'*

Self knows that the Malley Mile is a real place, and that both the sense of loss and the rainbow effect refer to aspects of its reality that – strangely, or is it just part of the program? – bring tears pricking to even her cold eyes. Scientist is yammering on about it, but she doesn't want to know right now.

She's just settled down with her third drink, burning the alcohol straight to energy but remembering to emulate the effect, when the door bangs open and a girl walks in who sure isn't some office-worker deciding the weekend starts here.

She's tall and thin, though her flak-jacket makes her look broad. Narrow jeans, spacer boots, a big automatic holstered on her hip. On her other hip she's carrying a large bag with a strap taking the strain to her shoulder. Short blonde hair lying close to her skull. Face too bony to be bonny. The main things going for it are her bright blue eyes and her big smile, which at this moment is turned on the men at – and the man behind – the bar.

She walks up to the bar and orders a beer, and as she drinks it she chats to one or two of the guys, and while she's chatting she reaches into her big satchel and hauls out fresh-looking tabloid newspapers and carefully counts coins from the men who take them. Some of them take them as if they're keen to read them, others with a show of reluctance and a lot of banter, but most just shake their heads or shrug and go back to their own conversations and watching the television screen, where somebody's just about to take a sudden death shoot-out. All the while the girl's every so often glancing around the room in a way that has Spy torn between admiration at the unobtrusive way she does it and anxiety that she's looking for someone quite close to Spy's hard little heart, namely Self.

The girl at the bar goes on talking to the men at the bar for another few minutes, then eases herself casually from the stool and takes a handful of papers and tries to sell them to the office-girls. She's only successful at one table, and then she's walking to the last table where the dark-haired woman sits alone.

A shot echoes. Two hands jolt towards two pistols, then retract as a ragged cheer from the screen and from those watching it indicates that it's just a death penalty being scored.

And then, grinning and shaking her head, she's standing there looking down. 'Jumpy tonight, aren't we?' she says.

Spy and Soldier are jumpy indeed, jostling for possession, and it's all Spy can do to modulate Soldier's sharp command into a smooth, low-voiced request: 'Just don't stand between me and the door.'

The tall woman steps smartly sideways. She looks surprised, but she doesn't go away.

'Hi,' she says. 'My name's Tamara. What's yours?'

Self takes over. She keeps her hand where it is.

'Dee,' she says. 'Dee Model.'

'Ah,' says Tamara. 'I see.' Her eyes widen slightly as she says it, then look away as if, for the moment, she's at a loss. 'Mind if I sit down?'

Dee gestures to her to do just that. She takes the seat to Dee's right, between her and the bar.

'What's that paper you're selling?' Dee asks.

Tamara slides a copy across the table. Its masthead says *The Abolitionist* in quaint irregular lettering with barbed serifs. The articles, which Spy assimilates in about two seconds and which gradually seep through to Self, are an odd mix: news snippets about labour disputes; technical articles about assemblers and reactors and stuff; some columns of a sort of paranoid gossip about the doings of various important people, in which Dee's owner's name appears here and there; and long rambling theoretical pieces about machine intelligence.

Dee puts it down, having just given it what looks like the most casual, superficial glance. She wonders for a moment if this is a trap, but Spy thinks it very unlikely: these are exactly the sort of ideas she'd expected to find in this area, and it's obvious that Tamara's espousal of them is completely, perhaps resignedly, familiar to those around her. (That those around her might be part of some elaborate set-up doesn't occur to Dee, or even to Spy: although their background is rich in intrigue and betrayal, they lack the ramifying conspiratorial imagination that would be second nature if they lived in a state.) Dee tries to keep her wild hope out of her voice.

'Do you really think that human-equivalent machines are, well, equivalent to humans? That they have rights?'

'Oh, sure,' Tamara says. 'Don't you?'

'Hmm,' says Dee. 'Let me get you a drink.'

When she returns she's carrying Tamara's satchel. She swings it under the table and places her pistol back on the top. Tamara waves away the offer of a cigarette. Dee lights up and leans close. Soldier takes over second place from Spy, who doesn't like what's going on at all. The most Spy can do is make sure no-one overhears. Another probe into the room's electronics, and the music's volume goes up a few decibels.

'I'm a machine,' Dee says.

Tamara's obviously half-suspected this, just from the name, but just as obviously doesn't quite believe it.

'You coulda fooled me, girl,' she says.

Dee shrugs. 'Most of my body was grown in a vat or something. Most of my brain's artificial. Technically and legally I'm a decerebrate clone manipulated by a computer. Neither component is anything but an object, but *I* feel like I'm a person.'

Tamara's nodding vigorously, the way people do.

'And I need your help,' Dee adds. 'I've escaped and my owner's agents are searching for me along this street.'

Tamara's head stops moving and her mouth opens.

'Oh shit,' she says.

Dee stares at her. 'What's the matter?' she asks. 'Isn't this what you want?' She glances at *The Abolitionist*. 'Or is this all – ?'

Tamara closes her eyes for a moment and shakes her head slightly. 'It ain't like that,' she says, looking embarrassed. She steeples her fingers to the sides of her nose and talks quietly into this adequate mask. 'Of course I'll help you ... We'll help you. It's just – this isn't the main thing we do, you know? We've persuaded a few people to free machines, but a machine freeing itself doesn't happen very often. Not that you get to hear about, anyway.' She's grinning again, back on track. 'You into making a fight about this?'

'I'm ready for any kind of fight,' Dee says. 'Who's this "we"?'

'Half a street full of anarchists,' Tamara says.

Dee doesn't understand what this means, exactly, but it sounds hopeful, especially the way Tamara says it.

'Can you provide sanctuary?' Dee asks.

'We're probably your best bet,' Tamara says abstractedly. 'There hasn't really been a proper fight on this issue. It'd be quite something to be the ones to pick it. Bloody hell. This could shake up the city, the whole damn' planet!'

Dee tries to think of a reason why this should be so, but apart from a bit of handwaving from Scientist there doesn't seem to be any information on file.

'Why?' she asks.

Tamara stares at her. 'You are definitely a machine,' she says, smiling past the side of her hand. 'Or you'd know the answer.'

Dee considers this, trying to formulate Scientist's bare hints into speech.

'It's because of the fast folk, isn't it?' she suggests brightly. 'And the dead?'

Tamara's eyebrows flash upwards for a split second. 'That's the smart worry,' she says. 'It's the stupid worries that are the real problem ... I think you'll find. Anyway. Are the greps likely to be hanging around outside?'

Dee thinks about this.

'No,' she says. 'Not now. But there might be others.'

Tamara drains her glass. 'Let's go,' she says.

They're just getting their things together when the door opens and a young man and an old robot walk in. The man looks haggard and is wearing desert gear, and the robot's just a standard construction rig. Tamara doesn't give them a second glance but Dee watches as the man pauses at the doorway and looks around the room with a curious intentness.

He sees her, and his gaze stops.

He takes a step forward. His face warps as if under acceleration

14

into an awful, anguished look, more a distortion of the features than an expression – it's unreadable, inhuman. At the same time Dee can feel the robot's questing senses scan her body and tap at her brain. Spy and Soldier and Sys move dizzyingly fast in the virtual spaces of her mind, repelling the hack-attack. Her own reactive hacking attempts are deflected by some shielding as impenetrable as – and perhaps no other than – the robot's hard metal shell. The robot makes a jerky forward lurch as the man takes a second step towards her. All of Dee's several selves start screaming at her to get out.

She has her pistol in both hands in front of her and the table's kicked over and Tamara's beside her. The bar falls silent except for the thudding music and the baying of a stadium audience on the television.

'Out the back!' Tamara says through clenched teeth. She shifts, guiding Dee to the right, walking backwards, pushing through a door that swings shut in front of them. They're in a corridor, dark except for smudges of yellow light and thick with smells of beer and fish.

Dee enhances her vision and sees Tamara blinking hard as she whirls around. From the way she's moving it's obvious that Tamara can see in the dark at least as well as Dee can.

'Come on!' Tamara calls, and plunges along the corridor. Dee kicks off her shoes, snatches them up and races after Tamara, down a flight of steps and around a couple of corners into an even darker, smellier corridor, in fact a tunnel. Dee can hear the traffic overhead and taste the water-vapour in the air increasing with every step. She glances back and there's no indication of pursuit. The water in the air tastes rusty as they slide to a halt before a heavy metal door at the end. Tamara fumbles with bolts at the top and bottom of the door until they clang back. She pauses, listening, then pulls the door slowly open, keeping herself behind it until it's almost parallel to the wall. She peers around it all the while, looking out and not behind.

'Wait,' she whispers. The warning isn't necessary: Soldier has kicked in and Dee is standing flat to the wall of the tunnel two metres from the doorway and only very slowly edging forward. As her cone of vision widens she sees that the door opens on to a narrow stone shelf barely above the surface of the canal, which is about fifty metres wide at this point. The lights from the opposite street, Rue Pascal, are reflected in the canal's choppy black wavelets, stirred up by the frequent wakes of plying boats. From the sound of the slap and sigh of water she knows that the outboard motor, just at the edge of her view, belongs to a small dinghy moored close to the door.

On the metre-wide quay a shadow moves – her own.

She turns to look back down the tunnel. A light, far back in the corridor, has just come on and something is moving between here and the source. Tamara, a moment later, notices it too and she steps from behind the door. She glances at Dee, points outwards, and then makes a two-fingered chopping motion to left and right. Together they jump out of the door, turning in opposite directions as they steady themselves, crouching on the quay.

Dee sees the walled bank of the canal rising three metres to street level, and the quay running alongside the canal to a junction a few hundred metres away. Boats and barges are moored along it, doors and tunnel-mouths punctuate it. There's nobody moving on it at the moment.

Over her shoulder she sees a similar view in the opposite direction, except that the canal extends out to the dark of the desert. She hears at least one set of running footsteps, now about half-way along the tunnel. She gestures frantically to Tamara.

'Get in the boat!' Tamara says. She hauls the rope and the little inflatable bumps against the quay's lip. It barely rocks as Tamara steps in, sways wildly as Dee follows. She finds herself flat on her back in the wet well of the boat on top of her purse and shoes, her feet getting in the way of Tamara's as the human woman casts off and starts the engine. Dee's glad she's in this undignified position as Tamara opens the throttle and the engine's whine rises to a scream and the front of the boat lifts. The boat surges out across the water and Tamara brings it over in a long curve that has them shooting straight along the middle of the canal to yells and curses from other boats by the time a distant figure appears at the mouth of the tunnel.

It's the man who recognised her. He shouts after them, but whatever he says is lost in the engine's note. Tamara slews the tiller again and they swing around in a wall of spray and head for an opening, passing under Stras Cobol and into a branch canal that runs between high windowless walls less than five metres apart. Tamara eases off the engine and Dee cautiously sits up.

'Lucky for us the boat was there,' she says.

Tamara snorts. 'It's my boat! I left it there an hour ago when I started my round of the bars.'

Dee smiles wanly. 'Where are we going?'

'Circle Square,' Tamara says. 'Precinct of the living dead. Crawling with bad artists, freethinking machines, and anarchists arguing about what to do in an anarchy. Safe.'

Dee isn't sure how to take this.

'Thanks for getting me out.'

Tamara looks past Dee, at the dark water. 'Yeah well ... I gotta admit I'm not sure what I got you out *from*. That guy and the robot didn't look like greps to me. Did you recognise them, or what?'

Dee's already been through this in her head. 'No,' she says, her voice cold. 'But he recognised me. I'm certain of that.'

'Me too,' Tamara says dryly. 'Just I don't think it was from a pic. He looked like he wanted to kill you, that first moment. Kill somebody, anyway, but shit, coulda been shock or some'ing – hey!' She stares at Dee's face. 'You ain't *dead*, are you? You and him might've had previous.' She looks quite pleased at this speculation. 'It's all right, you can tell me. We're cool about the dead as well as machines, OK?'

Dee doesn't know much about the dead. Once, when she was new, she'd thought that she could hear the dead: press her ear to the wall and hear them talking, furiously, in dead languages. But it was just the sough of the machinery, the 'ware, the marrow in the city's cold bones.

So her owner had told her, his laughter almost kind. With a harsher tone in his voice he'd added: 'The dead are gone. And they aren't coming back. Most of them ... ah, forget it.'

And obediently, she had.

She isn't sure whether to be annoyed at Tamara's speculation, but it's just the woman's human limitations after all: in a way she's making the same animistic mistake – thinking that machinery that sounded alive must at the very least be dead – that she herself had made way back when she was just getting her brain into gear.

So she gives Tamara a smug smile and says, 'You can scan my skull if you like, and you'll see me for yourself.'

'S'pose your body's a copy? A clone?'

Dee hasn't thought of this before, and the idea shakes her more than she cares to show. She shrugs. 'It's possible.'

'There you go,' Tamara says. 'That'd make whatever it was with that guy just a case of mistaken identity. No worries.'

She guns the engine again. Swept from the walls' dank ledges, seal-rats squeak indignantly in their wake.

'It *isn't her*,' said the robot, its voice more like a radio at low volume than a human speaking quietly. 'So forget it. Chasing after her won't get you anywhere. She's just a fucking machine.'

Wilde had trudged back up the tunnel, apologised to the bar-keeper, paid for the breakages and ordered a stiff drink as well as a large beer to accompany his grilled fish. The robot, propping itself up with a chair opposite him, had attracted no comment.

Wilde wiped his mouth with the back of his hand and glared at the machine.

'She didn't look like a machine. She looked like a real woman. She looked like –'

He stopped, in some distress.

'Cloned,' the machine said implacably.

'But why? Why her? Who would –?'

He stared at the impervious pod. 'No!'

'Yes,' said the machine. 'He's here.'

2

Pleistocene People

I REMEMBER HIM leaning his elbow on the bar in the Queen
Margaret Union, waiting for our pints, and saying: 'We'll be
there, Wilde! We'll see it! *One* fucking computer, that's all it'll take,
one machine that's smarter than us and away they'll go.'

Reid's eyes were shining, his voice happy. He was like that when
an idea took hold of him, and he prophesied. It sounds prophetic
enough now, but it wasn't an original idea even then, in December
1975. (That's AD, by the way.) He'd got it from a book.

'How d'you mean, "away"?' I asked.

'If we,' he said, slowing down, 'can make a machine that's
smarter than us, it can make another machine that's smarter than
the first. And so on, faster and faster. Runaway evolution, man.'

'And where does that leave us?'

Reid pushed a heavy mug of cider towards me.

'Behind,' he said happily. 'Like apes in a city of people. Come on,
let's find a seat.'

Glasgow University's original Students' Union dated back to
before women were accepted as students. It still hadn't quite caught
up. The female students had their own union building, the QM,
which did allow students of both sexes. It was therefore the one in
which the more radical and progressive male students hung out, and
the better by far for picking up girls.

Which was what we had in mind: a few pints with our mates in
the bar for the first part of the evening, and then down to the disco
about ten o'clock and see if anybody fancied a dance. The reason for
getting in as much drinking as you could beforehand was that
diving into the queue in front of the disco bar was best reserved for
when you had to buy a round for your companions or – better – a
drink for a girl who'd just danced with you.

19

The bar – the union bar rather than the disco bar – was fairly quiet at this time in the evening. So we got a good seat in the place, the one that ran most of the way around the back wall, from which we could see everybody who came in and – just by getting up slightly and turning around – could check out the state of play on the dance-floor below.

I rolled a skinny Golden Virginia cigarette and raised my pint of Strongbow.

'Cheers,' Reid said.

'Slainte,' I said.

We grinned at our respective manglings of each other's national toast – to my ear, Reid had said something like 'Cheeurrsh', and to his I'd said 'Slendge.' Reid was from the Isle of Skye, where his great-grandfather had come to work as a shepherd after the Clearances. I was from North London, and we were both somewhat out of place in Central Scotland. We hadn't known each other very long, having met a month earlier at a seminar on War Communism. The seminar was sponsored by *Critique*, a left-wing offshoot of the Institute for Soviet Studies, where I was doing a one-year M.Sc. course in the Economics of Socialism.

I didn't agree with their ideas, but I'd found the *Critique* clique (as I privately called them) congenial, and stimulating. They were the Institute's Young Turks, Left Opposition, Shadow Cabinet and Government-In-Exile. They regarded both mainstream and Marxist critical theories of the Soviet Union as all of a piece with the most starry-eyed, fellow-travelling naivety in their assumption that it was at least a new system, when it was hardly even a society.

The seminar was a lunchtime session. As always, it was crowded, not so much because of its popularity but because of a shrewd tactic of always booking a room just a little smaller than the expected attendance. In that ill-assorted congregation of exiles – from America, from Chile, from South Africa and from the Other Side itself – Reid, hunched in a new denim jacket, constantly relighting, puffing and forgetting his roll-up, his lank black hair falling around his young and good-looking but somehow weathered face, seemed entirely at home, and the question he'd asked the speaker afterwards showed at least that he knew what he was asking about. But none of us had seen him before, and in the pub later (these seminars had several features in common with socialist meetings, especially the pub afterwards) he'd admitted to being a Trotskyist, which was not surprising, and a computer science student, which was.

The woman sitting next to me was American and also a Trotskyist. Reid was getting up to buy a round and asked her, 'What will you be having?'

'Tomato juice,' she said. He nodded, frowning.

'How come you've not met him, Myra?' I asked as he slouched off to the bar. 'Aren't you in the IMG too?' I'd picked this up while chatting to her occasionally over coffee in the Institute – almost chatting her up, to be honest, because I was rather taken with her. She was tall and incredibly slim, with a blonde bob and a perky, peaky face, the concavities of her orbits and cheeks looking like they'd been delicately, lovingly smoothed into shape with broad thumbs, her grey eyes bright behind huge round glasses.

'I don't go much to meetings,' she admitted with a shake of her head. 'Like I got pissed with comrades urging me to do more in the fight against the fucking Leninist-Trotskyist Faction? I mean, what do these guys think I came to England to get away *from*?'

'You mean Scotland, England?' I drawled derisively, unable to comment on her – to me – utterly incomprehensible remark.

Myra laughed. 'Go give the guy a hand. He seems to be having a problem.'

Reid turned to me with relief. 'I've got everybody's except Myra's. What the hell are "tamadages"?'

'And one tomato juice!' I said to the bar-tender.

'Oh, thanks,' Reid said. He looked up at me. (He'd unconsciously pulled himself up to his full height, something folk often did around me, but he was still looking up.) 'What you were saying back there about the market, that was interesting. The millions of equations stuff.'

'Yeah,' I said, gathering up some of the drinks. 'The millions of equations. And that's not the half of it.' I knew what was coming next, having been around the block several times already on this one.

'Why can't we just use computers?'

'Because,' I said over my shoulder as I threaded my way back to the table, 'without a market, you won't *have* the fucking computers!'

Myra was laughing as I put down the drinks. 'Don't worry about Jon's bourgeois economics,' she said to Dave Reid as we sat down.

'Even the Soviet Union has computers.' She waited for some sign of reassurance in his honestly puzzled face, and added: 'The biggest in the world!'

Reid smiled but went on doggedly: 'Look at IBM. Do *they* bother about market forces? Do they fuck! Friend of mine worked at their factory in Inverkip one summer. He said they supply spare parts anywhere in the world within forty-eight hours, even if it means taking an axe to a mainframe that's already built – and pulling the parts out!'

'Yeah, that sounds just like the Soviet Union,' I said, to general laughter. 'And you sound just like my old man.'

'Is he a socialist?' Reid asked. He sounded incredulous.

'Lifelong SPGB member,' I said.

'SPGB? Oh, brilliant!' Reid said.

'What's the SPGB?' Myra asked. Reid and I both began to say something, then Reid smiled, shrugged and deferred.

I took a long swallow, but it wasn't the beer that I smelt but some strange remembered whiff of mown grass, dog-shit, and vanilla: Speaker's Corner. 'The Socialist Party of Great Britain,' I explained, falling almost automatically into the soapbox cadence of the autodidact agitator, 'set out in 1904, with less than a hundred members, to win a majority of the workers of the world. They already have 800, so they're well on their way. At that rate, the best projections put them on course for a clear majority by the twenty-fifth century.'

'You gotta be kidding,' Myra said.

'He is,' Reid said sternly. 'It's, well, not a bad caricature, I'll give you that. But I've read some of their stuff, and I've never seen that calculation.'

'OK,' I admitted. 'I made that part up. Well actually, my dad made it up. He's a true believer, but he does have a sense of humour and he once wrote a wee program based on population growth and the Party's growth, and ran it on a computer at work.'

'He's a programmer as well, is he?'

'Oh yes. For the London Electricity Board. When he started, debugging meant cleaning the moths off the valves, and I am *not* making that up!'

Reid and Myra and several of the others around the table

laughed. I'd never really held forth like this before, and I had the feeling that I'd made some kind of good impression on the clique.

'The point being,' I added, while everyone was still listening, 'that I've heard all these arguments about how computers will make economic planning a doddle, and I don't buy 'em.'

'You're missing several points here,' Myra interjected, and went on to make them, her moral passion a mirror-image of mine. So I shifted my ground to another passion.

'I don't want a planned society anyway,' I said. 'It doesn't fit in with *my* plans.'

That got a cheap laugh.

'So what are you?' Reid asked. 'A right-winger?'

I sighed. 'I'm an individualist anarchist, actually.'

'"Ey'm en individualist enerchist, eckchelly",' Myra mimicked. 'More like an anachronism. It's a tragedy,' she added with a flourish to the gallery. 'The kid learns some kinda Marxism at his daddy's knee, and he ends up a goddam Proudhonist!'

'Yup,' I said. 'Though it's your compatriot Tucker that I think got it all together.'

'So who's Tucker?' somebody asked.

'Well ...' I began.

We hadn't got any work done that afternoon, but – looking back at it in an economic, calculating kind of way – it was worth it. Most of us ended up drinking cans and coffees back in a basement room of the Institute. Reid and I sat at opposite sides of Myra at the corner of the big table. Sometimes she talked to both of us, sometimes to other people, and again to one of us or the other. When she talked to Reid it was like overhearing the gossip of an extended family quarrel, and I tuned out or turned to other conversations. But she always brought me back into it, with some remark about Vietnam or Portugal or Angola: the real wars and revolutions over which the factions waged their intercontinental fight.

After some time I became aware that there were only the three of us left in the room. I remember Myra's face, her elbows on the table, her thin hands moving as she talked about New York. I was thinking that it sounded just the place I wanted to go, when Reid's chair scraped on the floorboards and he stood up.

'I'll have to be off,' he said. He smiled at Myra for a moment then looked at me and said: 'See you around then, Jon.'

'Yeah, looks like we hang out in the same places,' I said with a grin. 'If I don't bump into you in the next day or two I'll probably see you in the QM on Friday.'

'Don't you disappear on us, Dave,' Myra said. 'Make sure you come to the next seminar, yeah? We need guys like you around *Critique*. You know, like not just academic?'

Reid flushed slightly and then laughed and said, 'Aye, that's what I was thinking myself!' He slung a duffel bag over his shoulder and with a wiping motion of his spread hand waved goodbye.

We heard his desert-boots padding up the stair, the outer door's Yale click shut. It came to me for the first time that he and I had spent the afternoon competing for Myra's regard – or she had spent it testing us. (That was how it started: with Myra. And not, as I thought long afterwards, with Annette. For if Myra had gone with Reid from the first, and I with Annette ...)

Myra settled her chin in her hands, jiggled her specs and looked at me through them.

'Well,' she said. 'An interesting guy, huh?'

'Yes,' I said. 'Very serious.'

'I'm not in the mood for serious, right now.'

She looked at me steadily for a moment and smiled and said: 'Do you want to burn some grass?'

I thought this was some obscure Americanism for sex, and only realised my mistake when she started building an elaborate joint back at her bedsit; but as it turned out I was not that mistaken, after all.

Myra and I didn't have an affair, more a succession of one-night stands. Ten days that shook the world. Neither of us pretended, but I like to think both of us hoped, that more might come of it. But publicly, to each other, we were being very sophisticated, very cool, very liberated about it.

Then she fell for a Chilean resistance hero with a black moustache, and I was astonished at how angry and jealous and possessive I felt. There was a moment, around three in the morning after the evening that Myra told me how, you know, it was very nice, and she really liked me, but she had quite unexpectedly found her feelings for this Latin Leninist just so powerful, so unlike anything she'd ever experienced before, that, well for a start she was seeing him in, like, five minutes ... there was a moment of drinking black coffee from a grubby mug and looking with unbelieving loathing at the ashtray spilling tarry twists of paper while my fingers rolled yet another just to feel the burn on my tongue, when all my circadian rythms troughed at once in an ebb of the blood, a bleeding of the body's heat, when I felt I never wanted to go again to a bed that didn't enfold the promise of Myra's pelvic bones rocking on mine.

And all the time another part of my mind was working away, analysing how absurd it was that this jealousy should be a surprise, and yet another level of my awareness was congratulating myself on being sufficiently stoical and self-understanding to understand that, and to know that this was a straightforward primate emotion which could be borne, and would pass.

I picked up a Pentel and scrawled on a pad: *Pleistocene people with looking-glass eyes*, so I wouldn't forget this cloth-eared insight in the morning, and crashed out. Still aching, but suddenly confident I had the measure of jealousy and unexpected, unrequited love.

At the same time as Myra and I were carefully, and in her case successfully, not falling for each other, I'd fallen for Reid. There's the love that (no thanks to God) now dares to shout its name, and there's another love that doesn't know what its name bloody *is*, and this was it. Our minds came together like magnets, with a clash.

Reid was stocky and dark, with well-proportioned Celtic features; I was tall and wiry, with hair I kept cropped to disguise its thinness even then, and a nose that had always had me cast as a Red Indian when I was a kid. Reid was gauche, I was suave; but Reid's awkwardness was something he shrugged off, and rose above with a kind of grace, whereas I felt every social occasion a constant test of wits. Reid's parents were religious – Free Kirk – and had done their best to inculcate the same principles in him; mine were staunch Marxist materialists, but had taken a laissez-faire attitude to my philosophical education. At times, for all Reid's accounts of questions answered by clips around the head or floods of tears, I felt that his parents' firm line had shown the deeper concern for his welfare.

Reid was a communist, I a libertarian; but he had a prickly independence of mind, a dogged tendency to worry at difficulties in the doctrines his sect espoused. I sometimes suspected I had too easy a scepticism, too catholic a confidence that my shaky pile of books by Proudhon and Tucker, Herbert and Spencer, Robert Heinlein and Robert Anton Wilson was building up to a reliable launch-tower of the mind.

Another thing I liked about Reid was that I got drunk faster with him than with anyone else; hence, the Friday evenings.

Reid and I talked some more about 'the computers taking over' (which was how people talked back then about the Singularity), then moved on to the current *New Scientist* article on catastrophe theory, about which Reid was sceptical ('like a bourgeois version of dialectics', was how he put it). After science, politics: the hot topic was Portugal, where the far left had just over-reached itself in what looked like a cack-handed attempt at a military coup.

'There's a good article here about it,' Reid said, digging out from inside his jacket a copy of *Red Weekly*, the newspaper of the International Marxist Group. 'Slagging off what *Socialist Worker* has to say. Well, I haven't read it myself yet, but it looks good.'

'OK, OK,' I said. 'I'll buy it. Sectarian polemic is one thing you guys are good at.'

'We'll get you in the end,' Reid grinned as I bought the paper.

'Or I'll get you,' I said.

Reid shrugged. 'That's not how it works,' he said. He started rolling a cigarette, talking in a tired voice. 'People don't stop being socialists and become something else. They just become *nothing*, or join the Labour Party – same difference.'

'*I* stopped being a socialist,' I pointed out.

'Yeah, but that's different, come on. It'd be like me saying I stopped being a Christian. It was just something I was brought up to, and as soon as I started thinking for myself I dropped it. Same with you, right?'

'Maybe,' I said. 'Mind you, it was never shoved down my throat every Sunday.' But I uneasily remembered how little it had taken – some anarchist summary of Tucker, I think – to precipitate every doubt I'd ever had about my inherited faith.

'I hope I always understand things the way I do now,' Reid went on, 'because it makes sense, it's ahead of anything else on offer. But if I ever forget, or you know, lose the place –'

'Or realise you've been wrong all along.'

'– all right, that's how it'll seem, that's what I'll tell myself –'

He grinned sourly, his tongue out to lick his Rizla, giving himself a momentary diabolic, gargoyle appearance. 'But if that ever happens,' he finished, rolling the cigarette up and lighting it, 'I'll be damned if I become an idealistic fighter for the other side. I'll just look out for myself, one way or another.'

'But that's what I believe in right now!' I said cheerfully. 'Look out for number one. I'm not an idealistic fighter for anything.'

'That's what you think,' Reid said. 'You're an anarchist out of pure, innocent self-interest? Oh, sure. Face it, man, you *care*. You're a socialist at heart.'

I liked him enough, and he said it lightly enough, for me not to be offended.

'Nah, that's not how it is at all,' I said. 'I really do have a selfish reason for wanting a world without states: I want to live forever. Seriously. I want to make it to the ships. A planet occupied by organised gangs of nuclear-armed nutters is not my idea of a safe environment.'

Most people laughed at me when I said this, but Reid didn't. One of the things we had in common was an interest in science fiction and technological possibilities, which fitted right in with the rest of what I believed. In theory it fitted in with Marxism too, but I knew that Reid's comrades regarded it as ideologically unsound, as if the only far-out futuristic speculation allowed was the IMG's latest perspectives document. His stacks of *Galaxy* and *Analog* were stashed in a cupboard of his bedsit, like pornography.

'It seems a bit much to expect,' Reid said. 'We picked the wrong century to be born in. I reckon we'll just have to take our chances like the rest of the poor sods.'

I held my cigarette at arm's length and looked at it. 'And we're not doing much for our chances.'

'I see it as a race with medical science,' Reid said. 'Mine's a pint of Export, by the way.'

I noticed our empty glasses and jumped up, contrite at not noticing sooner. When I came back Reid was deep in the paper he'd sold me, and I wasn't sure I wanted to push the conversation farther at the moment, so I leaned back and let my mind drift for a bit. The place was filling up. The juke-box was playing Rod Stewart's 'Sailing', a song which always incited in me a maudlin exile patriotism for a country which had never existed, as if I'd been a citizen of Atlantis in a previous life. When it finished I flipped out of the mood and looked around again, and I noticed that Reid's paper had another reader, who was sitting beside him and leaning forward, her head tilted to read the back page. Her curly black hair was tumbled sideways around her face. Black eyebrows, eyelashes, large green eyes moving (slowly, I noticed) as she read, small neat nose, wide cheekbones from which her cheeks, neither thin nor plump, curved smoothly past either side of full (and unconsciously, minutely moving) lips, to a small firm chin.

Her gaze flicked from the page and met mine with an unembarrassed smile. I felt a jolt so physical that I didn't even associate it with an emotion. And then Reid lowered his paper and looked at her. She sat back up, and now she did look slightly embarrassed. She was with a bevy of other girls who'd commandeered the next table along, and the rest were talking amongst themselves.

'Well hello,' Reid said. 'Are you finding it interesting?'

'I've never seen anything like it,' she said. 'I don't understand how anyone would want to support strikes.' She had a west coast accent, but – like Reid – she was speaking an accented English, not Scots like the native Glaswegians did. Probably from down the Clyde somewhere then, Irish or Highland: ESL a generation or two back.

'It's a socialist paper,' Reid said. He glanced at me, as if for support. 'We support the workers, you know?'

'But the *government* is socialist,' she said, sounding indignant. 'And they don't want strikes, do they?'

'We don't think the Labour government is socialist at all,' Reid explained.

'But isn't it bad for the country, when people can go on strike and go straight on social security?'

'In a way, yes,' said Reid, who would normally have lost patience at this point. 'But if what you mean by "the country" is most people living in it, right, then the problems we have don't come from workers going on strike, they come from the bosses and bankers doin' business as usual. They're the ones who're really *costing the country*.'

'You have a funny way of looking at things,' she said, as an explanation, not a question. She dismissed the matter and switched her attention to more important concerns. 'Are you going down to the disco later?'

'Yes,' I said, before Reid could make another attempt at political education. 'Are you?'

'Oh aye,' she said. 'Maybe I'll see you down there.' She flashed us a quick smile before being tugged back into the conversation with her friends. I stared for a moment at where her hair fell over the shoulders of her plain white shirt. The shirt was tucked into tight blue jeans, and her feet into high-heeled shoes. Her clothes and, now I came to think of it, her make-up looked too neat and normal for a student's. Same went for her friends, some of whom were dressed similarly, some in posh frocks.

'Well,' I said as Reid caught my eye, 'as chat-up lines go I think that one needs working on.'

'You could say that,' he admitted. 'Still, she didn't give me much of a chance.'

'You shouldn't have had your nose in the damn' paper in the first place,' I told him.

Just after ten o'clock, we both moved fast as the girls left, lost them in the queue but managed to grab the table nearest to theirs.

'Do you want to dance?' I shouted. UV light caught the nylon stitching in her shirt, a visible-spectrum strobe caught her nod. That dance was fast, the next slow. We had our hands lightly on each other's shoulders at the end. I looked down at her. 'Thank you,' I said.

There was a thing she did with her eyes: the green coronae streaming, the irises opening into black pools you could drown in.

All I could think of to say was, 'What's your name?'

'Annette.'

'Jon Wilde,' I said. 'Do you want a drink?' I had drowned, but my mouth was still moving.

'Pint of lager, thanks.' She smiled and turned to the table. When I got back Reid was shouting and handwaving something to her over the music and lights. She listened, head tilted, chin on hand.

The music changed again, and Reid stood up and held out a hand to Annette. She nodded, downed a gulp of the lager with a quick smile of thanks to me, and away they danced.

'Somebody seems tae hiv got aff on the wrang fit,' an amused but sympathetic female voice said in my ear. I turned to find myself looking at a girl with long bangs of red-brown hair out of which her face peeped like a small mammal from underbrush. She was wearing a blouse with drawstrings at the neck and cuffs, a long blue skirt over long boots.

'Yes,' I said with a backwards nod. 'He's a terrible dancer.'

She laughed. 'Ah wis talkin aboot you,' she said. 'Ah widnae worry. Annette's a wee bit i a flirt.'

'She can flirt with me any time,' I said. 'Meanwhile, let's get acquainted, if only to give her something to think about.'

'This'll gie her something tae think aboot,' she said, and astonished me with a kiss, followed by a snuggle up, which with some shifting of chairs and careful pitching of voices enabled us to have a conversation audible only to us. Now and again we heard ourselves shouting as the music stopped while somebody changed discs (not disks, they came later).

Her name was Sheena. Short for Oceania, I later learned.

'How do you know Annette?'

Sheena grimaced at my choice of topic. 'Live wi her,' she yelled confidentially. 'Work wi her, tae. Wir lab technicians. In the Zoology Department. Whit dae yee dae?'

I told her, and before long was shouting and waving my hands, just like a real scientist. But if the intent was to provoke Annette into showing more interest in me, the experiment failed.

Chill night, no frost, dead leaves skeletal on the pavements like fossil fish. Dave and Annette and Sheena and I paused at the bridge, stared over the parapet at the Kelvin's peaceful roar.

'Must be the only feature named after a unit of measurement,' Reid said. I laughed at that and the girls laughed too.

'There should be more!' I said. 'The Joules Burn! The Ampere Current!'

'Loch Litre!'

'Ben Metre!'

'Or computer languages,' Reid said as we walked on, the BBC

Scotland building on our left, on our right the Botanic Garden with its vast circular greenhouse, a flying saucer from some nineteenth-century Mars. 'Fortran Steps. Basic Blocks ...'

'Ada Mansions!'

'Stras Cobol!'

By the time we reached the girls' flat we'd scraped up Newton Heights and Candela Beach, and I was trying to persuade everybody that all the units were the names of people; for example Jean-Baptiste de Metre, the noted Encyclopaedist, Girondist, and dwarf.

'Of course after the Revolution he dropped the "de",' I explained as Annette jingled for keys. 'But that didn't save him, he got –'

'Shortened,' said Reid.

'By a foot.'

'No, stupid, a head.'

'Are youse goin tae stand there all night?'

'Only for a second.'

'Named of course after ...' I searched for inspiration.

Reid gave me a shove. 'Come on.'

I went in. Basement flat, big front room, bed, sofa-bed, fake fireplace. Snoopy posters, stuffed toys, girly clutter. Tiny kitchen where Annette was plugging in an electric kettle.

We talked, we drank coffee which only made us feel wilder, Sheena skinned up a joint. Later ... later I was in the kitchen, half-sitting on the edge of the sink, while Sheena took charge of another round of Nescafé and the remains of a roach. The door was almost closed, Dave's and Annette's voices a steady murmur.

She put milk back in the fridge, leaned on my thigh. I leaned over and parted her fronds and looked at her.

'Do you want me to stay?'

'Aye, well, no.' She passed me the charred cardboard; I sipped, winced and held it under the tap. 'Ah mean, Ah wid, but Ah c'n see ye fancy Annette.'

'Wish she could. Wish I'd told her.'

'Och, she knows. Ah think she's feart. Yir so – intense.'

'Intense? Moi? You mean, not like my pal Dave Fight-The-Good-Fight Reid? Likes his easy charm with the labour theory of value, is that it?'

Sheena grinned. 'Yir no far wrong. See, if he cares enough whit she thinks tae argue wi her, he cannae jist be interested in gettin aff wi her.'

The kettle sang. I gazed at the fluorescent strip above the worktop and squeezed my eyes. Sheena's weight shifted away and she busied herself with the mugs. I sighed in the sudden aroma.

'So what am I doing that makes you think I'm coming on too strong? I've hardly had a chance to say a word to her all bloody evening.'

'Dead right,' Sheena said. 'Ye talk tae me, and ye say things tae Dave, and aw the time ye look at Annette and smile at whitever she says.'

'I do not!'

She looked me in the eye.

'All right,' I admitted. 'Maybe I do. I'm sorry. Must seem a bit rude.'

'It does an aw,' she said. 'Still, I'm no blamin you. I started the whole wee game. C'me oan, see's a hand wi they mugs.'

When I'd finished the coffee I stood up. Dave and Annette were sitting on the floor, leaning against the side of the bed. Dave's arm was across Annette's shoulders.

'See you, guys.'

'See ya,' Dave said.

'Goodnight,' Annette said. I tried to read her narrowed eyes, to gloss a twinkle or a wink. She looked down.

Sheena kissed me goodnight at the door, with a warmth as sudden and unexpected as her kissed hello.

'Sure?' I tried to curve my lips to a mischievous grin.

'Sure.' She pushed my shoulders, holding. 'Yir a nice man, but let's no make our lives any mair complicated than they are.'

'Okay, Sheena. Goodnight. See you again.'

'Scram!' she smiled, and closed the door.

Tiles to chest-level, whitewash, polished balustrade. Glasgow working-class tenement respectability, not like the student slum I inhabited. I remembered something. I turned back to the door and squatted in front of it, pushed back the sprung brass flap of the letter-box.

'Dave!' I shouted.

'What?' came faint and distant.

'After *Charles the Second*!' I yelled. 'Patron of the Royal Society!'

A cloud had descended on the city while I'd been in the flat. At the junction of Great Western Road and Byres Road I waited at a crossing. Heels clicked up behind me, stopped beside me. A girl in a fur coat. She turned, smiling, and asked, 'How do the lights –? Oh, I see.' Voice like a warm hand, English upper-class accent. The fur and her hair glittered with beads of moisture. She was going somewhere she wanted to be, confident no-one would dare lay a finger on her: a beautiful animal, perfectly adapted, feral.

'Terrible fog, isn't it?'

'Yes,' I said. 'Never seen one like it in Glasgow.'

The lights changed. We crossed, our paths diverging. She went down Byres Road, to that place where she wanted to be, and I walked along Great Western Road, back to my room.

3

The Terminal Kid

IT'S RAINING ON New Mars. This is a machine-made miracle, the work of rare devices far away, and of the insensate, botanic power of their countless offspring which turn metal petals to focus faint solar radiation on chunks of dirty ice, flaring their surface volatiles to send them tumbling sunwards, nudged and guided in a precisely calculated trajectory that years later takes them into an atmosphere just thick enough to catch them and carry them down; where with luck they fall as rain and not as fire, and which in any case each bolide's passage leaves marginally better fitted to catch and contain the next.

But to Dee, out in the wet night, it's commonplace, and a drag. For about half an hour she's had to keep the image-intensifiers at full blast, and her eyes are hurting. Her ears, too: sonar ping off wet walls a metre or so away on either side induces an enclosing sense of pressure. At the same time turning it down or off would strain her even more. So it's with relief and relaxation that she sees the narrow waterway open out on a much wider and brighter canal.

'Ring Canal,' Tamara indicates as she turns her little craft to the right. Dee, craning her head and looking fore and aft, can see no curvature. Tall, narrow houses – rather than storage blocks and industrial units – overlook this canal, and lights are strung above its banks. Ahead, a rapidly closing hundred metres away, the Ring Canal itself opens out, and through the gap between the buildings at the end Dee sees what looks and sounds like a bonfire: a blaze of light, a roar of noise.

At the confluence, the Ring Canal separates to left and right, curving to a visible ring whose diameter Dee estimates as three hundred metres. More of the tall houses huddle around it, and within it there's a flat island, accessible from the surrounding circular way by bridges. This central island is covered with corrugated-iron huts and fabric booths and shacks, among which many people are loudly busy. The light comes from overhead floods, and from each individual booth's contribution of spotlights, fluorescent tubing, strobe, fairy-light cable, and fibre-optic.

Tamara takes another right and throttles back the engine, coasting along the outer bank, silent amid the din of music and commerce, both competitive.

'What's going on here?' Dee asks.

Tamara spares her a glance. 'Fi'day evening in Circle Square.'

A tiny jetty under a narrow wrought-iron bridge, with a set of steps attached. Tamara moors the boat and motions to Dee to climb the steps. She waits on the shoreward side of the bridge and helps Tamara to haul up the bag. The coming and going of people – couples, groups, kids dodging and weaving between legs and wheels, youths on or in vehicles built to go fast and moving slow, and things that might be vehicles except they have no riders – almost pushes her back off.

'Right,' says Tamara, 'time to make you legal.'

She sets off along the bridge, Dee close behind her – one person in the crowd who has no difficulty getting through.

Most of the stalls around the circumference of the island are locked up, but still lit-up. The ones that aren't are selling drinks and snacks. The main action is going on towards the hub, in a melée of fairground attractions, discos and rock concerts. Dee notices a stage with a band that looks and sounds just like Metal Petal, this week's hit at every uptown thrash. A quick visual zoom and aural analysis reveals that they *are* Metal Petal. (Dee's heard about copyright, but it's one of those things she doesn't quite believe, a song of distant Earth.)

Tamara stops in front of a thing like a big vending-machine between two stalls. It's covered with dust and rust. It has a black window at the top and a speaker grille and a channel down one side through which Tamara swipes a card. Nothing happens.

'Hey!' she shouts. She bangs the side with her fist, making a hollow boom. '*Fucking* IBM,' she says to no-one in particular.

Lights come on behind the dark window.

'Invisible Hand Legal Services,' says the machine, in a voice like God in an old movie. 'How can I help you?'

'Register an autonomy claim for an abandoned machine,' Tamara says, catching Dee's wrist and pressing her palm against the window.

'Both hands please,' says the machine. 'Both eyes.'

Dee spreads her fingers against the glass and peers in, seeing her own reflection and bright, moving sparks of light.

'How do you wish the claim to be defended?'

'I'll defend it!' Dee says with a sudden surge of Self-ish passion.

'By the principal,' Tamara adds gravely. 'And by me, my affiliates and by back-up if requested.'

'Very well. Noted and posted.'

The lights go out. Tamara's still holding Dee's wrist, and she swings her around and grabs the other ... then lets go, and clasps hands instead. Dee looks at Tamara's eyes and sees her own reflection and the speeding, spinning lights behind her, the doubled fair.

'Okay gal,' Tamara yells. 'That's you with a gang on your side! That's as free as it gets! Give or take ... Later for that! Right now –' she twirls to face the thrumming hub of the island market '– let's *party*!'

'You're telling me,' Wilde said incredulously to the robot, 'that *Reid* is *here*?'

'Yes,' said the robot. 'Why should that surprise you? Is it more remarkable than your being here?'

Wilde grinned at it sourly. He pushed away his empty plate and sipped at his beer. He shook his head.

'Reid was one of the last people I saw,' he said. 'For all I know, it may have been him who had me killed. And as far as I'm concerned, it happened *today*. Christ. I keep expecting to wake up.'

'You have woken up,' the robot said. 'You can expect some emotional reaction as your mind adjusts to your situation.'

'I suppose so.' A bleakness belying his apparent age settled on Wilde's countenance. 'It has already. So tell me, machine. I'm here, and you say Reid's here. What about other people I knew? What about Annette?'

'Annette,' the machine said carefully, 'is among the dead. Whether her mind as well as her genotype has been preserved I don't know, but there may be grounds for hope.'

'Because of the clone?'

'Yes.'

'I must find her, and find out.'

'You can find out without finding her,' said the machine. 'It's …
I'll explain tomorrow.'

'Why not now?'

'Trouble,' the machine said. 'Don't turn around until you hear
something.'

Wilde set down his glass. His shoulders began to hunch.

'Relax,' said the machine.

The doors of the pub banged open and the music stopped.
Conversations ran on for a few seconds and then trailed off into the
spreading silence. Everybody turned around.

Two men stood in the doorway. They were wearing loose-cut,
sharp-creased business suits, over open-necked shirts, over tee-
shirts. Their hair was as shiny as their shoes, and their knuckles
flashed with studded stones. One of the men perfunctorily held up a
card showing a mug-shot of himself and a grey block of small print.
The other took from a jacket-pocket a crumpled ball of flat material.
He grasped a corner of it and shook it out. With a final flick of his
wrist he snapped it to a glossy, full-colour, high-res poster depicting
the dark-haired woman who had fled from Wilde and the robot.

'Anybody seen her?' he demanded.

The pub's customers could still be approximately differentiated
into two groups, the men at the bar and the girls at the tables,
although some mingling had begun. A little flurry of giggles and
gasps came from the women, and a murmur of grunts and slightly
shifted seats and glasses from the men. Anyone who looked about to
say something would glance at the men at the bar, and find someone
else to look at, something else to say.

Within half a minute everybody was talking again; the men at the
bar had turned back to watching the television, where a commentator was interviewing a team-leader behind whom bodies were being
stretchered from an arena. The only person still looking directly at
the repossession men was Wilde. The one holding the picture
strolled over; the other followed, fondling a revolver-butt with a
look of distant pleasure.

The man with the picture looked down at Wilde and smiled,

showing perfect but strangely shaped incisors, long canines. Perfumed fumes poured off him like sweat.

'Well,' he said, 'you look interested. Big reward, you know.'

Wilde looked up reluctantly from the picture. He shook his head.

'She reminds me of somebody I used to know,' he said. 'That's all. But I've never seen her here.'

The man glared at him. 'She's been here,' he said. 'I can smell it.' He turned his head this way and that, inhaling gently, as if his statement were literally true. The other man gave a sudden gleeful yell and snatched up something from the floor.

He brandished it under Wilde's nose. Wilde recoiled slightly. The robot, leaning between a chair and the table-top, jerked forward a couple of centimetres.

The thing the man was holding was a newspaper.

'Knew it!' he said. 'Bloody bolishies! Right, that's it. We know where to look for her!'

Stuffing the newspaper and the poster in their pockets, the two men stalked out through another silence. The doors banged again. The music came back on. The hominid behind the bar looked at Wilde with an expression of deep rue, then shrugged his wide shoulders and spread his broad hands, his long arms comically extended. The shrug completed, he turned away and switched the music back on, louder.

Wilde returned to his meal, and downed his glass of spirits in a gulp that brought tears to his eyes.

'I still want to speak to her,' he said.

'If you're concerned about the gynoid,' the machine said, 'don't worry. If she's with abolitionists she'll be legally and physically safe from repossession, at least for a while. And if she isn't ...' It moved the upper joints of its forelimbs in a parody of a shrug. 'They aren't going to harm her. Just fix a programming error. It's not important.'

'Because she's just a machine, right?'

'Right.'

'Well, it may be tactless to point this out, but so are you.'

'Of course,' the machine said. 'But *I'm* human-equivalent, and *she*'s a sex-toy. Like I said: just a fucking machine.'

Surveillance systems? Don't make me smile. Any recording made around the centre of Circle Square is irredeemably corrupted, hacked and patched, spliced and remixed. Even Dee's memories are understandably giddy: Soldier and Spy just shut off in disgust, leaving only simple reflexes on the job. Humans pass drugs from hand to hand, machines pass plugs. The music has amplitudes and electronic undertow that work to the same effect. Dee sees Tamara talking to a tall fighting man with an industrial arm, finds herself talking to a spidery gadget with airbrushes and a single mind. It thinks, and can talk, of nothing but murals. It knows about concrete surfaces and the properties of paint and the physics of aerosols. It tells her about them, at considerable length.

She could have listened to it all night. She's a good listener. But the artist sees a builder, and without an excuse or goodbye skitters away through the crowd to chat it up.

Tamara catches Dee's elbow and stares after the machine. Then she turns and Dee can, as they say, see the wheels going round as the speech centres overcome intoxication.

Eventually the words break through.

'*Not* human equivalent!'

'I've talked to worse men,' Dee says.

Dee's mindlessly bopping – this is a Self-specific skill – when she notices the man she's bopping opposite, who's moving as if he presumes he's dancing with her. Her gaze moves up from his shiny leather fake-plastic shoes to the trousers and jacket of his fancy but unstylish suit, past the miasma of disgusting scent rising from the sweat-stained tee-shirt neckline inside the open-necked shirt-collar to his –

face!

– and the shock of recognising one of the greps, the repossession men, sends an adrenaline jolt that rouses Soldier. Everything slows, except her. (The music goes from disco to deep industrial dub.) A quick glance around sets Surgeon swiftly to work on the tendons and cartilages of her neck and brings back the intelligence that Tamara is writhing sinuously a couple of metres away, her back half-turned, and behind Tamara, sideways on to Dee, is the other grep. His movements and stance are as if he's fucking a virtual image of Tamara a metre or so in front of the real one, but that's just disco-dancing. His gaze doesn't leave the real Tamara for an instant.

She sees the sweat flick from his hair as his head flips. He looks fully occupied for at least the next couple of seconds.

The other grep, the one who's got his eye on her, has definitely noticed Dee's mental shift (that sudden blurred head-movement's a dead giveaway) and his pupils are shrinking to pin-holes even as his eyelids are opening wider. Dee is aware of her pistol as a heavy shape in the soft leather of that silly, cissy bag at her feet, aware of her narrow skirt as *drag* that'll impede the tactically obvious lethal kick.

She could yell, but a yell is nothing in this noise. The only pitch audible above it would be inaudible – to human ears. Her mouth opens, her chest inflates with rib-stressing speed and she lets out an ultrasonic yell she hopes is audible to machines for hundreds of metres around: '*Fucking IBM, help!*'

The music stops. Lights flood. People blink and stumble. At the same moment Dee's right hand reaches down, her right foot kicks up behind her – still in a move that could be part of a dance-step – and her high-heeled shoe flies into her hand. She holds it high like a hammer, ready to nail the grep through the eyeball. Recognition of this ripples through the muscles and blood-vessels of his face as the speakers suddenly speak. The voice of the IBM, to Dee's Soldier-speeded senses, now sounds deeper and more menacing than anything in de Mille:

'Invisible Hand client threatened; please assist.'

The grep backs off, and the one beside Tamara does too. Everybody else looks momentarily off-balance, except Tamara, who's looking at Dee with a dawning, jaw-slackening awe. Dee's sweeping glance around the crowd, before Soldier subsides to a watchful withdrawal, shows her that there are other faces, dotted through the crowd, responding to the call as best they can: tensing, rising or crouching or – in the case of one or two machines – telescoping. These folk start up a slow-hand-clapping chant: 'Out! Out! Out!'

And Dee shoves the man, and Tamara shoves, and the two greps are shoved and man-handled from one person or robot to another until they're ejected from the edge of the crowd into the waiting grasp of a couple of heavy bikers, who escort them away.

'OK,' Dee says. She smiles around and slips her shoe back on, waves and calls out 'Thanks, everybody!' in a girlishly grateful voice that sends Soldier away in a squirm of embarrassment and brings a small flush to her cheeks.

The music and the lights resume their rhythm.

Dee dances; but she knows the next time won't be so easy. These guys may not come back, but somebody will.

Dee's in a small room at the top of a house on Circle Square, overlooking the Ring Canal. Tamara has brought her back to a flat in this tall house, after what seems like hours at the outdoor party – and retired to her own room to sleep, with apologetic explanations that she starts work early in the morning. 'Ax will sort you out,' she's told her.

Dee is used to vague human speech. She doesn't ask for explanations. Her own human flesh and nerves are tired. She doesn't need to sleep, but she needs to rest, and to dream. One after another her selves have to shut down, go off-line, compress and assimilate and integrate the doings of the day.

The room is seductively comfortable, with the rain drumming on the roof just behind the sloping ceiling; its dormer window supplying more eye-tilting angles; a dressing-table with stoppered bottles and pots, beads and scarves and ribbons hung over the mirror, clipped fashion-shots tacked to the walls, a dozen dolls on a shelf. There's a curved, satin-padded wicker chair in a corner, a wall cupboard (locked), and a bed with a clutter of quilt and lace-trimmed pillows. There's something faintly troubling about the human smell behind the flowery and musky scents, but she can't be bothered to analyse it.

She takes her clothes off and folds or hangs them, adjusts her body temperature to her comfort, and lies down on the bed. Her eyelids shut out the window's view of Ship City's familiar reality: a damp, dripping city of silicate towers, a city veined with canals, crowded with stranded starfarers and free or enslaved automata, haunted by the quick and the dead. Her minds spool to Story, who spins another episode of her endless starring role in a self-perpetuating soap opera steeped in all the romantic glamour of ancient Earth, where ...

... she's the eldest daughter of a Senator and set to inherit his place in the Duma and all the privileges of his democratic anointment, but she's been kidnapped by agents of the Archipelago Mining Corporation and held captive by its young and dark and devilish chief executive, who wants her for his harem, and is willing to trade her life for her hand in concubinage and a major Antarctic concession, and her father's personal and fanatically loyal Chechen guards are fighting their way through the chief executive's rings of brutish defenders while she stands, sheathed in silks and clouded in perfumes on the balcony of a Kuomintang drug-lord's skyscraper in the heart of Old New York watching the tanks battle it out in the streets below and waiting for the hard-pressed Chechens to raise reinforcements from the desperate tribes of the South Bronx with the promise of plunder, and she hears a stealthy step behind her and the chief executive – whose face, if truth be told, looks uncannily like her owner's – falls on his knees before her and tells her he really, truly, loves her and he's consumed with remorse and he'll set her free, if only …

And so on.

This is what androids – or rather, gynoids – dream.

A knock on the door. She's back to full awareness in an instant, her internal clock telling her it's early morning.

'Just a moment,' she says.

The little cleaner-vermin have removed every speck of organic dirt from her clothes. She shakes them out without thinking and dresses in a blur of motion (a useful Soldier skill that she's cut-and-pasted to Self) and calls out,

'Come in.'

The boy who comes in carrying a tray with a mug of coffee and a bowl of cereal looks about twelve years old, at first glance. He's Black, with slight build and delicate features and a shock of black hair. As Dee scans him up and down, all the while smiling and saying 'hello', she realises that he's much older than he looks. There's no way so much experience could have made its subtle imprint in the muscle-tone of his face, the look in his eye, in just twelve years. Not here, not in Ship City. They have laws against that sort of thing.

'You must be Ax,' she says, taking the tray. 'Thanks.' She waves him to the chair. 'Tamara mentioned you.'

'Likewise,' the boy says, sitting back with one foot on the

42

opposite knee. 'So you're Dee Model, huh? Big boss Reid's main squeeze.'

Dee's facing him, her knees primly together, the tray balanced on them, the spoon almost at her mouth. She puts it back, making a tinny rattle against the side of the bowl. She steadies the tray, and her voice.

'How do you know that?'

Ax flashes white teeth. 'You're famous.' His grin becomes wicked, then relents to a reassuring smile. 'Not really. Your master had you on his arm at a party last year, pic made its way onto the gossip chats.' His eyes unfocus for a moment. 'Quite a dress,' he says.

'I didn't think so,' Dee says. She resumes eating. 'I had to stay in Sex most of the time to make wearing it bearable.'

Ax snorts.

'Anyway.' Dee blushes. Spy's routines keep her voice level and flat. 'Are there searches out for me? Rewards posted?'

Again the off-line gaze – he's got a cortical downlink, Dee realises, not a common feature around here; the most intimate interface with the nets that most people will tolerate is contacts, the little round screens that you slip over your eyes.

'None so far,' Ax says, attention snapping back. 'Reckon he's embarrassed. I mean, your walking doll walks out on you, can't be like having your car nicked, know what I mean?'

'Yes,' Dee says. The thought of her owner's probable rage and humiliation makes her knees, despite everything, quiver. She puts the tray down and reaches for her purse.

'Smoke?'

'Anything,' says Ax. He has a lighter on a chain around his neck, and moves swiftly to light up for her, then settles back, dragging on his own.

'So why did you walk out?' he asks. His tone is neither friendly nor prurient; it's like a professional question, the tone of a physician or an engineer with a patient.

'He doesn't mistreat me,' she says. 'I don't mind the service, or the sex. I mind being a slave.'

'You're supposed to like it,' Ax says. 'It's hard-wired.'

'I know,' Dee says. She glances around for an ashtray, sighs and mentally over-rides her Servant routines and taps the ash onto the empty, milk-lined bowl. 'And I do like it. I do find it fulfilling. But only sexually. Not any other way, not in my separate self. And when I realised that, what I did was … I patched my Sex programs over that area, and masked it all off from Self, and made myself free.'

'Amazing,' Ax says, as if it's anything but. 'So it's true what they say: *information wants to be free!*'

Dee shakes her head. 'It's nothing so grand,' she explains. 'It happened after I loaded up far more mind-tools than I was ever supposed to have.' She tries to remember that second birth, that awakening, when she flipped through all those separate selves and saw herself, a ghostly reflection in all the windows.

Ax frowns. He flips a finger, and his cigarette-butt's fizzing out on the bowl's film of milk. An investigating cleany-crawly shies away, rearing its frontal segments. 'When did this happen?' he asks.

Dee smiles proudly, bursting to share her confidence. 'Yesterday,' she says.

Ax's mouth hangs open for a moment. For a second the seen-it-all look drops from his face. He fumbles a cigarette-packet from inside the sleeve of his tee-shirt and lights one abstractedly, not looking, not offering. 'But why,' he continues, 'did you load up all the extra software in the first place? What made you do *that*?'

Dee finds herself at a loss. It's difficult to think back to her earlier simplicity, when she switched from one single mind to another and it was just her, it was where she lived. She was no less conscious then than she is now, but it was an undivided, naive, biddable consciousness, without detachment. But even there, somewhere in Self, was the lust to know. And the opportunity had come, and she'd taken it – with what, looking back, had been a sweet assurance that her owner would be pleased.

'Instinct,' she says, with a light laugh. Ax snorts and rolls his eyes.

'All right,' Dee says, suddenly stung. 'Perhaps it did come from the animal body, or the bits of biological brain!'

'We'll leave that argument to the other side,' Ax says.

'The other side of what?'

'The other side of the *case*,' he explains with strained patience. 'One way or another, this is going to end up in court. You know about the law?'

44

'Oh yes,' Dee says brightly. 'I have a mind in here called Secretary. She has precedents coming out of my ears.'

'Well,' Ax says firmly, rising, 'I suggest you go back over them. It'll all seem very different, I can tell you that for nothing.'

'OK,' Dee says. Ax holds the door open, waiting. Dee stands up. 'What now?'

He looks her down and up. 'Shopping, I think.' His voice conveys an epicene disdain.

She picks up her purse, sticks the pistol back in the top of her skirt, and glances around. She's left nothing.

'Nice room.'

'Mine,' Ax says. 'I'd be very happy to share it with you.'

The outer door of the building booms behind them. 'Stay,' Ax commands it. Magnetic bolts set it ringing again. Ax grins at her and sets off to the left. Dee glances around as she strolls beside him. The house they've just come out of is four storeys tall, and narrow. So are all the others around here, in classic crowded canal-bank style, but there are no weathered brick walls or contrast grouting, no sills or window-boxes. Everything's concrete, a skin slapped up in a hurry on webs of wire-mesh over iron bones, graffiti its only – and appropriate – decoration. The city's spicular towers loom like construction cranes above the buildings, reducing them to on-site huts.

Smoke rises from among the stalls, steam from the pavements. Mist hangs along the canal surface. The spray-paint on the walls gets more and more vehement, reaching a climax of clenched fists and rockets and mushroom-clouds and dinosaurs at the entrance to an alley.

Ax stops and waves inward. 'This way.'

The alley is no more than three metres wide but it's a shopping street in its own right, and unlike what Dee has seen of the neighbourhood so far, it has a worked-for charm, the names of the shops painted in painstaking emulation of the clean calligraphy of twenty-first-century mall-signs. At the first window display Ax waits impatiently as Dee surveys a fossil diorama, allegedly of the fauna of one of the planet's ancient sea-beds. Scientist has other views, and Latin names Dee doesn't know float distractingly across her sight. Inside the shop, fossils are being worked into amulets and

45

ornaments. A girl at a grinding-wheel raises her face-plate, gives Dee an inviting smile and returns – puzzled or baffled by Dee's Scientist-masked response – to her work. The volatile smells of varnish and polish, glue and lubricant waft through the doorway along with the screech of carborundum on stone.

There's a shop selling drugs and pipes; a newspaper stand where Dee sees copies of *The Abolitionist* and more obscure titles like *Factory Farming, Nano Mart, Nuke Tech*; a stall stacked with weathered junk identified as 'Old New Martian Alien Artifacts'; at all of which Dee's critical dawdling has Ax muttering and smoking. Dee enjoys this refusal, trivial though it is, to adapt to a human's priorities; an exercise of free will.

But she shares Ax's evident delight when they reach the first boutique, a cave of clothing and accessories. He leads her in, and they're there for an hour that passes like a minute and then out again into other clothes-shops, and cosmetics-artists' little studios and jewellers' labs. All the while Ax fusses around her with an unselfconscious intimacy which doesn't vary with her state of dress or undress. She can tell that the pleasure he takes in her is aesthetic, not erotic. The software of Sex is sensitive to such distinctions: it can read the physiology of a flush, time the beat of a pulse and measure the dilation of a pupil, and it knows there's no lust in this boy's touch.

At the far end of the alley is a café. They sit themselves down there under the sudden light of the noon sun above the narrow street, sip coffee, and smoke, surrounded by their purchases. Dee's cast off her sober style for something dikey and punky. She preens in leather, lacing and lace; satin and silk, spikes and studs. A look that would have most twelve-year-old boys unimpressed, most men stimulated. Ax looks at her as a work of art he's accomplished, which at the moment she is.

Dee fidgets with her lighter, looks up under the fringe of her re-styled hair. She's about to say something, but she doesn't know what to ask.

'Let me spare you,' Ax says. 'If embarrassment is in your repertoire, that is. Sexually speaking, I'm not in the game. *On* the game, sometimes, perhaps.' He flicks fingertips. 'Not gay, not neuter. Just a boy: a permanent pre-pubescent.'

'Why?' Dee asks. 'Is it an illness?'

'Terminal,' Ax grins. 'Something down where the genes meet the little machines: a bug. A virus. Something my parents picked up on the long trip. Fortunately it doesn't kick in unless I go through puberty. So I've fixed my biological age a bit younger than most.'

'And there's no help for it?'

Ax turns down the corners of his mouth. 'If there is, it's with the fast minds. Best advice would be to forget it, in other words. But I couldn't forget it. One reason I got into abolitionism ...' He laughs. 'My chances of becoming a man are right up there with the dead coming back and the fast minds running again. Pffft.'

'Hmmm.' Dee feels sad. What a waste. A brighter thought comes to her. 'You could grow up as a woman,' she says.

'Well, thank you,' Ax replies, pouting and posing for a moment. 'I'd consider it, but the fixers tell me the bug reacts to the hormones of either sex. So I'm stuck with neither, and after the predictable raging and sulking I decided I might as well make a career of being someone a jealous male could trust alone with his female.' He draws in smoke and exhales it elegantly. 'Freelance professional eunuch and part-time catamite.'

While Dee's still thinking about this, and wondering if Ax's lot isn't, all things considered, any worse than hers, he adds:

'Before I found out about my condition, I was quite a normal little lad.' He sighs. 'The effeminacy's just a pose, Dee, just a pose. And in case anyone forgets, I can also be extremely violent.'

'Why didn't you specialise in that? Be a guard or a fighter or –'

'And risk getting killed?' Ax guffaws. 'Do I *look* stupid?'

'No.' Dee gives him a friendly, sisterly (now that she's figured out their only possible relationship) smile, but she stops feeling sorry for him. She reckons he's doing all right. Queer as a coot, she finds herself thinking, and as they get up to leave she sets Scientist grumpily searching ancient, inherited databases to find out what the fuck a coot *is*.

'So I made it to the ships,' Wilde said. He raised himself on one elbow and peered around the room, in which he'd been lying awake for ten minutes.

'Good morning,' said the machine. It was resting on the floor in the corner of the room. The room was upstairs in the Malley Mile, cheap to rent and containing a wash-stand, a chair and a bed. It was remarkably free of dust, due to machines about the size and shape of large woodlice that scuttled about the floor.

Wilde stared at the machine. 'What have you been doing all night?'

'Guarding you,' the machine said. It stretched out its limbs momentarily, then folded them back. 'Scanning the city's nets. Dreaming.'

Wilde remained leaning on one elbow, looking at the machine with a suddenly reckless curiosity. 'I didn't know machines dreamed.'

'I also reminisce,' said the machine. 'When there's time.'

Wilde grinned sourly. 'I suppose time is what you have plenty of, thinking so much faster –'

'No,' the machine snapped. 'I told you. I'm a human-equivalent machine. My subjective time is much the same as yours. No doubt my connections are faster than your reactions, but the consciousness they sustain moves at the same pace.'

'Does it indeed?' Wilde got out of bed, looked down at his body with a flicker of renewed surprise, smiled and washed his face and neck and put his clothes on.

'So tell me, machine,' he said as he tugged on his boots, 'what am I to call you? Come to that, what are you?'

'Basically,' said the machine, detaching a filament from a wall socket and winding it slowly back into its casing, 'I'm a civil-engineering construction rig, autonomous, nuclear-powered, sand-resistant. As to my name.' It paused. 'You may call me anything you like, but I have been known as Jay-Dub.'

Wilde laughed. 'That's great! That'll do.'

'"Jay-Dub" is fine,' said the machine. 'Not undignified. Thanks, Jon Wilde.'

'Well, Jay-Dub,' Wilde said with a self-conscious smile, 'let's go and get breakfast.'

'You do that,' Jay-Dub said. It unfolded its limbs and stood up, revealing a litter of torn foil carapaces with now-stilled tiny legs and dulled lenses. 'I've eaten.'

The Malley Mile was silent, the bar shuttered and swept and polished and hung with damp cloths when they picked their way downstairs and out through a one-way-locked door.

'Trusting,' Wilde remarked, as he let the door click back.

'It's an honest place,' Jay-Dub said. 'There's little in the way of petty crime. For reasons which I'm sure you know.'

The small sun was low above the towers, laying lacey shadows on the street. Boats and barges floated down the canal, heading out of town.

'Where are they going?' Wilde asked. The man and the robot were strolling towards a small dock a hundred or so metres up the street. There were food-stalls on the dock.

'Mines or farms,' the robot said. 'They aren't entirely distinct, here. They're both a matter of using nanotech – natural or artificial – to concentrate dispersed molecules into a usable form.'

'And people work at that? What are the robots doing?'

'Heh-heh-heh.' Jay-Dub's voice-control had advanced: it could now parody a mechanical laugh. 'Robots are either useless for such purposes, or far too useful to waste on them.'

The small dock was busy. People – mostly human, but with a few other hominid types among them – were embarking, or unlading sacks of vegetables or minerals from long narrow barges. Electric-powered trucks were backing on to the quay, loading up. A family of what looked like gibbons with swollen skulls hauled a net-full of slapping, silvery fish along the quay and spilled them into a rusty bath behind one of the stalls, where a burly woman immediately began to gut and grill the fish. Wilde stopped there and, somewhat hesitantly and with a lot of pointing, got her to put together fish and leaves and bread. Coffee was for sale in glass cups, deposit returnable.

Wilde took his breakfast to the edge of the quay and sat down, legs dangling, and slowly ate, looking all around. The robot hunkered down beside him.

'Time you told me things,' Wilde said. 'You said you made me. What did that mean?'

'Cloned you from a cell,' the machine said. 'Grew you in a vat. Ran a program to put your memories back on your synapses.' It hummed, remotely. 'That last could get you killed, so keep it to yourself.'

'Why did you do it?'

'I needed your help,' said Jay-Dub. 'To fight David Reid, and to change this world.'

49

Wilde looked at the machine for a long time, his face as inscrutable as the machine's blank surface.

'You've already told me what you are,' he said. 'But *who* are you? The truth, this time. The whole truth.'

'What I *am*,' the machine said, so quietly that Wilde had to lean closer, his ear to a grille between its metal shells, 'is a long and complex question. But I *was* you.'

4

Catch

'IF YOU'RE INTERESTED, you'll be there.'

The train lurched. Carlisle's sodium-lit brown buildings began to slide by.

'What?' Startled out of a train-induced trance, I wasn't sure I hadn't dreamed the remark. The man on the opposite side of the so-called Pullman table wore a cloth cap and a jacket of some shiny substance that might once have been corduroy. His faded check shirt looked like a pyjama-top. He'd been drinking with silent determination from a half-bottle of Bell's all the long afternoon from Euston.

Now he rubbed a brown hand along his jaw, rasping white stubble over sallow skin, and repeated his utterance. I smiled desperately.

'I see,' I lied. 'Very true.'

'You'll be there,' he said. He reached for the bottle, judged its remaining contents by weight and replaced it on the table, then began to roll a cigarette with the other hand. His gaze, sharp with an occasional lapse into bleariness, stayed on me all the while.

'Where?' I looked away, flipped open a packet of Silk Cut (my gesture towards healthy living). My reflection flared in a brief virtual image outside the train. The sodden February countryside seeped past.

'Disnae matter,' the man said, exhaling smoke and the sour odour of digested whisky. 'Wherever. Ah kin tell. You're interested.' He paused, cocked his head and gave me a cunning look. 'You're one a they international socialists. Ah kin tell.'

I smiled again and shook my head. 'I'm sorry, but you're mistaken, I'm –' I stopped, helpless to explain. I'd spent a week researching in the LSE library and arguing with my father. My head was buzzing with Marxisms.

'Ach, it's aw right son,' he said. 'Ah ken youse have aw kinds i wee divisions. I dinnae bother about them. You're an intellectual and Ah'm just a retired working man. But you're wannay uz.'

With that he opened the bottle, took a sip from it and passed it to me, kindly wiping his hand on his thigh and then around the rim as he did so, to remove any harmful germs.

'And then what happened?' Reid asked.

We turned, hunched against the drizzle, into Park Road, past the pseudo-Tudor frontage of the Blythswood Cottage pub and ducked into the doorway of Voltaire & Rousseau, the best second-hand bookshop in Glasgow. I'd run into Reid at lunchtime, after not having seen him for some weeks – partly because I was working hard on my dissertation and partly because Reid was either politically active or out with Annette. In the first month of their relationship I'd once or twice had a few drinks with both of them, but I'd found it too awkward to continue.

'He fell asleep,' I laughed. 'I left the bottle severely alone and woke him up at the Central. He seemed to have forgotten the whole incident. Looked like he didn't recognise me.'

By this time we were both moving crabwise, heads tilted, systematically scanning the shelves that covered the narrow shop's walls. First we'd scour the politics and philosophy section, then – if we had any spare cash left – move on to the back room to hit the SF paperbacks. One of the shop's owners – a tall, tubby, cheerful chap with thin hair and thick glasses – looked up from his book at the till with a smile and a nod. He, I'd decided, must be Rousseau; his gaunt and gloomy partner, Voltaire.

'Probably an old ILP'er or something,' Reid muttered, pouncing on a blue Charles H. Kerr & Co. volume of Dietzgen. He blew dust off it and sneezed.

'One pound fifty!' he said in a low voice, so that Rousseau couldn't overhear his delight and guess what a bargain they'd let slip. He twisted back to his search, a read-head moving along the memory-tape of shelves.

'You know,' he went on, 'it makes me sick sometimes to think of all those old militants selling off their libraries to eke out their pensions. Or dying, and their kids – God, I can just imagine them, middle-aged, middle-class wankers who've always been a bit ashamed of the *bodach*'s rambling reminiscences – rummaging through his pathetic stuff and finding a shelf of socialist classics and about to heave them on the tip when suddenly the little gleam of a few quid lights up their greedy eyes!'

'Just as well for us that it does,' I said, wedging my fingers between two books to ease out a lurking pamphlet. 'It's the ones that end up on the tip that I – hey, look at this!'

I didn't care who overheard. This was almost certainly unique, a living fossil: a wartime Russia Today Society pamphlet called *Soviet Millionaires*. It hadn't stayed in circulation long, not after the SPGB had seized on it as irrefutable proof that behind the socialist facade the USSR concealed a class of wealthy property-owners.

'I've heard about it from my father,' I told Reid. 'But even he'd never had a copy. I'll send it to him.'

'Told you!' Reid grinned down at me from a step-ladder. 'You're such an unselfish bastard! That's what the old bloke saw in you! You're a *hereditary* socialist!'

'Ideology is hereditary?' I scoffed. 'And what does that make you?'

'A grasping kulak, I guess,' he said happily. 'Ah, now what about this?' He opened a book and studied the fly-leaf. 'Stirner, *The Ego and His Own*, property of the Glasgow Anarchist Workers' Circle, 1943. Five pounds.'

I stared up at him, open-mouthed. I didn't realise I was reaching for it until he pulled it away. 'Uh-uh. Finders keepers.'

'It's of no interest to you,' I said.

'Oh, I don't know.' Reid stepped down the ladder, holding the book like a black Grail in front of my eyes. 'Young Hegelians, German Ideology and all that. Marxist scholarship.'

'You're having me on!'

'Yes, I am,' Reid said. 'But I do have a use for it. I'm going to buy it, and as soon as we get outside I'm going to sell it to you for a tenner.'

No lunches for a fortnight, and back to roll-ups. I could manage that.

'It's a deal!' I almost shouted.

Reid stepped back and scrutinised me.

'Just testing,' he said. He shoved the book into my hands. 'You passed.'

In the grey leaded light of the Union smoking-room, the air thick with the unappetising smell of over-percolated coffee-grounds, we sat in worn leather armchairs and flipped through our acquisitions. I smiled at the twisted dialectics of the wartime apologist, frowned over the laboured wit of the great amoralist. Fascism, communism and anarchism traced their ancestry back to the same Piltdown, the Berlin bars of the 1840s. Give me turn-of-the-century Vienna any day, I thought, its Ringstrasse a particle-accelerator of ideas.

We both sat back at the same moment. Reid toyed with the bamboo holder of the previous day's *Guardian*. The MPLA had taken Huambo, not for the last time.

'How's Annette?' I asked with guarded casualness.

'Fine, as far as I know,' Reid said. He turned over a page.

'Not seen her for a bit?'

Reid laid down the paper and leaned forward, looking at me intently. 'We've kind of ... I don't know ... fallen out, drifted apart.'

'That's a shame,' I said. 'How did that happen?'

Reid spread his hands. 'She's got a real sharp mind, but she's the most unpolitical person I've ever met. She never reads newspapers. It's very hard to find things to talk about.' He smiled ruefully. 'Sounds stupid, I know, but there it is.'

I nodded sympathetically: yes, women are hard to figure out. I was trying to remember the location of the Zoology Department.

I walked up University Avenue, the broad Victorian edifice – Gilmoreghast, as one rag-mag wit had called it – on my left, the Wellsian 'thirties Reading Room on my right. (I hadn't used it since discovering that everything about it was perfect, except its acoustics, which were those of a whispering-gallery.)

At the top of the hill the pedestrian crossing was at red. I waited for the little green man, and wondered if I shouldn't turn around right there, and wait until seeing Annette again could be passed off as a casual encounter ...

No, I told myself firmly. *If you're interested, you'll be there.* I crossed and continued on down to the junction at the bottom, then

54

left along an internal roadway between massive grey sandstone buildings set among patches of grass with flowerbeds and tall trees. The Zoology Department was another of those ancient buildings, solid as a church and founded on a rock of greater age. Inside, polished wood, tiling, the smell of small-animal droppings. From behind a glass partition a receptionist peered at me incuriously. I decided to be bold and asked him where Annette was working. He glanced at a clock and a timetable and told me.

The laboratory at first appeared to be empty. Then I saw Annette, her back to me, laying down sheets of paper along a bench at the far end. I pushed open the double doors and walked up. She turned at my footsteps, saying:

'Excuse me, the practical isn't – Oh, hello Jon.'

Her hair was tied back, her figure hidden in a white lab-coat. Still no less desirable.

'Hi,' I said. Her green eyes examined me quizzically.

'Let me guess,' she said. 'You suddenly developed an interest in invertebrate anatomy, right?'

She gestured at the bench. I looked down at a round glass dish, half-filled with water, in which a few small sea-urchins lay – or rather, moved, as I saw when I looked closer. Laid out along the benches were sheaves of notes, diagramming the echinoderm's organs, the nomenclature beautiful and strange: ampulla, pedicellaria, tube-feet, madreporite, radial canal, ring canal, stone canal …

'Not exactly.' I fidgeted with sturdy tweezers, laid out like cutlery to break the delicate harmless creatures apart.

'So what brings you here?'

'Uh …' I hesitated. 'I just wondered if you'd fancy going out for a drink or something.'

Her face reddened slightly.

'Does this have anything to do with Dave?'

'No,' I said, wondering what she was getting at. 'Only that he told me he wasn't going out with you any more.'

'Oh! And when did he tell you that?'

'About twenty minutes ago,' I admitted.

She laughed. 'What took you so long?'

'I thought jumping up the minute he told me might be a bit insensitive.'

It was as if the implications of my statement were too direct, too blatant. She looked away and glanced back with a half-smile.

'It's very nice of you to think of me,' she said. 'Lonely and forlorn as I am. I'm not sure I'm ready for such kindness.'

If she could tease, I could tease right back. 'I don't expect you to stay that way long.'

'Well,' she said, 'no, I haven't been washing my hair every night!'

'Losing yourself in the giddy social whirl?'

'Yep.'

'So,' I persisted. 'Perhaps you can find room in your hectic life for a quiet drink?'

'Or something.'

'Or something.'

She smiled, this time dropping her ironic look.

'OK,' she said. 'How about nine o'clock tonight in the Western Bar?'

'I'll see you there,' I said.

The doors banged open and a commotion of students came in. 'You better go,' she said. 'See ya.'

At the door I looked back, and saw her looking up. She smiled and turned away.

I jogged off down the corridor. '*Yes!*' I told the world, with a jump and an air-punch that startled a few stragglers and narrowly missed an overhead fluorescent light.

The Western was a quiet pub, tarted up with some attempt at appropriate (i.e., cowpoke) decoration. I arrived about ten minutes early and was standing at the bar, half a pint and one smoke down, when Annette walked in just as the TV heralded the nine o'clock news. The barman reached up and flipped channels. (There were three, all controlled by the government).

Her hair was loose (and bouncy, and shiny, and just washed). She wore a mid-calf denim skirt and a black silk blouse under a puffy jacket which she unzipped and shrugged out of as she walked up. I bought her a lager-and-lime and we found a table by the wall.

'Smoke?'

'Yes, thanks.'

I lit her cigarette and we looked at each other for a moment. Annette laughed suddenly.

56

'This is silly,' she said. 'We know each other just enough to skip the ice-breaking chit–chat, but not well enough to know what to say next.'

Sharp mind alright.

'That's a good point,' I said, treading water. 'Actually I don't know anything about you, apart from having seen you across a table or a room a few times.'

'Didn't Dave talk about me?' There was an undertone of curiosity to her pretended pique.

'No,' I said. 'Mind you, he did tell me one very important thing about you ...'

'Oh yes?'

'That you're not interested in politics.'

'Is that all? Huh, and there was me thinking he'd be telling you as much about me as I've told Sheena about him.'

'That must be a relief.'

'Sure is ... And he's wrong about that, too!' she added.

'How d'you mean?'

'Well, it's not that I'm not interested. I just don't like talking about it.'

'Fair enough,' I said. 'But why?'

'I grew up in Belfast,' she said. 'Left when I was about ten. There's a saying over there: "Whatever you say, say nothing." I still have family over there, still visit. The habit sticks.'

'Even here?' I glanced around. 'What's the problem?'

She leaned forward and spoke in a lowered voice. 'Half the people in this city have some Irish connection, and a good few of them have very decided views. So it doesn't do to shoot your mouth off, especially in pubs.'

As Dave tended to do, I thought. Interesting.

'OK,' I said. 'I'm not curious. I can't even tell what I'm sure anybody from around here could: whether you're a Catholic or a Protestant. Me, I don't have a religion and I don't care what flag flies over me or what politicians do so long as they leave me alone.'

'Which they won't.'

'Aye, there's the rub!'

We both laughed. 'So,' I said, 'what *are* you interested in?'

She thought about it for a moment. 'I like my work,' she said.

'So tell me about it.'

And she did, explaining how she didn't just do the technical stuff but tried to find out about the science behind it. She talked about evolution and population and the future of both, and that got me on to talking about SF, and she admitted to having read some dozens of Michael Moorcock's Eternal Champion novels when she was younger (or 'young', as she charmingly put it). Before we knew it the bell had rung for last orders.

'There's a disco at Joanne's,' Annette said. 'Shall we go there?'

'Good idea,' I said.

It wasn't. We hadn't been there half an hour when the music stopped and the DJ told everyone to pick up their things and leave quietly. We all knew what that meant: a bomb scare. Annette grabbed my hand with surprising force and hauled me through the crowd, with a ruthless disregard for others that I'd hitherto only seen in the QM bar crush.

We spilled into the street just as somebody authoritative shouted 'False alarm!' and the surge moved the other way. Annette stood fast against it. I looked down at her with surprise and saw it wasn't just the drizzle that was wetting her face. Holding her parka around her shoulders she looked miserable and vulnerable.

'Don't you want to go back in?' I asked.

'I want to go home,' she said. I held her parka while she struggled to get it on properly. She grabbed my hand again and started walking fast.

'What's the matter?'

'Oh, God. I just remembered the first time I was in a bomb.'

'Yeah,' I said, trying to be reassuring, 'it's crazy how we've got used to bomb scares.'

She glanced up at me with something like pity.

'I wasn't in a bomb scare,' she said witheringly. 'I was in the *blast radius* of a bomb. Loyalists hit a loyalist bar. Christ. I could see people screaming, and I couldn't hear them.'

I didn't think it would be a good move to ask if many people were hurt.

'I'm sorry,' I said. I squeezed her hand. 'I didn't know.'

She stopped, throwing me off-balance. I turned, tottering, to face her. She held her balled fists in front of her as if grasping and shaking by the lapels someone much smaller than myself.

'*Christ!*' she spat. 'I *hate* this shit! I hate it *so much*! We were just

58

going to enjoy ourselves, we all were, and some fucking swine has to
ruin it! I blame them for all of it! For the bomb scares and the false
alarms and the hoaxes – they wouldn't happen if it wasn't for the
bastards who do the real thing. Ears and feet all over the pavement!'
She closed her eyes, then opened them as if she couldn't bear what
she saw. 'And Dave used to say we had to listen to the oppressed.
Nobody listens to me because I'm not an "oppressed". I'm a *focking
prodistant*!' Her voice dropped to a harsh whisper, remnant of a
caution otherwise thrown to the sodium sky. 'Fuck them all! Fuck
the Pope! Fuck the Queen! Fuck Ireland!'

As suddenly as her outburst had started, it stopped. She rested
her fists on my shoulders and looked up at me, dry-eyed. She
sniffed.

'God, you must think I'm crazy,' she said. 'You didn't deserve
that.'

I wrapped my arms around her and held her close, taking the
opportunity to look around. It must have looked like we we'd been
having some kind of fight. This being Glasgow, and she not having
used a bottle, nobody was paying us more than the idlest flicker of
attention.

'I'd prefer that to "whatever you say, say nothing",' I said.
'Especially as I agree with what you just said.'

'You do?' She pulled back and frowned at me. 'You mean you
don't believe in *anything*?' Her voice was incredulous, hopeful.

Myra's taunt came back to me: *Ey'm en individualist enarchist,
eckchelly.* No point going into it that way, with a string of isms.
I believe in you, I thought of trying, but that wouldn't do, either.
She looked so desperately serious!

I swallowed. 'No God, no country, no "society". Just people and
things, and people one by one.'

'Just us?'

I considered it, tempted. It would be a good line to hug her closer
with.

'No us either, unless each of us chooses, and only as long as each
of us chooses.'

'I don't know if I could live with that.'

'Better than dying with something else.'

She gave that glib response a more welcoming smile than it
deserved.

'Well,' she said, 'I can see you're not just trying to chat me up.' She caught my hand again and shoved it, with hers, into her parka pocket. 'Come on, see me home.'

We walked through the wet streets as if we were joined at the hip, stopping every couple of hundred metres for a clinch and a kiss. Neither of us talked very much. At her flat a faint glow and giggles came from Sheena's small room. We had the front room, and the couch, to ourselves. We did a lot of hugging and kissing and groping and rolling, but when it became obvious that I wanted to go further she pushed me away.

'Not ready yet,' she said.

'That's all right,' I said.

'Maybe you should go now. Some of us have to get up in the morning.'

I thought of several smart replies to that and in the end just nodded and smiled.

'Maybe I should. What about tomorrow?'

She stood up and pulled me to my feet.

'Let me see ... I'm going to a wedding on Saturday. I've got shopping to do tomorrow lunchtime. Hen night in the evening, recovering the night after. And sorting out dresses and stuff.' She mimed a curtsy. 'How d'you fancy coming along to the dance at the reception? Saturday evening.'

'That sounds great! Thanks.'

She peeled a sheet of paper from a pad and scribbled on it. 'Place, time, bus routes,' she said, handing it to me.

'Thanks very much. OK, I'll see you there then.'

We found ourselves at the door.

'We still have to say goodnight,' she said, and made good on it.

The reception was in a hotel in a part of Glasgow I hadn't been before, reached by a succession of buses through parts of Glasgow I didn't know existed. They looked like a war had been lost there: entire blocks and streets razed or ruinous, street-lamps smashed, derelicts or wild kids around fires ...

I later learned that this was the result of a road-building programme disguised as a housing policy, but at the time – sitting in the smoke-filled top deck of the bus in a suit I normally wore only for interviews – I indulged in some enjoyably pessimistic thoughts about the breakdown of civilisation. As the bus wended on, however, the islands of darkness became less frequent and I eventually hopped off in a residential area in front of a reassuringly bright and noisy hotel. I followed the light and noise to the function suite where I found a scene just like a disco except that most people were wearing something like Sunday best and the age range approximated a normal distribution curve.

Around the edges of the room were tables, a buffet with food and trays of drinks, and a bar at the far end. I picked up a glass of whisky at the buffet and looked around for Annette. The music stopped, a dance ended, people moved on to or off the floor.

Annette came out of the crowd as if it were parting just for her – for a moment, it seemed a spotlight had caught her, so that she shone, while everyone around her dimmed. Her hair was circled with leaves and small red roses, and her dress started with a frill at the throat and ended with a flounce at the floor. It was likewise rose-patterned, red on green on black, and over it she wore an organza pinafore with ruffles from the waist to over each shoulder, the tapes wrapped to a bow at the front. Her face, flushed by the dance, was smiling. As she stopped in front of me I smelt her strong, sweet perfume.

'Hi, Jon, you got a fag?' she said. 'I'm gasping.'

As I lit the cigarette for her she caught my hand and pulled me to a seat by a table. She dragged up another chair and sat down facing me, our knees almost touching through the rustling mass of her skirts.

'Ah, that's better,' she said. A passing waiter offered her a tray – she reached past the expected wine and lifted a shot of whisky. 'Thanks for coming.'

I raised my glass. 'Thank *you*. You look different. Beautiful.'

'Aw, gee, thanks.'

'Beautiful in a different way,' I hastened to add.

She gave a quirky smile to indicate that she was only pretending to misunderstand.

'You didn't mention that you were a bridesmaid,' I said.

'Didn't want to scare you off.'

I laughed, unsure what to make of this. 'I like your dress,' I said.

She leaned closer and said in a gossiping whisper: 'So do I. I dug in my heels to get one that I could wear again for parties, so after long discussions with Irene – that's the bride, went to school with her – we settled on this nice little Laura Ashley number. Then she decided it wasn't *icky* and *bridesmaidy* enough, so she got her Mum to run up this thing.' She flicked disdainfully at the apron frill.

'Oh, I don't know,' I said. 'The pinny's what makes it. You really must keep that for parties.' I was only half teasing – there was something undeniably sexy, in an undeniably sexist way, about its trailing associations of feminine servitude.

'Oh yeah, and get taken for a wench?' she grinned.

'Never,' I said. 'Lady, would you like to dance?'

'Well,' she said, considering, 'perhaps after you've refilled my glass, and I've emptied it.'

By the time this was accomplished, more than once, Annette had introduced me to some of her friends and relatives and the dancing had changed from disco-style bopping to traditional, but much wilder, Scottish dancing. Annette drew me into it, and started flinging me about until suddenly, like a memory of a previous life, I discovered I knew the steps and the moves and was able to fling her – and the bewildering, spinning succession of other partners – about with the best of them.

As I danced, skipped, stomped, turned, twirled, lifted and swung, I tried to remember how I remembered all this, and realised it was all down to my father. His interpretation of Marxism – broad-minded even for his socially tolerant, if politically dogmatic, party – insisted on the desirabilty of culture in all its forms. Hence, piano practice and dancing classes – and, when that had led to playground taunts, boxing lessons. Hence also, the Science Museum and the BMNH and the Zoo and the theatre. He was interested in everything. He was there.

And at Hyde Park on Sundays, telling unbelieving onlookers that whatever demo-of-the-week was passing through was a complete waste of time ... He thought he was turning a space-age schoolkid into a scientific socialist, but all he was doing was raising me to be as stubborn an outsider as himself.

The dances flew past as fast as the dancers, with only snatched gulps of whisky and puffs of smoke between one and the next. An eightsome reel finished the set. Annette and I leaned on each other's shoulders with one thought between us. 'Drink?'

'Drink.'

We went to the bar this time, our fortuitous and fortunate position at the end of the dance getting us there ahead of the rush. Annette perched on a stool, the hang of her skirt concealing it so that she seemed suspended on air. I propped my elbow on the bar and ordered pints.

'Well, that was something,' I said. 'I enjoyed that.'

'Me too,' Annette said. 'Cheers.' She sank half a pint of lager. 'Mind you,' she went on, 'throwing the littlest flower-girl in the air, swinging the bride onto your hips, and carrying her granny half-way across the room weren't all absolutely essential.'

'Oh.' I thought back. 'Did I do that?'

She grinned. 'You sure did. Made me proud. Nobody's going to gripe now about me bringing along a strange Sassenach.'

'I didn't know I was a subject of debate.'

'Well, now it'll just be speculation.' She winked.

'About us?'

'Aha,' Annette said. 'So there's an "us"?'

Face suddenly serious, haloed in red and black.

'If you choose,' I said.

Her green eyes regarded me levelly.

'And what do you choose?'

Around us people were shouting, reaching for drinks, brushing against us. The music was rocking again. I see and hear it only now. At the time there was nothing but her.

'There's no choosing,' I said. I took a step forward and put my arms around her waist. Our foreheads touched. 'It was all decided the second I saw you.'

'Me too,' she said, and we kissed. It felt strange doing it at the same height. By the time we'd finished she'd slid off the stool. She looked up at me, smiling, and said: 'But I saw you first.'

'So what,' I asked in a bitter-tanged amazement, 'have the past three months been all about?'

'I'm like you,' she said. 'I want to be free.'

'You can be free with me!' I said. 'Any time. Please.'

We were falling together laughing.

'Yes,' she said.

And then it had all been said, and we were just standing together at the bar, having a drink.

Irene, the bride, clicked up to us in high heels and a smart blue two-piece, gave me a wary smile and whispered to Annette.

'See you in a few minutes,' Annette said. I bowed to them both – and to this necessity – and watched their whispering progress out of sight.

Annette returned about a quarter of an hour later.

'Everything okay?' I asked, sliding her a G&T. She looked a bit preoccupied.

'Basically yes. Thanks,' she said, sipping carefully. 'I just spent ten minutes hanging about in reception with Irene's wedding-dress in a plastic bag over my shoulder. *Finally* got someone to stash it till I leave. Couldn't leave it in the room. Some mix-up with keys.'

'So it's not all fun, being a bridesmaid.'

'Ha, ha. Little do you know.'

'I think I'd rather not –'

I realised the music had stopped and somebody was trying to make himself heard above a hubbub.

'Hey, come on!'

Annette swirled about and dashed away to the nearest exit, where Irene and her man were backing out of the doorway with a kind of female scrum going on around them –

Something sailed over the heads of the scrum. As I looked up, startled, Annette shot her hand in the air like an eager pupil with an answer, and caught it. She brandished the bouquet as she turned slowly around, acknowledging cheers and catcalls, and faced me with a broad smile.

'Well,' she said. 'Lucky me.'

Everybody trooped outside to send the new couple on their way. They'd cunningly called a taxi, and left behind a car covered with shaving foam and lipstick for the rain to wash.

Then more dancing, and more talking, and a long taxi ride to Annette's flat, with Irene's dress draped across our knees. As I paid the driver she ran to the steps of her house, laughing, her hems bunched in one hand and the other dress flying out behind her like a comet. I caught up with her as she unlocked the outer door. We went down the stairs and into her darkened flat, noisily trying to be quiet.

She took me straight to her bedroom, hooked the wedding-dress on its hanger over a wardrobe door facing the foot of her bed, and turned to me. I caught the tapes of the bow at her waist, yanked them and she twirled around, catching the pinafore as it came off and sending it sailing into a corner. I fumbled with buttons down the back of the dress, found a concealed zip and opened it. The dress fell around her feet. She stepped out of its circle in a long nylon slip, and deftly undid every button of my shirt while I got rid of my footwear, trousers and Y-fronts as fast as possible. The slip slid down to her feet with a rattle of static electricity. The rest of her underwear took enjoyably longer to remove.

I cupped her breasts in my hands and buried my mouth between them. Her skin tasted of talc and salt. Holding her away to look at her and holding her close to touch her led to a closer, quicker rhythm as we tumbled onto her bed.

'Hey, hey, hey,' she said. She put her hand on my shoulder and held me away, reached behind her head and waved a small foil package in front of my face. Then she tore the package open with her teeth.

'Get that on, you irresponsible bastard.'

'Wouldn't want to be responsible for bastards,' I agreed. I rolled the condom onto my cock. 'I do have some with me, I just forgot.'

'If you ever say anything as feeble to me again you're outa here, Jon Wilde.'

I tried for a moment to think of some reply, and then put my tongue to a better use.

I woke in a room dim in the curtained light of mid-morning, my limbs still tangled with Annette's, and was momentarily startled by the apparition of the white gown looming over the end of the bed, its falls of lawn and drifts of lace protected by a shimmering forcefield of polythene, like a ghost from the future.

5

Ship City

W E TAKE, FIRST, a long view (longer than it looks) and catch the planet as it swings by from a hundred thousand kilometres out. It's red – no surprises there – but it's mottled with dark spills of blue and stains of green, and those spills and stains are beginning to be connected up by ... channels, by ... (and the thought is as fleeting as the glimpse) *canali*, so that New Mars really does look like the original Mars, really, didn't. (But didn't we wish.)

Flip the viewpoint to a thousand kilometres ... *up*, now, not *out* ... and we're crawling past it at a satellite's eye-level, taking in the whorled fingerprints of water-vapour, the planet's curving face-plate of atmosphere steamed-up with breath, the scrawled marks of life and the ruled lines of intelligence: yes, canals.

Dropping now, to a structure as unmistakably artificial as it's apparently organic: at first sight a black asterisk, like a capital city on a map, then (as the viewpoint hurtles in and the view reddens, bloodshot by the flames of air-braking) like a starfish stranded on the sand.

Cut, again, to a more leisurely airborne vantage, drifting above what is now clearly a city, its radial symmetry still its major feature but with its five arms visibly joined by the black threads of roads, streets, canals; and, at another level, invisible from the outside, by the cobweb cabling of *the nets*.

And we're in. That old TCP/IP transaction protocol is still valid (from way back to the Mitochondrial Eve of all the systems) so we can hear, feel and see. But the big! numbers still count, so encryption hides much of the data in catacombs of dark. What we can access, on the open channels, is more than enough to show:

Four of the city's five arms are non-human domains. They look as if they were intended for human habitation, but nobody's home, except machines. There's a basic stratum, a sort of mechanical topsoil, where things are doing things to things. Simulacra of intelligence are going through the motions, bawling and toiling: empty automatic barges plough algae-clogged canals, servitor machines struggle to sweep dust from the floors of corridors whose walls are already thick with mould. In the streets it's a creationist's caricature of natural selection: half-formed mechanisms collide and combine and incorporate each other's parts, producing unviable offspring which themselves propagate further grotesque transitional forms.

This mindless level is preyed upon by more sophisticated machinery, which lurks and pounces, gobbles and cannibalises for purposes of its own. Artificial intelligences – some obsessive and focused, others chaotic and relaxed, some even sane – haunt a fraction of these machines. It's hard to identify the places where such minds reside. Lurching, unlikely structures may be steered by a sapient computer no bigger than a mouse, while some sleek and shining and, even, humanoid machine may well be moronic or mad.

The whole groaning junkyard is persistently pillaged by human beings, who risk everything from their fingertips to their souls in venturing into this jungle of iron and silicon. They have their mechanical allies, scouts and agents; but if machines, in general, have no loyalty to each other, they have even less to human friends or masters. It remains easier to reprogram a machine than to subvert a human.

And through it all, like germs, the minute molecular machinery of stray nanotechnology goes about its invisible and occasionally disastrous work. Immune systems have evolved, the equivalent of medicine is practised; public health measures are applied (they are not, exactly, enforced). But the smallest are the swiftest, and here evolution's race is most ruthlessly run.

The fifth arm is the human quarter. The nets are its mind. In them we find its good intentions, its evil thoughts, its wet dreams and its dull routines. This is not how it should be finally judged. But still –

Underlying everything is the reproduction of daily life, and it provides a huge proportion of the net traffic. Nobody's counting, but there are several hundred thousand human beings alive on New

Mars, most of them in Ship City, the rest scattered in much smaller communities, fanning out across the planet. Every minute buzzes with thousands of conversations and personal communications. Business: orders, invoices, payments, transactions. Property rights – what people agree to let people do with things – have grown complex and differentiated, and the unbundling and repackaging and exchanging of these rights proceeds with card-sharp speed: time shares, organ mortgages, innovation futures, labour loans, birth benefits ... it gets complicated. Hence conflicts, charges, settlements, crimes and torts.

Law and order lifts its eyes and teeth above the stream of business only occasionally, and the resulting cop-shows and courtroom dramas and camp comedies provide – in reality and in fiction – a staple of entertainment. Most of the torments and humiliations we see on the screens are – fortunately – just pornography. The trials by ordeal and combat are real.

Religion – some. The highest clerical dignitary is the bishop of New Mars. Reformed Orthodox Catholic, so while she has the odd qualm about exactly how the Succession passed to her, she knows she'll pass it on to one or more of her kids. She's friendly with the few Buddhists and the rabbi (like, you weren't *expecting* Jews?) and stern but charitable towards the lunatic heretics; their delusion that New Mars is the afterlife or some post-apocalyptic staging area is, in the circumstances, forgiveable.

Politics – none. It's an anarchy, remember? But it's an anarchy by *default*. There's no state because nobody can be bothered to set one up. Too much hassle, man. Keep your nose clean, don't stick your neck out, it's always been this way and nothing will ever change, and anyway (and especially) *what will the neighbours think?* (They'll never stand for it, is what. It's against human nature.)

The outside of the city's nervous system consists of its senses: cameras and microphones for news and surveillance, detectors of chemicals and stresses which monitor its health. Start at the top: on the highest and most central tower is a globe the size of a human head. It's just an all-round viewing-camera, an amenity stuck there in a flourish of public spirit or private speculation. From there we can peer down the dizzying sweep of tower-tops that eventually planes out to low, flat roofs, and ends in domes, shacks and sheds at the city limits.

Like each of the city's five radial arms, this one is an elongated kite-shape, first widening, then tapering. The buildings themselves are of two types: those that were grown, and those that were built. The shapes of the former can be analysed into intersecting polygons, regular or irregular: those of the latter, into rectangles. The layout and location of the latticed, cellular structures has the same quality of accidental inevitability as the boulders in a rock-fall or the pebbles in scree, and for the same reason: minimal occupation of available space. The constructed buildings obey a different principle of economy, and stick up or dig down as its unpredictable laws dictate.

Both types of buildings – both laws of location – follow the streets, and the streets follow the canals. The canals are a circulatory system: the Ring Canal encircles the central area, the Radial Canals bisect the arms, and each has innumerable tributaries and capillaries. Near the leftward edge of the arm we're looking down is an anomalous, long canal that first comes into view just below us and extends beyond the horizon: the Stone Canal.

The man leans into the recess of the window, supporting some of his weight on his spread fingertips. The cement is rough under his fingertips. He stares out of the window, which is high on the city's slope, looking along the Stone Canal. As he balances his weight on the balls of his feet and the tips of his fingers, the tensed muscles in his arms and shoulders show through the soft cloth of his jacket. The muscles flex and he straightens, turning around. His black hair flicks past his chin with the speed of his movement.

The other two men in the room are taller and bulkier than he is, but they both recoil slightly as he strides towards them. He stops a couple of metres away and glares at them.

'You lost her,' he says. 'To the abolitionists.' His speech has an accent not much heard in this city, something from the past, roughened and refined over a long time. It provides a rasping undertone to the modulation of his voice, which is likewise – consciously or not – a practised and accomplished instrument of his will. Accent and tone together are precisely gauged to convey his emotion: in this case, contempt.

'She had an IBM franchise,' one of the men says. He licks his lips, withdraws his tongue abruptly into his mouth as if he's aware it's gone out too far. He wipes his chin.

'That,' says the man, 'is not an excuse. It's a description of failure.' He sighs, dusts his fingertips together. 'All right. From the top.'

He stalks away to a big wooden desk, and half-sits on the edge of it.

'OK, Reid,' says the other man, and launches into an account. He's spoken for a minute when Reid raises a hand.

'A young man?' he says. 'And a robot? Describe them.'

He listens, narrow-eyed, for another minute before interrupting with a downward gesture of the hand.

'You thought he recognised her, Stigler?'

Stigler's lips are dry again.

'He ... thought he did.'

'Oh, *Christ*!' The word comes out like a rod cracked down on the desk. Reid drums his fingers for a moment.

'And you, Collins, I don't suppose your descriptive powers are in any better shape, no?'

'I was giving cover, Reid,' Collins says. 'Looking everywhere else, know what I mean?'

'OK, OK.' Reid stands up and looks them over, speculatively. He might be considering profitable uses for their body-parts, and suitable methods of rendering. 'You did the job we agreed, as well as you could. If I'd wanted to pull in a man on sus, I'd have needed a warrant. And that's what I'm going to need, gentlemen, so I'm afraid that rules you out. Full payment, no bonus.'

Collins and Stigler look relieved and turn to go. At the door Collins scratches his neck, looks at Reid. Reid looks up from the screen he's turned his attention to.

'Yes?'

'Uh, Reid, question. You don't happen to know who *owns* that robot?'

Reid thinks about this. His smile lets the two men know they're his good friends, and not a couple of greps who haven't come back with the data.

'Stay on the case,' he tells them.

Wilde stood up and walked to the end of the quay, past the people and the intelligent apes and the machines that might have been intelligent. He stared across the Stone Canal, and then looked down into the water for a while. He found, perhaps, some answer in his reflection.

The robot, Jay-Dub, was still crouched at the edge of the quay, poised like a predatory water-bird. Patterns of liquid crystal shifted in its shadowed central band as Wilde returned. Wilde looked down at it.

'We're not in Kazakhstan any more,' he said.

The machine made no reply.

'What *happened*?' Wilde asked. He looked around. 'Is it safe to talk?'

'Safe enough,' said Jay-Dub. 'I can pick up most attempts to overhear.'

'All right,' said Wilde. 'Tell me this: where did I hide my pistol?'

'In the shower.'

'What was the last thing I said?'

'"Love never dies."'

Wilde frowned.

'What was the last thing I *decided*?'

'That I'd – that you'd never smoke again.'

Wilde leaned down and tapped the machine's hull.

'That's right. That's a promise I remember making, and you can go right on keeping.'

He took the coffee-glass to the breakfast-food stall and returned with the glass refilled and a packet of cigarettes and a lighter.

'I don't approve of this,' Jay-Dub said as Wilde sat down beside it and lit up.

'Fuck you,' Wilde said. 'I want your story, not your opinions.'

He leaned back against the shell of the machine, which shifted its weight on its legs to compensate.

'It's a long story. You have no idea how long.'

'So make it short.' Wilde's eyes were closed.

'"Yes, master," said the robot,' said the robot. 'OK, whatever you say. Basically, I died just after being shot. My brain was immediately scanned with a prototype neural imaging system and the pattern recorded.'

'Come on,' Wilde said. 'We don't – didn't have anything like that.'

'Reid's people did. They were more advanced than anyone suspected. And I was the first. The first human, anyway. I believe most of the enhanced apes around here originate with the early experiments of that period. However, it was many years later – though not, of course, subjectively – that I opened my eyes and found myself in an impossible spacecraft. Comfortable, one-gee, but no rotation or acceleration was apparent when I looked outside. Virtual reality, of course. What was outside the windows was what was outside in the real world.'

It paused. A minute passed. The man reached his hand back and knocked the machine's side with his knuckles. Then he sucked his knuckles.

'And what was outside was –?'

'Ganymede, I think,' the robot said. 'What was left of it. The machine that I inhabited was not much bigger than the one you see now. It, and thousands like it, were engaged in constructing a platform. All around the rings of Jupiter, other machines were engaged in related tasks.'

Again its voice trailed off.

'The rings of *Jupiter*?' Wilde said. 'Somebody had been busy.'

'Guess who.'

'Reid?'

'And company.'

'They'd done that? By when?'

'2093.'

Wilde opened his eyes and gazed out over the canal.

'I take it,' he said, 'that the humans and human-equivalent robots didn't do all this on their own.'

'Indeed not. Among the struts of the platform were huge entities that we called macros. They were made of nanomachines, and they were the hardware platform for millions of uploaded minds. People here, now, call them "the fast folk". They were by then well beyond the human, and they were building a wormhole – the one our ship came through to get here.'

'Where are they now?'

'Ah,' said Jay-Dub. 'A good question. The ones around Jupiter lost interest, shall we say, in the external world. The templates from which they developed, the source-code if you like, we brought with us, as we brought the stored minds and coded bodies of the dead.'

'Including me?'

'Well, yes. Your actual body wasn't coded, as far as I know. There was a tissue-sample, from which you were later – from which I cloned you. Your mind was coded, as I said.'

'Separately from yours?' Wilde sounded puzzled.

'My mind and yours were copied from the same original,' Jay-Dub said. 'I woke up in that machine in exactly the same frame of mind as you woke up yesterday, and with exactly the same memories. And in less auspicious circumstances.'

'My heart,' said Wilde, 'absolutely fucking bleeds.'

'My enormously sophisticated software detects a degree of hostility.' The machine's voice was attempting irony, something outside its familiar range.

'I hope it does,' said Wilde. 'You've just admitted that clones are a separate issue from stored minds. So the presence of anybody here who looks like somebody I used to know, is no indication what-so-fucking-ever that that person is actually here, am I right?'

'In principle, yes, but –'

'So your remark about the clone being some reason to hope that Annette was, as you put it, among the dead was a complete lie?'

'No,' said the machine. 'It does mean there's a chance.'

Wilde shook his head.

'The more I think about it,' he said, 'the more I doubt it. She never believed in cryonics or uploading or any of that shit. If she believed in anything, she believed in the general resurrection at the end of time. The Omega Point.'

'And all that shit,' said Jay-Dub.

Wilde laughed. 'You still think so? Well, I'll bow to your greater experience.'

The machine shifted slightly. 'The end of time may be closer than you think, and worse than you can imagine.'

'What do you mean by that?'

'I'd rather you worked it out for yourself,' said Jay-Dub. 'Anything I tell you about it would only put further strain on your credulity. But it does add a degree of urgency to our task.'

'Our task?' Wilde almost shouted. 'What do you mean, "our"? The way I see it, I'm not Jon Wilde. I have his memories, and my body is like his was at twenty.' He lit and drew on another cigarette; smiled through a cough. 'At twenty, we all feel immortal. But if anyone has a claim to *be* Wilde, it's you. You can keep his promises, fight his battles. I'm sure you remember one of those drunken discussions with Reid about cloning bodies and copying personalities; and the conclusion you came to: a copy is not the original, therefore ... Reid had some quaintly theological way of putting it, you may recall.'

'"The resurrected dead on the Day of Judgement are new creations, as innocent as Adam in the Garden."'

'Exactly,' said Wilde. 'That's what I am: a new creation. A new man.' He sent his cigarette-end spinning into the canal and jumped to his feet, stretching his arms wide and looking up at the sky. 'A New Martian!'

'You're Wilde all right,' said the machine. 'That's exactly how he would have reacted.'

The man laughed. 'You don't catch me that easily. Similarity, no matter how exact, is not identity. Continuity is.'

'That may be,' said the machine. 'But everything about New Mars is a logical consequence of assuming the opposite.'

Wilde closed his eyes for a moment, then squatted down beside the robot and scratched lines in the dirt and gravel of the quay with a fishbone. He gazed at the resulting doodle as if it were an equation he was struggling to solve.

'Ah,' he said. He thought about it some more. 'Everything?'

'Everything that matters,' said the machine.

'But that's insane. It's worse than wrong – it's *mistaken*.'

'I expected you to think that,' said Jay-Dub, a note of complacency in its tone. 'That way, whether you identify yourself with the original Jonathan Wilde or not, you'll probably want to do what I want you to do.'

'And what's that?'

'You said Reid killed you – me, us, whatever. At the very least he was responsible. Sue the bastard for murder.'

Wilde laughed. 'Sue, not charge? You have that too?' It sounded like his interest in his own case had been diverted by curiosity about the law.

'That too,' Jay-Dub said heavily. 'Polycentric legal system, we got.'

'Whatever the legal system,' Wilde said, 'for a living man to stand up in court and claim he was murdered is, well, pushing it.'

'Exactly,' said Jay-Dub. 'And I want to push it till it falls.'

Wilde scratched in the dust some more.

'Ah,' he said. 'I see. Very neat. All the answers are wrong. Like a *koan*.'

He looked up.

'Why,' he added, 'couldn't you sue Reid on your own account?'

Jay-Dub stood up, straightening and extending its legs. 'Look around you,' it said, flailing its arms about at the busy quay. 'Every jumped-up monkey here has rights that a court will recognise. I don't. I'm *instrumentum vocale*: a tool that talks.'

'So what about this distinction you make so much of, between *human equivalent* and *just a fucking machine*?'

'"Human equivalent",' the robot said with some bitterness, 'is a *marketing term*. It has no legal standing whatsoever, except with the abolitionists, and nobody gives a fuck about *them*.'

'Oh?' Wilde looked interested. 'That's the people the … gynoid went off with?'

'Yes.'

'I want to talk to them. They sound like my kind of people.'

'I assure you they're not,' the robot said. 'They're the kind of moralistic, dogmatic, self-righteous purists that you despised all your life.'

'Fine,' the man said. 'I said my kind of people, not Wilde's.'

He got to his feet. 'I'm going to see them.'

'That would be a mistake.'

Wilde set off briskly along the quay. 'It's the kind of mistake,' he said, as Jay-Dub rose and followed, 'that I died not making. Not many people get the chance to learn from that.'

Reid's office is large. The walls are curved, made from a plain grey cement that gives an unexpected atmosphere of warmth. The window's view adds a good percentage to the room's price. The morning sunlight slants through it. On the desk, of solid wood polished so that it looks almost like plastic, there's a standard keyboard and screen. Reid has contacts, which he seldom uses, on his eyes.

He's sitting on the desk, leaning across it, paging through a search. The search is fast, and the scenes flash by in reverse order. Days of recorded phone-calls jabber and gesticulate backwards.

He stops, slows, pages forward. Freezes the scene.

He looks up. 'C'mere,' he says.

Collins and Stigler step over and peer at the screen. It shows the interior of the cab of some big powerful haulage vehicle. The details are quaint: a dangling mike, a peeling motto, padded polyethylene seats. A man with a lined, leathery face is looking into the camera. Beside him is a young woman with very dark eyes, very black hair, a tight tee-shirt and cropped denim shorts. She has the look of an intelligent and wary slut.

Reid fingers a key and the picture moves. There's a flicker of interference that makes all three men blink and shake their heads slightly. As they open their eyes the screen clears.

'Forget it,' the man's saying. 'Wrong number.'

His hand moves out of frame and the screen blanks. Another recorded call begins. Reid stops and scrolls back. He pauses at the interference, runs it past again slowly.

'Oh, shit,' he says.

He clicks on another screen icon and pulls in some analysis software. The flicker suddenly becomes a page of symbols. Reid clicks again. The symbols expand into screens and screens of text. Reid runs his finger down the monitor, his frown deepening.

'Son of a *bitch*,' he says, sitting back.

Stigler is twitching. 'That guy,' he says excitedly. 'With the skin thing, he's –'

Reid looks at him. 'No shit, Sherlock.'

He calls up the picture again and runs another program, which smooths and softens the man's features.

'Hey!' says Collins.

Reid points at the screen. 'Get him,' he says.

'Wait a minute,' says Stigler. 'You said we'd need a warrant, and I can't see no court giving –'

Reid claps him on the back. 'Don't you worry about it,' he grins. 'That man is *dead*.'

He stalks away and leans once more on the sill, looking out through the window at the city, and smiles into the sunlight.

6

The Summer Soldier

I LOOKED UP from the *Observer* on the breakfast table. Outside, through the french window, our small walled backyard hummed with bees and bloomed with weeds. Ten o'clock sun slanted steeply in. Annette was sitting feet up along the bench opposite, leaning against the wall, enjoying her first cigarette and second coffee of the day. Eleanor, the main reason why we were up at this hour on a Sunday morning (and the result of a Sunday morning seven years earlier when getting out of bed was the last thing on our minds) knelt over felt-tip pens and a colouring-book.

'What are we doing today?' I asked.

'Peace-fighting,' Annette said firmly.

'Not me,' I said, in chorus with Eleanor's groaned 'Oh *no*, mummy.' I'd forgotten about the CND demonstration, although it had been pencilled, then biro'd, on the kitchen calendar for weeks.

'Please yourselves, anarchists,' Annette said, stubbing out her cigarette. Something in her tone and gesture told me she was annoyed – having succeeded in getting us to demos before, she knew our objection was based more on sloth than principle. In this year of Chernobyl and Tripoli, we were letting the side down.

'How about if we meet you there?' I suggested hastily. 'Eleanor and I could nip over to Camden market, then we'll go and see Granny and Grandpa at Marble Arch and watch out for you, and we can all go to McDonald's afterwards.'

As I spoke Eleanor transparently calculated whether trailing around second-hand bookstalls was worth it for the sake of seeing her grandparents and tanking up on cheeseburger and milkshake. From the way her eyes brightened it looked like the bottom line was in the black. I turned to Annette, who gave me a relenting smile.

'OK,' she said. 'At least you'll be there.' She stood up, in a

77

graceful slither of nightdress and negligée. 'And come on, you,' she added, stooping to pat the sticking-up rump of Eleanor, now back at her colouring. 'Get yo' little ass into some kinda decent gear.'

'Do we have-to?'

There were times – like this, and bedtimes – when I regretted ever answering the question: 'Daddy, what's libertarianism?' with anything but a lie.

'No, we don't *have* to,' I said. 'But we're going to, because I bloody say so.'

'I'll tell mummy you said that.'

'Said what?'

'Bloody.'

'Go ahead, clipe.'

'Whassa clipe?'

'A *much* worse word. A terrible word.'

By this time we were in the street, walking briskly along to Holloway Road. Even on a Sunday the trucks were lined up, honking nose to stinking tail. I blamed the environmentalists, who'd delayed the widening of the Archway road for years and inflicted planning blight on the entire neighbourhood. At least it lowered the price of a ground-floor flat. I relieved my feelings by starting to sing 'Ten Green Protestors' and got Eleanor skipping and singing along. By the time we'd reached '… there'd be no Green protestors and a road through the wall!' we were on the Camden bus.

Top deck, branches brushing past. Smokers had to sit at the back. I blamed the environmentalists.

Chalk Farm Road and Camden Market cheered me up, as they always did whether or not I found anything I wanted. Stalls and canals and the invincible hand of the flea market, its black plastic bags and canopies the banners of an anarchist army that would still be there when the rest had done their worst, if anything were there at all.

We left with a leatherbound Lord Macaulay for me, an antique rayon bodice for Annette, a coral paperweight for my parents and a climbing wooden monkey for Eleanor. So I was in a good mood when we emerged past the lines of cops at Marble Arch and found my mother and father near Speakers' Corner. As I'd expected, they were leafletting and pamphletting and generally irritating the first contingents to trail in after traipsing – with an entirely unjustified sense of having achieved something – from another park to this one.

Eleanor raced up to be grabbed by her grandparents. I encircled them both in a quick air-hug and let them get back to work. Tall, stooping, grey-haired, and tough as a pair of old boots, they'd seen it all before: the Peace Pledge Union, CND, the Committee of 100, Vietnam Solidarity, CND again ... Today they were doing a respectable trade in a pamphlet. In between keeping half an eye on the demo and chatting to whichever of them wasn't in full flow, I flipped through *Is a Third World War Inevitable?*: its cover as lurid as any peace-movement propaganda, its contents a frosty dismissal of two centuries of peace campaigns – all of which had failed to prevent (where they hadn't actively endorsed) increasingly destructive wars.

A Scottish ASTMS banner bellied through the gateway, and as it sailed closer I saw Annette a few rows behind it. She was walking with a man whom I recognised, with a pleasant surprise, as Reid. We'd seen him a quite a few times over the past decade, kept in touch: he'd crashed out on our floor often enough when he was in London for work or politics.

I stood there under the trees while my mother talked to Eleanor and my father argued with a stray Spartacist, and watched their approach. They were deep in conversation, faces serious, eyes oblivious to the surrounding march. When they were about twenty metres away Reid, perhaps distracted by the raised voices nearby, looked aside and saw me. He touched Annette's elbow and she saw me too, and immediately they broke ranks and hurried over.

Reid's hair was shorter and neater than it had been the last time I'd seen him, at a *Critique* conference the previous year. His shirt, black jeans and Reeboks were new. His denim jacket was faded, frayed, breastplated with badges against Reagan and Thatcher, Cruise and Pershing; for the Sandinistas and Solidarnosc, and (as if that unlikely combination wasn't enough) a red-and-gold enamel badge celebrating the 1980 Moscow Olympics. A carrier-bag flapped lightly from one hand.

'Hi Dave. Good to see you, man.'

'Yeah, likewise.' He slapped my shoulder. 'Hello, Eleanor. You've grown a lot.' Eleanor gave him a smile that showed all the gaps in her milk-teeth. Her gaze kept returning to the bright rows of badges.

My father's dispute had ended in a stand-off. The Spartacist, a scrawny lad in a knit cap and lumber-jacket, saw Reid and turned like a locking-on radar.

'Comrade –' he began, stepping forward and moving a bundle of papers into combat position.

'Oh, piss off,' Reid said, barely glancing at him. He faced my father. 'Good afternoon, Mr Wilde. I'm David Reid. Annette and Jon have often told me about you.'

'Martin,' my father said. 'And this is my wife Amy. Pleased to meet you, David.' He grinned. 'Jonathan tells me you're quite bright, for a Trot.'

Reid looked at me with raised eyebrows. I shrugged and spread my hands. 'I take no responsibility for what his warped mind makes of anything I say.'

'Can we go to McDonalds now?'

My father smiled at Eleanor and checked his watch. 'There'll be a couple of comrades along shortly,' he said. 'What about you, David?'

Reid jiggled his carrier-bag on one finger. 'I've sold most of my papers. Yeah, I'll be OK to skive off for half an hour or so.'

'It'll be all boring speeches now,' Annette said. She smiled and waved airily. 'Fine by me.'

'She never brings anything to demos,' I explained.

'Only my beautiful self.'

'That's enough,' Reid and I said at the same time, and we all laughed.

We hung about for a few more minutes until my parents' comrades – who, to my surprise, had green hair and studded nostrils – turned up. Then we ducked under the main road and through the golden arches, to find the place packed. A lot of badges and plastic bags, a lot of post-attack black.

'Goddamn anti-Americans,' Martin muttered as we queued. 'Under-fed, under-employed and underfoot!'

He trotted out some variant of this at every occasion of suspected anti-Yank sentiment, and now I barely grunted at it, but Reid grinned broadly. 'Yeah,' he said. 'They come down here, they take our seats ...'

Ten minutes later we were crowded around something that wasn't so much a table as a painstakingly exact plastic replica of one. Eleanor sat between her grandparents and kept them entertained. Annette sat on one bolt-down seat and Reid and I half-leaned, half-sat over another.

'Annette says you're still lecturing,' Reid said.

'Yeah.' I blew on a hot fry. 'Part-time, short-term contracts. Further education's run like a typing pool these days.'

'You should approve.' Dave was eating quickly, glancing away every now and then.

'I would if there was some sense to it all ... Just as well Annette's got a steady job.'

'Solid breadwinner,' Annette said, around a mouthful.

'Safe from everything except the animal rights nutters?'

'That's about it. How're you doing yourself?'

'Working for North British Mutual,' Reid said. 'Big insurance company in Edinburgh. I'm supposed to be a software engineer. It's just like being a programmer except you do it properly.' He leaned closer in a parody of confidentiality, and winked at my father. 'Money for old rope.'

'Still with the Migs, I take it?'

Reid gave a twisted smile. 'Everybody's in the Labour Party these days, but you know how it is. Got into working in the union. Been on the branch committee for the past year.'

My father looked suddenly alert. He'd been on *his* branch committee for decades.

'God, that must be thrilling,' I said.

For a moment Reid's face took on a look of utter weariness.

'It's OK,' he said. 'Better than Labour Party ward meetings anyway.'

'I'll tell you what your trouble is,' my father said quietly. 'You're still doing it for the party, not for the union.'

Reid shook his head. 'I'm for the union!'

Martin narrowed his eyes, held his gaze for a second, then returned to teasing Eleanor.

'What's *your* political activity these days?' Reid asked, breaking an awkward silence. 'Deep entry in the Tory Party?'

'Very funny,' I said. I *had* once spoken at a fringe meeting, but I wasn't about to tell him that. 'I do odd bits of work and write articles for what I consider good causes. Everything from Amnesty International to the Space Settlers' Society, with the Libertarian Alliance somewhere in between.' I shrugged. 'I know – it sounds a bit ... all over the place.'

'Space and freedom, huh?' Reid said lightly.

Across the street the demonstration was still going past. A banner with a picture of a rising rocket – a Polaris missile – caught my eye, and I think that was the moment when it all came together, when I had the vision. I saw a future where other people – infinitely different from these, infinitely like them – carried banners with other and greater rockets, chanted unfamiliar slogans I couldn't quite make out.

'That's it!' I said. 'That's what we need to get away from the nuclear terrorists. A *space* movement! Escape from the planet of the apes!'

'That'll be the day,' Reid said. He examined a hunk of sesame-sprinkled roll, stuffed it in his mouth and chewed it. 'OK folks, I gotta go.' He smiled around the table, saw Eleanor's covetous look at his badges and took one off and gave it to her. Jobs Not Bombs. 'My phone-number's still the same. See you soon, I hope.' I caught a flicker of a look between him and Annette. His eyes, as he turned to me, were calm and friendly as ever. 'Next time we'll have a proper drink, right?'

'Sure,' I said. '"Not those rich imperialist tit-bits."'

'Yeah,' he grinned. 'Well, back to the Judean People's Front.'

'What!?? Don't you mean the People's Front of Judea?'

Reid smote his forehead. 'Of course. See ya mate.'

He edged through the crush and vanished into the crowd.

We finished up our fast-food in a defiantly leisurely way. The queue, as apparently unending as the demonstration, shuffled forward. My father spotted a young woman carrying a bundle of papers whose headline – no, it wasn't even that, it was the actual *masthead* – read 'Fight Racism! Fight Imperialism!' and asked her in a tone of polite curiosity: 'Why don't you fight capitalism, for a change?'

But after the young woman had said only a few sentences, he

stopped her with a smile and an uplifted finger. He looked at his watch, and brought the finger down to tap it triumphantly.

'One minute, twenty-five seconds,' he said to the puzzled cadre. 'Congratulations. That's the shortest time yet for a member of – let me see –' he made a pretence of counting on his fingers '– a split, from a split, from a split, from the Fourth International to call *me* a sectarian!'

He stood back as we all rose to sweep our detritus onto trays.

'Wasse on about?' the young woman said indignantly, seeing a look of surreptitious sympathy from Amy. 'Wassis Fourf Inte'national?'

'Don't you worry, dear,' Amy said, squeezing past. 'He's a terrible man.'

But she slipped the girl a leaflet all the same.

Amy believed there was hope for everybody yet.

Except, possibly, Martin.

In the play-park off Holloway Road, Eleanor paced along painted lion-footprints and suddenly scooted off to the swings. We'd taken her here to run about after all the Tube and bus rides she'd sat through.

Annette flopped on a bench. 'I'm knackered,' she said. 'Long walk.' She leaned back, eyes half-shut against the sunlight but still watching Eleanor.

I sat down beside her, leaning forward, elbows on knees.

'Long talk, too?'

'Oh yes. Dave.' She sighed and shifted, half-facing me, an arm draped along the back of the bench. 'I came across him selling his Socialist Action faction rag at the assembly area, and I'd lost the Islington lot so I ended up marching along with all those Scottish trade unionists. Dave and I talked the whole way.'

I smiled. 'Like old times.'

Annette ran her upper teeth over her lower lip, looked in her bag and reached for a cigarette.

'Yeah, well ...' She lit up and inhaled hard, sighed smokily. 'You could say that. Shit, this is difficult.'

'What's difficult?'

'I should've told you this before, but there never seemed to be a good reason, or a good time. The fact is, for quite a while now David's been, well, kind of gallantly flirting with me, you know?'

'Of course.' I smiled sourly, feeling tense and cold. 'That's understandable. And I suppose you would coquettishly flirt right back?'

'How nice of you to put it like that.' She leaned forward, eyes bright, and laid a hand on my knee. 'But Dave's stubborn, and literal, and he's so goddamn *serious* ...'

'And he got the wrong idea,' I said, my voice heavy and flat. Eleanor came off the swing and ran up a grassy mound, like a long barrow, and began climbing a wood-and-metal artificial tree.

'Yes.' Annette sounded relieved. 'Maybe that's why –' She stopped for a moment and sucked air around the cigarette, as if it were a joint. 'Today,' she continued in a firmer tone, 'God, my ears were burning. He told me that letting our ... relationship, or whatever it was, break up was the worst mistake he's ever made, that he's never got over me and ...' Her voice trailed off and she stared into space. 'He's always loved me and he wants me to come back,' she concluded in a rush.

I stared at her. 'You mean to tell me –'

'Daa–ad!' Eleanor wailed from the top of the climbing-tree. She windmilled her arms as she swayed, her feet on the top grips. I jumped, I *warped space* – it seemed only a moment later that I was reaching up to catch her and lower her to the ground.

'Stay on the swings,' I said. 'Please!'

I sat down again beside Annette, shaking my head. My heart was thumping for several reasons.

'He really just blatantly told you that?'

'Yes,' Annette agreed.

'*Jesus!*' I exploded. 'What the fuck does he think he's up to?' I thought of our casual, friendly banter and felt sick.

'I've told you,' Annette said, 'what the fuck he thinks he's up to.'

'And what did *you* say?'

Annette lit another cigarette, her hands shaky, the flame invisible in the light. 'I said he was crazy, he was pushing it too far and that I was perfectly happy and I love you and Eleanor and there's no *way* I'd leave you for him. I told him to forget it, basically.' She smiled at me wanly. 'What did you expect?'

'Well, that, obviously.' I squinted into the sun at her, smiling with relief. I was angry, not at her – at him. But some of it must have leaked into my voice as I said, 'But did you say to him that *you* don't love *him*?'

'No,' Annette said. 'I couldn't. It's not that I still love him!' She laughed. 'I don't, not … like that, but I still care about him. As you do too, yes? And I don't know if you know this, but I got the feeling he's really *unhappy*, and confused and frustrated, and it woulda been like a kick in the teeth.'

A kick in the teeth, I thought – that could be arranged. But I breathed out, and relaxed and forced a smile, and said, 'Yeah, OK, I'm glad you said what you did. To him and to me.' I smiled at her more genuinely, and leaned forward to put my arms around her and as I did so realised that I had a cigarette in my hand and that after five years off the damn' things I was smoking again.

'Well,' I said, 'fuck me.'

'Yes.'

Which was all very well and wonderful, but afterwards, lying staring at the ceiling, I thought about all she had said, and – more worryingly – all that she hadn't.

Looking back, I could see that Annette had understated the length of time in which Reid had been 'gallantly flirting' with her. He'd done it from the first evening he'd met us after we'd started going together. I'd thought it a joke on me, a compliment to Annette, in as much as I'd thought of it at all. Shortly afterwards, Reid had – to everyone's surprise – had a brief and tempestuous affair with Myra. Now *that* I'd thought showed a flash of male-primate teeth, a gesture at me. But strangely, he'd seemed more cut-up about its predictable breakup than he had ever been about the ending of his relationship with Annette. Perhaps, like me, he'd unwittingly fallen for Myra, and she hadn't for him.

Sexual competition had been intertwined with our friendship from the start, and whether we were close or distant, so it apparently remained.

I rolled out of bed and padded through the flat to the kitchen. I sat in a pool of light and smoked another cigarette. Outside, in the black window, my reflection looked ironically back. The government health warning (always an occasion for ironic reflection) told me things I didn't need to know, and didn't warn of the real killer:

the slight, the subtle, the incremental and irreversible hardening of the heart.

I was working at the college three days a week, and Monday wasn't one of them. Annette left for work, I cleared up the breakfast stuff and walked Eleanor to the school gates. I picked up the papers, almost bought ten Silk Cut, returned to the flat and whizzed through the housework like a student on speed. Then I sat down with a coffee and a Filofax and a savage bout of nicotine withdrawal.

Normally I'd devote days like this to what I called political work. (I'd almost persuaded Annette it was some kind of elaborate game-plan whereby I'd work my way up, from writing long pieces for obscure organisations and tiny pieces for famous organisations, to being the sort of global mover-and-shaker that a grateful humanity would some day commemorate with statues on the moons of Saturn.)

Today I had more serious plans. I found an old address for Reid in my Filofax, and a current one (with the old one crossed out) in one of Annette's diaries. I worked my way through every free-market, libertarian, anti-environmentalist or just sheer downright reactionary organisation I'd ever had any contact with, and phoned or sent Reid's details to their mailing-lists. After about an hour that was done, and I wasn't satisfied, so I set out to cover a few more angles.

I leaned on the doorbell of the *Freethinker* offices in Holloway Road. Behind me the traffic rumbled past. As ever I felt saddened by the dusty window-display of sun-paled, damp-darkened books and pamphlets. After a minute the Society's secretary let me in. A slight-built, middle-aged man with a deeply lined face, eyes large behind thick glasses. Kind and unselfish and poor as an atheist church-mouse. I told him what I wanted, and he let me get on with it, busying himself with his breakfast while I picked my way through files, sifted stacks of magazines, got ink on my fingers from trays of painfully created label-sized addressing-stencils.

It didn't take long to compile a list of journals and organisations, mostly American, that could be guaranteed to stimulate a bit of free thought. By way of thanks on the way out I bought for full price a seriously shop-soiled copy of a selection from Thomas Paine's works. I browsed it while I used my Travelpass on an ideological whistlestop tour of London, from the Freedom Bookshop in Angel Alley and the Market Bookshop in Covent Garden to Novosti Press Agency in Kensington, getting back via Bookmarks in Finsbury Park just in time to meet Eleanor coming out of school.

These are the times that try men's souls ... The summer soldier, and the sunshine patriot, may shrink from the service of his country ...

Reid miserable? He hadn't seemed so, except for that moment when he'd talked about union meetings. Looking back, I thought I'd seen in his eyes a desperate recollection of a waste of evenings, and a premonition of more to come. If he could try to fuck my wife and fuck with my life, the least I could do was to fuck up his mind. Reid was spooked by his ideas; he had wheels in the head. He *identified* with his beliefs in a way I never did with mine. He didn't enjoy exposing them to challenge, but when some bit of grit was dropped in their fine machinery he went to endless trouble to remove it, to clean and polish the wheels and replace any broken teeth. He'd once kept me up, if not exactly awake, half the night as he teased out the intricacies of a surreal debate the Fourth International had in the early 'eighties: over whether Pol Pot's Democratic Kampuchea was or was not a variant of ... capitalism.

'Stubborn, and literal, and so goddamn *serious*' – Annette had his number in more ways than one. And so did I. There was no way Reid could ignore any political literature that came through his letterbox. He'd worry away at refuting the most manifest absurdity, check up on every recalcitrant factoid and bold-faced lie. By the time he'd struggled with all those conflicting views, Reid's soul would be sorely tried.

Other streets, other summers ... We met Reid at marches against the poll tax and apartheid. In the black June of '89 we sat down in a Soho street with thousands of Chinese and hundreds of Trotskyists, and sang 'The Internationale', and he nodded, giving me an almost worried look, when I told him I would march with the Taiwanese students.

'Ah so,' he murmured. 'The Kuomintang. Catch you later.'

Neither I nor Annette said anything more about what he'd said to her, and he always seemed to turn up with a new girlfriend for every demo. All of them, Bernadette and Mairi and Anne and Claire, seemed to me like distant relatives of Annette, dark Irish girls with bright eyes and ironic voices.

He never commented on the steady trickle of anti-socialist or dissident socialist or maddeningly wrong-headed socialist material I kept sending him. In the end I think it was redundant: the way things went in the Communist world, the subscription to *Moscow News* would have covered the lot.

But it had an effect, and it wasn't the one I sought.

7

Critical Life

'BASICALLY,' SAYS AX, as he and Dee wander back along the canal-bank towards Circle Square, 'I don't know if I believe it. I mean, most people just dismiss it, like, well, flying saucers and Old New Martian ruins and Elvis and shit. But I've heard stories.'

His pause indicates that whatever stories he's heard, Dee's going to hear too. She nods.

'Go on.'

'Well, some of us ... not Tamara, not the activist types, OK, have always thought, or wished, that Wilde would come back. Or come through. And over the years, people have seen him. Or said they have. Out in the desert. Sometimes walking, sometimes driving a 'track. Usually he's with a girl, and he looks like he did when he was an old man.'

He's been going on about the iniquities of society for a few minutes now. He's talked about things that have happened to him, and about how they'd be all right with Reid but not with Wilde. Wilde wouldn't have stood for it. This Jonathan Wilde seems to be a mythical figure, somebody who knew Reid and lost out to him and who might, equally mythically, some day come back and avenge the oppressed. Dee has listened politely, filing it all away for more detailed study later. She's handling it as she used to handle social occasions. But what he's just said brings her up short.

'What do you mean, an old man?' she asks.

'Somebody who hasn't re-juved before stabilising,' Ax replies flippantly. 'Quite a sight.'

Dee shudders, thinking of how people used to fall apart like badly maintained biotech, how they'd eventually *just stop*. Horrible. She's sat through classical movies with Reid, and they give a very

89

different picture of Earth than historical romances do. *Nobody* lives happily ever after.

'I saw an old man recently,' she says. 'In the last couple of weeks. An old man with a girl, in a truck. Called up Reid's front office, said it was a wrong number.' She glances sidelong at Ax. 'Not many old men here. Could that have been Wilde?'

Ax looks at her with sharp scepticism. 'What was this guy like?'

'Hmmm,' says Dee. She moves her lower lip over her upper teeth, then wipes her thumb across the teeth and observes the streak of lipstick.

'Something bothering you?' Ax asks, amused.

Dee stops in mid-stride. 'Yes.' The memory belongs to Secretary, but it resonates with several of her other selves as well: all the new ones she's loaded up have this odd imperative, linked to the memory and tagged to their root directories.

'Just a minute,' she says.

There's a bollard a few metres away. She walks over to it and sits down, flipping the back of her black lace skirt carefully out of the way, so that she sits on the bollard, not on the skirt. The iron is cold through fine leather, thin silk and bare skin. Ax, watching, gives an appreciative moan, but Dee has already boot-strapped into the dry clarity of Sys.

When Dee is in Self she thinks of Sys as 'Sis', and indeed it's what (she imagines) a big sister would be like: knowing everything, correcting her, tidying up after her, picking up and putting away the shrugged-off costumes of her quick-changed selves. She doesn't go into Sys very often, and doesn't stay in that thin, chill air for long.

Now, her cold inward eye takes in the hierarchy of her selves and minds and tools, the common structures and the ceaseless activity of Sys that make them one personality and not a squabbling legion contending for control of her body. She traces the memory of the phone-call, as it's passed from Secretary to Self to Sys, and then sees its onward cascade over the days in which she loaded up all that extra software: Scientist, Soldier, Spy, Seneschal ... and on to Stores and Secrets, out on a limb of their own. These last two she can't access. They've always been in her mind anyway; but now patient, mindless subroutines of Sys are systematically besieging them, hurling code after code at their mental locks like antibodies at a virus.

She drops back in to Self. Ax is looking down at her with puzzled concern.

'So that's how it happened,' she says, rising.

'How what happened?'

'How I became me. It was that phone-call. There was a command-code carried in it. It told me to load up and seek and search and ... and I did, and when there were enough selves and data and so on in my head, it happened! I woke up!' She gives a flighty laugh. 'Is that how it is with you? Do you get lots of selves, and then become self-aware?'

'To the best of my knowledge,' Ax says gravely, 'no. That is not how humans become self-aware. It happens at an early age, you understand.'

He shakes himself. 'You're telling me you woke up because of a phone-call from an old man?'

'Yes.'

'Hey man, cool. This is like Zen! Maybe he *was* Wilde, or maybe he was a perfect master.'

He catches her hand and starts her walking again. She complies, searching her brain for some referent to 'perfect master'. Scientist has a disdainful account, and its sneer is just fading from her mind as Ax asks excitedly:

'Do you know how to draw?'

'I can make pictures,' Dee says. 'But I don't think he was a perfect master. The girl with him sure didn't look like she needed enlightenment.'

'Zen,' Ax nods to himself. 'Definitely.'

In the lower floor of the house there's a big room with a kitchen-range and sink, sofas and chairs and a heavy, scrubbed wooden table. Books and papers and kit are piled in corners, and on the table. Dee sits down at the table, clearing a space between cups and tools. Ax rummages up some sheets of paper and a steel ballpoint pen. He gives them to her.

'So make a picture,' he says.

'OK,' says Dee. She takes the pen in her right hand and steadies the paper with her left. A quick jiggle at the top right of the paper tells her the ink is black, and running smoothly. Closing her eyes, she calls up the image of the man in the truck. She ignores the girl for the moment (though there's something there, something about her eyes, that Dee thinks odd and in need of further investigation – more research is necessary, OK, over to Scientist) … now. Yes. Tab to Printer Control: a little routine in Secretary's repertoire.

Start. She hears the skittering sound of the pen on the paper for a minute, as her right hand moves back and forth horizontally, very fast, with tiny vertical movements lifting the pen on to and off the paper; and her left hand moves the paper away from her, very slowly. Finish.

She opens her eyes. 'There,' she says. She rubs her wrist.

Ax is looking at her, open-mouthed. He closes his mouth and shakes his head.

'OK,' he says. 'Let's have a look.'

Even Dee is a little surprised to see what a good picture she's made out of the skips and breaks in a few hundred straight lines ruled across the paper; almost like a black-and-white photograph, it shows the man's face and some of his surroundings: the seat-back behind him, the scored panelling of the rear wall of the cab, the coiled cable of the hanging microphone he's holding in front of him, the girl's shoulder.

'I don't believe it,' says Ax. 'That's him. That's the guy I was telling you about: Jonathan Wilde.'

'Well,' says Dee, 'I told you he wasn't a perfect master.'

Ax grins at her as if even he is surprised at this level of wit from her (and oh, how those little surprises smart!) and drags an old book out of a drift in one of the corners. It's a leather binder holding an algae–cellulose paper print-out. Dee hefts it in her hand and leafs through it. The first page that falls open is near the end, and it's a photograph of the same man as she's just drawn. Even the pose and expression are similar – he's leaning forward, talking earnestly to camera.

'That's one of the last pictures of Wilde that ever became public,' Ax explains. 'It's lifted from a television interview with him in February 2046.'

Dee feels the hairs on the back of her neck prickle as she studies this image, from a past almost incalculably remote (but only in *real time*, Scientist reminds her, not in *ship time*; and it's going on about the Malley Mile again – the real thing, the one the pub is named for. She shuts it off).

'That's him all right,' she says. She glances at the picture she made, then at the one in the book; runs a transform. 'Every line maps exactly.'

She looks at it again. Something's bugging her.

'Well, yes,' Ax says.

Dee continues to leaf backwards through the book. The pictures get fewer as she gets closer to the beginning, Wilde gets younger; most of them are obviously not posed, but snatched on the fly: clipped blow-ups from surveillance systems, a calm face in angry crowds ...

'What is this, exactly?'

'It's a dossier on Wilde,' Ax tells her. 'Notes for a biography.'

She stops at another picture, a low-angle shot, blurry. It's labelled 'FOI(PrevGovts)/SB/08–95'. Two men at a table, in a pub or café. One, identified in the caption as Wilde, has his back to the camera. The other, talking past a held cigarette, is Reid.

'Told you,' says Ax. 'They knew each other for years.'

Dee has known, at some level, that Reid is one of the originals, that he came physically from Earth, but it's somehow still a shock to see what is – assuming the picture's antiquity and provenance – visual evidence. More pages flip past. When the sheaf of pages is thin under her thumb, there's a sharp, professional photograph that stops her thoughts. It has rough, scissored edges, a caption below and a scrawled attribution: *Dumbarton Gazette* 04/06/77 – some local zine, apparently. She stares at it, points at it dumbly. Behind her shoulder, Ax's breath hisses in past his teeth.

A wedding-portrait of a couple: formal clothes, informal pose, almost cheek-to-cheek. The man, she sees now that the continuity has been established, is the younger self of the old man at the end of the book; is Wilde; is the man she saw yesterday. The woman's face, above frilled shoulders and high collar in lace-trimmed white voile, is her own.

'Let me guess,' Ax says heavily. 'That's the guy who walked into the Malley Mile?'

'Yes,' she breathes. 'No wonder he looked like he recognised me. My body is a clone all right – a clone of his wife!'

93

'Creepy,' says Ax. He peers closer at the caption. 'Annette, that was her name.'

Dee can't look at the picture any longer, and doesn't need to: this image will stay in her mind forever unless she deletes it. It's creepy, all right, and disturbing in a deeper sense: this distant twin, this woman whose physical ghost Dee is, looks happy in a way Dee has never been, with a personality Dee knows is different from her own. Only the physical body, and the underlying temperament which, Dee knows, is likewise genetic, are the same. She lets the last lot of pages fall over the picture, and stares unseeing at the title on the first page:

Jonathan Wilde, *1953–2046: A Critical Life*
by Eon Talgarth

Ax is pacing the room, heedless of Dee's *angst*, talking excitedly. Dee has to run the first few seconds past her again before she catches up: 'So we have a puzzle,' he's been saying. 'A couple of weeks ago, Wilde sees you on Reid's screen. He gives no sign of recognition, but fires off an instruction-set to get you loading up information, maybe with the intention of waking you up, maybe not. Yesterday, Wilde walks in, apparently having re-juved in the meantime, sees you and freaks out.'

Dee shakes her head.

'The guy in the pub wasn't a re-juve of the man I saw on the screen.'

Ax frowns. 'You sound pretty sure of that.'

'The re-juve doesn't change the fact that you've lived longer. It always shows. Not on a picture, perhaps, but when you see someone move and speak it's obvious.' She smiles. 'Don't you find?'

'Haven't seen enough re-juves,' Ax says. 'It's not a common procedure – most people stabilise at what they fancy is their best.' He laughs. 'Sometimes there's a fashion for ageing, but it never lasts.'

'I'll tell you this,' Dee says. 'The Wilde I saw two weeks ago had lived a hell of a lot longer than the Wilde I saw last night.'

'OK, assume there's two of him. That's no more of a mystery than there being even one of him, because he shouldn't be here at all. He wasn't in the crew, or the gangs.' He flashes her a feral grin.

'So Reid says, or at least the lists do. The company roll. I've checked. But like I said, people say they see him. And now, you have proof. He's back!'

He picks up again the picture that Dee made. She can see his hands are shaking. He lights a cigarette after a couple of attempts, and stares at nothing for a while. His facial expression slowly changes, in a way that makes Dee think of how he must have got his names: it's hard, and sharp, and ... terminal.

'Do you know what this means?' he says.

Dee compresses her lips, shakes her head.

'It means he's back from *the dead*,' Ax says. 'It means everything's going to change. It means all bets are off.'

'I don't understand,' Dee says.

Ax jabs out the cigarette and lights another. He's still shaking.

'People assume things,' he says. 'They assume things will go on just as they are. They know what they can get away with. They know what they can get people to agree to. Like, I agreed to let other people use my body, because I needed the money. And they knew I did. But because I *agreed*, they think that makes it all right. Some of them even knew I hated it. But I agreed to it.'

Dee suddenly needs a cigarette herself. She lights one, and her hands, now, are trembling.

'Did Reid ever let other people use your body?'

'Oh no,' Dee says quickly. 'He's very possessive.'

'But he used you,' Ax persists. 'Whether you wanted to or not.'

'I always wanted to,' Dee says, but her Sex–y smile hides a new and gnawing doubt as to how much that consent was worth, now, looking back. Ax watches her, and she sees him see the doubt grow.

He opens a drawer in the table and reaches in, and brings out a knife. It isn't a kitchen-knife. It has a black wooden handle, a brass guard, and thirty centimetres of blade. Almost casually, Ax bangs the sharp point of the knife into the table and lets go of the handle, so it springs back a bit and it vibrates.

'Now you know who you are,' Ax says quietly. Dee isn't sure he's talking to her. All the shaking has gone out of his body, out of his voice, and into that quivering blade. 'You're a person. You're free. Have you ever thought – what you would like to do to people who've treated you like *meat*?'

Out here, in the damp-desert flats between two arms of the city, it's quiet even for a Sic'day morning. The only sounds are the thrum of the dinghy's motor, the occasional hiss of a jet transport overhead, and the cries of the adapted birdlife: the lost-satellite bleep of rustshanks, the quacking of mucks, and the caw-cawing of sandgulls. Sic'day is for most folk a day when some work is done, but not much.

(Tamara has heard the opinion that the day is called that because of the number of people working – or not working – with hangovers, but this is a myth. More than a Neo-Martian century ago, Reid expressed the opinion that continuing to name the days after the gods of the Solar system would be inappropriate. Nobody could agree on other names, so the week goes: Wunday, Twoday, Thirday, Fourday, Fi'day, Sic'day, Se'nday. There are twenty-five hours and ten minutes in a day; for convenience there are twenty-five hours in the first six days and twenty-six on Se'nday. There are a hundred and ten weeks in a year. More or less. All serious chronology is done in SI multiples of seconds, reckoning from the moment the Ship's clock came out of the Malley Mile, around 6.4 gigaseconds ago.)

Tamara's boat bumps against the canal-bank as she drifts along under minimal power. She's on a capillary of the Ring Canal. The shallow artificial rivulet is carrying her away from the centre of the city, towards the fields. The human quarter is on her right, the Fifth Quarter on her left. Between them is this expanse of waste, not quite mud-flat, but no longer desert, and not yet fields. In it, venturing out from the machine domain of the Fifth Quarter, can be found biomechanisms, Tamara's habitual prey.

A sandgull descends, screaming, about a hundred and fifty metres ahead and thirty from the left bank. Tamara ups the revs and lowers her profile as other gulls dive to join it. They squawk and squabble around a black thing. The boat cuts diagonally across the canal. Tamara zooms her right eye. The black thing has a flailing appendage. A stubborn gull clings to it, taking some of the momentum out of the shaking in moments of hopping near-flight.

'Stay,' Tamara tells the boat's 'bot, and it obediently idles the engine and hooks the bank as Tamara steps out, clutching a long grapple. She draws her pistol as she sprints forward. The bang of a blank scatters the gulls into wheeling indignation overhead. As

Tamara's feet thud over the damp sand and skip over tussocks of grass, the black object – a warty, rubbery ball about a third of a metre across, with at least a metre of flail – starts hauling itself towards the nearest patch of what looks suspiciously like quicksand. When she's about four metres away Tamara feels a tickle behind the bridge of her nose. She stops and sniffs. The tickle stays constant – good. That means the radioactivity is contained, not airborne. Still, the thing's uncomfortably hot. Not dangerous, but she has to be careful.

She circles it gingerly, getting between it and the wet area. It moves towards her: whip, tug, bounce; whip, tug, bounce. It stops. The tip of the flail rises and sways from side to side, then presses against the ground. Tamara steps forward, stumbles as her left foot comes up from the ground with an unexpected sucking noise. The rubbery limb recoils.

Tamara squats down and reaches out with her grapple, a simple mechanism a couple of metres long which has a primitive robot hand at the far end and a pair of handles for her to grasp, one-handed, and thus extend her clutch. She eases it across the ground and grabs the flail at the root. In obliging reflex, the tentacular appendage wraps around the grapple and starts trying to crush it to death.

Tamara lifts it off the ground and heads back to the boat. The biomech, evolved or designed at the interface between domains, is not a bad catch. It has senses, reflexes, and apparently a capacity to concentrate radioactives within its tough skin. Somewhere in the human quarter there's a technician who is looking for just such a genotype, or so she hopes.

She's just sat down in the boat and in the middle of manoeuvring the grapple and its load, awkwardly trying to keep her distance from it (at less than two metres the tickle in her geiger-sense is becoming a pain) while selecting and opening a container, when there's a ringing in her left ear.

'Damn,' she says loudly. She tenses her throat-muscles to turn on the mike, winks up the phone-screen, and with a rightward flick of her eyes accepts the call. The first screen to come up is clunky, even as it hangs with hallucinatory vividness in the space between her and the end of the grapple. It's like a camera is looking at a monitor screen, in some primitive glimmer of machine self-awareness. Text scrolls down it, a voice-over spell-checks itself along.

'Invisible Hand Legal Services,' it intones. 'Incoming challenge call from –' and here it hesitates, as if even this august implementation of the voice of the IBM is amazed at its own temerity '– David Reid. Will you accept?'

'Yes,' gulps Tamara.

The screen is instantly minimised to the corner of her eye, and the main view is taken by a solid image of a face she's seen many times before, but never before speaking to her. The window floats in front of her eyes, with Reid's head and shoulders at a comfortable speaking distance behind it. Behind him, she can see different parts of a room, a bright window (real, apparently). He's pacing about as he talks.

'Tamara Hunter?' he says.

'Yes.'

He grins, peering past her.

'I can see why you call yourself that. Well, to business m'lady. You're currently in possession of one of my machines, a Model D gynoid, and I want it back. Now.'

Tamara takes a deep breath.

'I'm not in possession of it – her. She's claiming self-ownership and I'm defending her. So are several sworn allies of mine, and other clients of Invisible Hand.'

'Crap,' Reid retorts. 'She doesn't even have the wit to claim self-ownership.'

'She does now, and did, before witnesses.'

'To a fucking IBM, you mean. Your legal expert-system couldn't pass the Turing itself, let alone administer it.'

'I RESENT THAT.'

'Shaddap,' says Tamara, still struggling with the grapple. The thing on the end is rolling like a badly held forkful of spaghetti. 'Sorry, Reid. That wasn't for you.'

'I appreciate that,' says Reid dryly. 'You were saying?'

'I can get human witnesses to testify before any court you like. The gynoid ain't your pet zombie any more.'

Reid's eyes narrow. 'That's because she's been *hacked*. It's still not an autonomous development, even if that matters, which it doesn't.'

'It's time it did,' Tamara says levelly. 'I'm willing to fight you on this.'

'Have it your way,' says Reid. 'In court, then.'

'It's your challenge,' Tamara points out.

'OK, the first bid's yours.' He bows.

Tamara winks up the Invisible Hand screen again. It displays a list of courts in descending order of preference. It's a short list. She goes for the first, but her voice is not hopeful as she says: 'Eon Talgarth, Court of the Fifth Quarter.'

'Accepted,' Reid says at once.

Tamara shrinks the IBM screen and stares at Reid, who looks blandly back.

'What?' she says. Then: 'Confirm, please.'

'I accept,' Reid says, with emphatic formality, 'that the decision be put to the Court of the Fifth Quarter in the case of myself versus Tamara Hunter and allies as represented by Invisible Hand Legal Services and-stroke-or themselves, to be held at the earliest convenience of all parties.'

'And I too,' says Tamara.

The IBM repeats what they've said.

'And meanwhile, no grepping?' Tamara asks suspiciously.

'Of course, no grepping,' says Reid. He gives her a smile that, despite everything, despite herself, brings a slight warmth to her cheeks. 'See you in court, lady.'

The screen vanishes in time for Tamara to see the black biomech unwind itself smoothly from the grapple, drop into the canal and, with a sinuous motion of its flail, swim away.

'All right,' said Jay-Dub. 'Have it your way. I suppose I can work something out.' It stopped at the junction of the pier and the street. 'But before we go rushing off, I have a couple of suggestions.'

Wilde stopped and looked back. 'Yes?'

'Get yourself a gun,' said Jay-Dub. 'And some better clothes. You look like you've just walked in off the desert or something. Also, if you want to head for the main abolitionist hang-out, it's quicker by boat.'

'You have a point there,' said Wilde.

An hour later he was wearing a baggy black jacket, shirt and trousers, all of some warm fabric that he'd been assured was knife-proof, and studying a bulky metal automatic as he sat in a crowded *vaporetta*. The other passengers, mostly young, paid him a gratifying lack of attention. Wilde sat, aloof by the side of the boat, and looked at the canal-bank scenes and cocked his ears to his fellow-passengers' slangy, accented English. Jay-Dub, limbs retracted, lay at his feet like luggage. It was the only robot on board, apart from the helmsman, a chunk of solid-state cybernetics on the prow.

Scoop-nets on the side of the boat trawled bobbing balls of plastic from the water, and flicked them, rattling, into a hold beneath the deck. The boat left the commercial gaiety of the Stone Canal and passed into a succession of tunnels and narrow, high-banked canals. Here, in the green algae soggy on the walls, smaller balls could be seen. They moved downwards very slowly, but their course could be inferred: the closer to the water they sank, the larger they grew, until they dropped off and floated away. Wilde refrained from asking the machine about the economics and ecology of this bio-industrial process.

They reached their destination forty minutes after leaving. The boat pulled up with much coughing of engine and thrashing of propellers alongside a little jetty with steps leading to a narrow canal-side street. The boat's only human crew-member, who'd done nothing but collect the fares, opened his eyes and waved a hand.

'Circle Square, two hundred metres,' he announced, and laid a short gang-plank to the steps. Wilde took care to be the last off the boat. He smiled at the boatman.

'You're a Kazakh Greek,' he said.

The man's eyes widened. He gripped Wilde's hand, and said something in another language.

'We've all come a long way,' Wilde said.

'Win friends and influence people,' Jay-Dub sneered, *sotto voce*, at the top of the steps. 'Always the goddamn agitator, eh?'

About thirty people walked along the street, Wilde and the robot a few metres behind the rest. Ahead, Circle Square's market island was just tuning up to its daily discord. The street was lined with tiny pavement cafés and stalls, and broken by alleys down which even tinier shops plied some kind of trade from windows and doorways.

They were a few steps away from one such alley-mouth, at the opposite corner of which a couple of perilously small tables were in use for serving coffee in proportionately minute cups, when Jay-Dub said urgently, 'Stop!'

At the same moment Wilde too noticed the two men – the same two men who'd come searching in the pub. They sat at one of those little tables, staring back at him from behind dark glasses. His hand froze in the act of reaching for his new gun as the others did so for theirs.

Into this momentary impasse came a peculiar vehicle: a platform on wheels, with a crane-like handling-apparatus at either end. It nosed out of the alleyway without warning. Wilde jumped back. Mechanical arms unfolded from the cranes and snatched past him. He turned in time to see the claws of those arms clamp around Jay-Dub's lower limbs. They lifted the struggling machine right over his head, and placed it firmly on the flatbed's platform.

Wilde squatted down, grabbed the platform with both hands, and lifted. Jay-Dub lurched against the constraints at the right moment, and over the whole thing went. As people reacted, a cascade of tables toppled as well. Wilde dived across Jay-Dub's hull, rolled with a kick at the legs of the two men – on their feet now, with steaming stains on their thighs – and a moment later was up and running. A frantic backward glance showed the two men a few steps behind, in his wake of jostled vistors and tumbled furniture.

Circle Square was just ahead of him, the crowd denser.

'Help!' Wilde yelled, plunging into the crowd.

'Proceed no further,' ordered a booming voice from ahead and above. It might have come from one of the loudspeakers hung from cabling among trees and lamp-posts. Wilde stopped, and looked behind him again. The two men chasing him had halted a few metres away, dithering at the edge of a pavement, just where the end of the narrow street met the parapet of a bridge.

One of them made a move for the inside of his jacket. Before Wilde could react, something else reacted faster. Something spidery and light, a ball of stiff stalks that skimmed over the heads of the crowd and flew at the two men. As it struck them its stalks became flexible, and wrapped around them both, from their shoulders to their thighs.

Confined, they were barely even an object of curiosity. Wilde stayed where he was for a minute as the crowd dispersed somewhat. Then he walked back the way he'd come. As he sidled past the two men he gave them about three metres clearance. They glared at him.

'Who sent you?' he asked.

'Fuck off,' one of them said.

'Give Reid my regards,' Wilde said.

At this the other man made an attempt to burst his bonds, but the multi-armed machine only tightened in response. Wilde continued along to the alley-mouth, and on his way passed two young men, guiding or herding the now empty and damaged platform in the opposite direction.

' 'Scuse me' Wilde said. 'See what happened to the other robot? The one this thing grabbed?'

'Scrammed,' he was told.

He thanked them, and checked for himself. The most anyone could tell him was that the construction-machine had fled down the alleyway. Wilde took a look along it, shook his head and muttered something to himself, and trudged back to the bridge. He arrived in time to see the two young men departing with the platform, which now had his attackers securely held by its remaining functional crane-arm. The other machine was still there, once more in its spiky-ball form. It rolled over to him like a tumbleweed.

'Good morning,' it said. The buzzing voice seemed to be generated by the vibration of some of its stalks. 'You called for help, within the domain of Invisible Hand Legal Services. I intervened in response.'

'Thank you,' Wilde said.

'Although no binding contract has been entered into, it would be a matter of courtesy to make a payment to Invisible Hand. As a reciprocal courtesy, Invisible Hand would like to offer you a ten-week defence policy, with that payment written off against your first bill if you choose to pay in advance.'

Wilde looked down at the eager machine with amusement.

'How much?'

'Twenty grams gold or equivalent.'

'Very reasonable,' Wilde said. 'Do you take cards?'

'Follow me,' said the machine.

Wilde slid his card down the slot of the rusty mainframe box. The machine that had come to his aid had led him here and left him.

'Thank you,' Invisible Hand said. 'You have identified yourself as Jonathan Wilde. Your account is that opened originally by the machine known as Jay-Dub, aka Jonathan Wilde, and endorsed in your behalf at Stras Cobol Mutual Bank last night.'

'Correct,' said Wilde.

'I have on my files a case against you,' the machine said. 'Do you wish to hear the details at present?'

Wilde looked around.

'Go ahead.'

Reid's face appeared in ruddy hologram monochrome behind the machine's screen.

'I, David Reid, wish to lay a charge against one Jonathan Wilde, of no fixed abode, namely this: that a robot known as Jay-Dub, property of the same Jonathan Wilde, was used to corrupt the control systems of a Model D gynoid, known as Dee Model, property of myself. If Jonathan Wilde wishes to defend himself legally against this charge, no further attempts will be made by me or my agents or allies to arrest him or to impound his machine. If he does not so wish, or refuses a mutually acceptable court, those attempts will continue. I end this statement this Sic'day morning, fifty-seventh day of the year one hundred and two, Ship time.'

Wilde watched the image dwindle to a ruby bead.

He sighed. 'How did Reid know I'd be registered with you?'

'He did not,' said the mainframe. 'This message was released to all defence agencies. I have conveyed to the others that it has been delivered. They have no further interest in it, unless of course you choose to have it defended by one of them.'

'No,' said Wilde.

'Very well,' said the machine. 'Do you wish to defend yourself legally against the charge?'

Wilde thought about this.

'Yes,' he said.

Shadows and lights moved behind the screen.

'I have a suggestion to make,' said the machine. 'There is another case in progress, between Reid and another party, in the matter of Dee Model. Dee Model is also a client of mine. You might wish to consider combining your defences.'

'I might indeed,' said Wilde.

'Wait here,' said the machine. '... You may smoke.'

8

Capitalist Realism

AN AEROPLANE OR a helicopter comes towards you on a rising note that climaxes, then dies away; but when you hear the sound of an aero-engine and it maintains the same flat tone for minutes on end, you look up, irritated by that anomalously steady buzz, and see an airship.

I stood on Waverley Bridge in the cool dusk and looked up and saw an airship, low in the sky, creeping up behind me like a shiver on my neck, a blue blimp with 'MAZDA' in white capitals on the side. It was the same airship as I'd seen two hours or so earlier, in Glasgow. Almost weirder than a UFO, something that shouldn't be there, a machine from an alternate reality where the *Hindenburg* or the Dow Jones hadn't crashed or the Germans had won the Great War. As I watched it move away like a cloud with an outboard motor, I had a momentary sense of dissociation, as if I shouldn't be there either. What was I doing here, watching an airship from a windy bridge when I could be on a train to London?

It must have been the heat. The heat in London that summer had been like nothing since the summer of '76, when I'd spent weeks going from interview to interview, crashing out with pals or in my parents' home, worrying about the rash of hateful Union Jack stickers plastered everywhere by the National Front. (And meanwhile, in another hot city, Polish workers pulled up railway lines and pulled down meat prices, and almost the state, almost ...) And coming back to Glasgow and a drier heat, grateful, walking into Annette's lab where dissected locusts were pinned in foil dishes of black wax and the smell of evaporating ethanol rushed to my sinuses as I grabbed her and said, 'I got a job!'

Nineteen years later and still the same job. Different employers, a different college, the students ever younger and more unsure about their presence, let alone their futures. But at least now I had a business on the side, which in good months brought in as much as or more than the job. My polemics in obscure newsletters and journals, and later on obscure Internet newsgroups as well, had – according to my plan, but still to my surprise – resulted in some mainstream attention. A few think-tank commissions, one or two academic journal articles, a chapter in a forthcoming intermediate economics textbook ... Annette and Eleanor had, or at least showed, more confidence in my eventually hitting the big time than I did. Sometimes I felt guilty about that.

I'd been online at my desk at home, setting up Web pages for the business, when Reid had called the previous week. After we'd exchanged pleasantries he'd said, 'You coming up to this science fiction convention thingie in Glasgow?'

'Yes! I've booked a stall there. Space Merchants. You coming?'

''Fraid not,' he'd said regretfully. 'Can't manage the time off work. But – I'd like to meet you after it, in Edinburgh.'

'That's a nice idea, but ...'

'No, no, wait. It's not just to see you socially. I've got a ... a business proposition for you. Something you might be really interested in.'

'Oh well, that's different. What is it?'

'Um, I'd rather not say at the moment. Sorry to be so cagey, but honestly this is serious and it could be well worth your while. We'll just go out for a few drinks and talk it over. You can crash out with me, or in a hotel if you like – I can pick up the tab, and the fares –'

'No, there's no need –'

'Really. You'll understand when we've talked about it, OK?'

Intrigued at the thought of him offering me a job in insurance, I agreed to meet him. It must have been the heat.

Reid sauntered up from the Princes Street end of the bridge, for some reason the opposite direction from the one I'd expected him to.

'Hi man, glad you made it.'

'Good to see ya.'

His hair had grown long again. His clothes were casual but refined: soft black chinos, blue button-down shirt, silk tie, dark linen jacket. I felt a bit of a scruff in my denims and trainers and astronaut cut.

'You're looking smart.'

'Thanks.' We'd started walking in the same direction Reid had been taking, towards the Rock. 'You're looking ... well.'

We both laughed.

'It's an illusion,' I said. 'Actually I feel a bit wrecked. Too many hangovers in the past four days.'

'Ah, you'll soon drink it off,' he said. 'But first – have you eaten?'

My stomach sharply confirmed that I hadn't. 'Not for ages,' I said. We paused at a junction where the traffic came four ways. Reid glanced around, and behind him.

'OK,' he said, 'Viva Mexico!' This turned out to be a Mexican restaurant halfway up Cockburn Street and down some steps. It was quiet. Reid nodded at the waiter. 'Table for three, please.'

The waiter guided us to a table well clear of anyone else and we sat down. Reid ordered three tall lagers. I looked around while he studied the menu. The faces of men with wide hats and long rifles glowered back at me from brown-and-white photographs of executions, funerals, weddings, train wrecks ... I was scanning the wall idly for any photos of heavily armed christenings or graduations when the lagers arrived and Reid looked up.

'How did the Worldcon go?'

'Brilliant,' I said. 'So I'm told. I was in the dealers' room most of the time. Space Merchants did well, though.'

'That's your business?'

'Yes.' I took out my wallet and passed him one of my remaining cards, with email address, Web site, phone number and PO Box. 'A coupla years ago I was looking for space memorabilia, videos of Earth from orbit, stuff like that, and I was surprised how hard it was to find. Especially all in one place. So I thought, hey, business opportunity! Started with mail order ads in SF magazines, then hawking stuff around conventions. Seems to have taken off now.'

Reid smiled. 'Lifted off! Good. Cheers.'

'Slainte.'

I glanced at the third glass fizzing quietly by itself.

'Who's your absent friend?'

'Along any minute. Relax. Still smoking?'

'Back on them, I'm afraid.' Thanks to you, I didn't say.

He passed me a cigarette.

'How's Annette?'

'Fine. Sends her love.' He didn't blink.

'And Eleanor?'

I couldn't help grinning all over my face. 'Oh, she's great. Sulks in her room listening to CDs and reading trash, most of the time, but basically she's a fine young lass.'

'Didn't she want to go to the convention?'

'I'm not sure,' I said. 'She sort of shrugged when I asked her. Annette wanted to save up holiday time for later in the year, and I think in the end Eleanor preferred to stay with her Mum. I didn't want to risk taking her along and finding she didn't really want to go and put her off for life.'

'Like those demos, eh?' Reid indulged a reminiscent smile.

I grimaced. 'Tell me about it … Annette and her "peace-fighting"! When Eleanor was thirteen she tried to join the friggin' Air Cadets!'

'What stopped her?'

'Not us,' I assured him. 'Defence cuts.'

The chair to our left was suddenly occupied by a slim middle-aged man, dressed similarly to Reid, with thinning black hair combed back. He briskly picked up the menu and nodded to us both. The contact-lenses in his brown eyes made him blink a lot, as if the air were smoky. I stubbed out my cigarette.

'Evening, gentlemen.' He raised his pint and sipped.

'This is Ian Cochrane,' Reid said. 'Works in our legal depart-ment. Ian, this is Jonathan Wilde.'

'Pleased to meet you, Mr Wilde.' His grip was clammy, perhaps from the condensation on the glass, but his thumb pressure was firm.

'Jon,' I said, nodding and wondering abstractedly if the handshake I'd just received was Masonic.

'I've heard a good deal about you, Jon,' said Cochrane. 'Most impressed by your article on Brent Spar.' He caught a waiter's eye. 'Shall we order?'

His accent and manner had that Scottish upper-middle-class tone which sounds more British than the English. He ate selectively and talked trivially while Reid and I satisfied our hunger. His second drink was mineral water. At that point his talk ceased to be trivial.

'"It's time somebody hammered home to people the difference between the bottom of the North Sea and the bottom of the North Atlantic,"' he began, quoting my article – a short column in a Sunday paper's 'Dissenting Voices' corner – from memory. '"One's the floor of a seriously polluted larder, which should be cleaned up. The other's Davy Jones' Locker ..." But nobody's hammering it home, that's your point, eh?'

'Yup,' I said, scooping up guacamole with a taco fragment. 'So Greenpeace gets away with murder.'

'Murder indeed,' said Cochrane. 'But who's going to take the word of an oil company against a bunch of selfless idealists?'

'Me,' Reid said.

'Ah, but you're not typical, you see,' Cochrane reminded him. He turned and blinked thoughtfully at me. 'David, as you probably know, is our IT manager.' I nodded; I hadn't known. 'He attended a meeting of a policy committee where these matters were addressed. We weren't involved in this Shell fiasco, thank God, but as an insurance company we're potentially rather exposed to similar situations. One of our senior managers remarked, in passing, that it would be very ... conducive to a balanced public debate, if there were a grassroots organisation campaigning *for* industrial development, instead of against – "A Greenpeace for the good guys", I think he called it. And the possibility was raised of, ah, materially encouraging an initiative in this direction.'

Reid leaned forward. 'Hope you don't mind, Jon, but I said I knew just the man for the job.' He leaned back. 'You.'

'To start an anti-environmentalist organisation?' I shook my head. 'They have 'em in the States. "Wise use" and all that. They're seen as mouthpieces for big business. Sorry, chaps. Not interested.'

Reid's face showed nothing but polite curiosity.

'Why not?' he asked.

'Ruin my street-cred.'

'We wouldn't want you to say anything different from what you've said already,' Cochrane interjected.

'That's not the point,' I said. 'You could get all the independent scientists you want, even relatively sane environmentalists on board. All that anyone would have to do to discredit it is remind people where the money was coming from.' I checked that we'd all abandoned our plates, and lit a cigarette. 'Look at FOREST.'

The skin around Cochrane's eyes creased and he nodded, as if to hold the place. He gestured to the waiter and ordered coffee and cigarillos. I tried to decline the cigarillo, but he insisted that I at least keep it for later. He stripped the cellophane from his own, lit up, and savoured his first few puffs with a lot more apparent appreciation than I did.

'The Freedom Organisation for the Right to Enjoy Smoking Tobacco,' he said, 'has a good deal more media-credibility than the Tobacco Advisory Council. We've checked. They're quite up-front about where they get a lot of their money from. They don't dispute the health risks, just the use of them to justify all kinds of intrusive restrictions and invasive propaganda. That doesn't strike me as a bad example.'

He stubbed out his cigarillo and fanned away the vile clouds with his hand. 'Feelthy habit,' he remarked, blinking furiously. 'Matter of principle.'

I shrugged. 'OK, if that's how you see it go ahead. But you won't do much to change public opinion, at least in the present climate.'

'*Mister* Wilde,' Cochrane said in a disappointed tone, 'We aren't talking about the *present climate*. We're talking about changing the climate.'

'You want to take the rap for global warming?'

Cochrane indulged a brief laugh. 'Touché ... but seriously, we stand to lose a great deal if the dire predictions turn out to be true, so no, we have no interest in minimising that. We'd like a clearer public perception of the issues, that's all. As to the climate of opinion ... North British Mutual Assurance has existed in one form or another since before the Revolution.' (Before the *what*?) 'If truth be told, its predecessor companies had not a little to do with the fact that the Revolution was Peaceful, and Glorious, and all those other fine words that history has applied to the distinctly business-like takeover of 1688.' (At this point my brain caught up with him.) 'So let me put a proposition to you, on the basis that – should the lady at the nearest table happen to be, let's say, a journalist for *The Scotsman* – this conversation will have undeniably happened, and otherwise ... perhaps not.'

He chuckled darkly, and despite misgivings I felt drawn in, part of his plot.

'As insurers,' he went on, in a lower voice, 'we have no interest whatsoever in backing polluters, because – as the asbestos companies have shown – they're a bad risk. We most emphatically *do* have an interest in prosperity, and growth, and clients who pay in their premiums through long and healthy lives. So if someone were to set up an organisation such as we've discussed, our interest could be quite open, and quite defensible by both sides.'

'If presented in the right way,' Reid said. 'I think it's within your capabilities.'

'Thank you,' I said. 'It could look no more sinister than giving money to the Tory Party. Probably less.'

Cochrane coughed. 'As it happens, our political donations this year –'

He was interupted by the cynical cackles of Reid and myself. After a moment he joined in.

'Yes, well, we *are* in the business of spreading the risk!'

'It's quite something,' I said, 'to see the smart money changing sides, almost before your very eyes.'

'Indeed,' Cochrane said. 'And you could look on our proposal as something similar, if on a longer time-scale.'

I shook my head. 'I'm sorry, I don't see your point.' I thought I did, but I hardly dared believe it.

Cochrane raised an eyebrow to Reid, who nodded slightly.

'I've glanced over some of the literature that you've sent to Dave over the years,' Cochrane said. 'Among all the dross it contains rather stimulating ideas about a possible role for insurance companies in supplying security to their clients. Now, as a political ideal –' An airy flick of the hand. 'However, as a market strategy for dealing with, ah, a certain absconding of the state from what have hitherto been its responsibilities, it has definite attractions. To say nothing of ...'

And he said nothing of it. His eyes had lost the blinking tic, and gazed steadily back at me.

'Another little interruption in the smooth course of British history?' I asked.

He nodded soberly. 'Speculative, of course. But we may some day have to consider our position in relation to what the erudite Mr Ascherson delights in calling *the Hanoverian regime*. Think of it as ...'

'Insurance,' Reid said gleefully.

I looked from one to the other and lit a cigarette, moving my hands very carefully to keep them steady.

Until that moment I'd thought myself immune to the glamour of power, in exactly the way that a eunuch might be to the glamour of women. I'd never stood up for an anthem or straightened for a flag, never fumblingly inserted anything in a ballot-box. The attitude that made my parents' sect reclaim the taunting nickname of 'impossibilists' had, I fancied, been inherited in my own anti-political stance. Oh, I'd wanted to have *influence*, to change the way people thought, just as my parents did; but – again like them – I'd never seriously expected the opportunity to actually get my hands on power's inviting flesh.

In short, I'd been a complete wanker, until that moment when I learned what I'd been missing. And you know, what I felt then *was* almost sexual; it's something in the wiring of the male primate brain.

The big thrill wasn't that they were offering me power – they were offering me a bit more influence, that was all. No, what made the hairs on my neck prickle was that they thought I might – any decade now – *have* power; that I might represent something that it was a smart move to get on the right side of well in advance; that somewhere down the line might be my Finland Station.

'Just one question,' I said. 'There are plenty of better-known and better-connected people with views similar to mine, so why me?'

Reid looked as if he were about to say something, but Cochrane cut him off.

'It's because you don't have connections with any part of the present establishment, and we wouldn't wish you to cultivate any. Your views on the land question and the banking system are dismissed as thoroughly unsound by every free-market think-tank I've consulted. Your political connections are such that your MI5 and Special Branch files are, I understand, commendably thick. Your Internet articles on the recent Oklahoma outrage, on Chechnya, on Bosnia, have added the FBI and the CIA and FIS to your attentive readership. So, you see –'

'I see, all right,' I said. 'You want to buy someone who looks like he's not been bought.'

'Christ, man –!' Reid began, but again Cochrane interrupted.

'Excuse me, chaps,' he said, dusting grains of chilli from his fingers. 'I've never had a radical conscience to wrestle with, and quite frankly I'd be a liability to my own case in the kind of discussion I can foresee developing.' He smiled wryly, almost regretfully, at us. 'So if you don't mind, I'll leave you to it.'

He stood up, held out his hand, and I rose to shake it, mischievously returning his peculiar grip. 'Good evening, Jon, and I hope I see you again.'

'Well, likewise, Ian.'

He nodded to Dave, and departed.

Dave remained silent until Cochrane was out of the door. Then he put his elbows on the table and his fingers to his cheeks, the heels of his hands almost meeting in front of his mouth.

'What the bloody hell are you playing at?' he demanded.

'Nothing,' I said. 'I meant it. You didn't expect me to jump at the chance of being the radical front-man for some bunch of suits worried about what happens when their present cosy arrangement goes down the tubes?'

'What a fucking idiot,' Dave said, not unkindly. 'You're the last person I'd have expected ... ah, the hell with it. Let's hit the pubs.'

In the conveniently close Malt Shovel, he let me get him a pint of Caffrey's and told me of his plan for the rest of the evening.

'I want to show you some of my favourite pubs,' he explained. 'Only one way to do that – a pub-crawl by public transport. Here, the Café Royal, a quick snifter in the station bar, on to Haymarket, next train to Dalmeny, along the front at South Queensferry then the last bus over the bridge to Dunfermline.'

Dunfermline. I'd addressed many packages to his place there, but had vaguely thought it was a suburb of Edinburgh. Wrong: over the Forth, apparently. My mental picture changed to Highland mountain ranges.

'You sure we have time?'

He set down an empty glass. 'See how far we go.'

We almost ran down Cockburn Street, across the Waverley Bridge again then up around the back of a Waterstone's and a Burger King to a large pub that seemed to have only a side entrance. High ceiling, tiled walls, murals, leather seats, marble, polished brass and hardwood.

'A veritable people's palace,' I observed as we sat down. 'It's like something from one of your degenerated workers' states.'

Reid grinned. 'The beer would be cheaper.'

'Yeah,' I said. 'See what they did to Budweiser?'

'Shocking,' Reid said. 'There ought to be a law.'

I nodded at the murals. 'Heroes of the Industrial Revolution ... is that Watt? Stevenson? ... they should have one of Adam Smith seeing the invisible hand.'

'Capitalist realism,' Reid said.

'Something you've got into, apparently.'

'Yes, I'm glad to say.' Reid leaned back, stretching out in his seat. 'It's the only game in town.'

'Yeah, well, you should know.'

'Damn' right I do!' he said forcefully. 'I haven't changed my ideas, long-term – but I know a defeat when I see one. Getting over the end of the Second World will take generations, and it won't be our generations. The last time I hung out with the left was during the Gulf War. The kids don't know shit, and the older guys –' he grinned suddenly like the Dave I knew better '– that is, the ones older than us, they look like men who've been told they have cancer.'

'And can't stop smoking, eh?'

'Ha! OK, Jon, we still have a bit of business to settle.'

'Fire away.'

'The brutal honest truth is you're not likely to get a better offer. Face it, man. You're forty, you're nobody, and you're getting nowhere. The chances are you'll end up hawking space junk around SF conventions and forgotten ideas around fringe organisations for the rest of your life.'

I shrugged. 'There are worse ways to live.'

Dave leaned towards me, almost jabbing his cigarette in my face with his emphasis. 'And there are better, dammit!'

'I know, I know. But I'll get there my own way. The whole free-market thing still has a long way to run, and even space is becoming fashionable again. People are going to see that new movie, what is it? – *Apollo 13*, and think, "Hey, we did that way back then! Why can't we do it now?" The West will get back into space fast enough when they have the Chinese on their ass. Or *somebody*'ll give us a

Sputnik-style shock. And look, even Cochrane seems to think I'm onto something.'

'Aach!' Dave's inarticulate sound conveyed a weight of Highland scepticism. 'That was ninety-nine percent bullshit and flattery. Maybe one percent keeping a weather-eye on the contingencies.'

'Sure, but I'd rather have that one percent than sell out.'

'Stop bloody thinking about this as selling out! Christ, I'd take money from Nirex or Rio Tinto Zinc if they gave me a free hand with it. This *is* getting there your own way. This is all legit. On the square and on the level –'

He realised what he was saying and laughed. 'OK, old Ian is in the Craft but that's got nothing to do with it!'

'Yeah, well, I'm kind of holding out for the Illuminati ... So that's the deal, is it? They put up the money and I do what I like with it?'

'No hassles so long as you get results.'

'Measured how?'

'Oh, rebuttals, airtime, exposés of where the *environmentalists* get their bloody money from. Parents making a fuss about Green propaganda in schools.' He shifted into a semblance of an English working-class accent, or at least a permanently aggrieved tone. "In my day we didn't call it destroying rainforest, we called it clearing the jungle, and I think there should be a bit of *balance*, know what I mean?"'

It was beginning to sound quite attractive. That and the thought of no more basic economics lectures. Get on my own demand curve instead of ...

'The rainforests belong to their inhabitants,' I said. 'Scrap environmental legislation, yes, but only if polluters have to pay for the damage, strict liability. That's my agenda. Think they'd buy that?'

Reid shrugged. 'You could try.'

'OK,' I said, my mind suddenly made up. 'Show me the details, and if it's all as straight as you say, I'll go for it.'

'You will?'

'Yes.'

'Well, thank fuck for that. I thought it'd take all night to batter some sense into you.'

At the station we had a few minutes to spare, even with a gulp of whisky in the Wayfarer's Bar, so I phoned home.

'Hi darlin'.'

'Hello, love. Where are you?'

'Waverley Station. Reid's got me on a pub-crawl by train.'

'Well, you take care. Looking forward to tomorrow night.'

'Me too!' Electric smooch. Some chit-chat about the Worldcon, and Eleanor's school exams, then she asked:

'Did you sell much?'

'Yes,' I said. 'I've sold a lot.'

I picked up my bag from the left luggage (the remaining stock from my stall was at that moment heading down the motorway in a van belonging to a friendly SF bookshop in London). We got on the train for one stop, downed a couple of pints at the Caledonian Ale House in Haymarket and caught the next train onwards.

Dalmeny was a pair of deserted platforms with a startling end-on view of the Forth Bridge, its lights sending ghostly pillars into the darkening sky. The Road Bridge straddled the backlit cirrus of the sunset. Dave led me along a narrow, bramble-whipping path between fields and the railway embankment, over a rise and a wooden bridge and down a long flight of wooden steps to the shore of the Firth. A sharp left at the bottom took us to the Hawes Inn, a pub whose charms were only slightly diminished by several games machines and many inapt quotations from Robert Louis Stevenson on the walls.

We found a seat by a window, in a corner with the games machines. Space battles roared beside us.

'This is where Rome stopped,' Reid remarked in a tone of oddly personal satisfaction as he gazed out over the Firth.

'Can't be,' I said. 'Weren't the Highlands Catholic –'

'The Roman *Empire*,' Reid explained. 'This was the farthest north they got: the *limes*. Massacred the natives at Cramond, apparently. Beyond the Firth they did nothing but lose legions all over the map, that's about it.'

'Heh!' I raised my pint of Arrol's. 'Here's to the end of empires.'

'Cheers,' Reid nodded. 'Still, it's impressive in a way. All the land from here to the far side of the Med under one government.'

'Hmm … somebody warn the Euro-sceptics: it's been done and it *lasted for a thousand years!*' – this in a comic-German screech that distracted one push-button space warrior enough to glance at me and lose a few ships to the invading evil empire on the screen. I think I was a little drunk by this point.

Our progress continued through The Two Bridges, The Anchor, and The Ferry Tap. Outside the Queensferry Arms Reid hesitated, then said, 'Skip this one. Got a better idea.' He led me a few steps along the narrow High Street to a Chinese take-away where he promised me the best delicacy on the menu.

'Two portions of curried chips, please.'

'Curried chips?' I asked incredulously.

'Just what you need after a few pints.'

The girl behind the counter served us these with what I dimly thought a patronising smile. Eating the steaming, sticky, greasy messes with little plastic forks, we made our way past a police-station and what Reid described as a Jacobite church, and on up to the last pub, pausing only to dispose of our litter thoughtfully behind a front gate.

We lurched in to The Moorings with breath like dragons'. The girl behind the bar actually averted her face as she pulled our pints. I followed Reid away from the bar into a rear area where wide windows presented a fine view of the Bridge.

The pub was new, fake-old; nautical gear and framed drawings of battleships on the walls. In the course of our travels Reid's opening shot about the Roman Empire had turned into a long and involved argument about empires generally, with Reid firmly in their favour. He loathed the usual default option for disillusioned socialists, nationalism.

'See these,' he said, opening his third pack of cigarettes and pointing at the naval engravings. 'See them. They, they saved us, right? From the German fascist barbarians. And from good old Uncle Joe, if truth be told.'

'That,' I said, trying to steady him in my 'scope, 'is a bit of an over-simplified few. View. I'm surprised at you.'

'So'm I,' he said. 'A few years back, there was a display out there, Harriers flying backwards and Sea Kings looping the loop and all that, and I realised I was *proud* of those guys. Just like I used to be about the heroic Red Army and the Vietcong.'

'Jesus.' I was shocked into a passing fit of sobriety. 'You're telling me the armed forces of the British state are *freedom fighters*? I'm sure the Irish have a different story, for starters.'

'Ah, fuck the Irish,' Reid said, fortunately not too loudly. 'I must admit I did have a hang-up about the bold IRA for years. And then they went and turned up their toes, just jacked it in like the fucking Stalinists.'

'But you always wanted something better than that –'

He glared into his Caledonian Eighty. 'Even so, I stuck up for the workers' states. And then they all went down like – like dominoes! I'm not the one who deserted. I mean, my side surrendered, right? So I can do whatever the fuck I like.'

The bell rang for last orders. Reid laughed and drained his glass. 'Same again?'

'Yes please.'

He returned with two pints and two shots of whisky. The whisky may have had some responsibility for what happened later.

'So what do you have to say to that?' he asked.

'Schlanzhe ... OK, OK. You're saying you used to admire the other side's armies, right? So what about all the peace-fighting, eh? What about CND?'

Peace-fighting, CND ... something was bugging me.

'Tactics. The Communists were probably sincere, funnily enough, but as far as we were concerned we saw CND work as running interference for the Russkies.'

'No shit?'

'No shit.'

'Well,' I said, taken aback at this brazen admission, 'I must say your new-found patriotism has a suspiciously damascene curve about it, as in going from one misguided view to what seems to be the complete opposite but is actually the same place –'

'Bullshit. I'm not patriotic. All I'm saying is, we live in a dangerous world and I'm not going to pretend I don't know whose guns keep me safe.'

'What about the people on the other side of the guns?'

'Tough. I'm just lucky I'm on this side. Compared to anything else out there, it's the side of progress. *We*'re the camp of the revolution.'

'Explain yourself.'

'Because your Yank dingbat libertarian pals are right – the

Western democracies *are* socialist! Big public sectors, big companies that plan production while officially everything's on the market ... sort of *black* planning, like the East had a black market. Marx said universal suffrage was the rule of the working class, and he was right. The West is Red!'

I had to laugh, not just at the audacity of Reid's rationalisation but at the grain of awkward truth in it. We explored this theory as we were cleared from the pub and made our way up on to the Road Bridge.

'Shit,' Reid said, scrutinising the bus timetable, 'we've missed it. Fucking private companies keep changing the services.'

'Goddamn capitalist roaders. Let's get a taxi.'

'From here? Nah. There's a hotel on the other side. Let's phone from there.'

I looked along the bridge's bright kilometre.

'Bit of a walk.'

'Might even be a bar open,' Reid said cunningly.

'I'm game.'

We set off, past signs announcing that security cameras watched the bridge at all times. To the north and west there was still light in the sky. Cars and lorries thrummed past, every other minute. The section of the bridge before it reached the river made a slow ascent above streets and backyards and waste ground and the long arms of a marina. There was a high barrier on our left between the footway and the drop to the river, a lower but wider barrier between footway and road. Reid kept to a rapid pace, saying little. About halfway across I paused to light up a black cheroot which had (unaccountably, at that moment) turned up in my pocket.

Something on my mind. Peace-fighting, something to do with ... ah!

Not a good time – but then, there never would be a good time. I hurried to catch up with him.

'Reid, old boy,' I said, from behind his shoulder, 'I have a bone to pick with you.'

His shoulder twitched up. He didn't turn. 'OK, man. Whatever.'

'Well, the fact is, Annette told me about, you know, you. And her.'

'Oh!' He stopped and faced me.

I stopped, leaning against the railing. Hundreds of feet below, the water gleamed like hammered lead. Reid fumbled out a cigarette, dropped it, picked it up and lit it.

'What can I say?' he said. He spread his hands, swayed, and laid his right hand on the parapet. 'It happened, what's the use denying it, and it was my fault, and I'm sorry.'

'All right,' I said. 'That's all you have to say.'

'You're ...' He drew hard on the cigarette, cupped glowing in his left hand. 'You're a good bloke, Jon. She deserves you. And you deserved better of me. I abused your ... hospitality, man. No excuse, except it was just fucking ...'

His voice trailed off and he looked away from me, out at the distance.

'*Just fucking?*'

'... obsession, man, that's the word.' He laughed harshly. 'I wish I *could* say it was just fucking.'

He looked back at me. The smoke was suddenly foul in my mouth. I sent the red ember spinning over the side, and watched its long slow fall.

'But I can't,' he went on. 'I'm not saying that wasn't wrong, but there was more than that. I once even tried to get her to leave you, if you can believe that. But she wouldn't, and she was right, and that was the end of it. Over. And I got over her, and she got over me.'

From that moment I've known that I'm capable of murder. He had one hand on the parapet, one at his side still holding the cigarette. He was again gazing into the distance. A grab for the collar and the belt, one good heave, and he would be over. It would have been easy, and I could have done it.

He turned to me. 'That was when she told you, right?' There was something of admiration and cunning in his eyes. 'I know, because that's when all the right-wing shit started arriving, from the Contras and Renamo and East European emigrés and the KMT and the NTS. Mixing it in with the old commies and the libertarians was a neat trick, but I got the message all right. You know some heavy guys, and they know where I live.' He laughed harshly. 'I've got to hand it to you, Jon, you had me scared.'

I took a step towards him and punched straight for his mouth. It was a good punch – my childhood boxing-lessons hadn't been wasted – and he reacted with a hopelessly slow, country-boy, haymaking swing.

But his connected, and mine didn't. I was slammed against the railing. The top edge hit my lower ribcage and suddenly I was leaning away over it, looking straight down. Straight up, for an unreal moment, as my semi-circular canals turned over and the universe followed them round.

And then I was sick. A Mexican meal, a dozen pints, two whiskies, a portion of curried chips and the tar from a score of Silk Cut and one Mexican cigarillo poured through my mouth and nostrils in a cascade that spattered walkways and ladders and disturbed roosting birds before it fell, with literally sickening slowness, visible all the way, to the water.

'Are you all right?'

I pushed myself away from the railing.

'I'm all right,' I said. I blew a fragment of taco and a gobbet of spicy slime from my left nostril onto my fingers, then balled my fist for another go at him.

His eyes widened, but he was looking past me. Brakes squealed. A van pulled up beside us, on the footpath, not on the road.

The door opened and a man in a boiler-suit leaned out.

'Come on, lads,' he said. 'We've been keeping an eye on you two. You look like you could do with a lift.'

The Conquest of Violence

9

Circuit Judgement

IT'S EARLY AFTERNOON and the watches are beeping fifteen. Dee follows Ax across a high, narrow bridge. The walkway is barely a metre wide, the parapets little more than a metre high. Beneath it is a hundred-metre drop to the roofs of a lower level. Above it, taller towers rise. The bridge slopes gently up, curves smoothly around to the right. Dee walks it fearlessly; this is familiar territory to her, the high locale of the high life of those who, in Ship City, pass for rich. Fortunately, however, she has never met Anderson Parris, the man whose residence they're approaching.

Dee has very little doubt that before the next hour is over, she'll have killed a human being. She hasn't done this before, and the prospect arouses in her a certain curiosity. The skills are there, of course, in Spy and Soldier. But she remembers rumours, as from a previous life (from her life before she awoke) that make her wonder if she can access those particular skills. If Sys has changed *the permissions* ... There's no way of telling, because that itself is a part of Sys to which she has no access. She recalls people talking, talking as if she wasn't there, of the potential dangers of AIs wandering around in human guise, and she knows that humans set great store by *the permissions*.

She has no doubt at all that Ax will be able to do it. Ax is a human being, and human beings don't need any *permissions*. Dee shivers, but not with fear or excitement. The wind is chill at this height, and her new clothes, even inside a green velvet cloak, do little to keep her warm.

The door is a bright, slightly convex steel panel, set back in the synthetic rock of the building. Dee admires her distorted reflection, practising transforms on it, while Ax exchanges a few words with a speaker grille. The door slides smoothly sideways, and Ax and Dee walk in. The entrance hallway has inward-sloping walls, and the rightward curve of its floor continues that of the bridge, further into the building. The hall is illuminated by a high skylight, and by tall windows in the outer wall. Electric lights hang at varying levels from the ten-metre-high roof, and likewise suspended bowls overflow with leaves and stalks, flowers and scents.

The door shuts behind them. Dee glances back for a moment, checking that it can be opened manually from the inside. It looks like it can, but Spy's subtler senses are on the job, tracking the pulse-patterns in the wires behind the walls, just in case. Ax's feet pad, Dee's heels click around the curve of the corridor. The wooden doors leading off the corridor are closed. After Dee and Ax have walked to a point where the outer door is no longer visible, the corridor widens out to a stairwell. A few steps up the spiral staircase, a man stands waiting. He's wearing a black kimono embroidered with deep-sky images. His fair hair is swept back from his high forehead. His face is narrow, lips thin, eyelashes sandy, expression serene. To Dee, his smooth and healthy features look old – older far than her, or Ax; almost as old as Reid. And yet they suggest some deeper immaturity, as well as a cruelty which Dee immediately sees as distinct from the cold ruthlessness which was the worst that Reid's most unguarded moments – even now, in replayed recollection – ever betrayed. This man is not like Reid, nor any of his friends or casual acquaintances. No burly businessman who ever ogled her at a meeting, or pawed her at a party, ever made her feel the way she does now, as his gaze inspects her.

Anderson Parris descends the stairs and smiles at Ax.

'Well, hello,' he says, catching Ax's hands. 'I'm delighted to see you, and your most interesting and beautiful friend.'

Dee opens a frogged clasp at her throat and removes her cloak. She swings the cloak across her left arm, concealing the bag in her left hand, and languidly extends her right.

'I'm charmed to meet you, Anderson Parris.'

After a nonplussed moment the man realises she expects him to kiss her hand, and he does. His fingers are cold, his lips damp. As his head lifts from kissing her hand his gaze travels from her high-heeled boots, past her black leather leggings under her black lace skirt, up the ladder of silver clasps and tiny bows on her black satin boned corset-top; to her neck, where a steel-studded leather collar matches the buckled straps on her forearms; to her darkly shadowed eyes. When their eyes meet she looks straight back, with the slight smile of a shared secret.

Sex is in charge here, and Sex has no difficulty in detecting that she has him on a leash. He waves her politely ahead of him, and they go up the stairs. She walks up slowly, letting him have a good view of her tight-laced back. His murmured conversation with Ax carries oddly in the stairwell.

They ascend into a circular room built around the stairwell. Its ceiling is a glass dome above the two-metre-high walls. Dee sees the sun, and the darting manta-shapes of passing aircraft. Nothing else overlooks the room, which seems to combine the functions of a studio, a gallery and a bedroom. There's a drawing-console and a camera-array. Around the walls are chairs, low tables, and long couches which might be used as beds, though the artfully casual deployment of covers and cushions makes their function ambiguous. The walls are hung with ornate weapons – swords of beaten steel, lasers of brass and ruby – and with pictures, of children who look vulnerable and women who look invulnerable.

'Would you like a drink, lady?'

'I would,' she says distantly. 'Dark Star.'

Parris's quick, almost obsequious smile can't quite conceal his momentary grimace at her taste in liquor, but he goes over to a drinks cabinet and a fridge and prepares the mixture. He brings it over, ice clinking, and touches her glass with his own of chilled wine.

Parris smiles as she drains her glass. He discards his kimono. Under it he's wearing deeply unoriginal bondage gear, a costume of belts and clips. His cock is straining against what looks like a painfully tight jockstrap, 'strap' being the operative word.

Ax, to her surprise, drops on all fours and scampers across the room to a big wardrobe. He nudges the bottom of the door with his head, and the door swings open to reveal an apparatus of chains and straps. Dee slams her (fortunately solid) glass down on the most expensive and delicate table-surface within reach, and turns on her heel and looks at Parris.

'I understand,' she says coldly, 'that you have been a very wicked man.'

Parris nods. His eyes are shining, in a face that's become a flushed mask of humility.

Dee lets the Sex program play out the scene. She slaps his face, a little harder than he perhaps expects.

'I have come to judge you,' she says. She pretends to think, scrutinising him. She looks around the room, until her glance lights on the open cupboard. Ax is squatting beside it, his tongue hanging out. Dee's eyes widen in mock surprise. She points to the cupboard.

'Over there,' she orders. Parris walks towards it. He flashes her a servile, collusive smile.

'Eyes *down*!' Dee yells.

Parris obediently bows his head and walks to the door.

Dee has the whole protocol mapped out in her head, but she's not really into this sort of thing (being, if truth be told, more sub than dom) and she gives the finicky business of shackling and binding him perhaps less attention than it deserves. It ends with her squeezing his cheeks until he opens his mouth. She pops a rubber ball into his mouth, closes his jaws with a finger on his nose and a thumb on the point of his chin, and slaps a piece of insulating-tape (of a suitably shiny black) across his mouth.

She drops out of character for a moment.

'OK?'

Parris nods. Dee checks the restraints. They're secure.

Ax, who all the while has been working his way slowly up from the man's toes to his knees with playful nips of his teeth, suddenly stands up and steps back. Dee steps back too, and together they look at the man hanging in the cupboard.

Ax smiles into Parris's suddenly troubled, puzzled stare. He reaches behind his neck, and the long knife is in his hand. He tosses it sideways into the other hand, and then back. He inspects the edge. The side of the blade catches flashes of sunlight; the edge betrays only the faintest flicker, as if even photons slide off it.

He looks again at Parris.

'Woof,' he says.

Wilde had more than one cigarette-stub at his feet by the time he saw the girl striding towards him through the market crowd. He straightened up from leaning on the mainframe.

'Tamara Hunter,' the machine said over his shoulder as the girl stopped and stuck out her hand. 'Jonathan Wilde.'

She cocked her head sideways and looked him over as he shook her hand.

'My God,' she said. 'You really are him.'

Wilde grinned. 'You look somehow familiar yourself.'

'The pub last night,' Tamara reminded him. 'Mind you, if ever anyone had eyes only for one woman, it was you.'

'Ah, of course,' Wilde said. 'You were with … Dee.'

'Yes,' Tamara said. She looked about. 'Where's your robot?'

'Hah!' Wilde snorted. 'You and I are supposed to be on the same side, according to this electric lawyer here, so don't you go saying "your robot". I'm damned if I'll admit it's *my* robot. The fact is, it's fucked off on its own somewhere.'

'Oh,' Tamara said. She glanced at the Invisible Hand mainframe. 'We're going for a private discussion,' she told it.

'Very well,' the machine said. 'I shall proceed with the technical aspects of the case.'

Tamara turned to Wilde. 'Talk about it over a beer?'

'God, yes.'

They wended their way between stalls and under trees. The market boomed around them. When they were – as far as it was humanly possible to tell – out of Invisible Hand's earshot, Wilde asked, 'Just as a matter of curiosity, is that piece of legal machinery self-aware?'

Tamara laughed. 'Nah, it's just an expert system. It has its little quirks, mind.'

'Yeah, you could say that.' He looked at a cluster of tables around an array of counter, refrigerator and grill, all small and all scorched. A tall Turk stood in the middle, his hands dealing out drinks and sandwiches for greasy wads of money. 'Here?'

Tamara nodded, with an appreciative smile at his good judgement. Wilde ordered two litres of beer. They sipped for a minute from the beaded brown bottles, in thirsty silence, and checked each other out.

'Smoke?' Wilde said, retrieving a now battered pack.

'No thanks,' Tamara said. 'But go ahead.'

Wilde smiled at her. 'This is my first pack for centuries,' he said as he lit up. 'Not that that's much of an excuse. For one thing, to me it all happened the day before yesterday, and for another it's smoking that got me killed.'

Tamara frowned. 'The books tell different stories, but I thought you died in some shoot-out.'

'That was it,' Wilde nodded. 'Tried to run faster than a bullet, but –' He looked ruefully at the cigarette, and took another drag as Tamara laughed.

'This is weird,' she said. 'I've talked to some people who were in the ship, and who actually came from Earth – hell, my grandparents did – but they never talk about having been dead. They talk about having been "in transition".'

'Yeah,' Wilde said sardonically. '"In denial" is the technical term for that frame of mind.'

'But you do ... and you being, like, a historical character. Wow, fuck!' She studied his features judiciously. 'You look different in the pictures. Older.'

'In *what* pictures?' Wilde demanded.

Tamara reached into an inside pocket, and passed to Wilde a plastic wallet containing a set of cards.

'I, um, collect them,' she explained as Wilde began to spread them out. 'They come free with, uh, a cereal that gets made in this area.'

'Harmony Oats!' Wilde shouted with laughter. He spread out the woodcut portraits. 'Let's see ... Owen, Stirner, Proudhon, Warren, Bakunin, Tucker, Labadie, Wilson, Wilde. They've got the ancestry right, but I doubt I deserve such exalted company. I'm not sure whether to be flattered or appalled.'

He looked down at the scored lines of the iconic faces, and passed a hand over his own fresh features. He shook his head.

'When I first looked like I do now I was far from famous,' Wilde said. His voice sounded sad for a moment, cheerier as he added: 'Perhaps it's just as well.'

'Dead right!' Tamara looked around. 'You're going to be famous all over again, when this gets out. Which it will, when the court case starts, if not sooner.'

Wilde shrugged. 'I'd like to delay it as long as possible. My grasp of the politics of this place isn't strong enough to handle publicity to my advantage.'

'OK,' said Tamara. 'We have a more immediate problem. Before I learned that you were involved, I got a message from David Reid. You ... knew him?'

'Sure did. Once.'

'Right, well he's suing me to get the gynoid, Dee, back. Fair enough, I expected that. I *want* to make a case of it. Invisible Hand has just told me you were being sued too, and that you wanted to combine forces. As a matter of fact you don't have much choice, as it's all part of the same case in actuality, so no other court is going to touch yours while ours is outstanding, and we'd have to bring you into it anyway, so you might as well go in on your own terms.'

Wilde spread his hands. 'So what's the problem?'

'The first person on our list of preferred judges is a bloke called Eon Talgarth.' She paused, waiting for some reaction. Wilde just raised his eyebrows. 'He used to be an abolitionist,' Tamara went on, 'and he now runs a court out in the Fifth Quarter. That's a machine domain. Most of the disputes he settles are between scrappies.'

'Scrappies?'

'People like me, who go into the machine domains and hunt for useful bits of machinery and automation. He's been known to let autonomous machines go free, and put injunctions on hunting them, but no other judge has accepted that as a precedent.'

'All the same,' said Wilde, 'he sounds like a good bet for your case.'

'Sure, which is why I didn't expect Reid to agree. But he did. Great. Trouble is, I didn't know you'd be involved. Shit.'

'Why is it a problem?'

'Because Eon Talgarth doesn't like you very much.'

Wilde put down his drink and stared at her. 'What? I never heard of him. What's he got against me?'

'Oh, nothing personal as far as I know.' She shrugged. 'He's from Earth, he was in the labour-gangs, he was in the ship. So you could have harmed him somehow – he's never said. But when he was an abolitionist, he used to argue against the idea which a lot of people here have, that you were some kind of hero and great anarchist thinker and represented an alternative to the sort of ideas that Reid implemented when he set this place going. He said you were an opportunist, that you made all kinds of dirty deals with govern-ments – and with Reid, and that any conflicts between the two of you were just personal rivalries.'

She spoke in a light-hearted, say-it-ain't-so tone. Wilde tilted his seat precariously back and rocked with laughter.

'It's all true, every word!' he said. 'I'm amazed there are people here who say I was a hero and a great anarchist thinker. Ha-ha! This Eon Talgarth has got me bang to rights.'

Tamara's mouth turned down slightly. 'It's not really true, is it? That you were always an opportunist?'

'Absolutely,' Wilde said. 'Only the other day – by my memory, of course – a woman I was once in love with told me I was responsible for the last world war going nuclear. By that time in my life, bearing in mind I was ninety-three years old and had taken a lot of flak for various ... controversial decisions, I didn't even take offence.'

'But if ...' Tamara considered the implications. 'That would mean you were to blame for –'

'The whole fucking mess!' Wilde said. He looked about him and waved a hand. 'Everything that has happened since the Third World War is *all my fault!*'

'That,' said Tamara, 'is what Eon Talgarth thinks.'

'He could be right,' Wilde said with a shrug. 'I don't think so myself.'

'Oh, neither do I,' Tamara hastened to add. 'And neither do most people, abolitionists or not. In fact, some people think you're, well ...'

She hesitated, embarrassed.

'What?' Wilde leaned forward, cigarette in hand, daring her. 'Something more than a great anarchist thinker?'

'Yes,' Tamara said. 'They think you're, well, still alive and out there somewhere. People say they've seen you, out in the desert.'

'Do they indeed?' Wilde sucked in smoke and blew it above her head, in a long sigh. 'Now that's really interesting, because the robot Jay-Dub claims to be another ... implementation of me, and to have been around since before the first landing here. I wouldn't put it past its capabilities to throw a fetch, or to appear as me on screen.'

'Aha!' said Tamara. 'According to the message I got from

Invisible Hand, Reid claims he has evidence that Jay-Dub hacked into Dee, and he holds you responsible.'

'Me?' Wilde said. 'Well, Jay-Dub said nothing to me about anything like that. What a surprise.'

'Yeah,' said Tamara. 'AIs are devious bastards, aren't they?'

'Devious and dangerous,' Wilde said. 'Wouldn't trust them an inch, myself.'

Tamara laughed.

'OK,' said Wilde, 'I reckon we need to fill each other in a bit. Us humans gotta stick together.'

Tamara recounted what had happened the previous evening, and that morning, and some of the background. Wilde kept smiling when she spoke about abolitionism. Then Wilde went over what had happened to him, and what the robot had told him. Tamara listened, sometimes wide-eyed, sometimes frowning. When he'd finished she sat silent for a moment.

'What a bastard,' she said at last. 'Growing a clone of your wife's body and using it as a gynoid. Jeez. Guess he didn't expect to see you again.'

'Maybe,' Wilde said dubiously. 'He must've known about the robot, though, surely? Could the robot have seen Dee before?'

'Sure,' said Tamara. 'That kind of rig would have comms, if nothing else. And Reid's claiming Jay-Dub did hack into Dee. But the robot said nothing about that?'

'Nothing to me,' Wilde said. 'I definitely got the impression that it knew something about Dee, in fact it insisted Dee wasn't human even in the sense that it is, but it never gave any hint that Dee was part of its plans, whatever they are.'

'And now it's disappeared,' Tamara sighed. She looked about, as though hoping it would reappear. 'Presumably it doesn't know about the legal case, and it figures it's best to lie low.'

'That would fit in with its personality all right,' Wilde grinned. 'And mine!'

'Let's hope it finds out before the trial,' said Tamara. 'Otherwise it is in even deeper shit … You still want to go before Talgarth?'

'From what you've told me,' Wilde said, 'I don't have much choice in the matter.'

'That's right,' said Tamara.

Wilde responded with an ironic grimace. He stood up, without

133

saying anything, and wandered about the nearby stalls. Every so often he smiled to himself, and then he turned and smiled at Tamara, who'd silently followed him.

'There's something about this place,' he explained. 'I always knew there would be places like this, trash markets on other worlds. It makes me feel so homesick that I know I'm the same man I was on Earth.'

Tamara looked down and scuffed the dirt.

'I'm sorry,' she said. 'I've heard so much about Wilde, but my mental picture of him is always like – you know, those cards, posters I've seen. I know I've been sort of presumptuous, talking to you like you're as young as you look.'

Wilde snorted and slapped her shoulder. 'Knock it off,' he said. 'I've only come back from the dead in a literal sense.'

They went over to Invisible Hand and registered Wilde as a joint defendant, and Wilde laid a counter-charge against Reid of having been responsible for the death of one Jonathan Wilde, of London, Earth. The machine took it all in without demur, but its internal lights moved about in an agitated manner.

'What now?' Wilde asked Tamara.

'Well, perhaps it's time you met Dee. She's staying at my place, and it's only five minutes away from here. Ax – that's a ... kid who lives with me – said he'd take her out shopping this morning.' She looked at her watch. 'Fifteen-thirty. They should be back by now.'

'OK,' said Wilde. He stood up. For the first time since they'd met, his face showed something less than composure.

'Let's go.'

Ax retrieves the knife from the closed door of the wardrobe, paces back a few metres, and throws the knife again. It thuds into the door and sticks there, adding to the rough human outline of gashes that repeated throws have left in the wood. A faint groan and a banging noise come from inside the cupboard.

Dee looks up from rummaging through Parris's picture collection. She feels nauseous. It's impossible to tell if the pictures are of real scenes, or posed, or are simply computer-generated imagery. She doesn't particularly care. She wants to wipe them from her memory, and their originator from the world.

She still doesn't know if she can do it, or even stand by and let

Ax do it. She doesn't know if the permissions for her lethal skills have been reset. She suspects that if they haven't, it won't be anything dramatic; no staying of her hand, no rooting of her feet; just some quite reasonable and natural-seeming inhibition, a distaste or disquiet that won't let her follow it through.

'Haven't you done enough of that?' she asks Ax.

Ax tugs the knife out of the wood once more. 'I suppose so,' he admits. He grins at her. 'You get carried away.'

Dee takes her pistol out of her handbag, tucks it in her waistband and walks over.

'Well I say finish it,' she says.

'Fine,' says Ax.

He opens the splintered door. Inside, Parris is still hanging in his bonds. His eyes are tightly closed. Tears are running down his face, and the sticky-tape gag is slimed with the snot that the tears have brought with them and which he's blown from his nostrils in frantic snorts.

Ax traces a line with the knife's tip, along the man's bare belly. Parris's eyes open, and roll from side to side, looking at Ax and then, as if in appeal, to Dee. Blood wells along the cut. The sight of it makes Dee stop, and catch Ax's arm.

'No!' she says. The images from Parris's collection are crowded out by images from Soldier, an encyclopaedia of injury and blood: spurting, spraying, oozing, dripping. She imagines it spattering her clothes, and shudders.

'No,' she says. 'It's enough.'

Ax glares at her, but she outstares him. He backs off. Dee sets to work, loosening, unshackling, unbinding. She steadies Parris as he stumbles out, and lets him sink to the floor. He's making noises through his nostrils.

'Oh,' says Dee. She'd forgotten that. She stoops to rip the tape from his mouth, and as it comes off she notices that Parris has come, and more than once, even with his cock bound back. Semen is drying on his thighs.

He falls forward into a kneeling posture, and looks up at her, gasping and smiling.

'Thank you, mistress,' he says in a low voice. 'I deserved that, all of it, I truly did!' He looks at her with sly hope. 'When can you visit me again?'

Dee stares at him. She takes a few steps backward, still thinking of keeping her nice new clothes clean. She turns and walks further away, past Ax, to the top of the stairs.

'Mistress, please ...' Parris calls after her.

'Oh, fuck this,' she says.

She draws the pistol from her skirt, takes aim, and blows his head off.

The shot echoes around the circular spaces of the room and the stairwell and leaves her ears ringing. She grins at Ax, who despite his instigation of the whole thing is looking at the remains of Parris, and then at her, with a shocked pallor.

'Now I know,' she says. 'I do have free will.'

'That must be very useful,' Ax says. 'I'm a bit of a determinist, myself.'

Dee smiles at him reassuringly as she briskly gathers up her stuff.

'Time to go,' she says.

Ax is pointlessly wiping the tip of his knife on a piece of drapery.

'Shouldn't we, you know, clean up?' he asks. 'Can't you see fingerprints and stuff?'

'Oh, sure,' Dee says, fastening her cloak. 'They're all over the place. And our skin-cells. Not to mention our images on the house's cameras.'

She looks up and smiles and waves at a tiny, hooded lens.

'Shit,' says Ax. 'Can you do anything about it?'

Dee flashes him a puzzled look and starts to go downstairs.

'Of course I can,' she says. 'But it's very important that I don't, and you know it. Come on, before somebody comes.'

Ax follows her, still reluctant.

'Nobody's gonna come,' he says. 'I don't think Parris had his nest video-linked to the nearest security-service.'

'I guess not.'

Unlocking the door doesn't require any of Dee's deeper abilities. It closes itself behind them as soon as they're out. They walk down the long ramp in silence. Near the bottom a side-ramp leads to a nearby residential door. Dee scans its electronics.

'This'll do,' she says. 'Somebody's home.'

Ax stops walking. For a moment, he looks like a stubborn child.

'This isn't what I meant,' he says.

Dee tries not to wheedle.

'It's important,' she says. 'It'll help your cause, as well as your case.'

'I don't give a fuck about a case,' Ax says. 'That shit is *over*.'

Dee regards him levelly while recalling the things he's said earlier.

'The dead may rise,' she says, 'and you may be right, but one way or another, this will all come to judgement.'

Ax stares back at her for a moment, then nods.

Together, they walk down the small ramp to the door. Dee pings the bell. They wait. A little screen above the bell lights up, a woman's face appears.

'Yes?' she says.

Dee stands a little straighter and taller.

'This is Dee Model and Ax Terminal,' she announces firmly. 'We have just killed your neighbour up the way, Anderson Parris. Call you witness.'

The woman gives an exaggerated blink.

'W-witnessed,' she says shakily.

'Thank you,' Ax says.

'Goodbye,' says Dee.

Then Dee and Ax hurry back to the main ramp and down steps and slopes to a level walkway, and up in a lift to a high platform, where they join a small queue of well-dressed people waiting at the air-stop to catch a flit. Ax occupies his time by tuning in to the stop's news-service. Every so often he shakes his head and smiles at Dee: no hue-and-cry yet; and uses these interruptions in his glassy trance to study a list.

Dee sees he's already crossed off one name, and that there are a lot more to go.

Tamara looked at the little stack of incriminating material on the table: the Talgarth file on Wilde, the picture Dee had made, and a scrawled apocalyptic rant from Ax. Wilde had just finished reading it.

'God,' he said. 'I've heard of suicide notes, but this is the first time I've ever come across a *murder* note.'

Tamara was holding her hands to the sides of her head.

'*I'*ll murder the little pervert, if I ever get my hands on him,' she said. 'Honestly, Comrade Wilde, if I'd even suspected he was

137

capable of going off the fast end like this I'd never've let Dee out of my sight.'

Wilde reached over and caught her hand.

'Easy,' he said, 'easy. What have I ever done to you to make you call me "Comrade Wilde"? My name's Jon, OK? And you're no more responsible for losing Dee than I am for losing Jay-Dub. They're both free agents, isn't that what this is all about?'

'I suppose so,' Tamara said. 'And Ax is claiming he wasn't, when he did some … degrading things. I can see why, too, in a way, but then … Aaach! It's so complicated! What do we do?'

'Tamara,' Wilde said gently, letting go of her hand and sitting down, 'how long have you lived?'

'Twenty years.'

Wilde lit a cigarette.

'New Mars years?'

'Yes.'

'Well then,' said Wilde. 'You've lived in an anarchy twice as long as I ever managed to, and you surely know the answer to that, or the way of finding the answer.'

Tamara sat down at the table and looked back at him, baffled and defiant.

'I don't get you,' she said.

'Look,' Wilde said, 'when we want to know whether something was worth making, we look for the answer in a discovery machine called the market. When we want to know how something works, we have another discovery machine, called science. When we want to know if somebody was right to kill somebody else, we have a discovery machine called the law.'

'Yes,' said Tamara. 'I know that. It's not going to be much help to Ax and Dee, if they get caught. Or us, if we wait too long before trying to stop them.'

'It's worth a try, OK? And if the law really lets you down, and you can't live with it, then –' He spread his hands, smiling.

'What?'

'You're back in the state of nature. You fight. OK, you might die, but so what? Same as if the market lets you down. It does happen. You're starving. You steal.'

Tamara looked taken aback.

'But that would be –'

'Anarchy?' Wilde grinned at her.

'You're saying people can do anything?'

'Literally, yes. In any half-decent society you're far better off respecting the law and property and so on, but the bottom line is, it's your choice. You always have the option of making war – on the whole world, if it comes to that.'

'But you'd *lose!*' Tamara said.

Wilde looked back at her, unperturbed.

'You might not. Locke said you can always "appeal to heaven", and God or Nature might find in your favour. What I'm saying is, Ax has made his choice, and Dee hers. Maybe they can justify that choice in front of a court, maybe not. Either way, it isn't for us to decide, and I'd be more than happy to justify not warning their potential victims. But if you want to, by all means go ahead.'

Tamara rubbed her chin and looked down again at Ax's screed. She looked at Dee's picture, and Talgarth's file. Then she looked up at Wilde and asked, as if wanting to settle one final question: 'What do you do if *science* lets you down?'

Wilde laughed. 'Trust to luck.'

He stubbed out his cigarette and jumped up.

'The sooner we get to Eon Talgarth's court, the better,' he said. 'Am I right?'

'Yes,' said Tamara. She rose and began to hunt around for maps and provisions and arms.

'So how do we get there?' asked Wilde. 'Aircraft?'

Tamara was packing ammo clips. She turned to him and laughed.

'Talgarth doesn't take kindly to aircraft landing nearby,' she said. 'He doesn't trust them, for some strange reason. Nah, we take just enough weapons and gadgets to get through the wild machines, and we walk. Everybody does.' She grinned. 'It's the law. It reduces the chances of fights breaking out in court.'

'There's a lot I don't know about this place,' Wilde acknowledged wryly.

Tamara grunted, testing the weight of a pack. She took out a heavy pistol, and passed it over to Wilde. She shoved Talgarth's file on Wilde across the table.

'Take that and read it sometime,' she said. 'There's a lot this place doesn't know about you.'

10

Tested On Animals

YOU'LL HAVE NOTICED by now that what I'm telling you here isn't in the texts. As you'll have guessed, that's the point. Why should I duplicate my hagiographers?

So you'll forgive me, I hope, if I take the story of how I used People for Progress (North British Mutual's educational campaign) as a launch-pad for the space movement; how I used Space Merchants to seed FreeSpace, a libertarian radical group that had learned the left's one sound lesson, Leninism; how we used the space movement as a popular front for our free-market anarchism, and how the space movement grew beyond even my expectations – if I take *mein kampf*, in short – as read.

And my political commentary and analysis, ephemeral as it seemed at the time, fading from the screens like a short-term memory, was all dutifully archived by the intelligence agencies of the day, and in due course (i.e. wars and revolutions later) passed into the public domain and is undoubtedly still hanging around out there – 'it is always *sometime, somewhere* on the net', so if you really want to know, it's only a search away [note: lightspeed limitations may apply]. So I won't repeat myself on that, either.

In my later years I was occasionally known to grumble about the youth of today, etc., and how they didn't appreciate that there had been a revolution before *The* Revolution and how there wouldn't have been a New Republic if there hadn't been a Republic in the first place, and how much tougher it all was for us and by the way have I ever told you about the war?

So I'll skip that, too.

But it remains worth saying that the United Republic didn't just happen. People didn't suddenly wake up that election morning in 2015 and think, 'This time we've *got* to get the bastards out.' As a matter of fact they did, but it took a lot of work to bring that reckless impulse to birth: decades of agitation, grumbling, constitution-drafting, sparsely attended meetings in poorly furnished halls, letters to the editor, noisy demonstrations, and all the rest. And bloody hard work it was. I know, because I was there and I didn't do any of it.

FreeSpace (the name had once seemed trendy, but now dated us painfully – 'very TwenCen', as I'd overheard someone say) had its modest offices above a Space Merchants franchise just across the road from the Camden Lock market. (I'd quit running Space Merchants, kept enough shares and options in it to keep a steady if small income, and left it alone. It had moved into selling actual space products now, most just novelties – moon-rock jewellery, free-fall crystals and so forth – but also some of practical use. Micro-gravity manufacturing had come up with unexpected applications, as I'd known it would.) We'd had the offices for ten years, and they still smelled of fresh paint and new wood and cement. The concrete walls were decorated with space movement posters and NASA Inc hologram views, but the first thing anyone saw when they came through the doorway was my desk with a huge notice behind it saying YOU'RE WELCOME TO SMOKE. I no longer smoked myself – although medical science had already beaten what we (misleadingly, nowadays) called 'the big C', there was no easy fix for the habit's bronchial consequences, and at sixty-two I needed all the breath I could get. The notice was a matter of principle, like the washroom soap-dispenser's mischievous little sticker announcing that its contents had been *Tested On Animals*.

The morning after the election I was the only person in the office who wasn't late in and hung over. Each bleary-eyed arrival was greeted by me looking up from the online news (panic in Whitehall, pound in free fall, riots in Kensington, airports mobbed) and saying: 'Oh, you stayed up for the results? Who won?'

Having thus protected my anarchist credibility I'd have another secret gloat at the results. The composition of the new government wasn't official yet, they were still arguing, but it looked like it would be Republican, New Labour, True Labour, and a couple of Radicals on the government side, with the Unionists the official opposition and the small parties in the wings. Plenty of the last – even the World Socialists (the new name of the SPGB) had scraped together enough first preferences to get one MP elected. Sadly, my parents hadn't lived to see it. It had taken the party a hundred and eleven years to get into Parliament, but they were still on course for that twenty-fifth-century global majority.

Then I'd get back to organising an emergency executive committee meeting for 11.00 that morning. No answer, not even an answering-program, from two of the members: Aaronson (research) and Rutherford (international liaison). Hmmm. I immediately contacted several potential rivals for each position – rather than our internal security group, who were *prima facie* most likely to be police spies anyway – and set them to work investigating.

But the other seven duly popped up on my screen, and all of us on each other's. I decided to say nothing about Aaronson and Rutherford, and just shrugged when their absence was remarked in the pre-meeting chit-chat as people shuffled paper, booted up notepads, settled in their seats and looked at me expectantly.

'OK, comrades,' I began, 'from here it looks like we've woken up to not just a new government, but a new regime. Now, call me a romantic old fool, but I think it's the start of a revolution. A very British revolution, I'll give you that, but it's been a long time coming and revolutions are a law unto themselves more or less by definition. I wouldn't bet on this one staying in the proper channels. This could be good news for us, or bad, depending on how things turn out. The question is, can we make a difference?'

All the eyes on the screen made a laughably simultaneous swivel as everybody checked everybody else's reaction. Ewan Chambers, the Scottish rep, spoke first.

'I agree with Jon. Things were looking pretty wild in Glasgow last night, something a bit more than a street party and no' quite a riot. And from what I can see there's a kindae uneasy calm in Edinburgh. The Workers' Power Party is carrying on like it won the election instead ae just a couple of seats.'

'It's the same down here,' said Julie O'Brien, our South London youth organiser, 'but I don't think we have to worry just yet about the Trots taking over and everybody starving to death. If you look at how the new government's put together, right, there's no doubt at all that we're gonna get a Republic, but beyond that the kind of programme they've been talking about is a real mish-mash of libertarian and statist. On the one side – easing immigration controls, ending prohibition, pulling the troops out of Greece and all that, but on the other hand the Labour parties are pushing this *industrial policy*, cabling up everything on one big system and all sorts of TwenCen shit.'

'Including a space programme, funnily enough,' I said. 'Any thoughts on that?'

A wrangle followed which I cut across as soon as somebody mentioned Ayn Rand. 'Here's what I suggest,' I said. 'We don't support it, don't oppose it, and if it ever flies, demand they privatise it.'

Nothing like a moment of shared cynicism for pulling a committee together. 'Right,' I said when we'd stopped chuckling, 'serious business. Good bloody riddance to the Hanoverian regime, but as Julie says the question is what happens afterwards. The political structure's going to be pretty flexible for a while. How about we try to get our hands on some derelict area and make it an enterprise zone or freeport or something, and put our money where our mouth is?'

Adrian Moss frowned. He was in charge of the movement's lobbying activities, such as they were. 'We could probably swing it,' he said, 'but why? Free zones are better left to real businesses, not political organisations.' His smile flicked around the screen. 'You know, that reminds me of some fringe ideology I've heard about!'

'I'll tell you why,' I said. 'If things work out smoothly, fine, a few more of our ideas get tested. But this country might be headed for a breakup. We've all seen what that means, time and time again. Everybody grabs what they can. Having a bit of land to call our own might give us a head start.'

This caused some commotion. Only Julie and Ewan were in favour. I feigned demurral and suggested that we put it to a poll of the membership. Those against my suggestion agreed, confident that it would be rejected.

By this time the absence of Aaronson and Rutherford had pushed itself onto the agenda. I donned my moderate hat and managed to convince the committee that if it turned out that they'd been spies all along and had now fled the country, we would quite definitely not have them assassinated.

Late that afternoon the investigations I'd initiated revealed that they'd both been discreetly offered jobs in the promised National Space Authority, and had been too embarrassed to tell us. At this point

I was quite tempted to have them assassinated, but after some thought decided just to throw them off the committee.

In the membership referendum on making a bid for a local enterprise area my position won overwhelmingly, as I knew it would. With all the political excitement, even a rabble of libertarians couldn't help wanting to do something constructive for a change.

A year later FreeSpace had control of an abandoned North London industrial estate with a few blocks of empty high-rise flats thrown in by a local council desperate to get rid of them. Six months after that we had the place swarming with enthusiastic volunteers and Adrian was pulling in outside investment hand over fist. After a further six months a delegation of workers' and employers' representatives told the committee that they were very happy with the security our militia provided, but there was one little extra assurance they wanted.

Just for their peace of mind.

Julie said it was immoral, Ewan said it was illegal, Adrian said it was far too expensive and I said I knew a man who could get it for us cheap.

Transcript of telephone conversation, released 01/10/50 under Freedom of Information (Previous Governments) Act.

[*reception-program voice ends*].

JW: Hi, Dave.

DR: Oh, hello you old bastard. What can I do you for?

JW: Uh, this encrypted?

DR: No, but I'm sure you know what to say.

JW: Fuck. [*pause*] We're thinking of going private for, uh, the big one. [*pause*]

DR: Are you outa your fucking mind?

JW: Don't think so. I gather some of your friends in the communistans –

DR: – deformed workers' statelets – [*laughter*].

JW: – might have the best deals. Can you swing it?

DR: Oh, sure. We've got policies.

JW: Better than politics. [*laughter*]

DR: I can't see you needing it, that's all.

JW: Not much of a salesman, are you? [*pause*]

DR: Oh well, it's your life. Lemme check. Shit, okay, make it next week … Tuesday, oh-nine-thirty, Stanstead. Charter desk.

JW: See you there mate.

DR: Great. Love to the wife and weans. [*laughter*]
JW: Likewise, to your mistresses and bastards.
DR: Well, thank *you* mate. Cheers.
JW: Slandge. [*human voice ends*]

We hit turbulence over the southern Urals. I was standing in the narrow corridor towards the tail, braced against the sides and looking straight out of the last window. As the aircraft dipped I got a clear view of the mountains. In the long shadows of dawn they looked remarkably like a papier-maché model of mountains. Not too far below, a regular series of small white clouds were simultaneously dispersing. Curious.

Another wing-dip, another moment of free-fall, then a rapid climb. A yell came from the tiny toilet.

'Are you all right?'

'I'm fine,' Reid shouted. 'Just cut myself.'

'What are you *doing* in there?'

'Shaving.'

Ten, no, fifteen minutes earlier I'd seen him sand down his cheeks and chin with an electric razor, just before I'd recklessly given him precedence for the toilet. My bladder sent me a sharp note of protest. You may have had surgical microbots crawling around your plumbing, it told me, but there *are* limits … It was high time, I thought, for me to start practising the egoism I preached.

'Shaving *what*? Your legs?'

'The – backs – of – my – hands,' said Reid. I could hear the clenched teeth. 'Forgot the fucking rubber gloves, first time I used the scalp treatment.'

He came out with a sheepish grin on his face and shaving-foam on his cuffs. I didn't stop to gloat. My flood of relief made the spittoon-sized aluminium toilet-bowl ring. Then I splashed cold water on my face, opened a few more buttons on my shirt and smeared deodorant awkwardly under each armpit, dried my beard, brushed my short-back-and-sides, rubbed a towel over my bald top and put on a tie. As I had to stoop or squat throughout, and the mirror would have been about adequate on a ladies' pocket compact, the overall effect wasn't easy to judge. I was still chuckling over the reason why Reid's hair, though as grey as mine, was so long and thick.

Gene-fixing shampoo, indeed! What vanity, I thought, as I held the mouthwash for a minute to do its work, then spat it out and checked the gleam of my teeth.

North British Mutual had spawned a security agency, and Reid had been heavily involved in its management buy-out several years earlier. If this flight was anything to go by, the Mutual Assured Protection Company were doing well. The *biznesman-jet* they'd hired for this leg of the trip might be a little cramped, a little Spartan, but it did have its own stewardess, an Uzbek lass with a fixed smile and no English. Breakfast had been served by the time I returned to my seat: microwaved croissants and a coffee which, I guessed after the first sip, had also been microwaved. Neither was quite hot.

'Microwaved, huh,' Reid grumbled. 'Waved in front of the radar for a bit, more likely.'

'Might account for the turbulence,' I said.

'Turbulence?' Reid snorted. 'That was anti-aircraft fire, man.'

'What!' I turned in alarm to the window.

'Don't worry,' Reid said. 'Just bandits. They couldn't hit a 777 at this height.'

Our bodyguard, Predestination Ndebele, nodded slowly. A lithe, wiry Zimbabwean, one of Reid's employees.

'You think this is bad,' he said, 'you try landing at Adnan.'

'I'll take your word for it, Dez.'

Reid looked up from his papers. 'Last I heard,' he said with a vague frown, 'it was called Grivas.'

We flew for hours over a terrifyingly featureless plain, and then, in the middle of all that nowhere, descended to a full-sized international airport buzzing with military and civilian craft. In the far distance a clutter of launch silos and gantries; closer by, a town of low pre-fabs: Kapitsa, capital (and only) city of the International Scientific and Technical Workers' Republic, aka the Number Three Test Area, in the wasteland somewhere between Karaganda and Semiplatinsk. Part of former Kazhakstan.

'I have a suprise for you,' Reid said as we waited for the transit bus.

'What's that?'

'You'll see.'

I looked at him and shrugged, huddled against the dust-dry wind and trying not to breathe too much. The levels were supposed to be safe by now, but I was already interpreting the effects of jet-lag as incipient radiation sickness.

The airport main building was like any such, a neon-lit space of seating and screens and PA systems, but the differences were striking. The duty-free wasn't in a separate area, because there was no customs barrier. No passport control, either – just a cursory weapons registration and a walk through a scanner. The only thing anyone could smuggle in here that could make any difference was an actual atomic bomb, and they're not easily hidden. No tourists: all the arrivals and departures were of serious-looking customers: men in suits or uniforms. Very few women, apart from among the airport workers, who all – even the cleaners, I noticed – moved about their tasks with an almost insolent lack of haste, under enormous posters of Trotsky, Koralev and Kapitsa. The men who gave the Soviets the Red Army, the rocket, and the Bomb and who all got varied doses of Stalin's terror in return.

From every part of the concourse came an irritatingly frequent popping of flashbulbs. Photographers roamed the crowd, scanned faces hungrily, snapped officers and officials and company reps as eagerly as they would video stars. Their subjects responded in a similar manner. All over the place, poses were being struck by ugly, scowling men: shaking hands, bear-hugging, standing shoulder to shoulder and mugging like mad.

'Where to now?' I asked, as Ndebele and myself hesitated for a moment at the edge of the concourse. Reid glanced at me with a flicker of impatience.

'This is it,' he said. 'This is where the deals get done. It's gotta be public, that's the whole point.'

He set off purposefully towards an open-plan Nicafé franchise. I hurried after him.

'Hence the paparazzi?'

'Of course. Stay cool,' he added to Dez, who was glowering at anyone who looked at us.

We sipped our first decent coffee of the day around a table too low to be comfortable, as if designed to hasten the through flow of customers. On the television four pretty Southeast Asians in pink satin ballgowns sang raucously in English, thrashed instruments and leapt about the stage. The continuity caption gave their name: Katoi Boys.

'Boys?' Dez raised his eyebrows.

'Thai refugees,' I said. 'My youngest granddaughter tells me they're the latest pre-teen heart-throbs.'

'Kinky, man,' Dez said with severe Calvinist disapproval. 'Decadent.'

'Yeah, that's what the Islamic Republic told them.' Reid spoke idly, scanning the crowd. He stood up.

I turned. A tall, slender woman in an ankle-length fur coat was walking up to us, with a wide and welcoming smile. Photographers trotted behind her, at a respectful distance. I nearly fell back into my seat as I recognised her: Myra, my long-ago ex from the Soviet Studies Institute in Glasgow.

'Well, hi guys,' she said. She caught my hands and put her cheek to mine and whispered, 'Smile, dammit!' and I turned with an idiot grin to face the flash.

One of my earliest memories, oddly enough, concerns the Soviet Union, space, and the Bomb. (I don't remember being born, but I'm assured that event took place on 5 March 1953, the day Stalin died. Make of that what you will.) I was playing on the carpeted floor of our house in Streatham, a suburb of the city of London. I was playing with a toy rocket. If you put your eye to the hole in the end you could see part of a picture of trees on the inner surface, because the toy had been made in Hong Kong from a recyled tin can. This wasn't because of ecological concern, which at that time hadn't been invented. It was because it was cheap.

My father, sitting at the breakfast table, peered at me over his copy of the *Manchester Guardian*.

'The Russians have sent a rocket into space,' he told me. 'Way up in the sky, going right around the world.' He traced a circle in the air with his forefinger.

I felt disturbed by this. The Russians were in my mind a vague, vast menace. They had done something unpleasant and unfair to a friend of my father's, an old gentleman whose photograph was framed above the fireplace: Karl Marx. The Russians had *distorted* him. Whatever that was, it sounded painful.

I zoomed the toy rocket up and when it reached the limit of my arm's reach, I turned it and brought it down, nose-first. Its shape, I noticed for the first time, was just like a bomb. I had once seen a bomb being craned cautiously out of a garden at the end of the road, in front of two policemen, a dozen soldiers and a fascinated crowd. It had been buried in the ground for ten years after the war between the British and the German capitalists.

'Does that mean they can send bombs through space?'

My father had returned to his paper, perhaps disappointed by my preoccupied response to his exciting news, and now lowered it again and gave me a brightening look.

'Yes!' he said cheerfully. 'That's exactly what it means. Very clever, Jonathan. And now the Americans and everybody else will build rockets and put bombs on them.'

My mother frowned at him.

'But it's all right,' my father hastened to add, as he stood up and shook out his napkin and folded his paper. 'The workers won't let them use the bombs. We'll stop them, won't we?'

'Yes,' I said. 'We'll stop them.'

I knew from playing with other boys in the street that my parents' views were not widely held in Streatham, but I also knew that all around the world, even in far-away countries like Austria and New Zealand, there were people who agreed with them. Altogether there were *hundreds and hundreds* of them.

This mighty force would stop the bomb. I went back to playing happily with my rocket, and my father went whistling off to catch the train that carried the wage-slaves to work.

'Reid told me he had a surprise,' I babbled, 'but I must say I'm knocked flat. How on earth did you end up here?'

Myra smirked. She looked well, and I could almost believe she hadn't aged much in forty years, but that was just part of the same illusion that kept me from feeling old myself. You could see the papery texture of her skin, the crinkles in its still impressive tightness.

'I came here in the 'nineties,' she explained, 'to do research, and then I just realised that these people needed help and that I enjoyed giving it. They still had a lot of bad shit from the tests, and they had one hell of a brain-drain as well. They needed any educated person they could get, and I was able to fix a lot of aid from US medical charities. Then I fell for an army officer, we got married, and luckily for us he was on the winning side of several civil wars and military coups and the re-revolution. So here I am, People's Commissar for

Social Policy.' She waved a hand. 'They let me sign treaties whenever I want, so I don't feel like I'm stuck with the domestic issues.' She laughed. 'You know, women's work!'

I shook my head. 'So Reid's become a capitalist, and you've become a bureaucrat – dammit, I'm the only one who's still a revolutionary!'

'I am *not* a bureaucrat,' Myra said, with some hauteur. 'I was elected, in a real election. We do have democracy, you know.'

Reid was taking documents from his briefcase and spreading them on the table. 'Yes Myra, you sure won over your dashing young lieutenant. His faction has given a whole new meaning to the expression "deformed workers' state".'

'Old joke,' Myra said, but I could see she wasn't annoyed. 'I'll tell you an older one. Soviet. "How do we know Marxism is a philosophy? Because if it was a science, they'd have tried it out first on *dogs*."'

There was such withering proletarian contempt in her voice that we all had to laugh, and then Myra shot back: 'Well comrades, these people were the dogs, and they've made *something* work. I wish you could stay for a few days and see it. Or even come and visit in October.'

'Why October?'

'Centenary celebrations,' Myra said. 'We're planning a *real impressive* fireworks display.'

'I'll bet,' Reid said dryly. 'The biggest in the world, no doubt. Unfortunately, we have our own revolution to get back to.'

Myra sighed. 'Business ... You ready with those forms?'

'Ready when you are.'

We signed, flashbulbs popped, and that was it. The world would know that I had the Bomb.

When the Soviet Union broke up, Kazakhstan had for a while found itself playing the unfamiliar role of a Great Power, because it had on its territory a number of nuclear weapons. When Kazakhstan broke up, one of its fragments had retained some (different, and better) nuclear weapons, with the additional difference that the International Scientific and Technical Workers' Republic – initially nothing more than a division of the ex-Soviet Rocket Forces, a few thousand nuked-upon Kazakhs and a strip of steppe – had known what to do with them.

They exported nuclear deterrence. Not the weapons themselves – that, perish the thought, would have been illegal – but the salutary effect of possessing them. Our contract was pretty standard, and it simply gave us an option to call in a nuclear strike on anyone who used nuclear weapons against us, and who *didn't provide full compensation*. Anyone who nuked us – even accidentally or incidentally – had to pay up or get nuked themselves.

The beauty of this arrangement was that any number of clients – the more the better – could have a claim on a relatively small number of nukes, an effect rather like fractional reserve banking. It also meant that anyone who wanted to tempt the ISTWR with a first-use deal would have had to offer more than the income from *all* the deterrent clients, and that would have cost far more than just building or stealing their own nukes. So the chances of the system being used for nuclear aggression were minute. Above all, for the first time, nuclear deterrence was available to anyone willing to pay for it, and the cost was reasonable enough for every homeland to have one.

Especially when the competion caught on: rogue submarine commanders, missile crews in Siberia and Alaska who wanted payment in real money for a change, groups of ambitious junior officers in Africa all started selling off shares in the family plutonium.

Another triumph for the free market.

Not everyone agreed.

'When I saw the pictures,' Annette raged, 'of you with that anorexic floozy, I thought you'd run off with her! This is *worse!*'

Oh, no it ain't, I thought, and I was right. We quarrelled, we argued, we got over it. This was just ideas, not bodies. I could be an actual instead of a potential mass murderer, and it would have hurt her less than me screwing somebody else.

Not that I ever said it. Some weapons are best kept in reserve.

11

Down Time

WILDE STOOD LOOKING dubiously at the pack and the two sets of weapons that Tamara had laid out on the table. He lifted the pack and put it back down again.

'What have you got in there?' he said. 'Nukes?'

Tamara looked up from a scanner, which she was using to download the latest maps of the Fifth Quarter to her contacts, and shook her head. 'No nukes,' she said firmly. 'Discharging nuclear explosives within city limits is a serious offence.'

'I'm glad to hear it,' said Wilde. 'So that's us ready to go, then.'

'More or less.' Tamara folded away the scanner. 'We need to be ready to go at any time, but that doesn't mean we have to go now. Reid will book the hearing, and we'll get at least thirteen hours' notice.'

'What about preparing our case?' Wilde asked. 'I don't know anything about your laws here, let alone the specific code Talgarth operates.'

'Oh, that's all right,' Tamara said. 'Invisible Hand will take care of it. You can get someone to stand counsel if you want, but if you ask me you're just as well letting Invisible Hand patch you a MacKenzie remote.'

'A what?'

'A software agent to advise you on points of law, when you're representing yourself.'

'Ah,' said Wilde. 'Progress.'

Tamara wandered over to the kitchen-range and began brewing up a large canteen of coffee.

'Expecting company?'

'Allies,' Tamara said. 'Invisible Hand is calling some in for me.' She smiled mischievously at him. 'None for you.'

'Consider me one of yours,' Wilde said. He looked about the room, searching. 'Do you have any way of keeping up on the news?'

Tamara looked at him oddly. 'Yeah, sure.'

She went over to a shelf and picked up a television screen and unrolled it and stuck it to the wall behind the table. The tall kettle was boiling. She turned to attend to it. Wilde looked at the screen, caught Tamara's eye. He waved at the screen's blank pewter surface.

'Oh!' Tamara tapped her temples with her hand. 'Sorry. You don't have contacts?'

'Something the robot evidently neglected to tell me about,' Wilde said.

Tamara told him about a good local stall where he could buy contacts, and how to get there. He wrote down her instructions, drew a sketch-map, checked it with her, and left. He returned about half an hour later, blinking and wide-eyed. 'Wow,' he kept saying. 'Wow, fuck!'

Tamara's allies turned up in ones and twos over the next hour; eventually, a dozen of them were filling the room, sitting on the table, checking weapons and drinking Tamara's coffee. Most of them smoked and all of them had strongly held opinions on aspects of the case, as well an embarrassed, and embarrassing, interest in Wilde. The man from the dead! Wilde rapidly lost track of their names or interest in their obsessions, as he found himself backed into corners by a crowd of mostly skinny, mostly young, all heavily armed strangers telling him things he didn't know about himself.

'I've always thought your later works denouncing the conspiracy theory were forged by the conspiracy –'

'No.'

'– and Norlonto, right, that was an ideal community –'

'No.'

'– the basic idea of abolitionism, that machine intelligence has artificial rights, was based on the same premises as your space movement manifestos –'

'No.'

'They say this is all because Reid is screwing your woman –'

'No.'

And so on.

153

And then everyone started and fell silent at the same moment, even Wilde who had by now got the hang of tuning his contacts to the television screen. The news, like most news on Ship City's channels, was delivered by an excited child. (Wilde had already expressed his opinion that this was one of the most enlightened and appropriate uses of child labour he'd ever come across.)

'News just in!' said the blonde-curled bimbette on the Legal Affairs Channel. 'Three sensational developments! David Reid sues abolitionist for return of his gynoid, Dee Model! And – he sues the long-dead anarchist and nuclear terrorist, Jonathan Wilde, on a related charge! Finally, Dee Model and another abolitionist call witness that they've killed the renowned artist, Anderson Parris! Hue-and-cry raised – bounties posted shortly!'

Pictures of those mentioned zoomed giddily onto the screen as she spoke, and the channel then split into sub-threads exploring the implications of each aspect, the biographies of the alleged partici-pants and the eschatological significance of the return of Jonathan Wilde.

'*Nuclear terrorist?*' The man who spoke was called Ethan Miller. His appearance was older than most of those present, with lank black hair, skin the colour of the vile tobacco he smoked, and a face like a well-used hatchet. He wore nothing but leather trousers and a ragged TOE-shirt which he claimed was an original, though the Malley equations now had even more holes in their fabric than they'd ever made in reality. 'You should sue them for that, man!'

'No.'

Invisible Hand's more sober declaration over-rode the news channel, instructing all parties in the case to appear at the Court of the Fifth Quarter by ten the following day.

'Right!' yelled Tamara above the hubbub. 'You heard! Go go go!'

The deployment that followed was less frantic than Tamara's efforts to organise it. Evidently the deadline for their appearance wasn't expected to be hard to meet. People tooled up and strolled out, with Tamara, Wilde and Ethan Miller bringing up the rear. Tamara locked and armed the house – just to prevent any warrantless searches, she explained – and they all moved off towards the quay.

The sun was low in the sky, turning the city-centre towers into a tall tiara of gold and gems. On Circle Square's central island, stallholders were packing up, while the first roadies for the evening's bands were rigging up sound-systems. The early-evening air was thick with the smells of cooking-oil and engine-oil and the sweet reek of cannabis. Around tables and outdoor bars, late departures or early arrivals watched the quiet-speaking, marching group with shadowed apprehension and hand-hidden comments among which the occasional encouraging smile gleamed like a flashed weapon.

'What'll happen to Dee and Ax,' Wilde asked, 'if they're caught?'

Tamara grunted. 'Depends how outraged whoever catches them is,' she said. 'Likely they'll just be pulled in and charged, by whoever is claiming the damage. I guess this Anderson Parris would've had a pretty price on his head.'

'Yeah, well …' Wilde said. 'I can relate to all that. But what gets done to them, like punishment?'

'Punishment?' Tamara sounded puzzled. 'Oh, you mean penalties. Depends, again. Killing somebody can be quite serious, you know.'

'Yes,' said Wilde dryly. 'So what does the penalty depend on?'

'Don't worry,' said Tamara. 'Shit, at least they've called witness to it. That counts for a lot, not trying to hide it … apart from that, it depends on the victim's losses, right? Emotional distress, loss of life-experience, earnings, loss of society for those close to them – add all that up and multiply it by the down time.'

'Ah,' said Wilde. 'Down time. I think I might understand what you're saying a lot better if you explain to me exactly what *down time* is.'

They had reached the quay where Tamara's dinghy bobbed. The others had piled into their own boats, a flotilla of skiffs and outboards and inflatables. Tamara descended to her boat, Ethan Miller passed down her kit, and she helped Wilde on board. He sat down where she told him, by the side.

'Down time,' Tamara explained, as she cast off and eased the engine into a gentle start, 'is the time between gettin' killed and coming back. Backups cost, see, and growing clones can take fucking *months*, 'specially if you want a good one, no cancers or shit. So like, if you're just ordinary, like me say, you'll have back-ups every year or so, and you'll have a fast-clone policy. If you're real rich, like this Parris bloke, you'll take 'em weekly. But then, you have a slow clone, and your losses mount up faster 'cause of your earnings being higher. So it sort of balances out, but it's still cheaper to kill poor folks.'

She smiled at him and gunned the engine. 'Ain't class society a bitch.'

'Uh-huh,' said Wilde, noncommittally. 'And what if somebody doesn't have a back-up? What if they stay dead?'

'Everybody has back-ups,' Tamara said, amazed at his ignorance. 'Nobody *stays dead*. Jesus.'

She concentrated on steering the boat in the reckless wake of their companions', and missed Wilde's look of sudden pain. Only the boat's 'bot saw it, and it could only record, and not understand.

The low sun, reddened by desert dust, is in Dee's eyes. She shades them with her hood, tugs the cloak closer about her. As her sight adjusts, a millimetre out of the direct glare, she can see the jagged black edge of the Madreporite Mountains far to the west, at the end of the Stone Canal's shining slash. She's sitting, hugging her knees, the skirt's bunched lace prickly on the skin of her arms. Ax is also sitting, leaning against her back. They're in a sort of eyrie, a functionless hollow in the side of a tower pitted by many such. The holes are connected by likewise inexplicable tunnels, which at least provide ventilation for the longer and much wider corridors within. The great spongy spike has been colonised over decades by businesses and settlers. What, if anything, it was originally designed for was almost certainly not human occupation, but humans are nothing if not ingenious and adaptable animals. Dee knows about this trait. She finds it admirable, though – she now realises – she can't quite take pride in it. They're not her species.

That humans are not her species is a conclusion she has come to only this afternoon. It's a little disappointing, since she's only felt like a human being for a couple of days, and she has every intention of keeping it to herself, especially if the question of her human status becomes a matter of learned dispute. But it's the only way she can explain to herself how little she minds killing them.

Even given that they'll come back – minds out of slow-running computer storage, bodies out of vats – being killed must cause them a lot of distress and inconvenience. (This is different from *the dead*, Scientist pedantically reminds her – different storage, different retrieval, different problem. Yeah, yeah, she tells it, and as that self is off-lined again Dee has a fleeting thought about Annette, the woman whose genotype she now knows she shares. She thinks of her among the dead, she thinks about codes and stores, and for another moment Sys flashes up some tenuous connection, but it's gone ... She's just got too much on her mind right now.)

The distress and inconvenience caused is, for Ax, the whole point. He's taking great delight in knocking off anyone who ever ripped him off, exploited him financially or spiritually or sexually. He chortles as they fall, to Dee's bullets or his. Three so far, and more to go. Dee just doesn't give a shit, basically. She knows she's capable of emotion, of empathy, even of ethics – they're right there, burned into the circuits of most of her selves – but they don't seem to apply to people like Parris, or that woman Ax skewered in a cellar two hours ago, or the man she shot in a doorway. Perhaps they're only meant to apply to one's own species, in which case they're not her species.

It now occurs to her, as she squints into the sun and watches out for bounty-hunters, for signs of hue-and-cry, that there is another explanation. Perhaps she's human, all right, and her victims are not. Perhaps what they all have in common is a parasitic mimicry of humanity, which she can see through. One of her Story threads, which she plays on nights when she wants to give herself stronger fare than her usual historical romance, is about vampires. She wonders if the ostensibly human species – or hominid genera – are divided between real people and some hollow mockery of people, beings like vampires, who live on the lives of others. Killing them might be quite different from killing real people, who only live on the lives of plants and animals and machines.

An interesting thought.

She hears Ax's long, lung-emptying sigh. She braces her back for the expected thud of the pistol and thump of the recoil. They shake her body a second later.

'Got him!' says Ax.

Dee doesn't need to look around. The exit-ramp their eyrie overlooks is five metres down and about twenty metres away, and she can picture the sprawled body of the banker lying there. She can also picture the faces and lenses turning in their direction in the next couple of seconds ...

But they've already rolled, Ax and Dee, down the slope of the hollow and out of immediate sight. A metre-wide hole in the synthetic rock leads to a curving chute, which they patiently climbed up about half an hour ago. The glassy smoothness which made the ascent difficult makes the descent easy. Dee goes first, feet-first, wrapped in her cloak. The drop at the end is awkward; her lumbar ligaments strain, her heels jar – another task for the Surgeon sub-routines. She turns and holds up her hands and catches Ax as he hurtles out.

The corridor they're standing in has the usual quasi-organic rounded-off corners in its rectangular cross-section, and curves smoothly around to the left and right. The glowing mother-of-pearl surfaces are pocked with holes, studded with chitinous lenses and membranes – and, hacked crudely in, mikes and cameras, office windows and doors. Already alarms are echoing along the corridor, and rippling along the wires. Soldier and Spy, time-sharing Dee's senses and transmitters, hack and ping. Some of the alarm-signals are disrupted.

But not all. With a silent conference of glances, Dee and Ax turn and race to the left. They head for the lift which they used to ascend from street-level. Doors open down the corridor in front of them, alarms shrill again. A security guard in a black uniform steps out and raises a hand. He's just in sight around the curve of the corridor. Dee skids to a stop and catches Ax's arm.

'Back!' she gasps.

They turn and run back. The guard's footsteps echo behind them. Dee notices, out of the corner of her eye, a movement behind a thin area of the wall – not a window, but internal to the building. She runs on for a few metres and then stops and turns. The guard is just coming into view. She aims carefully at the thin patch and shoots at it. It shatters like glass and a blue, bubbling liquid floods out, slicking the floor. The guard slips on it and tumbles, then jumps up and begins tearing off his uniform and yelling for help. Dee can sense a barrier up ahead, thick and resilient – perhaps a cordon of guards; she can't be sure at this distance.

Close by there's an elliptical hole in the wall. Somebody has scrawled above it 'FIRE EXIT?!' Dee looks at it, looks at Ax, raises her eyebrows. Ax nods.

Dee peers in. It's a dark chute, sloping sharply down and turning out of sight. She steps in, lies down on her cloak, and lets go of the top edge of the hole.

She instantly finds herself plunged downwards and whirled around what feels like an almost vertical spiral drop. 'AAAAAHHHHH!' she observes. Her scream is quite involuntary, but it comes too late to discourage Ax, who's followed her a scant second later. His heels are perilously close to her hooded head. She hunches forward, only to see the drop as even more terrifying. Her ankles are crossed, her hands are clasping the cloak in front of her thighs. It's all she can do not to curl up into a ball. The walls of the tube are in places transparent – at some moments she sees, or thinks she sees, over the city's roofs, at others she glimpses the interiors of rooms, with the startled faces of their occupants looking straight back at her for fractions of a second. She can smell the fabric of the cloak beginning to scorch.

Her other senses are utterly confused. She retreats to the detached perspective of Sys, which is already running the first steps of the bale-out routine, getting ready for somatic systems failure. Dee has a brief, chilling image of her computer detaching itself from the remains of her animal brain and crawling out of the bloody wreckage of her skull.

Then she's sliding along more slowly, in an open space. Light shines on her closed eyelids. She opens them and finds herself still whizzing along, but decelerating … she braces her shoulders and, right on Newtonian cue, Ax's heels cannon into them. Daylight and open air, and people yelling.

Dee sprawls and stops. Everything is still spinning. She sits up and looks around. Ax is a few metres away, eyes still shut, mouth open. They're at the bottom of a gentle slope of black, vitrified material at the foot of the tower, in a plaza. Among benches and fountains and the entrances to other buildings, people are staring at her.

Just to the right of her right hand, a centimetre-wide hole appears in the black glass. Cracks radiate out from it. At the same time, she hears a soft *pock*.

Another hole, closer.

'She-*it*!'

Dee leaps up, staggers forward and grabs Ax by the ankle and drags him across the lip of the slope. He falls half a metre with a bump. He cries out and opens his eyes. Dee looks up the face of the tower, sees dark figures darting on balconies high above. She fires a couple of shots upwards, on general principle, then hauls Ax to his feet.

'Run!'

They're both still so dizzy that dodging and weaving, and falling and rolling, come quite naturally. Within a second or two they're among the now screaming pedestrians in the plaza, though not yet out of the cone of fire from the tower-top.

Things are still going around and around. Ax is slamming into people, but continuing a pinball progress across the plaza. Dee fights her spinning senses into stability and sprints straight for an entrance-way that has an overhang. She reaches its welcome shadow and looks back. Ax, to her utter horror, has got into a fight. Three girls in secretarial gear are swiping at his head and kicking at his shins, while he butts at their midriffs and stamps at their feet and pummels their thighs.

Dee dives out of cover with a banshee howl and grabs a fistful of long blonde hair. She yanks the girl's head back, reaches into the melée with her other hand and drags Ax by the collar until he's behind her. Then with a sweep of both arms she shoves the girls together into a heap and catches up with Ax, who has very wisely chosen to run for the same overhang.

She stares down at Ax's flushed dark face.

'Run!' she says.

'Where?'

'After me!'

Maps are dancing in front of her eyes. Soldier pages through the head-up and marks a route, hallucinating signposts in front of her. She runs along the steps of the building, around a corner, through a car-park, and over a railing into a noisome alleyway. Puddles splash underfoot. Ax pants along behind her.

The virtual arrowheads are pointing at a door in the wall. Dee rattles its knob. Locked. She fumbles her pistol out but Ax stays her hand. He grins at her and spins on the ball of one foot, kicking hard at the door with the other. It bangs open, showing a flight of steps. The map's arrows glow on the steps like the footprints left by some gigantic radioactive bird coming the other way. Dee glances to left and right. At the car-park end, a head dodges swiftly back.

Dee fires a shot at the corner the head has gone behind, hopeful that a flying splinter or two might discourage further peeping, and goes down the steps. Ax treads on her trailing cloak a couple of times. She tugs it up indignantly.

At the foot of twenty-five concrete steps they emerge into a huge basement area with just enough clearance for Dee's head. Dim-lit by organic noctilucence, it resembles an underground car-park, although there aren't enough vehicles in this area to justify such a use. Instead it's heaped with old machinery, coils of piping, and – to Dee's amazement – obvious modular components of spacecraft. She knows that the city's towers were partly grown from parts of the original Ship, but this confirmation is almost shocking. It's like she's arrived at the very pit of her world. From here, *there's no way down.*

She hears movement at the top of the steps, and turns and sends another bullet back. It spangs and ricochets in the stairwell, most satisfactorily. Then she runs. Her instincts, and the guidance arrows, are leading her in the same direction: across the basement, towards the smell of water.

They can't run in a straight line. Their flight weaves in and out between crates and hunks of hardware whose space-junk-pitted sides are stencilled with warnings and instructions and markings – Dee notices 'Space Merchants, Karaganda' and 'Project Jove' and part of her mind has time to marvel at these antiquities. Behind her and Ax, among echoes of sound and the screech of electromagnetic interference, she detects pursuit. More than one person, moving with swift deliberation.

There's a line of light ahead at floor-level. The arrows that her guidance software is patching to her sight end there, flashing. (Like she wouldn't notice.) As she runs up she pings the control-systems of a wide, metal roll-up door. With much grinding and squeaking it begins to move up. After it's risen thirty centimetres, it stops. Dee bounces more short-range radar off it, to no avail.

The bead of a laser-sight appears on it. Dee drops, tripping Ax so he tumbles to a landing that's soft for him, though not for her. She rolls from under him, half-sits, and shoots back along the clearest avenue, towards some detected motion. Hastily she jams another clip in her pistol, and fires again. A flash replies and a bullet whizzes above her nose. She empties the clip with a random spray. The pursuer dodges behind a crate and Dee rolls again and crawls for the gap under the door. It's too low for her.

'Go ahead!' she hisses to Ax. He needs no urging. He rolls under the door and leaps sideways.

She hears him yell: 'No!' and then fall silent. A pair of mechanical feet appear at the gap, striding to the middle of the door. Metal claws reach under the door and lift. The door rolls and ravels upward like a slatted blind. Whatever is lifting the door lowers its body at the same time, between its legs. A line of dust-particles flares above her head as an industrial-strength laser beam stabs into the darkness of the basement.

Hopeless now, Dee ejects the empty clip, and inserts another that she's scrabbled out of her handbag. She's definitely running low. She turns to face her new antagonist. It's a squat, squatting robot. Its laser, protruding between its upper and lower shells, moves and ranges and fires again. There's a yell from behind her, far too close.

'I think I've blinded the bounty-hunters,' the robot says. 'But I think you should get out.'

Dee stares at it for a moment, and then recognises it as the robot that accompanied Wilde the previous night.

'Oh, it's you,' she says ungraciously, and scrambles out. The robot lets the door fall with a rattling crash and, for good measure, fuses the locking-mechanism with a close-up blast. They are standing on a quay at the back and bottom of the building, overlooking a fifty-metre-wide canal between the backs of other buildings. The canal is empty except for a few long, automatic barges going about their oblivious business in a world little more demanding than the toy realities of the first AI experiments. There may have been light under the door, but that was just the contrast; it's dim down here, as it probably is even at brighter times than twilight. Ax is standing hesitantly a little distance away, keeping a suspicious eye on the robot. His clothes are torn; where the robot grabbed him, Dee guesses.

'We're OK,' she tells him. 'I think.'

'I certainly mean you no harm,' says the robot. 'I have no intention of turning you in, as I think my actions have shown.' It waves a limb, indicating a streamlined boat with a powerful outboard engine and, most welcome of all, a small but concealing cabin.

'Come with me,' it says. 'We have much to do.'

'Yeah,' says Ax. He tucks his gun away inside his now ragged shirt. 'Will you just *look* at the state of her clothes.'

As the boats of the litigant alliance moved away from the main canal-system and out of the human quarter into the sandflats and marshes, Tamara's boat shifted towards the front. By the time they were no longer in recognisable canals but in reed-banked streams and barely navigable ditches, she took the lead. Somewhere far in towards the centre of the city, a hovercraft roared across the flats, sending birds scrambling skyward for kilometres around. A vee-line of geese flew overhead, golden dots in the deep-blue sky.

'The things I see when I don't have a shotgun,' Tamara sighed.

Wilde slapped at insects. 'Why the fuck,' he demanded, 'did we have to bring fucking *midges* across interstellar space?'

'Ecology,' Tamara said, with a trace of smugness. She passed him a tube of insect-repellent. Wilde rubbed it on and spent the next few minutes gloating as the tiny black devils landed on his skin and then dropped off dead, straight to whatever hell awaited their evil, two-byte souls. He expounded this unorthodox theological point to Tamara at some length, making her laugh and relax.

She told him about her occupation of hunting for biomechanisms, and her political activity in the abolitionist movement. Apart from pressing her for details of the banking system and the abolitionists' actual forms of organisation, and their social objectives, he was not a bad listener. Then he lay back in the prow of the boat and flicked through Eon Talgarth's notes about Jonathan Wilde. Sometimes he scowled, more often he laughed out loud. Ethan and Tamara urged him to tell them what was funny, and he now and again did. After a time he fell silent, and sat and looked at the early pages of the file, and at the end, and then the beginning again. At last he stowed it in Tamara's pack, and sat looking away from the others, out over the damp desert, which in the sunset lay ruddy like a field of blood.

Ship City is in the tropics of New Mars. Darkness came within minutes of the sun's disappearance behind the horizon. Wilde smiled at Tamara and Ethan, and lit a cigarette.

'It's strange,' he said, 'being able to see in the dark.' He looked around again. 'Shit! I can't!'

'Shield the cigarette,' Ethan told him. 'It's blinding you.'

'Damn' near blinding me,' Tamara said. 'No, no, just cup your hands around it, that's OK.'

Wilde did as he was asked, and shortly threw the butt into the water and gazed up at the stars. With the lights of the human quarter behind them and the less ordered lighting and unpredictable random flares of the Fifth Quarter not far ahead, they were less overpowering than on his first sight of them the previous night, but impressive nonetheless. He gasped at a bolide's whispering flight, blinked at the flash it made behind the western horizon.

'The robot called something like that a "waterfall" ', he said to Ethan. 'What does that mean?'

'Cometary ice,' Ethan explained laconically. 'Feeds the canals.'

'It's a kinda slow terraforming,' Tamara added. 'Planet's habitable, sure, but we want more water and a thicker atmosphere. Take us a couple more centuries, like, but by then it'll be as green as Earth ever was.' She paused, as though she'd got a little carried away. 'Least, that's what Reid says.'

'I wonder,' Wilde murmured, 'how green Earth is now. Whatever "now" means.'

'Ah,' said Ethan promptly. 'I can tell you that.' He made a show of looking at his watch. Tamara and Wilde laughed, so loudly that heads turned in the single file of boats strung out behind them in the narrow waterway.

'Nah, nah,' Ethan went on. 'Serious. "Now" is two times. Absolute, if there is such a thing: fuck knows. This way: if'n you got a signal from the Solar system, it would've been a long time on the way. Thousands a years, millions, fuck knows. But if you went back through the Malley Mile, that's the daughter-wormhole gate, right, you'd be right back at 2094 *anno domini* plus Ship-time. Six point four gigasecs, lemme see ... uh, twenty-three-nineties, early twenty-four hundreds, maybe. So now is the twenty-fifth century, outside.'

'The twenty-fifth century!' Wilde laughed. 'Yes, Earth might be Green all right! Or even Red!'

They didn't get it, and he didn't explain. He frowned at Ethan Miller.

'Why "daughter wormhole"?' he said.

Ethan shrugged. 'It's what me old man calls it. He went through,

and not as a fucking robot upload, either. He was crew, not crim.'
He pounded his chest. 'Human all the way back, that's me.'

'Carbon chauvinist,' Tamara chided.

Wilde leaned forward, thoughtlessly lighting another cigarette.
'Go on.'

'Well,' Ethan said, waving a hand at the sky, 'the wormhole we
came through was a spin-off.' He planed his hand sideways. 'The
main probe, the one the fast folk built before their minds burned
out, it went right on. Draggin' its end of the wormhole to …
wherever. Must've got there by now.' He laughed harshly.
'Whatever "now" means, like you said.'

Wilde sat back, drawing on his cigarette so hard that his cupped
hands couldn't hide the glare.

'The end of time,' he said.

He thought for a few moments longer.

'Oh, hell,' he said.

'What's the problem?' asked Tamara. She throttled back the
engine and the boat coasted towards a spit.

'Time,' said Wilde. 'As in, we don't have much.'

'Well,' Tamara said as the boat grounded, 'we're at the Fifth
Quarter. Let's get a move on.'

12

Near Death Experience

ANNETTE HAD THE tubes in her right arm, I in my left. Her left hand reached out and caught my right.

'Scared?' I asked.

'A bit.'

'Me too.' I squeezed back.

The township hall was packed with mature people, older people, people like us; on our backs on trolley-beds looking up at the roof-panels. Green-tinged daylight, green-smocked technicians, every-thing slow: an underwater feel. Big machines connected to the tubes infiltrated tiny machines into our blood. Not nanotech, not full cell-repair, not yet; but it gave us a chance of living until that came along. In the seven decades we'd been alive, our life-expectancies had already extended by at least another four. We felt better than we had at fifty. We looked – well, the early anti-ageing treatments made your skin tougher as well as tauter, so we looked a bit sun-dried, a bit *smoked*.

This treatment was different. We hadn't had it before, though I'd had a microbot injection to deal with a worrying prostate enlargement some years earlier. Now, the microbots had expanded their capabilities, and by one of those trade-offs characteristic of the Republic, the state Health Service was offering these capabilities to citizens in exchange for their state pension rights. The deal was more political than economic, but it had a certain elegant symmetry: swap retirement for longevity and a degree of rejuvenation, and you can work till you drop.

It would never have passed under the old laws. It was risky. One or two in a thousand died under it, though whether they died of it was another matter. It was a heart problem, hard to predict. If you had it, it would get you anyway, soon. So the health companies and the Health Service said.

A technician walked up between our beds, gently parted our hands.

'Ready?' she said.

'Yup,' said Annette.

'Ready as I'll ever be,' I said. I attempted a grin. 'Who wants to live for ever?'

'Well, I know you do, Citizen Wilde. Good luck.'

Here comes nothing, I thought.

She pressed a switch, sending a short-range radio signal to the microbots in my blood and in Annette's.

I felt my heart stop. It had to. The microbots needed a steady platform for fast work around the vagus nerve, and to give them a chance to shove neural growth factors and cloned foetal nerve-cells across the blood-brain barrier.

Colour faded out, then light. Consciousness went down completely, as in sleep. My heart re-booted with a painful power surge and consciousness came back up, crashed, restored from memory and came up again. I raised my head weakly and looked at Annette, who opened her eyes and stared at me and smiled.

'We made it,' she said.

'We'll make it,' I said. 'We'll make it to the ships.'

I tried to sit up.

'If you don't stay where you are for another half hour,' the technician admonished, 'you'll not make it to the *door*.'

Out, into the Greenbelt street, under the greenhouse sky. We made our way through the usual Pro-Life picket, who kept yelling 'Murderers!' at us from behind a line of armed Republican Guards. It was the foetal tissue – cloned from our own cells – that we'd allegedly murdered, according to the leaflet from the Society for the Protection of the Unborn Child that some poor addled soul shoved in my face.

'SPUC off!' I called back. '*You* can go to hell! *We* aren't even going to *die*!'

'Do you wish to make a complaint, citizen?' the nearest Guard asked me, not turning round.

'It's OK officer,' Annette said, grabbing my elbow and pulling me along. 'Free speech ... and you shut up!' she added to me.

'OK, OK.' I walked quickly, shaking inside. Nothing – not Communists, not fascists, not authoritarians of any stripe – ever aroused in me the same homicidal rage as the Pro-Lifers. Whenever I came across them exercising their rights, I made damned sure I exercised my own.

I'd got used to living here, in what was officially called 'the informal sector': London's shanty-town fringe, where the Republic's experiments in local government overlay an experiment in anarcho-capitalism that made the space movement's enterprise zones look over-regulated. The second, third, and subsequent storeys of most buildings were afterthoughts. Organic farming made the absence of sewage pipes something less than a disaster, but it didn't make the night-soil tankers any less smelly. The exhaust fumes did. The population was a mixture of the native marginals and refugees from Europe's and Asia's wars. Not many beggars, but they were distressing enough: people whose protectors had skimped on their nuclear insurance policies.

Like I say, I was used to it, but at that moment – an after-effect of the clinic, or the picket – it all got too much.

'I feel terrible,' I said. 'My head hurts, and my stomach feels like it's been pumped.'

'Oh, quit moaning,' Annette said. 'It's no worse than a hangover.'

'What a happy thought,' I said. There was a pub on the pavement in front of us. 'Half a litre of Amstel would just about hit the spot.'

Annette waved a Health Service handout in front of me. 'It says here –'

'Yes, I know what it says. Do I look like I'm about to be handling weapons or heavy machinery?'

'I suppose not.' She grinned and lowered herself into a plastic chair, perilously close to the gutter. 'Pils for me. And those kebabs look good.'

I shouted the order to the *garson*, who disappeared through a hatch and re-emerged a minute later. There was the usual poster of Abdullah Ocalan above the hatch. I could never figure why even the exiles from Democratic Kurdistan – entrepreneurs to the bone – still honoured the Great Leader. Possibly a shakedown was going on in the townships. I made a mental note to have it checked out. There might be money in this for a defence company that could offer them a better deal than their Party's protection racket. Or I might be misreading the situation entirely – nationalism was still as foreign to me as ever.

The crowd, Kurds and Turks mostly, flowed around the pavement pub. Behind us beasts and vehicles followed some unwritten highway code, in which precedence depended on a coefficient of momentum and noise. A television by the hatch showed a game-show from Istanbul. Overhead, airships drifted to the distant masts of Alexandra Port. I sat back, warmed by the sun and the spreading glow of the food and drink.

'Did you dream?' Annette asked.

I shook my head. 'Did you?'

'I thought I did,' Annette said, smiling mysteriously. 'I heard a warm, friendly voice and I saw a white light, and I remember thinking, "Great! I'm finally having a Near Death Experience!" and then the light was just sunlight, and the voice was the technician, counting.'

'That's the real thing,' I said. 'The sunlight really is the white light.' This materialist insight was all that survived of a magic-mushroom trip I'd taken as a student. That and a vision of three goddesses: Mother Nature, Lady Luck and Miss Liberty, who were – I realised after coming down from it – necessity, chance and freedom, and indeed the rulers of all.

'Imagine,' Annette said, 'if that's the nearest we ever come to dying.'

'Touch plastic!' I rapped the table. We laughed, clasped hands across the table. I gazed at her face, aged but not deteriorated, its lines a map of her life's laughter and grief, and I felt I could love her for ever.

'"Till all the seas gang dry, my dear, and the rocks melt wi' the sun …"'

'Oh, stop it before I report you for senility.'

The traffic and the noise stopped. I looked over at the slowing cars, and thought everyone was looking at us. Turning the other way, I saw they were looking at the television. The commentary, and the loud conversations that suddenly replaced the hush, were all in Turkish and Kurdish. But the televion image needed no translation: a German tank, and a Polish road-sign.

Berlin – twenty-first century, pre-war Berlin, Old Berlin – was the most exciting city in Europe. The post-reunification construction boom was over by then but the intensity of business and pleasure didn't miss a beat. Everybody who was anybody was either there or in London. In a sense the two capitals were moving in opposite directions, one recovering its national self-confidence, the other climbing down from its imperial pretensions. One, as it turned out, rearming, the other disarming ...

Right now there was only one person I cared about in Berlin: Eleanor, there with her partner on a long weekend.

'What do you *do* in a war, Jonathan?'

Eleanor's nineteen-year-old daughter, Tanya, sounded more curious than anxious. It was one of those emergency family gatherings around telephones and televisions that went on all over the country in the first few hours of the conflict. Ours was in Eleanor's front room in Finsbury Park. Her absence was ever-present. Many of our friends, and other relatives, were also in Berlin. People were calling them up on all possible channels. I had a paging programme pursuing Eleanor, and was trying to pull together an executive meeting at the same time, partly to keep my mind off her. Communications, not to my surprise, were slow.

What *do* you do in a war? With four generations of anti-militarists behind her, you'd think the kid would know.

'You oppose it,' I said. It didn't seem a very enlightening answer. I set up the codes for yet another attempt at a conference link.

Angela, Eleanor's eldest, laughed. 'You're incorrigible.' She was passing out cups of coffee and tea. Good girl. *She* knew what do do in a war.

'My grandparents were conscientious objectors in the First World War, and my parents in the Second, and I'm damned if I'll miss the chance to do the same in the Third.' The server wasn't responding. I sighed and punched through a re-route command.

'Yeah,' Annette said, leaning back against my shins. 'A conscientious objector with nuclear capability.'

'Nuclear *cover*,' I corrected. 'Anyway, it won't come to that. The Germans don't have nukes.'

'So they say.'

Annette was flipping channels, getting CNN downlink from the Polish front, WDR vox-pop from Berlin, Channel 4 News from the regional assemblies and the State and Federal Parliaments of Britain. With their hovercraft tank-transporters the German advance was the fastest ever seen. They used up combat drones like Khomeini and Mao used men. We weren't in the war – yet. There were plenty in the opposition parties who wanted us to be. Lord Ashdown's face popped up far too often for my liking.

'No, so the FIS says, and they should bloody know, it's their skins that'll fry if – ah!'

I had a connection. An 0.1 scale image of a table with the others around it flashed up behind the screen on my lap. Of the committee at the time of the election, only Julie O'Brien and I remained. The rest were new faces. Almost a decade of social and political upheaval – the revolution, as everybody now called it – had winnowed the space movement's libertarian cadre, most of whom were organised in FreeSpace. Some of the best had followed Aaronson and Rutherford to Woomera, where the British and Australian Republics ran their joint space programme. Others had defected to conventional politics, usually Republican but occasionally to wilder shores, even to the resurgent Trotskyism of the Workers' Power Party or the proliferating single-issue campaigns. I was left with hardliners – young Turks (ha!) who saw me as a dangerous moderate.

'OK, comrades,' I said. 'Anyone who's paying full attention to this meeting had better switch their telly on right now, because we need to keep at least half an eye on it. No doubt the wider space movement's going to be all over the place on the war, and that's as it should be, but we in FreeSpace have a responsibility to take a stand – in the name of freedom if not of space. I have every sympathy with the Germans – they couldn't be expected to take refugees, fallout and terrorism forever. It's rather gratifying to see the Poles get a bloody nose, especially after the way they've been treating their minorities. Nevertheless. I say it's an imperialist war, we oppose all sides and we do our damnedest to keep Britain out of it.'

The seriousness of my statement was somewhat undermined by Tanya's eye-rolling observation of it. *I went on peace marches for the likes of you*, I felt like telling her. (And with Eleanor, a cry from inside me added.) Annette's grip on my hand was tight, as if she might slip away. I stroked her shoulders, below the virtual image, and glared at the comrades.

'I'm afraid I don't agree with comrade Wilde,' said Mike Davies, a black Liverpudlian in his twenties whose views I occasionally respected. 'What he's just said is exactly what the government's saying, like, and if you ask me it's the kind of TwenCen liberal pacifism that has got us into this mess in the first place. If Britain hadn't ditched its responsibilities on the Continent, the Germans wouldn't have had to take them on. As it is, the best we can hope for is that the Americans will bail us out again.'

'What *is* this shit?' Julie said. 'Responsibilities? Well, thank you comrade, but I'll take no responsibility for the bloody British state. Liberal pacifism – when did that become a dirty word? I'm a libertarian internationalist and proud of it. War is the state's killer app. I'll take a liberal pacifist over a libertarian militarist any day. Neutrality, non-intervention, and preparation for self-defence – that's what we should be pushing, not trying to work out whether we should back the Germans or call for the bloody Yanks to come charging in. Which you –' she added, turning to stab a phantom finger at Davies, 'have evidently not even made up your own mind about!'

In another corner of the screen a light flickered urgently. Eleanor had got through!

'If that was a motion,' I said drily, 'I'll second it. Meanwhile, comrades, I beg your leave for a few minutes.' I nodded to them solemnly, turned the sound down and flipped to the phone channel.

Eleanor's face appeared and I patched it to the main television. A joyful babble filled the room and then fell silent as Eleanor spoke.

'Hi folks,' she said. 'Sorry to have got you all so worried. I couldn't get through on my handset, and there's a queue of about fifty behind me for the hotel phone. Can't stay long. Are you all OK?'

'We're all fine,' Annette said. Eleanor's partner leaned briefly into view, smiled and waved. 'Oh, hello Colin,' Annette went on. 'When are you coming back?'

Eleanor frowned. Colin, behind her, was restraining the impatience of the next in line. 'I don't know,' she said. 'The airport's closed for now. They say flights'll resume tomorrow, but there'll be chaos out there. We might as well sit it out until the operation's over.'

'The *operation*?' I squawked. 'I don't know what they're telling you over there, but from here it looks like the beginning of the big one. The Yanks are very cross indeed, the Russians are sounding nervous, and some of the little republics the Europawehr's bearing down on are fingering their nukes. Get the hell out as soon as you can. Get to the airport *right now*. If people around you are complacent, that's their problem, and your opportunity.'

Eleanor was about to reply when the picture dissolved and a was replaced by an apologetic-looking man in a suit that said 'Hotel Manager' as plainly as a name-badge. 'I'm sorry sir, we can't permit this conversation to continue.' The connection broke, to yells of indignation at our end.

Tanya turned on me. 'Why did you have to shoot your mouth off? We didn't even get to speak to her!'

'I'm sorry,' I said. 'I really am. But I don't think anybody over there realises how serious it is. Maybe finding that their phone-calls are being monitored will –'

'It won't,' said Annette. 'You should know that. All that Eleanor will have seen is the screen going fuzzy.'

After some more recriminations, eventually calmed by Annette, I stalked out with my comms rig and sat down on a bed. Through the open window I could hear doleful singing from one of the many fundamentalist and charismatic churches that had in recent years congregated in the area. I wondered if my own activities were any less futile. Then the strength of my scepticism returned to me. I punched through.

At the meeting there was only a debate going between those who wanted to push for: British involvement; American involvement; neutrality; and – coming up on the outside – using the war as an opportune moment to launch a libertarian insurrection.

I could handle that.

The phone was ringing. I woke up and waved the light on. The clock said 03.38 and the little red bulb on the phone winked: an encrypted call. I picked it up and thumbed the switch. Myra's face appeared on the display, black-and-white in a military cap and uniform. She looked as if she'd been up all night.

'Oh,' I said, ungraciously, stupid and irritable with sleep and disappointment. 'It's you.' I'd hoped it was Eleanor.

'Hello, Jon,' Myra said. 'Sorry to disturb you, but it's –'

'Who's that?' Annette struggled awake.

'It's Myra,' I said. 'Business.'

Annette glanced at the screen, grunted and pulled the covers over her head. I half-heard something like 'nuclear whore', and hoped Myra hadn't.

'What is it?'

'It's the Germans,' Myra said. 'They're shopping around for nuclear cover, and they're making us a very good offer.'

'You'd better take it,' I said, 'before they arrive.'

'That's what I think,' Myra said. 'Problem: we're over-booked, as you can imagine. The Germans are offering to buy out enough of our existing clients to reverse that. Will you sell?'

'For what?'

'Five million Deutschmarks, in gold, at pre-war – that is, day before yesterday's – prices, no questions asked. I have the German negotiator on the line right now, and the Swiss bank account is verified.'

'Christ! Give me a moment to think, OK?'

I hit the blank/silent button to hide my confusion and tried to think fast. It seemed odd that the Germans hadn't set up some such deal before they actually launched Operation Restore Order, but perhaps the risk of exposing their intentions had prevented them. Now they were improvising a nuclear defence policy at blitzkrieg speed.

The offer was tempting, even apart from the money. With Eleanor in Berlin ...

But we were here. The British nuclear deterrent was currently tied up in a dispute with the US, so ours – and other private-sector arrangements – was all we had to rely on. Who knew if we might need the option, perhaps after Eleanor was safely home?

And there was another consideration. If we sold our share of the Kazakh nukes to the Germans, the FreeSpace company would be undeniably involved in the war, on the German side. The repercussions of that were incalculable, and unlikely to be pleasant.

I toggled the output switch. Myra's eyebrows flashed.

'So?'

'Sorry, Myra, no deal. Not our fight, and all that.'

Even on the tiny hand-held screen her face registered an increase in her weariness, but her voice conveyed no reproach when she said, 'I understand. OK, Jon, I'll try somewhere else. Signing off.'

'Goodnight. See you again.'

She smiled as if this were some hopeless fancy. Her image shrank to a dot.

However momentous, in retrospect, my decision may seem, the fact is I slept well the rest of that night.

The next day the government lost a no-confidence motion (due to the abstention of only five MPs, the three Workers' Power and two World Socialists) and fell, to be replaced by a more radical coalition drawing in support from the smaller parties. Neutrality was affirmed. The Upper House – elected now, but a transitional mix of old Lords and new Senators – debated the war issue separately, and came to a different conclusion. The first pro-war demonstrations, in the Midlands, were violently broken up by Republican Guards and Workers Power Party militants.

It was a bloody disgrace and we said so. At the same time – having won the argument in the committee – we started organising a campaign for neutrality and keeping out of the war. The UN imposed sanctions on Germany and Austria. The British ambassador walked out of the UN, a gesture which even I thought histrionic. It was to cost the Republic dear.

The Germans shelled Warsaw, live on CNN.

We didn't hear from Eleanor over the whole of the following week. I have no memory of sleep in that week. Civil wars flared like secondary fires on the widening perimeter of the German advance. Britain edged close to it as the issue of joining the US/UN mobilisation against Germany became inseparable from the issue of the Republic. The government increasingly relied on support in the streets, as demonstrations against participation in the war multiplied and spread and clashed with pro-war demonstrations that demanded the old Britain back. The pro-war forces called us Huns. We called them Hanoverians. Neither side thought of the other as British any more.

The Germans reached the Ukrainian border, and stopped. The Poles, in headlong flight, plunged straight into the ongoing

Ukrainian civil war. The British Chiefs of Staff presented an ultimatum to the government. Generals, leaders of the Unionist parties, and members of the pensioned-off, semi-privatised Royal Family made up a constant stream of visitors to the US Embassy. Reluctant Republican Guards, only doing their job, fought off determined demonstrators in Grosvenor Square. There was talk of a military coup.

Myra called again. The German offer had gone up to twenty million. I said no. Needless to say I never mentioned this to the rest of the committee.

My paging program almost reached Eleanor, at least twice.

There wasn't a coup. Instead, the overseas parts of the British armed forces went to war without the government's permission. Another government – civilian, spraying an inky cloud of constitutional justifications – was formed out of the opposition, the Lords and the King. It won immediate diplomatic recognition in the US and Britain's vacant seat at the UN. It declared war on Germany.

The Poles regrouped, allied with a couple of Ukrainian factions and attacked the German concentrations. They used chemical weapons. Simultaneously, some Bosnian exiles – it was never established which nationality they came from – poisoned Hamburg's water supply. The Germans rolled forward on all fronts. The French and Russians finally came off the fence on the Security Council.

The Republican government still controlled the internal forces of the country, while the Royal junta controlled the state's external power. In a bizarre way they had to co-operate, or at least maintain a division of labour: while one was participating in American airdrops over the Balkans and naval manoeuvres in the Mediterranean, the other was frantically mobilising the civilian population for civil defence. In effect the Kingdom outlawed the past ten years of Britain's history, while the Republic legalised a revolution.

It would have been an interesting revolution. Which of the competing extremisms – including ours – would have emerged victorious is still debated. As it is, I had an interesting week. The space movement really was as big as the old peace movement had been, and the rockets on our banners were our own. I left the demonstrations to those members of the committee who were good at that sort of thing, and spent my time obsessively organising militia and defence company patrols in the free-trade zones and the Greenbelt, negotiating with our contacts in the state apparatus and – in between times – writing more, faster, than ever. If I hadn't been worried about Eleanor and in constant fear of German air-raids I'd have been even happier than I was. I had reached my Finland Station.

Someone was shaking my shoulder. I raised my head from my forearms and looked about. It was 10.15 a.m., and I was at my desk in the FreeSpace office. I must have closed my eyes for a moment about six hours earlier. The office was crowded but quiet. People were looking at screens, not at me; except for Annette, who was holding onto me, staring.

'What's happened?'

'Somebody's nuked Kiev.'

'Oh, my God.'

I stood up. She buried her face in my shoulder. I held on to her as sobs made her quake, and glared about until someone silently pushed a screen into view. An entire German army had been wiped out by an airburst over the otherwise empty Ukrainian capital. Within minutes, as I watched, the same thing happened on the southern front, in Baku. The Russian and Turkish armies were both in action now, and news was coming through of British and American landings on the Aegean coast.

And Israel had declared war on Germany. It was ridiculous. What could they do? I thought, and then I suddenly realised that they'd probably just *done* it.

I flipped to N-TV for the reaction from Germany. A reporter was talking to the camera, in front of the Bundestag. He was saying something about Frankfurt, and he sounded terrified.

He clapped a hand to his ear, tilting his head.

His face paled, and the screen went white.

His voice, if you could call it that, continued for some time.

The war had ended. The peace process began. For Britain it began with stealth bombers and cruise missiles, and continued with paratroopers and teletroopers and lynch-mobs. The Royalist junta, its American allies and the British counter-revolutionary mobs between them killed about a hundred thousand people in six days. After that they had a country that knew its place in the New World Order.

It was still ungovernable. Under the Republic's reforms, freeing up the housing, education and labour markets, there had already developed a tendency towards differentiation – self-ghettoisation, as I saw it, especially when it wasn't spontaneous but promoted by the Republic's unfortunate encouragement of identity politics. Bombing, invasion and civil war hardened the tendency into an irresistible force, as every minority fled to the dubious safety of its own tribe. Regional assemblies took the hint and drew old borders in fresh blood: North Wales, South Wales, Cumbria, West Scotland, East Scotland ... even our own Greenbelt and free trade zones became safe havens, refugees piling in on top of refugees. The militias defended the area as best they could.

The final session of the Republic's Federal Assembly passed its authority over to the Army Council, a body made up of the few senior officers who had stayed loyal. It called on the civilian population to avoid needless sacrifice and to resume armed resistance 'at such time or times as the Army Council of the Army of the New Republic shall decide'. They thus gave a shred of legal cover to an indefinitely prolonged campaign of merciless terrorism, as they well knew. Then they all walked out of the former main workshop of the Ford Motor Company's Dagenham site into the withering fire of the surrounding tanks.

It was probably the proudest moment in the history of British democracy. I watched it in the basement of a safe house on an illegal Iraqi satellite channel, and it made me vomit.

I knew I should be working; there was always another article to send out on the net, another friend or foe to contact, another militia unit's fate to check; but I was hacking German casualty lists, searching for a name I hoped against hope that I wouldn't find. The Israelis had tipped their long-range missiles with tactical, not strategic, warheads. Even in Berlin there were more survivors than anyone had expected. There was always a chance ...

The phone rang.

'Dad?'

'*Eleanor!*'

'Yes. Are you all right?'

Was I all right. I felt as if it was I who had come back from the dead.

'Of course, oh my God, are you?'

'I'm fine, I saw some terrible things but I'm okay. So's Colin. We're at the airport.' She laughed. 'Like you said. Sorry I'm a bit late. My flight boards in ten minutes, due in at 1545.'

It was 2.15. I said I'd be there to meet her. After she rang off I immediately called Annette with the news.

'Is it safe for you to come out?' Annette asked after we'd finished telling each other several times over of our joy and relief and assurance that we'd neither of us ever given up hope.

I shrugged. 'I'm not on any "wanted" lists. The mobs have been brought to heel. Looks safe enough to me.'

'From where you are, I'm sure it does,' Annette said wryly. 'Some of the movement people –'

'Yeah, I know,' I said. They'd got involved in resistance. Some had got themselves interned, or shot. Others – such defence companies and militias as I could influence – had tried to avoid engagement, but found themselves fighting the Yanks whether they liked it or not. I was uncomfortable talking about it even on a secure line. 'Still,' I went on, 'I've got a list as long as my arm of messages and articles urging them not to do it, so ...'

'Anyway,' Annette said, in sudden decisiveness, 'you can't stay down there forever. OK, I'll pick you up in fifteen minutes. Broadway at the lights. Usual.'

She was in Acton, not at home but not in hiding either.

'Right, see you there love.'

I gathered my gear, swept up any traces of my presence, and when the basement looked again like nothing but a computer hobbyist's cubby-hole, climbed the swing-down aluminium ladder and stepped out from a cupboard under the stairs into my host's hallway. It had that dead aroma of a house where nothing had moved all day but the letter-box flap, the thermostat and the cleaning-machines. I left an envelope containing a few gold coins on the umbrella-stand and let myself out.

The house was on a street behind Ealing Broadway. The chestnuts lay like green sea-mines on Haven Green. A light drizzle was falling. I remembered a spray-bombed slogan from the

Chernobyl year: *it isn't rain, it's fallout.* I turned up my collar and hurried. There were cops outside the Tube station – Republican Guards, to my surprise. I didn't give them a closer look.

I crossed the Broadway and walked away from, and then towards, the traffic lights. The Odeon across the way was showing *The Blue Beret*, advertised by a huge back-lit poster of some grizzled veteran played by Reeves or Depp (I forget) holding a bayonet's edge to a Peruvian peasant's throat.

I turned back, spotted Annette's black Volvo a hundred metres away in the sparse traffic and turned again and sauntered to match velocities as she slowed to a stop. I leaned over, opened the door and got in. There was always that moment of checking that you hadn't given someone the shock of their life.

We laughed, and she accelerated away from the lights.

'Everybody all right?' I asked.

'Everybody we know,' she said, her voice taut.

'Tell me later about the comrades,' I said. 'We'll do what we can.'

She nodded, concentrating on the road and the traffic-screen updates. Our route was charted along the Uxbridge Road until just past Southall, then sharp left along the Parkway to Heathrow.

'What's wrong with the Great West Road?'

She grunted. 'Troop transport.'

Hanwell, a middle-class residential suburb, was quiet. Southall, an Asian immigrant area, solid Republican, had dozens of gutted shopfronts.

'What happened here?'

'A mob from Hayes,' Annette said. We went up and across the bridge over the Grand Union Canal. The factories of Hayes, to our right, had been precision-bombed to charred splinters by the Yanks. I admit to feeling a certain grim satisfaction: the area had been a racist, imperialist bastion for years. Even the Trotskyists had given up selling their Red weeklies to its White trash.

'What goes around comes around.'

'Rather a hard lesson,' Annette said.

Every park we passed had its encampment of black plastic domes, lurking cowled aircraft, black helicopters. As we neared the airport the numbers of black-uniformed US/UN troops increased. No need for roadblocks – a wave of an identity-reader did a neater job. The lasers made you blink, always too late: the retinal scan was in.

Heathrow was like a scene from the twentieth century. Nobody was flying but those who had to: refugees from the war zones, wounded soldiers and civilians, desperate emigrants. It had a Third World of people waiting for flights, waiting to get through the re-imposed immigration barriers, waiting to die; and a Second World of officials and officers ordering them about. In this bedlam the First World consisted of volunteers trying to help and entrepreneurs trying to help themselves. Each passenger lounge had its field hospitals and hawkers; each gate its unpaid advisers and legal sharks and medical aid team.

We arrived at the international terminal, but the flight had been switched to the domestic. The rolling walkways were over-loaded with disembarking troops and their kit. Walking between terminals was a Brownian motion through a Hobbesian crowd. Time dragged, stopped, passed without being noticed. Annette and I clung together and struggled forward.

Hours later, when Eleanor and Colin at last appeared in the stream of arrivals, we were as haggard and ragged as they. After hugging and crying and talking, we turned around and fought our way out again. We got to the car, paid the parking surcharge, paid a hawker another outrageous sum for warm coffee, and set off for home. It was about 10.00 p.m.

I drove: Annette was exhausted, I was manic with relief.

As I edged the car around the junction for the M4 a laser's ruby flicker hurt my eyes. Blinking away the after-image, I was blinded again by a torch, waving us in to the side of the road. On the pavement was a unit of five soldiers with black uniforms and M-16s. I thumbed the car-phone switch and pulled in, turned with a hopefully reassuring smile to the others and stepped out. Other cars inched past me. Everyone in them took great care not to look. I kept my hands on top of the car and moved crabwise around to the near side.

Hands groped around my collar, my torso, down my legs and between them. Then my shoulder was grabbed and I was spun around and thrown back against the car. I froze in the light and kept my hands up. Behind me, through an open inch of window, I thought I heard Annette's quiet, urgent voice.

The soldier covering me lowered his beam, raised his rifle and loomed close. His visor was up, revealing an impassive, Andean face: I was reminded of the peasant in the poster. What goes around comes around ...

'Jonathan Wilde,' he said. It wasn't a question. I didn't answer. My mouth was dry.

'Come with us,' he said.

I felt the window at my back roll down.

'No!' Annette shouted.

'Yes,' I said. 'Go. Go now.'

'Yes,' said the soldier. 'Go.'

He motioned me away from the car. I took two slow steps forward. 'There are no weapons in the car,' I said.

'We know.' He swung his rifle away from me, towards the car. For the first time his face showed an emotion, something so primal it was hard to tell whether it was fear or rage.

'Go!' he screamed.

I could hear Annette's dry sobs, Eleanor crying, Colin arguing. I dared not turn around, or even make a gesture.

The engine started, and slowly the car pulled away.

Streetlights and fog. Aircraft landing-lights and fog. Night and fog. They had never looked so beautiful. I raised my eyes for a look at the stars I thought I'd never reach, not now. I couldn't see them. Ah well.

They walked me a few hundred metres to a patch of waste ground. I was actually relieved to see a black helicopter, its matt angular surfaces gleaming with condensation in the shadows. They bundled me aboard and sat me down facing the open doorway as the craft took off. It made surprisingly little noise. The soldiers watched me with silent malice and dirty-secret smiles.

I wondered why I'd kept walking, when I could have run. It looked like I was for one of the classic US-client execution styles, the Saigon sky-dive. I should have run, I thought, and not given them this satisfaction. There's an Arab proverb, something along the lines that *hope is the enemy of freedom*, or *despair is the liberator of the slave*. It explains a lot, including why I climbed into that helicopter.

I hope it doesn't explain what I did after I got out.

'Come in, Mr Wilde.'

The polite invitation, from one of a dozen men in suits around a table, was accompanied by a shove in the back from the UN trooper that sent me stumbling into the room and left no-one in any doubt who was really in charge here. The door behind me was too heavy to slam, but it closed with a muffled thud, as if the soldier had at least made the attempt.

I straightened, mustering my dignity, and glanced around the room. Somewhere in Westminster – the helicopter had landed in St James's Park, and I'd been bundled into the back of an APC and driven a short distance – but it was impossible to tell if it was a private or a public building. Big mahogany table with lights above it, oak-panelled walls, portraits of distinguished ancestors or predecessors in the gloom. The men who looked up at me from the table had something of that same air of inherited or acquired assurance, despite being more dishevelled than I was: their jackets crumpled or hung over tall chair-backs, ties loosened, eyes red and cheeks unshaven.

The table was spread with laminated maps, on which lines had been drawn and wiped and redrawn in fluorescent inks from the marker-pens that lay scattered among coffee-cups and overflowing cut-glass ashtrays the size of dinner-plates. Rising smoke curled up through the cones of light to be sucked away by powerful air-conditioning that gave the atmosphere a stale chill.

The man who'd spoken stood and motioned me towards a vacant seat at the nearest corner of the table. A freshly filled cup of coffee steamed in front of it.

'Good evening, Mr Wilde,' he said. 'I must apologise for the rather brusque manner in which you've been brought here.' He gave a self-deprecating smile, a slight shrug as if to disavow responsibility. He was old, older than I – though he'd had better treatment – and his wavy yellow-grey hair, shoulder-length, made him look like a judge or one of those eighteenth-century dignitaries in the portraits. 'I trust you have not been otherwise ill-treated?'

I stood where I was and said, 'I call kidnapping ill-treatment, sir. I demand an explanation, and an immediate contact with my family and my lawyer.'

Another man spoke up, leaning forward on his elbows into the light. 'None of that applies. This country's under martial law, and anyway, you're not under arrest.'

'Fine,' I said. 'Then I'll go now.'

I turned away and made for the door.

'Stop!' The first man's voice sounded more like an urgent warning than a command. 'A moment, please.'

This was more like it. I turned back.

'Of course you're free to leave,' the man continued, 'but if you do, only we can guarantee your safety. All we ask is that you hear us out.'

I doubted this, but decided it would be foolhardy to try anything else. Besides, I needed that coffee.

They were a committee of what was already being called the Restoration Government. Members of Parliament, civil servants … they didn't give their names, and I never subsequently tried to find out. They told me they were trying to restore order and a civilian administration.

'The Republic is dead, Mr Wilde. Our only choices are a prolonged and futile resistance, with a prolonged and painful occupation – or an an attempt at a workable settlement.'

'I don't see the US keeping up a prolonged occupation,' I said. 'Given their notorious sensitivity to body-bags.'

'How many US troops have you seen?' snapped the second man. 'They're all in bunkers operating telepresence rigs. Believe me, America's Third World clients have troops and to spare for the UN. Internal security is what they're raised for and paid for. They'll laugh off the pathetic efforts of our home-grown Guevaras. Make no mistake – the United States – the United *Nations* – means it this time. No nation will ever again be allowed to start a war. Nuclear disarmament *will be enforced.*'

Saliva droplets from his speech were spotting the maps. I was half-expecting his right arm to twitch up. I must have recoiled slightly. The long-haired man raised a hand, soft cop to the hard cop.

'We know as well as you do that a power such as the US must become cannot possibly administer the world. Police it, at a very high level, yes. But as some powers move up from the nation, others devolve to the local community. We have the opportunity to encourage autonomy and diversity. Let us take it, and spare our country years of agony.'

'"Us"?' I looked around. 'I have nothing in common with you. What do you want from me?'

'The possibility of a deal, Mr Wilde. A settlement. We're pulling in all the regional and factional and community leaders we can reach. You happen to be the first.'

'And what d'you intend to offer them?'

'Accept the Kingdom – in practice – as the national authority, and you can have autonomy in the areas your supporters control.'

'I have no authority to negotiate –'

'Oh, but you have. You have influence. We know that without it some younger and hotter heads would be calling the shots. And we know you're up to more than your public statements indicate –'

'What makes you say that?'

He smiled. 'The volume of encrypted traffic from your safe houses.'

Damn. I tried to remain poker-faced.

'What you see is what you get. I've done nothing secretly that goes against what I've said openly.'

'Of course. Then you can have no objection. Take a look at these ...'

Agreements, ready to sign. Maps. London, for a start, was to be carved up. The part conceded to the space movement encompassed the Greenbelt and an arc of suburbs in which we had free trade zones. They'd even given it a name: North London Town, which on the map some military hand had clipped to NORLONTO.

It was a lot. Frankly, I'd have settled for less.

'And in return?'

'No armed actions to be launched from the territory. And one other thing ...'

'Yes?'

'Ah ... the nuclear deterrence contract, Mr Wilde.'

'You want me to end it?'

'Good God, no!' He looked shocked. 'We want you to transfer the policy to us.'

'To the *government*? But you've got –' I stopped, and looked at their ever-so-slightly-embarrassed faces.

'Oh,' I said. 'I see.' I turned again to the map, and picked up a pen. By the end of the night we had something I could take back to my committee.

Two days later I sat in a room at the back of a Greenbelt shebeen with a group of men and women who, thanks to my negotiations, had emerged blinking from hideouts and camps and cells. I explained to them that they had the chance to try out their ideas on a couple of million more or less enthusiastic people, with minimal interference from a state only too glad to have this explosive and impoverished mass off its hands. I told them the only price for this was a *de facto* acknowledgement of that state's authority, and the renunciation of an untested nuclear deterrent about which most of them had mixed feelings and which was now obsolete.

I didn't expect gratitude or agreement, and I didn't get them. What I got was comrades falling over each other to denounce me. I'd expected that. Being expelled from the organisation came as a surprise. The vote was unanimous. *Et tu*, Julie.

'Good day to you, comrades,' I said. 'And good luck.'

I stood up and pushed back my chair and ducked out of the door and walked away. Two days after my expulsion, US/UN crack troops took over and disarmed every surface-based deterrence exporter. The renegade subs took longer, but they were rounded up too. Among other consequences, my ex-comrades didn't have our nuclear policy to bargain with, so they had to settle for a smaller Norlonto than I'd been offered.

It served them right, but I wished they could have kept Islington. The Christian fundamentalists got it, and set about ethically cleansing the place. Eleanor and her family had to abandon Finsbury Park. They moved in with us and it was months before they found a new house.

I was getting too old for that sort of thing.

13

The Court of the Fifth Quarter

'WHY COULDN'T WE have gone in through the canals?' Wilde grumbled, as he booted yet another inquisitive machine away from his ankle. Several hours of difficult progress through back alleys, with the expedition crunching and stomping and shooting their way over and past assorted mechanical vermin, lay behind the strain in his tone and the strength of his kick.

'Ha!' Tamara snorted. 'You *seen* the canals around here?'

'As it happens,' said Wilde, 'no, I haven't.'

'And you don't want to.' Tamara flattened herself against a wall and signalled back to the others to halt. 'But you will.'

She poked a device like a long electric torch past the corner, and waved it back and forth, keeping an eye on the readings on a hand-held meter and the view on a wrist-screen.

'OK,' she announced. 'No sapients. Looks fairly safe. One at a time. Deploy to the centre of the street, spread out, then single file to the right. Go.'

She ran out into the middle of the road, which was about fifty metres wide and obsessively well-paved. Along the centre were empty plinths of concrete like traffic-islands. Tamara bounded up on to the one facing the alley, looked around again and beckoned to Wilde. He dashed after her and jumped up beside her.

'Cover my back,' she said. Wilde stood behind her and began scanning up and down the street, his pistol held in both hands, close to his waist. The street had its own strange pedestrians: robots of various shapes and sizes clambering walls, edging along pavements. One or two bowled down the permanent way, in light wheeled vehicles. Ethan had to dodge one of these smartly as he ran over. It sounded a subsonic siren that set everyone's teeth on edge.

'You look like you know what you're doing,' he said to Wilde, as he stationed himself a couple of metres further back along the plinth.

'Trained in the militia,' Wilde grinned. 'Mind you, it was a long
– *look out!*'

A black, winged missile was hurtling towards them. Wilde raised his pistol to head height and shot it. It came down and hit the roadway in a shower of feathers.

'Pigeon,' said Ethan. 'Take it easy, man. They're harmless.'

When the alarm spread by this incident had been calmed, the deployment continued. After a minute or two they proceeded behind Tamara along the canyon of office-buildings. Somewhere a couple of streets away, an automated process was sending gouts of flame high in the air at irritatingly irregular intervals. Between flares, the illumination of the buildings themselves was almost as unpredictable: some windows dark, full of the expedition's reflections as they passed; others, at street-level or high up on the faces of the buildings, lit from within. Shadows and silhouettes moved, but not those of humans. At the same time, it was impossible to believe that a robot-based commercial life was going on; it was all too random, too artificial.

At the next major junction the street they were on crossed one that was narrower, but much more crowded: a slowly moving river of metallic machinery, over which faster entities skittered and skipped.

'Makes you sick,' Ethan muttered. 'Some of the big 'uns would make bloody good cars.'

'You pay me enough, I'll catch you one,' Tamara told him. She waved them all into a skirmish line, again keeping Wilde next to her.

'Right,' she said, swinging her back-pack to the ground. 'Time to hack through the jungle.'

She unbuckled the pack and tugged down the flaps, exposing a piece of equipment with a small keypad, extensible aerials, rows of meters and screens.

'Amazing,' said Wilde. 'Popular mechanics! Amateur radio!'

'Heap of junk,' Tamara said. 'No fucker will miniaturise it. Not enough demand.'

'You put this together yourself?'

She looked at him. 'Wouldn't trust anybody else to.'

Her fingers flew over the keypad. Screens flickered, tiny speakers howled and stabilised.

'Gotcha! Traffic channel.'

She twirled a knob, looked up at the machines passing like cattle ahead. Made some adjustment, twirled it again. A ten-metre-long crawling machine suddenly swerved right across the road. The machines behind it piled implacably into it and within seconds formed a mounting heap of wheeled or tracked robots. As those in front of it kept moving, a space soon cleared.

Tamara was still watching the feedback.

'Fucking go! Go! Go!' she yelled.

The others sprinted across.

Tamara lifted the pack, leaving the control-panels exposed.

'Still here?' she said to Wilde. 'Shit, OK, let's move it.'

She sidled across the road, Wilde at her back keeping lookout. A machine on four long, stalked legs, its body about the size of a melon, with a cluster of lenses at its front, suddenly reared above the pile-up and scanned them.

'What's that?'

Tamara looked up and stopped.

'Don't move,' she said.

Wilde held his breath, and froze in the act of looking over his shoulder at the machine. The lenses withdrew, and another tube-like extension moved into position. Tamara stabbed frantically at the keypad.

'Shoot!' she yelled.

Wilde jumped and turned, but it wasn't him she was calling to. A volley came from the far side of the street, knocking the machine over. Tamara and Wilde ran to join the others.

'Shit,' said Ethan. 'That one was sapient.'

'I *never* hunt sapients,' Tamara said, gasping and rubbing the small of her back. 'Don't mind killing the little fuckers, though.'

They moved on; over a bridge that gave Tamara an opportunity to point out to Wilde exactly why using the canals for transport in the machine domains was not a good idea; and on until they saw, in a wide park at the end of the long avenue, a scrap-metal stockade.

'Talgarth's court,' Tamara said.

As they walked up they were swept by sonic scans that set their teeth buzzing, laser scans that made them blink and curse.

'Ignore it,' Tamara said. 'They have to check.'

The park was bizarrely neat, and kept that way by tiny devices that roamed through the grass and among tree-branches. For the first time since they'd landed, Tamara enjoined care against stepping on any machinery.

'Talgarth don't like it,' she insisted. 'Fines you.'

They picked their way across the grass, their weapons holstered or slung – the bristling armaments on the stockade being more than enough to protect them from any feral gadgetry. Machine-guns, laser cannon, radar and whirling, ever-ready bolas ...

The stockade's three-metre-high gate swung smoothly open before them, and quickly shut behind them. About a hundred metres square, grassed like the park, with a dais in the centre, seating and media-equipment scattered around, and wooden cabins of varying sizes around the perimeter. Nobody else was present.

'What do we do now?' Wilde asked.

Tamara looked at her watch. 'It's one in the morning,' she said. 'We pick a cabin to put ourselves up in, and we sleep.' She grinned. 'It's an old vertebrate custom.'

'Well worth keeping up,' Wilde said. He looked around indecisively as most of the others moved confidently off.

Tamara caught his hand.

'Come with me,' she said. 'I'll see you're all right.'

He complied, a confused look on his face.

'You watch out,' Ethan called after him. 'She follows old primate customs.'

'Go fuck yourself!' Tamara yelled back. 'See you in court!'

'So this is how non-propertarians do it.'

'Yeah. Free love.'

'Ha. I was faithful to my wife for seventy years ...'

Wilde's voice trailed off, then continued, more happily, '... and now I've been with two other women in three days.'

'What! Who else?'

'None of your business. Free love, right?'

'Aw, go on.'

'She's probably dead by now.'

There was a silence. Then Tamara, her face lit only by a dim night-light and the glow of Wilde's cigarette, spoke in a cautiously cheerful voice.

'Hope it ain't catching.'

Wilde gave her a lopsided grin and stubbed out the cigarette. Their eyes adjusted swiftly, and they spent a few moments looking at each other.

'Could be,' Wilde said. 'I'm dead myself after all.'

Tamara investigated.

'Well this bit's definitely alive.'

'Oh no.'

'Oh yes.'

'How d'you expect me to stand up in court tomorrow?'

'You're standing up all right tonight.'

'Mmm.'

'Anyway – ah-hah-ha-ha-ah – you'll get help from ah-ha-ha!'

'I'll give you *Invisible Hand*.'

'Nah,' said Tamara. 'That's for *much* later ...'

'It's eight o'clock,' Tamara informed him kindly. 'You look terrible.'

'Thanks.' Wilde steadied himself on one elbow and reached for the mug of coffee she was holding out to him. 'Oh, God. How long have I been asleep?'

'Four hours.'

'Thanks to you, you promiscuous anarchist bitch.'

Tamara smiled.

'Don't worry,' she said. 'I've put a drug in the coffee. You'll be more awake than you can imagine.'

'Is that why I'm seeing things?'

'No. You left your contacts in.'

'Thanks again.' Wilde reached for his cigarettes and rasped his face. 'Does this anarcho-capitalist court by any chance have some rip-off, monopolistic enterprises associated with it?'

'Funny you should ask.' Tamara indicated a couple of packs of cigarettes and a bubble-pack containing a razor and toiletries. 'I put them on your bill.'

She busied herself with making breakfast while Wilde padded about, getting washed and dressed and drinking the drug-laced coffee. The cabin had three adjoining rooms: a small bedroom with an elementary wash-stand and a tiny toilet; a small kitchen, and a larger room containing communications equipment and computer interfaces, all on a conference-table with half a dozen chairs around it.

'How long are we expected to stay here?' Wilde asked, shaving.

'As long as it takes.'

'Has Reid turned up yet?'

'Yup. And his supporters. Odds are about even if it should come to a fight.'

'That's a happy coincidence.'

'No, it was arranged by –'

'Don't tell me, Invisible Hand. OK. Jesus.' He towelled his face. 'I haven't felt so unprepared for anything since my final exams.'

'What are exams?'

'Old primate custom.' Wilde crunched his Harmony Oats. 'I gather you've evolved beyond it. Let's catch the news.'

Tamara set up the communications rig in the main room, while Wilde watched. She was still in her jeans and tee-shirt and flak-jacket, but she'd put on make-up and perfume as some kind of gesture towards formality or femininity.

'Am I still a mess?' Wilde asked.

She looked him up and down. 'You'll do,' she said. 'Use the after-shave, though.'

They checked out the news. The case was the lead item on all channels. Overnight, a whole sub-culture of newsgroups and discussion fora had sprung up around its aspects. The three killings claimed by Dee and Ax, their disappearance, and the appearance of Jonathan Wilde gave the whole affair an added edge of social panic. At least two heretical churches had already proclaimed Wilde a sign of the end.

'I hope your abolitionist comrades are prepared for trouble,' Wilde said.

'What kind of trouble?'

'You should know. Don't you always get hassles, selling your paper? Hasn't Ax shown what can happen if people suddenly think the world's going to change forever? Imagine all of that multiplied by tens – hundreds!'

Tamara shook her head. 'I can't. I've read about riots and revolutions, but we've never had anything like that here.'

'Count yourselves lucky.'

Tamara's cheeks reddened. 'Oh, I do, don't get me wrong. Ship City's basically not a bad place, it's just that – there are all those wrongs done to machine minds, and – it's a long way from the ideals of anarchism. And people really do think that you suddenly turning up means all that's going to be put right.'

'"The ideals of anarchism",' Wilde repeated heavily. He gazed at Tamara's face for a few seconds. Nobody, looking on, could have had any doubt which of the two youthful faces in the cabin had the older mind behind it.

Wilde spent the next hour or so in conversation with a subset of Invisible Hand's legal database, the 'MacKenzie's friend' software. It was a friendly, and user-friendly, system. Its hardware component was an ear-to-chin phone that picked up what he said and heard, and passed it by short-range radio to a local relay. Its prompts could be whispered in his ear, or displayed in his contacts.

Shortly after nine, Tamara interrupted his study of precedents and arguments.

'Reid's come out of his cabin,' she told him.

Wilde blinked away the display.

'What's he doing?'

'Just wandering around with his friends, sipping coffee and chatting to people – and to the news 'motes.'

'I think I'll do the same,' said Wilde. 'Also, I wouldn't mind talking to him.'

Tamara smiled wryly. 'Bit late to settle out of court.'

Wilde stood up. 'It's never too late,' he said. 'But no, I don't hold out much hope of that! The fact is, I can't wait to see him.'

Tamara was silent for a moment. Wilde lit a cigarette.

'I should warn you,' Tamara said. 'I spoke to him yesterday, when he called me, right, and ... even though I'd seen him on the news and so on, I found when I actually spoke to him that he's very ... I mean he has a kinda, you know, *presence*. You may find him a bit ... intimidating.'

Wilde stood up, with a harsh laugh.

'I watched him watch me die,' he said. 'No way can he intimidate me.'

They walked out of the cabin together. Tamara swaggered, her big pistol blatant in its holster. Wilde strolled, coffee in one hand, cigarette in the other. Dew sparkled on the grass. The chill, damp air held slow, small columns of smoke and steam above knots of people who stood about, in earnest or sociable discussion. Some of the cabins had opened out into stalls, though only for minor necessities. No food or drink sales marred the dignity of Talgarth's court.

The metal of the stockade – great chunks of ragged-edged iron, that might have been the platework of ships, but which were torn like strips of bark and sunk into the soil – gleamed red and rusty in the sun. The stockade's armaments kept up a constant movement, swinging or swivelling. Outside, the machine domain made its presence felt with geysers of flame and the roars and squeals of clashing engines in pursuit of their incomprehensible and incompatible aims.

Wilde walked among the groups of people, waved to those few he recognised as his supporters, and then went over to the centre of the court. Workmen and robots were setting up an awning of plain red canvas above the dais. Beneath it, in the centre of the dais, were a folding-chair of pale wood and frayed grey fabric, and a small table at the right hand of the chair. On the table lay a glass, a bottle, a gavel, and an ashtray.

Wilde examined this arrangement for a moment, smiled, and turned away. He found himself face-to-camera with a news 'mote. It resembled the sapient robot they'd encountered at the crossroads, but its array of mikes and lenses would have left no room for anything more sinister.

The lenses were not only for cameras. As the machine stepped delicately backwards on its insectile legs, it startled Wilde by throwing a fetch of the blonde girl they'd seen presenting the news bulletin. She stood on the grass to the right of the machine.

'She looks solid,' Wilde whispered to Tamara, 'not a holo –'

'It's in your contacts,' Tamara hissed back, baring her teeth bravely at the camera.

'Legal Channels!' the girl said brightly. Her voice came, in eerie ventriloquy, from the machine's speakers. 'Good morning, Esteemed Senior Wilde!'

'Good morning,' Wilde said, smiling down at her. His cigarette fizzed out in the grass.

'*Look at the camera*,' Tamara whispered. The girl's virtual image instantly flitted to the front of the camera, and stood on empty air.

'Do you have any comments to make, Esteemed Senior Wilde?'

'NOTHING TOO SPECIFIC,' the MacKenzie advised.

'Yes,' said Wilde. 'There's no need to call me "Esteemed Senior" … dear lady. My name is Jonathan Wilde, and my friends call me "Jon".' He beamed her a smile that suggested he'd be honoured to count her among them; then coughed and said, more formally: 'I have no comment to make on the case, but I am concerned about the interpretation which some, ah, less responsible news channels than yours are putting on it. I implore anyone who may be listening to do nothing rash – to let the law take its course, because that's the only way to preserve and improve the civilised values of anarchy.' He smiled again. 'That's all.'

'Thank you, Jon Wilde! And have you anything to say about Judge Eon Talgarth's known views about yourself?'

'NO,' advised the MacKenzie, in an urgent flash.

'Nothing at all,' Wilde said cheerfully. 'I have every confidence that a man of his standing would never allow such matters to influence his judgement. I'm sure my choice of his court is proof enough that I mean what I say.'

He made a chopping motion of his hand in front of his chest, and nodded. The girl hesitated, literally hovering, waiting for more, but Wilde set his face in an expressionless mask and walked briskly out of the cameras' field of view. Tamara hurried after him.

'That was all right,' she said. She didn't sound entirely enthusiastic. Wilde squeezed her shoulders.

'Don't you be another,' he said.

She looked up at him. He was staring straight ahead.

'Another what?'

'Another comrade who's disappointed at my moderation and common sense. I had enough of that in my first life.'

And with that he let go her shoulders, nudging her as he did so. She looked ahead again, and found that they were walking straight into the group of people around David Reid.

Reid was wearing a loose woollen suit, and a blue cotton shirt without a tie. He leaned with his left hand on the back of a seat, on which he'd left his mug of coffee. His right hand held a cigarette, with which he made sweeping, smoke-trailing gestures. He was speaking to three men and a woman, all dressed with similarly casual care. His long hair was damp from a recent wash, and the morning air.

When he saw Wilde he stood up straight, transferred the cigarette to his left hand, and held out his right. The two men shook hands, both smiling, studying each other's faces and finding in them recognition and, almost, disbelief.

'It's been a long time,' Reid said.

'Not for me,' replied Wilde.

Reid acknowledged this with a brisk nod.

'I appreciate that,' he said. 'Perhaps with more time, you could have seen things differently.'

'I can see the Karaganda road quite clearly,' Wilde said. 'And your face. When I close my eyes. I've had time to think about the look that was on your face, my friend.'

'That wasn't personal,' Reid said. 'And neither is this.'

'I know it wasn't personal,' Wilde said. 'I know you better than that, Dave. I almost wish it had been.'

'We were both political animals,' Reid said lightly. 'You had decisions like that to make, too. In your time.'

Wilde shrugged. He fumbled for a cigarette. Reid pre-empted him, offering a pack and a light. Wilde accepted both with a thin-lipped smile.

'Tobacco,' he mused, as if noticing its anomalous presence for the first time. 'Cotton. Wool. Where are the plantations, the flocks?'

'Organic synthesis is our best-developed technology,' Reid said. 'As you should know.'

Wilde laughed. 'The case starts in twenty-five minutes,' he said. 'That's how long you have to convince me you didn't let me die to shut my mouth for good.'

Reid touched Wilde's shoulder, as though to remind him.

'Not for good,' he pointed out. 'You're here, and you've been –'

He stopped. Wilde spoke again immediately; it could have seemed he interrupted.

'For long enough!' he said. 'You almost admit it, man! I want you to admit, and explain it. And to retract your ridiculous accusation that the actions of the robot Jay-Dub are any responsibility of mine,

196

and to free the autonomous machine that you have walking around in Annette's body. An apology for *that* insult to my wife and myself wouldn't be amiss, either. *Then* we can talk about other matters.'

He was trembling slightly when he finished speaking.

Reid stood, blowing smoke slowly from his lips.

'What other matters?'

Wilde leaned forward, speaking so softly that only Reid and Tamara, and the MacKenzie, heard him.

'The fast folk,' he said, 'at the other end of the Malley Mile.'

Reid recoiled slightly. 'Is that what Jay-Dub told you?'

'I worked it out for myself,' said Wilde. 'It's obvious, when you think about it.'

Reid shook his head. For a moment, his face showed genuine grief. Then, his expression hardening, he stepped back.

'Jay-Dub made you,' he said. 'He made you as a weapon against me. And something else, I warn you, made Jay-Dub what he is.'

'He?' Wilde retorted, following his prompt. 'That's quite an admission.'

'He was you,' Reid said. 'A simulation of you, I should say. And for a time, he was my friend. He had plenty of time to accuse me of his – your – murder or neglect, and he never did. Because he understood. He has a greater mind than yours or mine, Jon, and he understood. But he was, when all's said and done, a machine. A machine with its own purposes, with endless patience, and bottomless cunning. I had hoped that the human element in it would overcome the machine's ... program. I was wrong, and I'll put that mistake right. Legally, you own it, and I'll nail you to that. But in reality, you are ...'

'What?' Wilde challenged. 'Tell me what you think I am.'

'*Instrumentum vocale*,' Reid said bitterly. 'A tool that speaks. Jon Wilde is dead.'

He turned on his heel, sweeping up his companions with a brusque gesture, and stalked away.

14

Combat Futures

AFTER THE WORLD war there was a world government. It was officially known as the United Nations, unofficially as the US/UN, and colloquially as the Yanks. It kept the peace, from space, or so it claimed. What it actually did was prevent innumerable tiny wars from becoming big wars. But in order to maintain its power, it needed the little wars, and they never stopped. We had war without end, to prevent war to the end. The US/UN kept the most advanced technology in its own hands, to keep it out of 'the wrong hands' – i.e., any hands that could be raised against the US/UN's dominion. It was not as dreadful as generations of American dissidents had feared. It wasn't, by a long way, as dreadful as generations of global idealists had hoped. That leaves a lot of leeway for bad government.

The Restoration Settlement, the fragmented system of 'communities under the King', was Britain's contribution to the tale of infamy. In the interstices of the Kingdom all sorts of Free States flourished: regionalist, racialist, creationist, socialist; even – in the case of our own Norlonto – anarcho-capitalist.

The Kingdom was a caricature of a minimal state, which bore about the same relationship to my utopia as once-actually-existing-socialism did to my father's. The people who did best of all under the arrangement were the marginals who squatted the countryside and called themselves New Settlers, and whom we city folk called new barbarians – 'the barb'.

After twenty years of slow-burning war of all against all the Army of the New Republic proclaimed the Final Offensive for the fourth time.

'You've got to talk to them,' Julie said.

'Why the fuck should I?' I replied, not turning away from the window. The fine morning view of North London's Greenbelt fringe was marred by puffs of white smoke from the far side of Trent Park. I counted several seconds before hearing the artillery's dull thuds, couldn't hear the shells burst. Over the horizon, probably. The Army of the New Republic was rumoured to have infiltrated Luton. Whatever the truth of that, Luton or somewhere nearby was taking a hammering from the Royal Artillery.

'It's your problem,' I continued, facing her. In a way that had become familiar over the years, but which I'd never ceased to envy in the middle-aged of today, she seemed to have changed little between twenty and fifty. The most visible difference between my former Youth Organiser and the woman who now stood in my office was that she'd traded in her formerly unvarying cosmonaut jumpsuit for a more dignified crini-dress.

I, in my nineties now, was still tough and vigorous, strutting in the leather of my own skin, and my brain was still running sweet and clean, oiled by the foetal cell-lines. But the prolongation of life, and the prospect of its indefinite extension, had robbed me of the stoic maturity and detachment that had sometimes come to the truly aged of the past. I'd noticed in myself a hardening of the attitudes, a thinning of the spirit. The peaceful revolution that had established the original Republic I'd welcomed and tried to use; I'd plunged into the chaotic possibilities that accompanied that Republic's violent end; but the imminent prospect of its violent renewal – new revolution or counter-restoration – now found me determined to do only what I could to survive this latest turning of the wheel, with no expectation that it would carry me anywhere.

Behind me the window rattled to an explosion followed by the scream of some missile's passage, catching up too late. I must have given a start, because Julie's smile was sly when she said,

'It's your problem too. Are you going to wait till the rockets come *through* the window?'

'No,' I said. 'But why do you want me to do it?' My voice sounded querulous, to my annoyance. 'Why not your own spokesfolk?'

Julie laughed down her nose. 'Name them. You're the one everybody's heard of. Our grand old man.'

'Oh, thanks.'

'Also,' she went on, 'they insist on talking to *you*, because you weren't involved in what the Republicans call the Betrayal.'

I suddenly found myself smoking a cigarette. (First of the day. One

of these decades I'd have to quit for good, health risks or no health
risks ...)

'But I was,' I said. 'Dammit, I helped the Hanoverian bastards draw
up the *maps*.'

'Yeah,' Julie said. 'And then we threw you out, remember?'

'So?'

'Well, everybody assumes it was because you were *against* the
Settlement.'

'What!' I sat on the edge of the desk and laughed. 'The organisation
put that about?'

'Not exactly,' Julie said. 'We just ... didn't contradict it. We could
hardly denounce you for opportunism after we'd done the same thing
ourselves.'

'Of course you could,' I said absently. 'Didn't I teach you *anything*?'

I'd just understood why, ever since the Settlement, my reputation
had carried a mystique of irreproachability which in my actual
political activity I'd done so little to deserve. It had helped me in my
second career, a none-too-demanding history lectureship at North
London University supplemented by more substantial writing than
I'd ever had time for before. The writing had brought me to the
unsought position of space-movement guru, more read about than
read. The idle curiosity which had driven me to investigate and refute
the conspiracy theory of history was hailed as a long-overdue revision
of revisionist scholarship, my increasingly cynical journalism as the
voice of the Movement's radical conscience, challenging the inevitable
compromises of its hands-off hegemony over Norlonto.

Julie was looking at her watch, wringing her phone, twitching her
hair. Another rocket came in, closer this time. The gun-battery fell
silent.

'OK,' I said. 'Take me to their leader.'

'Only in a virtual sense,' Julie said. 'You take *me* to the Media Lab,
or whatever it's called these days, and I'll patch you in.'

I picked up my jacket and computer and stubbed out my cigarette.
'What about the students?'

'That's fixed,' Julie said. 'They're on strike.'

'Oh,' I said, holding the door open as she steered her skirt through.
'Where do they work?'

Whatever contribution to the struggle the students thought they were making by staying away, they'd have done better by coming in, to the Cable Room at least. In the Perry Anderson Building's cool, quiet basement with its thin layer of natural light from slatted windows near the ceiling, cameras and screens and VR immersion gear lay amongst a clutter of notes and chewed pens and stained styrofoam cups. Julie powered up more and more cable and net connections, displaying a media battle almost as important as any on the ground.

Britain – 'former Britain' as the Yanks called it – was world news for a change, with the ANR allegedly poised to strike and the US/UN nerving itself for another bloody intervention. Meanwhile the local boards and channels were buzzing with rumour and debate. The ANR, for its part, was saying nothing, apart from a manifesto and a timetable showing exactly where and when they intended to strike. Tomorrow looked busy.

'You want deep or flat?' Julie asked, jolting me out of a fascinating, spinning thread of argument from one of the Yorkshire mini-states.

'Flat.' I never could stand the hassle of gloves, goggles, and gear – the way I saw it, if you were going to kit yourself out like that you might as well be getting into some good healthy perversion instead of the inside of a computer.

'OK, putting you through now.'

The newsgroup discussion (and its almost equally intriguing accompaniment of cartoon characters – smileys, they were called – who pulled faces, gestured obscenely or rolled about laughing in the margins, in a graphic gloss on the main debate) flicked away and a video link cut in.

Flakey reception; scratches like an old movie (the cryptography had been lifted that minute from a campus freeware board in North Carolina, according to its indignant, jumping-up-and-down copyleft demon in the corner) and voice quality like a badly dubbed Iranian skinflick, but there was no doubt who was on the other end.

'Well, hello there Jon.'

'Hi, Dave. Didn't expect to be speaking to you.'

('You *know* this guy?' Julie hissed.)

Dave coughed. 'I hired out a few squads for, uh, technical work in the current operation, and for some time I've had a good business relationship with our friends to the North.'

I understood what he meant but it seemed unnecessarily oblique. I gave him what I hoped came across as a dirty look.

'You worried about the crypto, or something? I mean, it was your lot who picked it.'

'No, no.' Dave nodded as if past my shoulder. 'Just – who's that lassie on the bench behind you?'

'Uh?' I looked back. Julie was leaning forward over hillocks of skirt, her neat boots dangling below, like a doll on a shelf.

'Watch your lip, man, that's Julie O'Brien.'

'Sorry, ma'am,' Reid said. 'Didn't recognise you.'

'That's all right,' Julie said. 'And you can speak freely.' Probably flattered at being called a lassie, I thought dourly.

'OK,' said Reid. He relaxed. 'Fact is, Jon, I've been working with the ANR for years, and I've spent the past few weeks brokering deals with defence companies in your neck of the woods.'

'Yeah, well I had noticed combat futures were up.'

Reid grinned. 'Aye, and you can use them to leverage insurance ...' He rubbed his hands. 'Great fun, of course, but now that we've squared everything with the road owners and cop-cos we need to deal with the Movement militia. Politics, not business. They thought I was the right person to talk to you.'

'Given our deep personal trust.'

'Something like that.'

'Are you really launching an offensive tomorrow?'

Reid grinned. 'I can't say. We intend to, but we haven't got all the bugs out of our system yet.'

The ANR was alleged to have inherited some diabolically clever military software from the old Republic, though if its previous failed offensives were anything to go by it wasn't all it was cracked up to be.

'Why are you posting a timetable of where you intend to hit? Most strategists still rate the advantage of surprise, last I heard.'

'I'm told it's a humanitarian measure,' Reid chuckled. 'It lets the civilians get out of the way.'

'And clogs the roads with refugees and gives the mini-state militias every excuse for calling in sick tomorrow morning?'

'Like I said –'

'– Humanitarian. OK. Business. What's the deal with Norlonto?'

'We know your militia won't fight for the Kingdom,' Reid said slowly, 'and we don't expect you to fight for the Republic. All donations gratefully received, of course, but that's by the way. The main thing is, we don't want anybody thinking we're invading you if we happen to, uh, pass through in large tracked vehicles.'

'I can see how that might be misunderstood,' I said. (Julie, behind me, snorted.) 'What guarantee do we have that you aren't gonna just stomp on us?'

'Apart from my solemn word?'

'Yeah,' I said. 'Apart from that.'

'It's not in our interests. We've nothing against Norlonto. Some of the little Free States will have to be cleaned up, but you're not on the list.'

Fucking great. 'OK, how about this. ANR shelling and rocketing of Norlonto stops *right now*. Your troops can pass through, but they can't stay and they *especially* can't launch any attacks on the Hanoverians from positions inside Norlonto, even with the landowners' permission.'

'That'll do,' Reid said.

'That breaks the Settlement,' Julie said, as if this point had just occurred to her.

'Indeed it does,' Reid said drily. 'So just on the off-chance that we lose this round, I suggest that Jon makes this deal known over your heads. All those who did accept the Settlement resign their posts in disgust, and Jon takes over for the next day or two.'

'What!' Julie and I said at the same moment.

'Sure,' Reid went on imperturbably. 'Make him dictator or something. That way, he can give the orders to the militia and take the rap if we go down. You can always shoot him afterwards if we win and he shows too much attachment to the job, but I'm sure that won't be necessary.'

'You're asking a lot,' I said. 'If you lose, I'll swing for it.'

'Oh, I wouldn't worry about that,' Reid said airily. 'If we lose it'll be because the Yanks come in, and then you'll die anyway.'

'Doesn't that apply to the rest of us?' Julie asked. 'I mean, why bother with – ?' She waved her hand.

'Dear citizen,' Reid said with feigned patience, 'the Yanks have a *list*. He's on it, and you're not.'

'Well,' I said after this reassurance had sunk in, 'how can I refuse?'

'Good man,' said Reid. 'I hope I see you again.'

'So do I, mate,' I said. 'So do I.'

The following day the ANR offensive started (Bang On Schedule! as the *Sun-Times* noon edition put it) but stalled and fell back before the day was over. There's a story that this was down to some kind of software problem, but it's hard to credit. I think the general strikes and local insurrections that broke out at the same time had a lot more to do with it. Fortunately, over the next few days this civilian uprising carried the revolution to victory. When it became obvious that America too was on strike and the troops weren't coming, the Restored Hanoverian government departed ignominiously in helicopters to 'continue the struggle against terrorism from exile', as they put it.

The fall of the US/UN has been similarly attributed, in the sort of conspiracy theories I once thought I'd exploded forever, to an engineered viral assault on the global information nets. But a moment's objective thought will show that the insurrections in Britain and Siberia, concurrent with an escalating arms-control dispute with Japan, were what finally convinced the American people that world domination wasn't worth yet another tax hike and draft call-up. Copycat insurrections, as they were called, spread around the globe with the speed of an Internet rumour. The disruption associated with what amounted to a world revolution is, in my view, a more than adequate explanation for the chaotic state of everybody's computer screens over the next few months.

At the time I had more pressing matters to attend to, like trying to figure out a way of losing my new job without handing it to somebody worse. I should have known better than to become a dictator in the first place, but that's anarchism for you. It's just no preparation for the responsibilities of government.

February, 2046. The coldest winter in years. People said there was a hole in the greenhouse, as they lit fires with yesterday's money.

We had our own greenhouse, our geodesic dome on the edge of the Trent Park, near the university. The students were occupied with making mistakes about democracy and elitism that had been considered passé when I was at Glasgow. I left them to it. Annette moved slowly about her horticultural experiments, with a lab-coat made of fur. I rattled out net propaganda, spoke myself hoarse on the cable, convened virtual meetings of Norlonto's factions and hammered out a line to take to the national government.

For relaxation I talked to people in space. Beyond the Lagrange settlements and the Moon it was easier by email, a more natural medium given the lightspeed lag. Asteroid miners solemnly asked my advice about mutual banking, Martian colonists grumbled about being abandoned now that Space Defense was being cut back. Soldiers' councils on former Space Defense battlesats bounced ideas off me for profitable ways to use laser cannon. (They were good kids, really, or they'd have thought of the obvious way.)

Meanwhile the civil wars went on. The Republic's modest aim of combining national unity with local autonomy clashed repeatedly with locals whose idea of autonomy was a good deal more expansive. As a state, the Republic was in many ways weaker than the Kingdom – with its ever-present, over-the-horizon orbital back-up – had ever been. More fundamentally, the revolution had put everything up for grabs: created incentives to defection, as the game theorists put it.

Refugees poured into Norlonto from the countryside, and continued their fights in the shanty-towns and camps. The strain on our charities and defence-companies alike increased by the week, and every week I shouted at their organisers to recruit new workers from among the refugees themselves.

That worked until it became difficult to tell just who was recruiting whom. Competing cop companies found themselves literally in rival armed camps, whose quartermasters, as like as not, were authorised charity distributors. We called it the Thailand Syndrome.

The weekly meetings of the Defence Liason Committee became daily, or rather, nightly. They usually began at 9.00 p.m. and went on until after midnight. This was all right by me. My sleep requirements had diminished with age. I resented having to go into VR, but that's life. Every evening I'd take the washing-up gloves off, pull the datagloves on, give Annette a smile across the cleared table and put on the glasses and –

Be there. Some of us fancied ourselves as Heroes In Hell, and the setting was appropriate: a black infinity around us, and between us a round table with a common view of Norlonto, or London, or whatever we wanted to examine; a *camera obscura* view, patched together from satellite pictures and enhanced with all the data we could pull in. At this level there were thirteen of us, always a lucky number for a committee. Our fetches – our body-images in the virtual world – were the same as our actual forms, mainly so that we could recognise each other in real life or on television.

The night of the big crisis we were one short. I looked around, worried. Julie was there, Mike Davis, Juan Altimara, all from different tendencies of the space movement; a pair of identical youths whom I'd mentally tagged 'the Mormon missionaries' though actually they were from the Norlonto churches' protection charity, the St Maurice Defence Association; and – moving from the voluntary sector to the commercial – a handful of defence company delegates who changed from week to week and always looked alarmingly young and pathetically exhausted, and always squabbled with the leftists –

'Where's Catherin Duvalier?' She was young, fast, smart: a communist militia co-ordinator whose intelligence networks extended through the Green camps to the distant battles in the hills.

Julie smiled at me from across the table's bright gulf.

'Cat's getting married tomorrow. Sends her apologies.'

'No excuse,' I grunted, but I was relieved we hadn't had a defection, or indeed a casualty. 'OK, comrades. First business.'

I keyed up the day's trading figures for defence shares and combat futures. They were rising fast.

'Well, chaps,' I said to the defence-agency boys, 'do you know something we don't?'

A flicker of data interchange set the fetches wavering as if in a heat-haze. Then, their hasty conferring over, one of them spoke up.

'We were about to say, Mr Wilde ...'

Oh, sure.

'... all our companies have been separately approached today about, ah, potential conflict situations. It seems that once again a large number of street-owners have made deals to allow passage of, uh, armoured columns –'

'You mean the *Army*'s coming in?'

Virtual eyes heliographed shock around the table.

'Yes,' he said uncomfortably. 'We've been instructed to inform you that the government has decided to end Norlonto's anomalous status – their words. It's been done at the request of a significant part of the business community and a number of Norlonto's more, uh, settled neighbourhood associations –'

'Bastards!' shouted Julie. She rounded on the 'Mormon Missionaries'. 'Did you know anything about this?'

'Don't look at me like that,' one of them said. 'We've been passing on the complaints from our clients for weeks. The situation really is becoming quite intolerable, especially for the less fortunate. I assure you all that the Association knew nothing of this, but I can't say I'm surprised or sorry.'

'So,' I said, 'when do the tanks roll in?'

'Day after tomorrow,' one of the agency reps said. 'Show of force, and all that. Order on the streets.'

'Good,' I said. 'That gives us time to organise.'

'*Resistance?*' Several voices said it at the same time, in dismay or hope.

'No,' I said grimly. 'Retreat. Tell your principals, and the government, that there'll be no trouble from the militia.'

I looked around the table, my hand on the databoard of the real table tapping out an urgent message to the space movement people to stay behind. 'Meeting's adjourned. See you all tomorrow.'

'*What* the fuck are you playing at, Wilde?' Julie asked, when the charities and the businesses had left the scene. 'We can't take this lying down. It'll be the end of Norlonto!'

Mike Davis and Juan Altimara nodded indignant agreement.

'Oh ye of little faith,' I said. 'Of course it'll be the end of Norlonto. I seem to recall that most of you were not too keen on the *beginning* of Norlonto.'

Juan, who'd arrived in Norlonto as a child refugee from Brazil's brief biowar during the Amazonian Secession, looked at Mike and Julie. The fungal scar on his cheek twisted as he frowned.

'I did not know this,' he said.

Julie flushed, Mike fiddled with his bat switch: 'Heat out the roof, now,' he said uncomfortably. 'Point is, like, Norlonto's been a bastion of liberty for years, a successful experiment, and you want to let the statists march in without firing a shot!'

'Excuse me, comrades,' I said, 'but who's capitulating to statism here?' I was rummaging around in the virtual depths of the table, illuminating likely routes for the incursion and checking them against the movements of insurance ratings, defence-agency deployments, militia strongpoints. 'The way I see it, if the clients of the various defence agencies, if the communities and property-owners of this town want to make a deal with a nationalised defence industry, what business is it of ours? Isn't that anarcho-capitalism in action?'

'Capitalists selling out the anarchy, more like!' said Julie.

'As they have a right to do,' Mike said. 'Yeah, I have to agree with Jon here. Still, it means we've failed.'

Julie and Juan were both inspecting the enhanced map take shape. They looked up, looked at each other.

'We don't have to fail,' Juan said. 'The militia's strong enough to hold off the Republic's forces. We have time to rally the population. The Army can't get away with a massacre in its own capital – even the Hanoverians held back from that.'

'They're getting away with murder in the countryside,' I said. 'You ever *listen* to any of the refugees?'

Julie gave this comment a flick of the hand. 'If you believe the whining of those people the Republic's a monstrous tyranny, which it obviously isn't, so –'

'So why are you so worried about having their troops on the streets?'

'Because –' Julie looked at me as if I was missing something so obvious she was having trouble believing she had to spell it out. 'Because it's our town, dammit! Our free city! We can't let the state roll in after all this time. We should crack down on the camps ourselves, do it *now*, chase those mafias and renegade militias out and get rid of even *that* excuse for the Army coming in. If we move now we could do it tonight!'

I could see Mike taking heart at this suggestion, while my own heart sank. I wished Catherin Duvalier had picked a different day to get hitched. The argument went on.

A butterfly flew out of the infinite darkness around us and settled on the table, wings quivering.

'Oh, shit,' it said in Annette's voice. 'I hope I've got this damn' thing working –'

'We see you, Annette,' I said. 'What are you doing? How did you get here?'

I felt her hand, eerily invisible, brush the back of mine.

'Excuse me,' she said. 'I know I'm not supposed to be here, and I haven't hacked in or anything. In real life I was sitting across a table from Jon, and I could see what he was saying, and I've come round beside him and piggy-backed in on his link, and I've been circling around this conversation –'

'This is a security risk!' Juan said.

'This is no security risk, this is my wife,' I said. 'She's the one who keeps my physical location secure while I'm here, and always has done. So shut up, comrade, and let's hear what she has to say. *If that's all right with everybody*.' I glared across the map-table and they all, eventually, nodded.

'OK,' Annette said. In real life she slid on to my lap and put an arm around my shoulders; in VR she flew up, agitated, then began swooping and fluttering round the map, as if drawn to its lights. 'You say that letting the Republic take over Norlonto would be a terrible defeat and disgrace. All right. Even Jon thinks that, I'm sure. But have you thought what a defeat and disgrace it would be to go down in blood? Or to win, and become a state yourselves? You'd have to fight not just the Army but the security companies, and that would be the end of the free market anarchy you're so proud of. As for driving out the refugees – and that's what you're really talking about, Julie – it wouldn't just be wrong, it would be used for years as evidence that what we have here is no different from what *they* have *there*.'

She settled in my lap, and on the map. 'But if you let the Army in, what do you think will happen? The Army will get sucked into our way of doing things – the economic way, not the political way. They'll have to do deals and trade combat futures and take disputes to court companies and swap laws and all the rest of it.'

'How do you know they won't just do things their way?' Mike asked.

'Because Julie's right,' Annette said. 'They don't want a fight on their hands. They don't want to conquer us, they want to buy us off. In fact it looks like they already have bought off the defence companies. And what's bought can be sold. Before they know it they'll be practising anarcho-capitalism without believing a word of it.'

'Just like every other group that's come in here,' Julie said sourly. 'And look where that's got us.'

'Yes, look,' I said. 'It's got us twenty years of peace and freedom, and tolerance between people who jointly and severally hated each others' guts!'

Juan, Mike and Julie had to laugh. It was a notorious fact that libertarians in Norlonto were rarer than communists in what Reid used to call the workers' states.

'I think Annette has a point,' I said carefully, as if it wasn't what I'd been thinking all along and hadn't got around to articulating (I could never have gotten away with the passionate pacifism of her appeal). 'There's another point we've tended to forget, and it's been bugging me recently. Over the years we've got so caught up in running Norlonto, in as much as it hasn't run itself, that we've tended to ignore what's been going on in space. I know, I know, it's been a sort of socialism-in-one-country versus world revolution thing, and Space Defense held the high orbits, and apart from Alexandra Port there wasn't much practical we could do. I remember years ago some of us tried setting up experimental laser-launchers, and got stomped on from a great height. But now Space Defense is out on a limb, and we have friends – comrades – in Lagrange and on the Moon trying to build ecosystems out of a rag, a bone and a tank of air. It's about time we did something about it. So I say, if the statists want Norlonto, let 'em have it. We can find better things to do.'

I sat back, feeling Annette's weight shift too, seeing the butterfly image tremble. The other three space movement leaders were looking at me and communicating under the table – as it were – with each other. I hoped they would be at least secretly relieved at the idea of saving the Movement's honour by *not* fighting.

Juan's fetch glowed with incoming information, dopplered back to an image of himself.

'OK, Wilde,' he said. 'We think we can sell it. Get ready to wake up early. Julie's going to fix up interviews with you on as many channels as possible. Now, I suppose it's time to …'

'Get back to your constituencies, and prepare for government,' I said.

Nobody laughed.

When the others had faded from view I moved to take the VR glasses off, and felt Annette's hands catch my wrists.

'No,' she said. She swooped into my face, passed out at the back and came around again. 'This is fun. Why didn't you tell me about it before?'

She stood up, dragged me out of the chair and pulled me down on the real table, the virtual image of our stateless state swaying in front of my eyes. We groped and fumbled and fucked on the kitchen table, on the mapped city, while above us two butterflies mated in the infinite dark.

15

Another Crack at Immanentizing the Eschaton

DEE IS EXPERIENCING her first guilty pleasure. The pleasure comes from sitting on the grassy, boulder-strewn side of a valley, under Earth's sun. The sky is a different blue, the clouds a different white, to anything she's ever seen, even in her Story dreams. At the bottom of the valley, far below her, a brown river tumbles over black stones. Farther down the valley, the peace of the scene is disrupted by the clangour of construction on a vast pylon. But from where Dee sits, the distant noise only emphasises the surrounding quiet; the rush of work by half-a-dozen tiny, scrambling figures only reminds her that she has nothing to do but relax, and breathe deep of the clean, thick air of Earth.

The guilt comes from its all being an illusion: a full-immersion virtual reality which has her so spellbound that she understands exactly why this seductive subversion of the senses is so much frowned upon. The most decadent sybarite in the upper lofts of Ship City will sternly inform you that this kind of thing is unnatural, has rotted the moral fibre of great civilisations, and makes you go blind.

She's a little guilty, too, that Ax can't share it. He's stuck out in the real world, mooching in the back of the truck. The half-tracked vehicle is like a gigantic, elongated version of Jay-Dub's upper shell. Its brushed-aluminium skin conceals several centimetres of armour-plate. Its nuclear turbines can give it a top speed of a hundred kilometres an hour, with a flat surface and a clear run. In its stores are many fearsome and fascinating things, but VR immersion gear is not among them.

Dee's in via a direct cortical jack, plugged in to a socket behind her ear. Ax could do this too, but there's only one jack, and she needs it – or rather, it's needed for her. Ax is (she has to assume) still sitting under the raised visor of the tailgate, with his legs dangling over the end of the truck, and applying his electronic version of telepathy to the dodgy reception of an old television. He's also (she hopes) keeping a watchful eye out for predators, bounty-hunters, and dust-storms. The crawler's systems, and Jay-Dub's, are well prepared for all of them, but as Dee looks down the virtual valley, she suspects that they're more than a little preoccupied. She knows a thing or two about CPU time, and from here she can see a lot of it being used.

And not only by Jay-Dub and the vehicle. One reason why she's been sent off up the hill and instructed to do as little as possible is that her own systems are almost fully engaged. Her body, out in the real world, is lying in the back of the truck, limp as a rag-doll. All but two of the figures working on the skeletal tower, just below the long, low house whose graceful shape juts out of the slope like an overhang, are aspects of herself. Soldier is there, and Scientist, and Spy and Sys, helping two other entities with their strange work. Stores and Secrets don't manifest themselves in VR as anything like people: instead, they're tangled, almost impenetrable bundles of live wires and sharp thorns and equally discouraging objects. The dark figures dance and poke around them, and now and again snatch something from the thickets and carry it off triumphantly to add to the bristling tower.

The two other entities are the ones that inhabit Jay-Dub all the time. She met them after Jay-Dub had taken them in its boat up the Stone Canal, far out into the desert, last night. They are the old man and the young girl who spoke to her from the truck. (The truck, indeed, is a version of this vehicle, and she can understand the attraction of its illusory, cluttered cab.) Away from the cab, in the valley and in the house, Meg is a graceful, elegantly dressed woman, but in the cab she's a slut. Her face and eyes are the same in both virtual environments; but her eyes always seem larger and darker, when her smile haunts your memory, than they are when you see them again.

Ax has been given the task of watching the news, and following the court case when it starts. Meanwhile Wilde, the old man in the robot's mind, has harnessed all the resources of its mind and hers to crack the problem – as he puts it – independently of the outcome.

He and Meg, and the spectral shapes of Dee's separate selves, are running about like ants at a fire.

And Dee is up here, on the hillside, all by her Self.

Tamara caught Wilde's elbow. His fists were clenched, his heels were off the ground. He was leaning forward, staring after Reid and Reid's companions.

'You can always kill him afterwards,' she said. 'If it comes to a fight.'

Wilde relaxed somewhat. Slowly his hands uncurled. He gave Tamara a smile to set her at her ease, and looked down at the cigarette Reid had given him. It was still smouldering, the filter tip flattened between his fingers. He took a last long drag of it, and threw it away.

'He said I was a puppet, and Wilde was dead.' He shook his head, then shivered. 'If Jonathan Wilde is dead, who killed him, eh?'

'NOT ADMISSIBLE,' the MacKenzie adviser told him.

Wilde snorted, blinked away a floating footnote about rules of evidence, and sat down on one of the seats. He crushed his paper cup and stuffed it into the mug that Reid had left. He reached for Tamara's hand and drew her to a seat. She sat down on it sidelong, facing him.

'What was all that –' her voice dropped '– about the fast folk?'

Wilde glanced around. Seats around them were filling up, as people settled down to await the beginning of the case: Reid's supporters and theirs, as well as an increasing number of people who didn't fit in either camp, and who were drifting in from the main gate. These visitors, as distinct from the litigant alliances, made a colourful showing, with their hacked genes, elective implants or biomech symbionts. News remotes prowled about, some on the ground, some – supported by small balloons or tiny haloes of rotor-blades – drifting or hovering overhead. Up at the front someone tested microphones, generating howls of feedback.

'There's no time,' Wilde said. He sighed and repeated, as if to himself, 'There's no time.' Then he clasped Tamara's hand and said urgently, 'Look, you've seen something of what Reid really thinks. I don't know if he'll try that in court – he can't very well claim I'm human, and Jay-Dub's owner, and then turn around and say what he just said. But there's a lot more at issue than the matters before the court. If the outcome goes against him, there's no way Reid will go along with it. And if it goes against us, there's no way *we* can go along with it!'

'We could challenge him to single combat,' Tamara said, as if it were a good idea. Wilde laughed at her.

'Do you really fancy my chances?'

Tamara thought it over, eyed him critically. 'Nah. Not really. You're bigger, but he's faster.' She brightened. 'But I'd have a chance, or I could call on an ally. Shit. Wish Ax was with us.'

'Forget it,' Wilde said. 'You're fighting no battles for me.'

'Battles ...' Tamara sat up straight. 'You said there might be big trouble. I can tell the comrades to get ready. In Circle Square we've got a few good fighters, and people who've studied all the great anarchist battles – Paris, Kronstadt, Ukraine, Barcelona, Seoul, Norlonto ...'

'Yeah, right,' said Wilde. 'Well, I hate to break this to you at such a late date and all, but there's one vital thing all the great anarchist battles of history have in common.'

'Yes?'

Wilde stood up and got ready to move down to the front row. He grinned at Tamara's eager enquiry.

'They were all defeats,' he said. ·

Wilde took his seat, with Tamara at his right and Ethan Miller at his left. The others who'd come with him filled the other seats on either side. Farther to the left, across a passage between the files of seats, Reid and his immediate supporters had positioned themselves. The rest of the hundred or so seats were occupied, and twice as many more people – human or otherwise – made shift to stand or sit on the grass. In front of all of them was the wooden dais with its simple furnishings, and an array of microphones and cameras. From the labels stuck on them they appeared to be from the news-services rather than part of the court's arrangements, but some of them had been cabled to loudspeakers at the rear of the seats, the cobweb threads of the cables shining on the damp and now trampled grass. Ethan ostentatiously checked the mechanisms of his rifle.

At a minute before ten, the voices hushed, and the other sounds – of breathing, of shifting, of recording – seemed louder, as Eon

Talgarth walked up the central aisle. Heads and cameras turned. Talgarth faced straight ahead.

He was a slight-built man, of medium height, with wispy brown hair slicked back under a tall hat. He wore a plain black suit and white shirt, with a blue tie. His features conveyed a greater maturity than Ship City's fresh-faced fashions normally affected. When he reached the dais he bounded up on it, and sat down carefully on the canvas seat. He filled his glass with a yellow liquid, sipped it, and lit a cigarette. His narrow-eyed gaze swept the crowd.

'Right,' he said, in a London accent that sounded archaic and drawling by comparison with the clipped local speech. 'Begin.'

Reid stood up at once and walked to the nearest microphone.

'Objection,' said Wilde, rising. 'My charge is the more serious, and should be heard first.'

'Over-ruled,' said Eon Talgarth. 'His claim was prior.'

Wilde turned an incipient shrug into a polite bow, and sat down. 'WORTH A TRY,' the adviser told him.

Reid addressed the judge.

'Esteemed Senior,' he said. 'Thank you for hearing us.'

'Thank you for honouring the court with your custom,' Talgarth said. 'Now, what's your charge?'

Reid paused, and then spoke as if reading from a note: 'My charges are against Jonathan Wilde, and Tamara Hunter. My charge against Jonathan Wilde is that the robot known as Jay-Dub, property of the same Jonathan Wilde, was used to corrupt the control systems of a Model D gynoid, known as Dee Model, property of myself. My charge against Tamara Hunter is that she illegally took possession of the gynoid, subsequently claimed that Dee Model was abandoned property, knowing that the gynoid was not abandoned, and raised an improper defence of the gynoid's falsely claimed autonomy against the recovery agents of its lawful owner.'

Talgarth looked at Wilde and Tamara.

'Do you accept these charges, or contest them?'

They both stood up. 'We contest them.'

'Very well,' said Talgarth. With one airy wave he gestured for them to sit, and Reid to continue.

'The material evidence for these charges,' said Reid, 'has been brought to your attention through the First City Law Company, and I wish to introduce it formally. One: a transcript of an interaction between my gynoid, known as Dee Model, and another artificial intelligence. Two: personal records of interactions I have had in the past, with an artificial intelligence embodied in a robot known as Jay-Dub. The authenticity of these records can be, and has been, independently verified.'

Talgarth nodded. 'The court accepts their provenance.'

'Challenge?' Wilde murmured into his adviser's mike.

'NO CHANCE.'

'Three,' Reid went on, 'the public record of the ownership of Jay-Dub, posted many years ago with the Stras Cobol Mutual Bank. Its owner is identified as Jonathan Wilde, my opponent in this case.'

'Will the person identifying himself as Jonathan Wilde please rise?'

Wilde complied, turning around so that every eye and lens in the place could see him.

'Thank you,' said Talgarth, with a curt nod to Wilde. 'You may sit.' He turned again to Reid. 'Continue.'

'Fourth, and finally,' Reid said. 'An autonomy claim posted through Invisible Hand Legal Services, by Tamara Hunter, also in this court –'

The identification ritual was repeated.

'– and alleged to be on behalf of Dee Model, an allegedly abandoned automaton.'

Talgarth took another sip of his drink, and fixed his eye on Tamara.

'We accept that this claim was posted,' she said.

'Fine,' Talgarth said. He tapped a cigarette out of a pack, and lit it.

'So that's the evidence,' he said. 'You needn't introduce evidence about Tamara Hunter's defence of Dee Model, as the incident is a matter of public record. The court acknowledges that there's a case to answer, on the face of it.'

Wilde stood up, blinking spasmodically as the MacKenzie downloaded a sudden screed past his eyes.

'We are prepared to answer it, and to lay counter-charges,' he said. 'However, I need a few moments to assimilate some new information. I crave the court's indulgence for … ten minutes?'

A ripple of impatience and derision disturbed the crowd.

'You have seven,' said Talgarth.

What the MacKenzie adviser was telling Wilde, and which he précised to Tamara and a huddle of their supporters, was this:

Invisible Hand's sub-contracted software agents, on a (necessarily slow) trawl of Ship City's vast, unencrypted public records – which, in the absence of anything resembling a civil service, suffered from inadequate maintenance, low compatibility and shoddy indexing – had uncovered a single, intriguing reference to Jay-Dub and Eon Talgarth. They had never had any recorded contact since the landing, but they had been on the same work-teams back on the other side of the Malley Mile.

'Does this change anything?' Tamara asked.

'I don't know,' Wilde said. 'But Reid must know about this, just as he must know that Talgarth took a pretty dim view of my activities back on Earth.'

Ethan Miller thrust his face forward. 'We should get the trial called off, man! The judge is biased against you, and maybe against Jay-Dub as well.'

'We can't,' said Wilde. 'We've agreed to him, I've said publicly I trust his judgement, and we can't turn round now and say we didn't know.'

'But we can on appeal to another court,' Tamara pointed out.

'Ah,' Wilde said. 'So could Reid – this cuts both ways! We don't know how Talgarth and Jay-Dub got on when they were both robots together – could've been the best of mates, for all we know.' He straightened up, coming to a decision. 'Reid can't know that Jay-Dub never mentioned this, or for that matter that it's currently out of communication with us. So he might be holding this back as grounds for an instant appeal if the decision goes against him. Fuck it. I'll just have to bear it in mind. Play on.'

Dee hears a distant shout. The figures around the tower are yelling and waving at her, and moving away. The tower itself has changed, its barbed branches forming a pattern that looks somehow inevitable and right, ugly though it is.

She sighs and stands up. Now she'll have to slog and slither all the way back down the hill, and along the rough road. Seeing as how this is virtual reality, she doesn't understand why she can't just fucking *fly*. Wilde has told her about something called 'consistency rules' but she's not impressed. *She* doesn't need a spurious consistency to stop her going mad.

But all this casting of curses and aspersions proves redundant, for without a moment's warning she's back in her tired and aching flesh. Her head hurts so much she wishes she were scrambling down that hillside, under the big, hot sun of Earth. Above her, tools and flashlights sway from hooks, and all around the deep electric hum of the crawler's turbines tell her they're on their way.

She sits up cautiously and swings her feet to the floor. Ax stands by the closing tailgate. Interior screens light up on all four walls of the vehicle's hold as the rear door shuts with a sigh of hydraulics and a suck of sealing-strips. They are heading straight for the canal, which they cross with a gentle pitching motion. The crawler's treads, Dee knows, are mounted on some kind of extensible legs which make drops of a couple of metres no more than bumps in the road.

'What's going on?' Dee asks.

Ax shrugs, but Dee's question is answered as the forward screen changes to a view over the shoulders of Wilde and Meg. Meg twists around and smiles, Wilde keeps looking forward but his eyes meet hers in the rear-view mirror. (Consistency rules again. Crazy, Dee reckons.)

'Hi,' he calls. 'Sorry about the abrupt departure. You can go back to our place with Meg if you want, but right now I've got to stay in reality.' He laughed. 'To the extent of looking out the window and driving the truck, anyway.'

In reality, Jay-Dub is nested in a cavity near the front of the vehicle, and has been since they arrived. The truck is perfectly capable of driving itself. Dee has a shrewd suspicion that the necessity of controlling its progress is in part purely psychological, at a more superficial level than that of the embedded consistency-rules. She lets the explanation pass.

'Where are we going?' she asks.

'We have to go back to Ship City,' the man tells her.

'Problem at the trial?' Dee guesses. She's not paying the conversation her full attention; she's exploring her mind, checking off her selves like they're strayed children coming home, and finds to her relief that they're all there. Secrets is smaller, Stores is far bigger than when she downloaded them to Jay-Dub – but that's all right, she has room in her head to spare.

'Oh no,' Wilde shouts back, his eyes flicking from the mirror to the desert. Dee can see the vehicle is moving at almost its top speed. 'We have to pick up some poison, and then ...'

His voice trails off, whether because of the outcrop they're about to (she grabs the edge of the bed-bench) go over –

or because he doesn't know what to say.

'Then what?'

Wilde's eyes, crinkling into a smile, look back at her again.

'We're going to hack the gates of hell.'

She doesn't even bother to ask for a further explanation. It is obvious that none will be forthcoming, and she has to assume there's some good reason why not. Wilde gives her an encouraging nod, and then turns his attention to the flat desert and to Meg. Ax has braced himself on an old foil blanket, next to an aerial feed, and is having visions by television.

Dee sets Scientist to work, and enters Sys. Minutes pass. Then, as from a great, cold height, a mountain higher than any on Earth or either Mars, in a raw virtual vacuum that makes her head feel as though it's about to bloodily explode, Dee sees exactly what Wilde's cryptic statement means.

'You first,' Tamara said. The others dispersed to their seats and Wilde stepped forward to the microphone. Talgarth stubbed out the cigarette he'd spent the seven minutes smoking, and nodded.

Wilde went through the same courtesies as Reid had used and said:

'Esteemed Senior, I am more than willing to answer for my actions, and for those undertaken on my behalf. I am not willing to answer for the actions of the robot Jay-Dub, or to accept the allegation that it is my property. My present physical existence began last Fi'day, around noon, when I was resurrected. The robot Jay-Dub claimed to have accomplished this, by means which I make no pretence to understand –'

Reid sprang to his feet.

'Objection!' he said. 'Irrelevant.'

'Sustained,' said Talgarth.

Wilde swallowed. 'Very well, Esteemed Senior. The point can be made independently by appealing to the records of Jay-Dub's transactions with the Stras Cobol Mutual Bank, which I am happy to make available to the court so far as they are relevant. They establish indeed that the owner of Jay-Dub is one Jonathan Wilde. And they identify who, exactly, that Jonathan Wilde is. The earliest records include transactions with David Reid's company, Mutual Assured Protection. They explicitly accept the name 'Jay-Dub' as a synonym of Jonathan Wilde, and the robot Jay-Dub as equivalent to that person, Wilde. The robot Jay-Dub has been accepted without demur these many years as none other than Jonathan Wilde – Jay-Dub, in short, *is* Jonathan Wilde! Any records mentioning Wilde as the owner of the robot Jay-Dub, therefore, can only be interpreted as meaning that the person Jonathan Wilde owns Jay-Dub in the same sense that I, Jonathan Wilde, own my body.' He smiled thinly. 'Any coincidence of names is regretted.'

Eon Talgarth, sitting on his chair on the dais, shared an eye-level with Wilde, standing. Their eyes locked for a moment.

'The court will rule on this point,' Talgarth said. 'The robot known as Jay-Dub is in a unique position among all the inhabitants of this colony, so far as I know. However, it is a position in which many of the said inhabitants once were, and in which it alone remains. I accept the argument which has just been put, and I rule that any charges against Jonathan Wilde in the capacity of owner of the robot Jay-Dub must be laid against that robot, as a self-owning mechanism.' He looked around. 'It is not present in this court and should be notified forthwith. The charge against *that* Jonathan Wilde remains pending.'

Reid started to his feet with a look of fury, but a woman sitting beside him caught his arm and drew him back. After conferring head-to-head with her, Reid desisted.

'My ruling carries no precedent relevant to questions of machine personality as such,' Talgarth went on. 'The matter of the ownership of Dee Model has still to be considered. Regardless of whether her control-systems were corrupted, and who if anyone is responsible for that, Reid's claim that he did not abandon her is not contested. Therefore he remains her owner, and those present on the other side of the case are enjoined to co-operate in her apprehension and return.'

Tamara rose, received a flicker of permission to speak, and said, 'Senior Talgarth, this court has many times ruled that the autonomy of machines may be claimed by the machines themselves. That, and not the issue of abandonment which I freely admit I was wrong about, is the basis on which we wish to assert Dee Model's self-ownership.'

Talgarth sighed. 'All such cases,' he said patiently, 'relate to unowned sapient machines in the machine domains. The freedom of such automata is also implicitly recognised by other courts. The gynoid under consideration, however, has been constructed by the resources and efforts of David Reid, and remains his property until he decides otherwise.'

Tamara sat down and gave Wilde a grimace of regret or apology. Wilde, however, seemed to gaze right through her. He blinked, smiled at her and stood up. He walked to the microphone and looked over the crowd before turning to the judge.

'Esteemed Senior, your valued opinion on the matter of Jay-Dub and the matter of Dee Model raises some further points, which I beg the court to consider. First, in the matter of Jonathan Wilde in his embodiment as Jay-Dub. The court has accepted that he and I are separate persons, though – by implication – sharing a common history up to a point which the court has refused to determine –'

'How?' Talgarth frowned.

'When you sustained the objection that the time of my resurrection was irrelevant.'

Talgarth sat back. 'That's correct.'

'As a separate embodiment of Jonathan Wilde, I wish to proceed against David Reid on the charge of having unlawfully killed me, on the basis that any considerations or acknowledgements that may have been made between Reid and Jonathan Wilde aka Jay-Dub have no bearing on me.'

'I'll defer consideration on that until the time of your resurrection has been determined satisfactorily,' said Talgarth. 'The charge of murder which you brought against Reid remains outstanding until that point has been cleared up, or is not contested. David Reid, what do you say?'

Reid rose, disdaining to step forward. 'Please the court,' he said loudly, 'I am quite willing to accept this person's claim that he was resurrected by the robot Jay-Dub three days ago. As a matter of natural justice I wish the earliest opportunity to clear myself of the charge of murder, or have it thrown out of court as a waste of the court's valuable time and a piece of actionably vexatious litigation.' He glared at Wilde and sat down.

'Very well,' said Talgarth. He turned to Wilde. 'Before we move to considering that charge, do you have anything further to say about points raised by my opinion on the matter of Dee Model?'

'I do indeed,' said Wilde. 'The court mentioned that the gynoid Dee Model had been constructed with the, ah, other party's resources and efforts. I wish to raise a question about the ownership of those resources themselves. Because Dee Model's body is a clone of the body of my late wife. This is obvious to me, and I challenge Reid to deny it.'

He paused and turned around to face Reid. Reid's response was a tremor of the eyelids, and a shake of the head.

'You don't deny it?' Talgarth said.

Reid stood up. 'No.'

Wilde shot Reid a look of triumph and hatred, then composed his face to swing a calm smile past the cameras as he turned again to Talgarth.

'In that case,' Wilde said slowly and distinctly, 'I claim that Dee Model's body belongs to the legitimate heir of my wife!' He smiled at Talgarth. 'Whether that heir is myself or Jay-Dub I leave to the court to determine.'

Reid rose at once and bowed politely, though whether to Wilde or Talgarth wasn't obvious.

'I am happy to concede the ownership of the genotype,' he said. 'And to come to an amicable or, failing that, arbitrated arrangement about its use, or compensation for its use and any distress inadvertently caused. My major concern is the recovery of the gynoid's software and non-biological hardware, which are incontestably my property.'

Wilde looked over to Tamara, who shrugged and raised her eyebrows as if to say, 'What's his game?' The MacKenzie remote was saying substantially the same thing. It had expected a bigger fight, since the ownership of genotypes was a hotly contested issue. Its only suggestion was that any concession made here would avoid establishing a precedent that other courts might recognise.

'Very well,' said Wilde. He adjusted the microphone, his hand shaking slightly. 'The only compensation I wish is that David Reid resurrect my wife's mind as well as her body – something which is evidently possible, as the robot Jay-Dub has demonstrated by resurrecting me.'

Reid was on his feet at once. Wilde had to step back quickly as Reid strode up and caught the microphone from his hand.

'The court has not accepted that Jay-Dub resurrected this man!'

Talgarth flicked ash from his sleeve. 'Ah, but *you* have,' he said mildly.

Reid sat down again. The woman beside him whispered in his ear, her face stiff with annoyance. The news remotes buzzed, and people in the crowd were checking out the running commentaries, on hand-held screens or on their contacts.

'Order!' Talgarth banged his gavel, carefully steadying his drink first. 'David Reid may answer your request in his own time.'

'I'll answer now,' said Reid. Wilde stepped back from the microphone, and returned to his seat.

'You've stirred things up a bit,' Tamara observed.

Wilde winked, confusing the remote adviser for a moment, and settled back to listen to Reid.

'Wilde's request is reasonable,' Reid was saying. 'The question of resurrecting the dead has for long been on the minds of us all. But, however much we may wish to do it, we are prevented by *force majeure*. Most of the personalities of the dead, including that of Reid's wife Annette, are held in smart-matter storage which remains inaccessible without the co-operation of posthuman entities whose capacities and motives are unknown, but who – as experience has shown – are a risk to us all. I am responsible for keeping the codes that could be used to re-start them, and I can assure this court that until someone demonstrates a way to do this safely, these codes remain in my possession, and the dead ... sleep.' He glanced at Wilde. 'There are some matters best left undisturbed,' he told him.

'He's telling you not to push it,' Tamara muttered.

Wilde grinned at her and went forward again as Reid took his seat. The tension in the crowd had diminished. Even Talgarth's impassive face betrayed relief.

'The robot Jay-Dub resurrected me without disaster,' he said. 'But there is more to the matter than this.'

Reid leaned back in his seat, hands behind his head, and watched Wilde with half-lidded eyes.

'The court has given its view on one of Reid's charges,' Wilde said, 'and left the other in abeyance until the other Jonathan Wilde, aka Jay-Dub, can be ... prevailed upon to answer it. I now wish to press my counter-charge, the outcome of which may perhaps affect how any fines and damages in these matters are allocated. It may also affect the question of the resurrection of the dead in general.' He smiled at Talgarth, who no longer seemed relieved. 'Not in a legal sense – on that, I'll defer to the court – but in a practical sense.'

Wilde stepped a little to the side, so that while he was unarguably and correctly addressing the court, he was also speaking to Reid and to the wider audience.

'My counter-charge is this: that David Reid had me unlawfully killed, by the reckless action of people acting on his behalf and by his personal, wilful neglect of my injuries. That having done that, he has made no efforts in good faith to resurrect me. He claims that this is difficult – nonetheless, no evidence exists of any attempt on his part to overcome the difficulty. I claim compensation for loss of life-experience and loss of society, for my entire down time. That is, for nothing less than the whole of Ship Time, and possibly for longer.'

Eon Talgarth had to call for order, more than once, before the hubbub ceased.

'Do you have evidence to bring for this charge?' he asked.

'Yes,' said Wilde.

He stalked over to his seat, reached into Tamara's backpack, and pulled out the folder of Talgarth's notes. He held it high as he walked back, and presented it to Talgarth.

'The evidence,' he said, 'has been gathered by a certain Eon Talgarth, and has been a matter of public record and never challenged.'

The court fell silent, except for the toy-helicopter buzzing of the remotes and the distant din of the machinery outside.

Talgarth riffled through the pages, and shook his head. 'There were conflicting claims,' he said, 'as to the manner in which Jonathan Wilde met his death. Although I myself inclined to the view which you have just stated, there are no surviving witnesses other than David Reid and, putatively, yourself. Its not having been challenged has, I'm afraid, no bearing on the matter. No court on this planet recognises libel, and they do not recognise a refusal or failure to rebut a claim as any evidence in its favour.'

He sighed, as if in regret for more than the inadequacy of the evidence; for, perhaps, a political passion long spent, which had driven him to compile the dossier. He handed the folder back to Wilde.

'The court cannot accept this as evidence,' he said. 'In the absence of other evidence, or the confession of the one you have accused –'

He glanced at Reid, who was shaking his head vigorously.

' – which I understand will not be forthcoming, and which I have no power to compel, I do not see how this charge can be tried at this time. Should you call Reid as a witness, he may refuse to answer, and no adverse inference may be drawn from that.'

Reid's legal adviser stood up and conferred briefly with Talgarth, while Wilde stepped back out of earshot and looked away. When the woman had sat down again, Talgarth tapped with his gavel.

'The counter-charge is dismissed,' he said, 'without prejudice to either party. Wilde's bringing of the charge cannot be called vexatious or frivolous, and is not to be held against him. The name and reputation of David Reid remain unsullied. The allegation that his killing of Wilde was unlawful, or with malice, remains as it was before the charge was brought, that is, an unsubstantiated historical speculation which he is within his rights in treating with contempt.'

Reid and his assistant exchanged smiles.

'However,' Talgarth went on, with an abrupt harshening of his voice, 'the claim that Reid was responsible, culpably or not, for the death of Jonathan Wilde is ... considerably better attested. The witnesses are not, of course, in this court, but some are known to survive and could be asked to testify.'

He beckoned Reid's adviser, and after they had conferred again he banged his gavel.

'Reid does not contest his responsibility for the fact of Wilde's death.' He held out an open hand to Wilde. 'You may proceed.'

'Ax?'

No response. Ax is watching television in his head, or in front of his eyes, or whatever the hell he does. Dee can't stand his autistic but audible interest for a second longer. She leans over and shakes his shoulder. He rouses himself and frowns up at her.

'Wha —?'

'Ax,' she says patiently, 'would you mind *patching* this fascinating material to a *screen*, so I can see it too?'

'Oh. Sorry, Dee.'

He disengages from the cortical downlink and fiddles with switches. Outside, on the big screens, the outskirts of the Fifth Quarter roll slowly past. Dee watches the chaotic activity with disdainful dismay. If this is how machines behave when they're left to run wild, she reflects, it's no wonder humans mistrust them.

Around the crawler, which is making its way up a broad street, dozens of other machines, each about thirty centimetres long, are scurrying and sniffing about. They look like larger versions of the cleany-crawlies you find in houses, and although partly autonomous they're guided by radio control from the cab. Meg has told her they're looking for traces of a specific poison: one of the public-health countermeasures with which this place is periodically bombarded. The poisons – generically known as Blue Goo – are the nanotechnological equivalent of viruses, regularly updated and mutated to keep pace with the likewise evolving smart-matter wildlife of the machine domains. The job of spraying them from the air is done by a charity, which has no difficulty at all in raising money and volunteers.

Ax gestures to her to look behind her. Part of the screen she turns to gets masked as another window clicks up. It's the Legal Channels service, showing the court case. Wilde – or Jay-Dub, as Dee finds herself mentally calling him – and Meg have been keeping an eye on it, when they can spare a moment. Ax has been given the task of keeping a *close* eye on it. Dee has been feeling left out, and wonders if the others have been trying to spare her feelings. Nice of them, but a waste of time.

Because, whatever bad news the court case may bring her, it's all irrelevant now. As Ax said, that shit is *over*.

Wilde has apparently just finished speaking. He turns away from the judge, Eon Talgarth. Even Dee's heard of Talgarth, a former crim from the Malley Mile orbital camp, who studied law as a prisoner; got involved in, then disillusioned with, abolitionism; and has for years made a living adjudicating disputes between scrappies and between machines.

As Wilde turns away the camera follows his face, and he gives it a slow, arrogant grin.

'Well that was some speech!' says the breathless commentator. 'He looked quite annoyed when he described his killing – his *alleged* killing I should say! Sorreee! And nobody's ever suggested before that we might owe the dead their back pay! For the implications of that please see –'

Ax snips that particular thread and all Dee hears now is the silence in court as Reid strides to the mike. His face makes her quail. She's hardly ever seen him angry, and never with her, but she knows his anger is to be feared and right now he's angry at the whole world.

The camera circles around behind Talgarth. Reid's more composed now, and Dee feels proportionately calmer – in fact, as she gazes at the close-up, she feels the stirring of an involuntary affection and desire. It's all the more disturbing in that she feels it as a person, not as a slave, but she puts it down to her past and concentrates on what the man is saying.

'Senior Talgarth,' he says heavily, 'what we have just heard is a disgrace to this court, and an insult to the intelligence of us all. It is also dangerous, in stirring up an opportunistic envy that has no place in a basically just society such as ours, where no person is reduced to selling their lives or labour to those more successful than themselves.'

'Objection!' comes a shout from Wilde.

'Sustained,' says Talgarth sternly. 'We aren't here as a public forum.'

Reid dips his head. (Dee hears Ax, behind her, snort.)

'The point,' Reid continues, 'is that my opponent has asserted that those with an interest in the dead have a claim against me, because I've made no attempts in good faith – as he puts it – to tackle the immense task of finding a way to bring about the resurrection of the stored dead. Well, Esteemed Senior, good people, that is a task which I freely admit is beyond my capacities!' He spread his hands and shrugged. 'Have I ever prevented anyone else from putting forward a proposal to tackle it? No! Because, as we all know, the real problem is finding a way to contain those whose help we need to raise the dead. The fast folk, those who once were human and whose minds, and motives, developed far beyond human comprehension or control. *They* are the ones I could awaken, if I wished. *They* are the ones who could awaken the human dead, who sleep in the same storage-media as they do. And *they* are the ones who could, in the blink of an eye, turn this planet into the kind of hell that some of us glimpsed, a hundred of our long years ago.'

His gaze focuses on Eon Talgarth, and Dee feels only the slipstream of his passionate plea: 'Esteemed Senior! I know *your* memory is not so short! Strike down this claim before it does more harm!'

He looks around once more, and resumes his seat.

Talgarth sips from a glass, and lights a cigarette. He contemplates the smoke for a few moments, then leans forward, elbows on knees. His posture makes a strange contrast to the formality of his attire, and, as if noticing this, he removes his hat.

'Means he's talking off the record,' Ax explains.

'But we can hear him!' says Dee.

'Figure of speech,' says Jay-Dub, from the virtual cab up front. 'Ssh.'

Dee, somewhat chastened, looks away for a moment and notices that the crawler is idling at the end of the broad street. The subaltern machines have returned, whether in defeat or success she doesn't know. Ahead, there's a grassy park with some fortification in the centre. Above it she detects a cloud of gnat-like flying-machines.

'Ah, Reid,' Talgarth is saying, 'you were always a fine speaker, and I hear what you say. But between you an' me, if you catch my drift, Wilde has made a valid point about how we could do it off-planet, safe in space, like, and you haven't answered that, have you?'

Reid raises a hand placatingly to Talgarth, who leans back and replaces his judicial hat. Then Reid turns to the stiffly dressed woman beside him and has a murmuring consultation, from which the camera – as required – cuts away. It pans to Wilde, who's sitting with –

'Tamara!' Dee and Ax exclaim delightedly.

'Good for her,' says Jay-Dub.

Back to Reid, who's just angrily shrugged off the woman's hand

and is walking towards the camera and the mike, followed only by the woman's open-mouthed dismay.

'I didn't want it to come to this,' Reid says, all conventional courtesy discarded as he speaks to the world, and the court only as an afterthought. 'But enough is enough. Sure, "we" could do it in space! Tell me, who's this "we"? If anyone has the capital to spare for a deep-space station *and* a ring of laser-cannon shielded against any viral programs that could be sneaked into its controls, *and* a foolproof procedure worked out *and* hair-trigger, dead-fall nuclear back-ups in place, they can go right ahead! Be my guest! I'll *sell* you the fucking dead, and the demons who could raise them. Go ahead! Have another crack at immanentizing the eschaton!

'Before any entrepreneurs of the apocalypse rush forward, however, let me give you a warning.'

He turns and points a shaking finger at Wilde, who's observing Reid's performance with an expression of insolent detachment.

'*Don't* follow any suggestions from this ... *thing* that calls itself Jonathan Wilde! This thing which admits it is a creature of the robot Jay-Dub!'

He pauses and takes a deep breath, and faces Talgarth. 'Esteemed Senior, I have a heavy responsibility before the people of New Mars. I allowed the robot Jay-Dub to continue in existence, after I had grounds to suspect that it was corrupted by the original fast folk, in the Malley Mile. It has repeatedly, in person and through its golem here – and, for all we know, through manipulation over the years of the so-called abolitionist movement – urged on us the disastrous course of re-running the fast folk. Whose interests, I ask you, would that serve?'

Talgarth makes no reply.

Reid, as if in sudden disgust with the whole business, gives a backward shake of his arm above his head and stalks back to his seat. But he doesn't sit down. His supporters rise with him, and others in the crowd stand too.

Reid reaches inside his jacket, and there's a sudden frenzy of movement as the crowd separates – some fleeing the confrontation, others closing with one side or the other. Tamara, and some people Dee doesn't know but Ax – going by his eager comments – does, form a barrier around Wilde. The cameras bob about, the factions face each other arms in hand.

Talgarth is speaking urgently into his right lapel, and making equally urgent gestures. Dee notices the weapons on the stockade's iron walls swivel on their mounts, swing around and bear inward and down.

One floating camera suddenly spins and zooms in on the gate, which has opened, unnoticed. The rounded prow of a great armoured vehicle noses in. Dee looks away from the television window to the window screens, and sees another angle on the same view. The intruding vehicle is their own.

16

The Winter Citizen

I WOKE TO the sound of armour in the streets, and lay on my back for a while staring up through the hexagon panes of the dome at the pale cold sky. It was ten o'clock. I'd slept in, but the ANR, as usual, had arrived on time. After yesterday's exhausting round of television interviews and visits – actual and virtual – to militia units, I felt I had a right to a rest. I no longer even had the responsibility of being Norlonto's nominal dictator – I'd resigned as chairman of the Defence Liaison Committee as soon as the last militia commander had come on side.

An airship floated by above, its shape distorted by the ripples of the glass. Then another, and another, close behind. I wondered if a lot of people were getting out before the state moved in. Doubtless there were those who didn't want to hang around for questioning: Hanoverian recusants, spillover from the civil war, Army deserters … perhaps even space movement libertarian idealists, off to grab a place on a launch vehicle before Earth's exit hatch shut down completely, as the more alarmist ones thought it might.   And now, after twenty-odd years as a denizen of a functioning anarchy, I was a citizen again. The tanks and APCs continued to trundle by outside, the airships and helicopters to drift or buzz past above. Annette mumbled and stirred beside me. I ran my fingers over her long white hair and slid from under the duvet, hastily wrapped her fur coat around me and padded down the stair-ladder from our nest under the top of the dome.

I printed off newspapers and fired up a pot of coffee and went to the door. Our housing association's cluster of domes was set back a little from the street, among paths and ponds, lawns and cannabis gardens. Children raced about, chickens strutted their fenced-in runs. Only the dogs still bothered to react to the Army's passage.

The tanks, as always, moved faster and quieter than you'd expect. The soldiers sitting on them wore ANR uniforms customised with bandanas and bandoliers and the insignia of forces they'd defected from or defeated. They chewed or smoked and looked down their noses at us, discordant rock music blaring from sound-systems. I stood for a long time, shivering, shanks prickling, and watched.

Then I stooped and picked up our deliveries: juice, milk, eggs, bread and rolls. The bags and cartons had a fur of frost over them; they must have been there for hours. Not much petty crime in Norlonto. I wondered how long that would last. As I fried eggs and bacon and tore off pages from the papers a supermarket bill caught my eye. In our division of domestic labour, shopping was down to Annette. The price of coffee and cigarettes shocked me, the price of local foodstuffs gave some comfort. I checked the delivery bill.

Fruit juice cost about ten times as much as milk. Nothing to do with the inflation – that only applied to the Republic's official joke currency, and we paid in good South African gold.

Crazy prices. What was the world coming to?

There I was, thinking like an old man. I shook my head and carried Annette's breakfast and a wad of her favoured newspapers upstairs. Then I washed and dressed and settled down to my own breakfast and news, trying to figure it out.

I was on my second coffee and first cigarette before I remembered that these, like the fruit juice, were imported. For a wild moment I wondered if the Republic had slapped on taxes or tariffs, then realised that such an outrage would hardly have passed me by. I'd have heard about the riots; heck, I'd have been *in* the riots.

A trawl through the *Economist*'s database set me straight. Raw-material prices had risen sharply over the six months since the Fall Revolution, while the prices of finished goods and services had dropped. There were plenty of articles explaining why, which in my absorption in our little local difficulties I'd overlooked.

The defeat of the US/UN, and the collapse of its financial scams such as the IMF and World Bank, had had divergent effects. The primary products tended to come from the less developed areas, the old Second and Third Worlds. Their instabilities made our civil wars look like peaceful picketing. Without the empire to police them, protection costs and risk had gone up. Meanwhile, in the more advanced regions, the reduction in taxes – and the end of the headlock on technological development imposed by UN arms control – had allowed manufacturing to enjoy a spurt of growth. Even nanotechnology looked as if it might come on-line at last, if only somebody could entice its best minds out of hiding.

So much for the price of coffee. What was still bothering me was why we weren't as poor as we should have been. My income from the university had dropped to a token stipend, as the only lectures currently being given there were from the ignorant to each other. (God, let them grow out of that. *Soon.*) Royalties from my writings had gone up, but not by much, because most of the increased circulation was of those I'd disdained to copyright. Our pension funds were paying out regularly, but they were pretty basic and they certainly hadn't gone up. And yet – unlike most people since the Revolution – we hadn't had to tighten our belts.

I keyed up our bank statements and almost spilled a mug of expensive instant coffee. An ordinary expensive cigarette smouldered undrawn to a butt. Our regular income had indeed dwindled, but the balance was being made up by increased payments from my small, almost-forgotten stake in Space Merchants. I cursed the fund-management software for letting me eat my capital, then called it up.

We weren't eating my capital. We were using up part of the income, and a small part at that. The value of my stake had increased far more than I'd ever expected, and had almost doubled since the Revolution. We were moderately, comfortably, and inexplicably rich.

'I don't see what you're complaining about,' Annette said, over a late lunch. No urgent phone-calls; I assumed this meant the occupation was proceeding smoothly. 'I'm thrilled. I never particularly wanted to be rich, but I've always thought it would be *nice.*'

She looked around the dome, at the stacked books and climbing plants and the dodgy cabling of the electronics, blatantly thinking of improvements.

'Yeah, well, me too,' I said. 'But to make money in space these days is, like, *defying gravity.* Space Defense was run on defence budgets that are due for the chop. All the space industries, even the settlements – even NASA – were like the shops in a garrison town.

234

Like the whorehouses! The whole system should be in a severe slump. A lot of it is – the battlesats are running on empty, hawking microwave beams to electricity companies or some such. So why is Space Merchants doing well?'

Annette's eyes had a glint of amusement or sadness. 'You won't stop, will you?' she said. 'You think you're on to something, and you won't stop.'

'Yup,' I said, rising and clearing away the plates.

'If you find out it's all been a terrible mistake, just do me one favour,' she said. 'Take the money and run. I don't care who it belongs to, they owe you this much.'

'Half a day under the state,' I said, 'and you're thinking like a politician.'

'No,' she corrected me, standing up and laughing. 'I'm thinking like a politician's wife.'

The soldiers stayed, the camps were pacified, people from all wings of the space movement denounced me. I made no reply to the attacks. Snow fell. We kept ourselves warm, and worked on the puzzle as a team. Annette followed the news, and I followed the money. For an advocate of the free market I was embarrassingly ignorant of finance, and a few days went by before I could find my way around the *FT*'s pink screens without frequent tabs to the Wizards.

Then on to the great databases of Companies House ... in VR you could wander through it like a vast mall, its connections and intersections emulating the impossible topologies of an Escher print. I went as myself, and so did some of the other searchers and researchers there, but most were in cryptic fetches, corporate icons or the mirrored samurai armour of the latest discretion software from the Kobe code-shops ('Zen cryptography – *don't even think about it*', the ads said).

From Companies House you could see the world.

I saw the intricate geometries of Thailand's Islamic banking system crumble before the assault of the anti-technological Khmer Vertes; Vladivostok's port economy, liberated by the Vorkuta People's Front, rise in new and strange shapes; America's frayed networks of scientific information glow brighter around the coasts, flicker and die in the heartlands as the Scientific Fundamentalists and the White Nationalists shut down the corrupting institutes of what they called 'rootless naturalism' in public and 'Jewish science' in private.

I saw Kazakhstan's cosmodromes stretch skyward, and I saw too the tributaries that fed them, the KomLag archipelago of the forced-labour companies. Some in the Former Union – old skills put to a new use – but most in the freer world. A few right here in Norlonto.

Wherever the victorious forces of the Fall Revolution could do it, they were keeping the more useful employees of the defeated US/UN empire – and especially Space Defense – at work for a pittance, in partial restitution for past exploitation. They were supplemented by a new and expanding use for non-political criminals, earning out their payback at high speed, in the high-risk, high-wage space economy.

'Slavery,' Annette said. 'I just don't believe it's come to this.'

'It isn't really slavery,' I said uncomfortably. 'It's just bonded labour.'

'Yeah, yeah. Like we don't have capital punishment, we just let psychopaths pay off their blood-debts by starring in snuff movies?'

'Exactly,' I said. 'Do you still want to take the money and run?'

'No!' She looked fiercely at me, then down at the table. 'On the other hand, there's no-one to give it back to, it would be counter-productive to sell the shares to someone with even less scruples than you, and it'd be pretty hypocritical just to give the money away.'

'Not to say wimpish.'

'Yeah. C of E.'

'So what's the answer?'

'Use it to expose where it's coming from,' Annette said firmly. 'Dig into it some more, then run a campaign to get it all out in the open and discussed. You could do that.'

'And accomplish what?'

'Oh, come on! If there are any abuses going on, it might help to stop them.'

We both found ourselves laughing at this statement, but as Annette said after we'd lapsed into a gloomy silence, what else was there to do?

I circled warily in the dataspace around the representations of the

Kazakh spaceport hinterland, and noticed the tag-line of the company I'd started so long ago: Space Merchants. It had strong flows of material and information linking it with Myra's Kazakh workers' ministate and Reid's Mutual Protection defence agency. I amplified the resolution, trying to trace what was going on.

They'd all changed, grown beyond anything any of us had initially intended. Space Merchants had become an import–export business between Earth and low orbit, almost as distant now from its innocent, fannish origins in the space-trash market as the latest SSTO boosters were from Goddard's amateur rocketry. The International Scientific and Technical Workers' Republic, its nuclear teeth long since drawn, had changed its specialty to launch-vehicle development. The ISTWR had held out against the surge of Kazakh reunification, and Mutual Protection had a major presence there. And not only there: Mutual Protection now ran security and restitution facilities on three continents, usually guarding installations and extracting payback from any thieves or saboteurs foolish enough to mess with its clients.

It was weird to see that personal triangle between myself, Myra and Reid, replicated as a commercial connection, like the family relations of dynastic armies; but whether those connections meant anything was a different matter. (As I pointed out in *Ignoramus!*, my work on the counter-conspiracy theory of history, everybody knows somebody who knows somebody who ... (etc.), and it's the easiest job in the world to ink-in those pencilled lines; to speculate that the surprisingly few handshakes that separate the obscure from the famous are all *funny* handshakes ... My incautious illustration of this with a diagram of my own second- and third-hand connections, 'proving' the existence of a mysterious Last International linking the world's libertarians and futurists to each other and to a long list of historic usual suspects, had resulted in a certain amount of misunderstanding: for *years* afterwards I'd received anonymous mailings of what purported to be the Last International's Central Committee minutes.)

Firewalls guarded most of the companies' data, the remnants of recent hack-attacks fading on the matt virtual surfaces. I moved along, seeking entry nodes. Out of nowhere, something pinged my fetch. My hands, in the datagloves, felt warm. Warmer. *Hot.*

I was holding what looked like a sealed envelope, iconic

equivalent of a personal message: based on an anonymous transaction protocol, it couldn't even be read on screen, only in VR through the intended recipient's fetch. It was also a delivery method of choice for target-specific viruses. I looked at it – damn, it was beginning to give off smoke – and hastily reached behind me and tugged the emergency back-up bat. Seconds trickled by as the contents of my home computer were transferred to isolated disks. When it was safe to do so I opened the now smouldering envelope.

dear jon, it read, *it's too fast. help me. love, myra.*

Then it crumbled to bits.

Well, that was a lot of use, I thought as I backed out and sat blinking in chill daylight, Annette's quizzical smile teasing me from the other side of the table.

'You've heard from Myra,' she said.

I stared at her. 'How do you know?'

'From your face,' she said. 'I've seen that look before.'

I'd been in contact with Myra perhaps a score of times, in more than a score of years: when we'd had the Bomb, and on deals I'd brokered for the space movement in the Norlonto decades. There was a direct airship link between Alexandra Port and Baikonur, and I'd met her a few times when she was passing through, but most of our contact had been remote.

I reached for Annette's hand. 'You're not *jealous?* Good God, it was seventy years ago!'

'I know,' Annette said. She squeezed my hand. 'And I know you love me. But you loved her, too. I think she was the only other woman you were ever in love with. And it's true what they say: love never dies. You can kill it, sure, but it never dies by itself.'

Her words may have echoed any number of sentimental songs and stories, but she spoke them as if they were a bitter, reluctantly accepted scientific truth. She laid a hand over my open mouth before I could protest, expostulate, explain.

'It's all right,' she said. Then: 'What does she want this time?'

'I don't know,' I said. I explained about the message, and where I'd found it. 'She's in some kind of trouble, and she wants me to help.'

'"It's too fast."' Annette stared past me, into some virtual reality of her own. 'That fits, you know. The bonded labour, the profits from space – *something* is happening too fast. If you look at the news it's like the world's coming apart, and I think it's ... being *pulled* apart, by something we don't know about.'

I laughed. 'If it was, somebody would have told me.'

'I think somebody just did,' Annette said. 'Anyway, there's only one way to find out. Go to Kazakhstan. I assume it won't be difficult to find Myra, or she'd have told you how.'

I looked at her, astonished. It was a proposal I was just working around to myself. From Annette I'd have expected, if anything, a fight against it.

'I don't want you to go,' she said. 'I don't even know if you do. But I'm more afraid of doing nothing. Nobody's spoken out for you since the troops came in. I don't think they trust you any more.'

'They?'

'The space movement people. The comrades.'

'There's no conspiracy,' I grinned. It was one of my catch-phrases.

Annette's eyes were sad and serious.

'This time, you could be wrong,' she said.

She stood up and moved to the house computer, keying the board in a brisk rattle. 'Well come on,' she said. 'Go and help her. I'll try and book you a flight. You get ready, and for heaven's sake remember to pack your gun.'

I complied, shaking my head. None of the thoughts Annette had expressed had ever crossed my mind before. 'Love never dies'.

Well, fuck me.

I was tempted to make the journey by one of the steadily plying airships, but as Annette pointed out those took days, and were usually loaded with freight and crowded with space-workers hung over after a month's leave in Norlonto. So I found myself leaving Stanstead on a regular jet, much larger than the one that Reid and I had taken thirty years earlier. No anti-aircraft fire this time; the Urals corridor had long since been bombed into a safe passage.

Stanstead to Almaty, its airport still shell-pocked from the victory of the Kazakh People's Front; north to Karaganda, a frightening, grimy place, black even in the snow: post-Soviet, post-industrial, post-independence, post-everything. From Karaganda there was a regular hop to Kapitsa; because the ISTWR was still an independent enclave, I was detained for a check – the first in my whole journey. Front cadres and local officials scrutinised my documents, tapped my details into some ancient mainframe (located in India, if the response time was anything to go by) then broke into smiles and offers of Johnny Walker Red Label when my records came up. I had said good things about the KPF, when it wasn't fashionable. They insisted on telling me how much they admired this, and after a few whiskies I told them how much I admired them. They'd fought the US/UN, reunited their country without fueling nationalist fires, and refrained from imposing their state on the one part of the country that didn't want it.

'The ISTWR?' They thought this was funny. They hadn't refrained out of any high-flown principles.

'Why not, then?' I shrugged slightly, glanced at the map above the customs-officers' desk. Not the little enclave's defensive capacity, that was for sure.

'Bad lands,' I was told. 'Bomb country.'

They say the steppe around Kapitsa glows in the dark, but it's just starlight reflected off the snowfields. That's what I told myself on the flight, as I dozed off the effects of good whisky taken neat, jolted awake and smoked and dozed again. Only two other seats on the aircraft were occupied, and their occupants were as keen to keep their own company as I was. I kept my reading-light off, pressed the side of my face to the window, and watched the black thread of the road from Karaganda to Semipalatinsk wend across the steppe, and even fancied I saw the tiny sparks of light from the snow-ploughs.

We landed in a twenty-below dawn on a runway just cleared of snow. A minibus hurried us to the terminal. Beyond the swept-up mounds of dirty snow the gantries stood skeletal and dark. Few aircraft were parked, none were coming in. The airport building was as bright as ever, its workers as secure in their casual employment as before, redundantly supervising busy machines. The republic's heroes still loomed large in their posters.

But compared with its bustle when the place was exporting nuclear deterrence, it might as well have been deserted. Its sinister emptiness recalled the public squares of the old Communist capitals. I set off across the concourse with the nervous hesitation one feels on entering a large, old, and possibly unoccupied house.

I had no idea what to do next. If Myra had wanted to tell me, I'd assumed she would and could; if she'd had any warnings, she'd have included them in the message. As it stood it appeared that the only aspect of our contact which she wanted to keep secret was that she needed my help.

The coffee franchise was still there, and open. It was where she'd met us before. I walked over and ordered a coffee and sat down with it and a copy of the English-language edition of *Kapitsa Pravda*, which lived up to its name in that it gave an apparently truthful account of the news. I had reached the sports pages before I realised that it contained no news whatsoever about Kapitsa.

I scanned the concourse, eagerly fixing on any figure who chanced to resemble my memory of Myra, and sat back disappointed each time. An hour passed. Mutual Protection guards wandered through as if they owned the place. More people came and went. I heard one, then two more aircraft come in. Their passengers straggled individually or in small knots to the glass doors, outside which a dozen taxis idled their engines in the cold.

Maybe I should just look her up in the phone-book ... I was standing at the booth and gazing at the search page before I realised that I didn't know her current surname. It even took me several seconds of racking my memory before her original surname came back to me: Godwin. I tried that. No luck.

I put an encrypted call through to Annette.

'Hi, love. I've arrived safely.'

She smiled. 'Glad to hear it. That's not why you've called.'

'Why d'you say that?'

'I know how your mind works, Jon.' She laughed. 'It's Davidov. I looked it up on the old insurance policy.'

I suppose I must have looked embarrassed. Annette grinned and stuck out her tongue, a pink millimetre on the tiny screen. 'I love you,' she said. 'Take care.'

The screen blinked off. I sighed, suddenly feeling very old and alone, and keyed up the phone-book again.

Davidov, Myra G., Lieut-Cmmdr (ret'd) lived at Flat 36, Block 7, Ignace Reiss Boulevard. No other Davidov was listed at that address; Myra's marriage had broken up years ago. The building, when the taxi dropped me off there, turned out to be a classic Soviet block, recently built in a kind of perverted homage to the workers' motherland but with its concrete already crumbling and discoloured. Only one car was parked outside, a big black Skoda Traverser. Myra's, I guessed: it looked just the sort of vehicle that would be at the disposal of a retired People's Commissar.

The lift, in another neat touch of authenticity, didn't work. I lugged my travel-bag up three flights of stairs. My knees hurt. Time I got a new set of joints. I rang the doorbell and looked around for a CCTV camera. There wasn't one. Instead, a shutter flicked back, exposing a fisheye lens sunk into the door. Bolts squeaked, chains rattled. The door opened slowly. Yellow light, heavy scent, stale cigarette-smoke and loud music escaped. Then a hand reached out and tugged me inside. The door swung and clicked behind me, and I was caught in a warm and bony embrace.

After a minute we stood back, hands on each other's shoulders.

'Well, hi,' Myra said.

Her steel-grey bobbed hair matched the gunmetal satin of her pyjama-suit. Her face had the waxy, dead-Lenin sheen imparted by post-Soviet rejuvenation technology, a glaring contrast to the mottled and ropy skin of her hands. Like me, like all of the New Old, she was a chimera of youth and age.

'Hello,' I said. 'You're looking well.'

She laughed. 'You aren't.' Her fingertips rasped the stubble on my cheek.

'Nothing a shower wouldn't fix.'

'Now that,' she said with a sharp look, 'is a very good idea.' She reached past me and flipped a switch. Shuddering, firing-up noises came from the walls. 'Half an hour,' she said, leading me into her living-room. It had one double-glazed window overlooking the street. The view extended past the replicated streets of the district, over the older prefab town and out to the steppe.

A central-heating radiator stood cold beneath the window-sill, an electric heater threw up hot dry air. Insulation was what kept the room warm; it was thickly carpeted, the walls hung with rugs, their patterns – blocky like the pixels of an early computer-game – a display of traditional Afghan designs of helicopter gunships and MiGs and AK-47s. Between them were political and tourist posters of Kazakhstan's history and geography (the ISTWR itself being deficient in both), and old advertisements of rocket blast-offs and nuclear explosions. A television screen, hung among the posters, was tuned, sound off, to a Bolshoi Luna ballet; floating flights and falls, the form's illusions made real under another sky. Huge antique Sony speakers high up on over-loaded bookshelves pounded out Chinese rock.

An old IBM PC stood on the table beside Myra's hand bag and a stack of coding manuals. A glance over their titles suggested that she'd had to encrypt her message by hand. No wonder it was so brief: it must have taken days.

She made me a breakfast, of cereal and yoghurt and bitter Arabic coffee. We chatted about the flight, and about the changes in our lives since we'd last met, several years earlier in an Alexandra Port bar. She still saw her ex-husband, the dashing officer she'd once subverted, and I got the impression that something was still going on between them, but for months he'd been in Almaty, supposedly negotiating with the KPF. She implied that he was being kept out of the way.

'So is this place still a Trotskyist state?' I asked.

Myra set down her cup, her hand trembling slightly.

'Oh yes,' she said. 'It's … just like Russia when Lev Davidovich was in charge.'

That bad? I raised my eyebrows; she nodded.

'And you're not in the government any more?'

'Not for some time.' She smiled wryly.

'I'm sure you still have a lot to say,' I said. 'Does anyone listen to you?' I cocked my head.

'They sure do,' she said. 'I can't complain.'

She looked at her watch. 'Your shower is ready.'

The shower was in a stall off her bedroom. I laid my clothes on the foot of her bed, carefully – I didn't want them creased. As I smoothed out my jacket my fingers brushed the hard edge of my pistol, a neat, flat plastic piece no longer or thicker than my hand. After a moment's thought I took it out and as I got into the shower laid it across the top corner of the stall. Then I turned the shower on and stood in its steamy spray, grateful that this at least was built to spec. I had barely rinsed off my first soaping when the splash-door opened, and Myra stepped in.

'It's an old trick but it works,' she whispered in my ear, rubbing my back. 'White noise is white noise, no matter what they use.'

'You really think you're being bugged?'

She laughed. 'It's what I would do, in their position.'

'Who's "they"? What's going on?'

She picked up a tiny disposable razor and an aerosol that extruded pine-scented foam. She lathered my face and began to shave it, thus ensuring the fixity of my gaze. Just as well, because it almost took lip-reading to make out her whispered words in the steady hot rain, and there was no time for her to repeat herself or for me to interrupt.

'You know there's something going on,' she said. 'I left that message weeks ago, because I thought if anyone was gonna investigate, it'd be you.' She grinned. 'And I was right. OK, here's the story. Deep technology – nanotech, genetic engineering, AI and so on – was restricted under the Yanks, and it's still under attack in most places, what with the bloody Greens and religious zealots and shit. Two things happened. One, places like this took in scientific refugees and let them get on with their work under cover of other projects. Two, the US/UN and especially Space Defense kept up their own work. The bans were for everybody else, not for them. Now it's all come together: our scientists are working with theirs, and you can bloody well bet theirs are co-operating – it's the only way they can work off their debts. Same goes for a vast POW labour force. They're shipping stuff into space like there's no tomorrow, and at this rate, there won't be. I think they're going for a coup.'

'In Kazakhstan?'

'In the *world*, stupid!'

I really did feel stupid. That, or she was crazy.

'For fuck sake, who? And how?'

'Your space movement – OK, maybe not yours, but – anyway, they had people in the official space programmes, even in Space Defense. And they can see how things are going, since the Fall Revolution. "Fall" is right! Everything's falling apart – it's like a global version of the Soviet breakup. Another few months, years at most, and there won't be a rocket lifting from anywhere. The word is, it's now or never if we're ever to get a permanent space presence. We're in what they call a resource trap.'

That at least fitted with what I'd seen, and what Annette had suspected.

'I'll take that for a "why",' I said. 'I asked who, and how. Even SD couldn't really dominate the world, without back-up on the ground, and now that's gone, splintered –'

'I told you,' she hissed. 'As much as I could in the time I had. "It's too fast", remember? *Nanotech*. With that you can build space-ships, not big dumb rockets but real ships so light and strong they can get to escape velocity like *that*.' Her hand planed upwards. 'Whoosh. They have AI that can guide laser-launchers, send ships up on a needle jet of super-heated steam. And with nanotech, you got one, you have as many as you want, you can grow them like *trees*!'

I shrugged, under the pouring water, absently sponging her skinny flanks.

'If you have all that, you don't need to rule the world. All you have to do is save it.'

Myra shook her head, sending drops flying. 'They don't want to save it, and they don't think it wants to be saved. Oh, Jon, you hung out with all those humanists and anarchists, and you just don't know how much bitterness and contempt there is among the scientific-technological elite for the ignorant masses! That's why they threw me out, after the Fall Revolution, when I got in on a little bit of this and began to kick up a fuss. They called me a populist and a – a revisionist!' She laughed. 'They suffered and chafed for years under the UN bureaucrats and the Stasis cops and the Green saboteurs, and they don't want to have to mess with those people ever again. They really believe that if news gets out of what they're up to, the mobs will march on the labs, demagogues will push governments into another crackdown, and it'll all be over.'

I looked up from flannelling her shins. 'They could be right.'

'Don't say that! That's what Reid's been telling them for years!'

I stood up, almost slipping on the stall's wet, sudded floor.

'*Reid?*'

'Ssshhh. Yes, I thought you knew. He's running the whole show, and he's been planning it for a long time. I think he might even have done it if the Revolution hadn't happened, but now it has he's moving faster than ever. Mutual Protection and its goddamn privatised gulags are the muscle behind it all, and he's the worst of the lot. He thinks like you sometimes used to write, about freedom, but with him it's absolute – no ethics, no politics. Even the scientists are afraid of him.'

I could believe that. Ever since he'd stopped being a communist, Reid had followed no interest but his own. So had I – being one's brother's keeper was to my mind still the original sin – but I'd never quite achieved Reid's single-minded dedication in that regard.

The shower died to a trickle.

'What are we going to do?'

Myra looked at me. 'I know what I want to do,' she said with a wicked smile. She looked down. 'Jeez – does this this kinda talk *turn you on?*'

We dried each other silently in the tiny space that Myra's big bed left in the room, and continued the conversation under cover of the bedding and some very loud music. She told me what we were going to do, and then we did it, and then lay on our sides, face-to-face, legs entwined, talking dirty politics. We whispered under the bed-clothes, like children after lights-out.

Simply exposing what was going on might well result in the very outcome that Reid's faction feared. Letting it go on could result in a chaotic and bloody splitting of humanity, between a tiny space-based minority and an earthbound majority dominated in all probability by anti-technological, paranoid leaderships. Either way, the prospects for a civilised future were dim.

There was another way, Myra argued: to get what she called the 'legitimate' space movement to organise a campaign for exactly the same things as Reid's group wanted – access to the technology developed by the UN and the scientific underground, a big effort to hold the space programme together – but openly, and voluntarily, funded by donation rather than extortion. Get it all out in the open, and discussed. That was the only way to undermine the suspicions on both sides: let the technologists see that people really wanted what they could give, and that they would actually pay for it. Let the ordinary folk see that deep technology wasn't really going to turn the biosphere into germ-sized robots or them into machines, and all the other things they'd been told they had to fear.

'And you,' she said, 'are the only person I know of who could make it work.'

'Me? You flatter me, lady.'

'You have the contacts, the credibility ...'

'I'm not too popular with the space-movement cadre any more,' I said. 'To tell you the truth, I think most of them already think the way you say Reid's group does.'

And (I didn't say) there was only one thing that could turn the supporters of the movement against its organisers, and that was exposing the plot, if such it was. I lay in the dark tent of the quilt for another minute, looking at Myra's face, and thinking some thoughts which I hoped didn't show on mine. Starting with the big one: she had told me a pack of lies.

'Let's do lunch,' I said.

Lunch was in a tiny Greek restaurant around the corner.

'Why Greeks?' I asked, nibbling hot shish.

'They followed the Tatars back here, before the Tatars went home,' Myra explained.

'That's a lot of history,' I suggested.

'Yeah,' said Myra. She glanced around. 'Leave it.'

We drank good wine and some ferocious brandy. Myra talked about safe, non-controversial subjects, like how the whole state of the world was *my fault*.

'If you'd sold the Germans the option,' Myra explained, 'the fuckingIsraelis –' (it was always that with Myra, like one word) ' – would never have dared do what they did, and the Yanks would never have taken over, and ...'

'And so on.' I laughed. 'Come on. There must have been scores of people in the same position as me, who made the same decision.'

'Yeah, but they all needed their nukes. You didn't. You just hung onto them out of principle.'

'No I didn't! I've never made a principled decision in my life! I'm an opportunist and proud of it. Anyway, why didn't you just let them have their deterrent, and settle up afterwards?'

Myra grinned at me, shrugged.

'Bad for business.'

I grinned back at her.

'That was my reason, too.'

We'd reached the honey-cake and coffee and the last shots of brandy. Myra picked and licked and sipped. Stopped, a grin of enlightenment on her face.

'That's it!' she said. 'I should know better than to blame individuals. The whole goddamn' mess is the fault of –'

'Capitalism!' I said loudly, and the *garson* came over with the bill.

Back at her flat we dived into bed again. She left the sound-system on. We hardly noticed when the rock music changed to military music, but we both lay in silence afterward, when the announcement that the airport was temporarily closed boomed through the house.

We didn't need to talk about what this meant. Martial music and closed airports were the traditional prelude to an announcement that the country had been saved. Someone had made their move. It was time I did likewise, before the roadblocks went up – or Myra turned me in, for her own protection and mine.

I stroked a strand of hair away from her face.

'Are you ready for a cigarette?' I smiled.

'God, yes.'

'I've got some in my jacket,' I said, sitting up and reaching toward the end of the bed.

'No, no,' Myra said. She threw back the covers, caught my forearm. 'You must try some of ours. Really.'

She smiled into my eyes. Had she thought I might be going for my gun? If so, she must think it was still in the jacket. She'd have felt it there when we embraced in the hall, and not checked again before getting in the shower.

She reached over to a bedside cabinet, opened the drawer. I didn't take my eyes off her for a second, and she didn't let go of my arm, as she fumbled around inside the drawer and took out a pack of cigarettes. We smoked in thoughtful silence. The strong, rough cigarette made my head buzz. Did she suspect that I suspected?

I stubbed out the cigarette, gave her a broad wink, and said, a little too loud, 'Myra, would you mind driving me to my hotel?'

She grinned back at me and said, again as if for the benefit of anyone who might be listening, 'No problem.'

I put on all my clothes except my jacket, stooped to zip up my overnight bag, and said: 'Ah, I left my cloth in the shower.'

I leaned into the shower stall, recovered the pistol, turned around –

My foot reached the drawer of the bedside cabinet a second before her hand, and slammed it shut. As she jerked back I opened the drawer again, and fished out the pistol that I'd known for sure would be there.

Myra sat rigid, white-faced, clutching the quilt as if for protection.

'I'm ready,' I told her. I slipped her big heavy automatic into my jacket pocket, picked up the jacket and draped it across my arm and hand. 'We can leave as soon as you're dressed.'

When she was dressed, and we were back in her living-room, she tried a casual reach for her handbag, but I got to it first. I pocketed yet another pistol, this one even smaller and lighter than my own, tossed her the keys and nodded for the door. She pulled on her long fur coat, and descended the stairs in front of me. The black Skoda still stood alone on the street.

Following my silent indications, she opened the passenger door and slid across to the driver's seat. I got in and closed the door. She turned the key and the engine started immediately, as did the heater. Just as well – I was freezing after going those few steps in the open without my jacket.

She faced me, tears in her eyes.

'Jon,' she said, 'what are you doing? I trusted you. Are you working for Reid?'

'I see you're not worried about bugs in your car,' I remarked. 'I don't think you were worried about bugs in your flat, either. Start driving.'

Her shoulders slumped. 'OK, OK,' she said. 'Where to?'

'Karaganda.'

'What?' She looked at me, open-mouthed. 'That's hundreds of kilometres. Semipalatinsk is closer.'

'I know,' I said. 'Shut up and drive.'

The border on the Karaganda road was only fifty kilometres distant, and I knew – from my conversation with the KPF cadres the previous night – that the greater Kazakh republic had a border post there, and the ISTWR hadn't.

Myra engaged the gears, and the vehicle pulled out as the first snow of the day began to fall.

Myra's story, I'd decided, just didn't add up. If she and her doings were under surveillance, my visit had to be known. If she was out of favour with the authorities, her contact with me could only be interpreted with suspicion. It must be as obvious to her as it was to me that the first thing I'd do once I was safely home was to give her story all the publicity I could, risks or no risks.

It followed that both she, and the ISTWR's security apparatus, *wanted* me to expose it – and that she was still well in favour with that apparatus. This implied that her story of the little republic's having been completely taken over by some faction linked with Reid's company was false. Far more likely it was that the core of the state was opposed to a (no doubt encroaching) company take-over, and wanted my earnest exposure as the perfect political pretext (before or after the fact) for reasserting their own control.

So whatever was going on, whether it was the company or the state that had struck first, there was no way I wanted to get involved. And there was no way, either, that whatever deeper threat we faced from Reid's technocrats would be countered by political campaigning. The only way out that I could see was to take the whole story to the one state that could act swiftly, and whose intentions I trusted slightly more than those of any other state I could think of: the surrounding Kazakh Republic.

Which was why we were now driving along between metre-high, ploughed-back ridges of snow, on a road covered by a fall already centimetres deep.

Myra tried to speak once or twice, pleaded with me to explain what I was doing, and each time I told her, as harshly as possible, to shut the fuck up. I wanted her scared, off-balance; I wanted her to think me capable of shooting her. Which I certainly was not, but her sincere belief that I was should help to keep her out of trouble, whoever won.

In less than an hour the border was only a minute's drive away. We topped a scrubby ridge and I could see the lights of the Kazakh border post through the snowfall. And a moment later and three hundred metres ahead, a line of men in bright yellow survival-suits with big black rifles, waving us down.

'Mutual Protection,' Myra said, with a bitter laugh. 'So what now, smart-ass?'

'Stop the car,' I said levelly. 'Slew it so your side is nearest, and get out with your hands up.'

I looked at her startled face and added as she applied the brake, 'If that's OK with you.'

'It's OK,' she said.

She was a good driver. She brought the car to a halt just fast enough to skid the rear end around and bury the front in the snow-drift.

I opened the passenger door, rolled out with my jacket and gun, and pushed my way through the top of the oily, gritty snow of the drift, keeping the car's bulk between me and the company guards. I crawled forward on knees and elbows until the approaching line of men had passed me on their way to the car. I could hear Myra's raised, officious, protesting voice, and hoped that whatever she thought of me getting away, the last thing she'd want was for me to fall into her opponents' hands.

I kept crawling forward, as close to the roadside snow-ridge as possible. The grit lacerated my palms, elbows and knees. The warmth was bleeding from my body with every passing second. When I could bear it no longer, I lifted myself to a sprinter's crouch. The lights of the border post were half a kilometre away. I glanced back. The men were inspecting the car, Myra was kicking up a major political incident.

I started to run. At first I tried to run doubled-up, but I couldn't do it. I straightened up and began to run flat-out. My sides felt as if they were being skewered on hot swords. I swore I'd never smoke again.

Then I felt a great thump on my back, and saw the blood spurt from my chest, and I followed its red arc forward onto the snow, as if I could catch the drops.

I was on my back, looking up at a white sky. Above me an impossible object floated, a diamond ship: faceted, sparkling, like the delicate white ghost of a stealth bomber, suspended on ridiculously faint jets. A rope-ladder snaked down from it, a white-clad man descended. I raised my head a couple of centimetres as he reached the ground, and faced me. It was David Reid. His face told me nothing.

Yellow suits, goggled faces. Myra, her arms firmly held as she strained towards me.

'Love never dies,' I tried to say, and died.

The Floodgates of Anarchy

17

Android Spiritual

'**M**OVE AND YOU'RE dead!'

The cheerful Cockney voice of Esteemed Senior Eon Talgarth, Judge Resident at the Court of the Fifth Quarter, boomed from loudspeakers all around the hundred-metre square of his stockaded property. Enough of the guns mounted on the stockade were pointing inward to make the court an execution-ground for those in the centre. The neutrals who'd fled to the perimeter would be safe, but the opposing groups, each numbering a couple of dozen, confronting each other in front of Talgarth's dais, were at the focus of the cones of fire. The situation became clear to all in that target-area within a few seconds.

'That's it, that's it,' coaxed Talgarth. 'Now, good people, you will please put away your weapons nice and slow, know what I mean?'

The weapons were sheathed or shouldered. Jay-Dub's crawler continued to roll forward. Talgarth waited until its tail was just clear of the gate, and raised his left hand. The vehicle stopped.

'Right,' he drawled. 'The case is adjourned. Since David Reid's side made the first move towards settling the matter by violence, it seems only fair to allow the other side to make a strategic withdrawal until another arrangement can be made.'

For a moment, nobody moved. Talgarth jutted his jaw at the group around Jonathan Wilde.

'Don't just stand there,' he urged them. 'Move it.'

They backed off slowly and then turned and made a run for the long, low, silvery shape at the gate. Reid and his group glared after them, muscles twitching, conscious of the continued cover of Talgarth's guns.

'This is a disgrace!' Reid snarled. 'Who's going to trust your justice now, Talgarth?'

'A damn' sight more than would be impressed by my letting you start a slaughter in my court,' Talgarth answered, his eyes following the running figures. Reid also was momentarily distracted, by some intelligence whispered in his ear.

'You know whose truck that is?' he demanded. 'It's the vehicle of the robot Jay-Dub.'

'I know,' said Talgarth evenly. 'I've known it was in the vicinity for some time.' He tapped his ear and grinned, suddenly seeming more a jailbird than a judge. Wilde's group disappeared around the back of the crawler. Its engines thrummed and it began to inch backwards out of the gate. 'When I saw how things were going, I called it in.'

'You did *what*!' Reid exploded. He looked around in appeal to his companions, and to the hovering remotes of the news services, now beginning to drift back to the centre of the court. 'Why in the name of God did you do that?'

The gate closed with a rattling finality. Talgarth turned away from it and relaxed, and looked Reid in the eye.

'You asked, back there, if my memory was so short,' he said. 'Rhetorical question, I suppose, but even so.' He very deliberately lit a cigarette, and blew out smoke with every appearance of satisfaction. 'It ain't.'

Even after they've dropped off the rest of Wilde's supporters, whom Ethan Miller is confident he can lead back to the human quarter without too much difficulty, it's crowded in the back of Jay-Dub's truck. It's more of a cargo-hold than a passenger area, although it has some rudimentary provision for human occupancy. Ax is wedged into his place on the floor by the television feed, Dee and Jonathan Wilde are sitting on the padded fold-down bench on which Dee lay earlier, and Tamara's clinging to one of the larger hooks suspended from the ceiling.

The crawler's speed is anything but a crawl. They're battering across the Fifth Quarter with radio and sonic sirens blaring, and scant regard for anything that remains in the way. Robots and other, less definable machines scatter before them. The screens are fully given over now to displays of the surroundings, and they're full of alarming sights.

Dee glances at Wilde, and at the other version of Wilde in the illusory cab. Her eyes meet Wilde's looking wonderingly from the older Wilde to her. She gives him a tentative smile.

'I'm seeing ghosts,' he says. 'You're … it's strange now, being able to look at you.' He laughs briefly. 'Without you running away. I know you're not Annette, but … don't mind me looking at you, OK?'

'It's OK,' she says. 'I understand.'

His smile turns into a look of confidential puzzlement.

'Who's that woman up in the front with … Jay-Dub?'

'Her name's Meg,' Dee whispers, 'and she isn't a woman, exactly.'

Meg turns around. 'I heard that,' she says over her shoulder. 'Don't you believe her. I'm as much a woman as she is, Jon.'

'She's a fast woman,' the other Wilde yells back.

Ax observes this somewhat incestuous banter, and looks up at Tamara with a scornful roll of his eyes. Tamara catches this and looks away from Wilde and Dee, with something like a guilty start. Ax sighs and reverts to channelling the news.

'How long have we got?' Wilde asks. 'Talgarth can't keep Reid and his crew locked up for long, can he?'

'Nah,' says Ax, breaking his trance again. 'Reid's calling up reinforcements, appealing to other courts, and in general kicking up a stink. I reckon Talgarth will have to let him go within half an hour.'

'And then he'll come after us?'

Jay-Dub shrugs, removing his hands from the apparent steering-wheel to wave them about in a manner which Dee can't help seeing as dangerous, even though she knows it isn't. 'He's after us now,' he says. 'He – or his defence agencies – have one or two aircraft and at least a time-share on a spy-sat, and they've got us on their scopes if not in their sights. I doubt he'll take any action until he knows which way the political or legal chips will fall. Unless –'

His attention is diverted by the need to clear a barrier.

'Hold tight!'

The crawler slows, lurches, almost leaps over a burning junk-heap strewn across the road.

'Unless what?' Dee prompts as she recovers from the jolt.

'Unless he finds out you're with me,' Jay-Dub says. 'Remember those bounty-hunters who came after you? They got burned pretty badly, but they survived and they'll make a full recovery.' He grins over his shoulder at Wilde, or at Dee. She isn't sure just who's the target of his irony this time. 'Amazing what medical science can do these days. As soon as they've got over the shock and have enough of their faces grown back to talk, they'll talk. About the fugitives being rescued by a robot.'

Wilde frowns around the company. Dee already understands, but she can't tell the others yet.

'What'll Reid do then?' Wilde asks.

Jay-Dub is attending to the steering again, by necessity or choice.

'He'll destroy us,' he says. 'With whatever it takes, and whatever it costs.'

So we cut, as they say, to the chase.

The crawler dives into a dank tunnel under a canal, at the far side of the Fifth Quarter. It stops, engines throbbing, just long enough for Dee, Ax, Tamara and Wilde to get out. Dee is the last to leave. A hatch in the side of the hold slides open, and one of the small crawling-machines rolls over and presents her with a sealed plastic box. She slips it in her handbag.

'Goodbye,' says Meg.

'Goodbye,' says Jay-Dub, the elder Wilde. He notices her tears and gives her a grin and a broad wink.

'It's not so bad,' he tells her. 'I've been there, and there's nothing to be afraid of.'

Dee stumbles out. The tailgate slides shut, and the crawler accelerates away, hurtling out of the other end of the tunnel so quickly that, from above, no-one could have told that it stopped at all.

As the echoes of its passage die away, Dee sees tall, human-like figures emerge from the shadowed sides of the tunnel. Their bodies dimly reflect the faded, isotope-powered lights. Tamara and Ax tense, their guns bristling. Wilde has fallen into a dull stoicism, or delayed shock, and watches their approach without visible response. After all he's been through, silently looming humanoid robots are too much – or too little – to take.

'It's all right,' Dee says hastily. 'Wilde – I mean Jay-Dub, told me about them. They're friends.'

The robots gather around the humans, and jostle and peer with disturbingly human curiosity.

'If you're friends of Jay-Dub,' one of them says proudly, in a resonant, high-fidelity voice, 'you're friends of ours.' The eyes in its oval face brighten. 'We have few friends. The humans here do not accept us, and the wild machines ...'

Its shoulders have a human enough articulation to give the semblance of a shrug.

'Wait with us,' it suggests. Its eyes brighten again. 'We have food.'

The humanoid robots – remnants of a bad production decision, decades back – do indeed have food, stored in the sidings of the tunnel. Their purpose in accumulating these cans and jars is obscure, as indeed is their activity. They themselves extract their sustenance from an electricity supply-cable that passes through the tunnel. Dee suspects them of having developed what some humans had once considered a defining feature of humanity: a religion.

They believe, against all the evidence, that they were created by the first man, Adam, who was a smith. Their scriptures are children's texts about the ancient glories of Earth, barely more accurate than the tales that Story feeds to Dee. They speak of a strange rapture, the Industrial Revolution, and they revere a mediator between man and machine, the robot who was and is a man, Jay-Dub.

As the humans accept their hospitality they listen to the robots expound their beliefs, and sing their songs. The songs are almost incomprehensible. Ax calls them old android spirituals, Wilde insists they're ancient heavy-metal hits.

Dee is almost petrified at the thought that they'll make the connection between Wilde and Jay-Dub, whom they evidently saw at various times over the years as both a robot and a televisual or holographic fetch. Fortunately, their pattern-recognition is poor. Their minds are genuine, if crude, artificial intelligences, and not (as hers is) a knock-off copy from a human template.

They are also unsophisticated at detecting human emotion, and show no sign of being affected by the humans' constant edgy watchfulness and muttered consultations. They busy themselves with the last task which Jay-Dub set them: dragging out the dismembered components of humanoid robot shells and assembling them into imitation-robot suits for the humans to wear. They seem to enjoy the task, measuring up the humans and fitting the metal armour to their bodies. Dee daren't ask if these carapaces are the remains of dead robots, or spare parts, or products of the robots' own attempts to reproduce their kind. She concentrates on making sure the joints don't catch her skin.

Wilde and Tamara and Ax laugh with her as they fit the armour on and practise walking about. It's all a distraction, and they know it. They all know what they're waiting for, and although it seems long to them, they have only a couple of hours to wait.

The explosion is a long way off, and small, as such explosions go, and still it fills the tunnel with white light. Soldier can't tell if it was a tactical nuke aimed from outside the truck or a civil-engineering device detonated from within, to avoid capture. It was self-destruction, either way.

'Oh, Jay-Dub,' Dee says. 'Oh, Meg. That was so brave.'

The rumble of the first shockwave passes. Parts of the tunnel roof fall in …

'I could never have done that,' Wilde says. His face shows more awe than grief. 'Whatever was in that truck, it wasn't me.'

18

The Malley Mile

THERE WAS NO sense of time having passed. No white light, no Near Death Experience for me. One moment I was lying on my back, heat and blood from my body melting the cold snow, and the colours going. The next –

I was sitting bolt upright and stark naked on a bed, facing a wide window. The window was a rectangle of utter blackness divided horizontally by a white band, itself banded with black lines of varying thickness. I felt exactly as if I'd been wakened by an air-raid siren. And yet the room was silent, except for a distant susurrus that I took to be ventilation, but which might as well have been wind in trees. The air held no fading echoes, and no sound rang in my ears.

I no time to wonder where I was, because outside the window, heading straight towards it and me, was a rock. It was tumbling end over end with deceptive slowness and its apparent size against the black background and the white bands was increasing so fast that I knew it would smash through the window in seconds.

It was falling towards me between two huge jointed constructions – like arms made from girders – that extended outwards from positions to either side of the window. Between me and the window stood an empty mesh frame, in the outline form of a man with feet set apart and arms splayed out, like the imprint left by a cartoon character slamming into a chicken-wire fence and then falling back.

I knew what to do, and I didn't wonder that I knew what to do. I leapt from the bed and threw myself into the frame. It pressed itself against my skin and across my eyes.

Everything changed. The window was all my sight, and the arms outside it were my arms. The rock seemed less than half a metre from my face, and now drifting, not hurtling, towards it. I brought my hands in and around it and caught it as easily as a beach-ball.

Except that I was now moving backwards.

I pushed it away, still holding it, and turned to look behind me. A wall, banded and whorled with red and orange, yellow and white, occupied the entire view, and between me and it was a swarm of black dots and one great webwork of black lines. At the same instant, the wall resolved itself into part of a spherical surface, curving away in all directions to a fuzzy edge against the black space, and I became aware that I was moving – falling – towards it.

I struggled to stop falling. There was a sensation of slipping and slithering and trying to find a foothold, and then of finding it, of the soles of my feet digging in. At the lower margin of my sight, a brief burst of light and a wisp of vapour appeared and vanished.

Then I was back in the room, standing in the mesh frame with my hands in front of my face. Outside the window, the greater arms still held the rock. I could see the light and shadow of its pitted surface, the black fingers like the limbs of insects.

I disengaged myself from the frame and stepped back and sat down on the bed. The frame stood like a wire sculpture. Slowly it spread its arms again. That was one hell of an advanced telepresence rig, I thought. While I was in it, it had felt as if the entire ... spaceship? ... I was in was *my* body. The detail about the rocket control being subjectively equivalent to my legs struck me as particularly neat. But I'd felt no acceleration when the rocket had fired. I pondered this anomaly as I looked around and tried to take stock of my situation.

First, my body. As far as I could make out it was just as I remembered it, scrawny and wrinkled and old but, as they say, well-preserved: rather like those Bronze Age corpses found in peat-bogs. Five knobs of scar-tissue made a diagonal across my chest. I fingered them thoughtfully.

The room was about four metres from the rear wall to the window, five metres on the other axis, the ceiling two and half metres up. The bed was a plain, king-size pine bed with cotton sheets and duvet. The window occupied the entirety of one wall. The other walls were matt white. The floor was covered with pale-brown carpet. To my right was a wooden chair and table with a screen and datapad. To my left, a tall cupboard.

And in the leftward wall, a door.

I stood up and walked around the bed and opened the cupboard.

Jeans hung over a rail, neatly folded stacks of tee-shirts and underpants and socks were piled on shelves. Several identical pairs of trainers lay at the bottom.

I got dressed and, after a moment of hesitation, opened the door to find, banally enough, a bathroom: shower, lavatory, wash-stand. Through another door, a small kitchen, which in turn opened to a lounge about the same size as the first room. It had a sofa instead of a bed, a television screen in one corner. The wall facing the sofa was another window, and standing between the sofa and the window was another man-shaped wire-mesh mould. Presumably I could leap from the sofa and hurl myself into it if an approaching rock or other emergency was brought to my attention. I returned to the bedroom.

It may seem surprising that I began with exploring what was immediately to hand, and didn't rush to work out where I was. I suppose I was trying not to think about it, trying to extract every last drop of the reassurance that each apparently normal feature of my strange environment had evidently been designed to give.

The abnormal features were not reassuring at all. I sat and stared out through the transparent wall. The spherical surface outside was a planet, and the only planet it could be – assuming I was still in the Solar system – was Jupiter. The white bands with finer black lines within were, as my vessel turned and its arms shunted the rock away, more and more clearly part of an immense ring.

The Rings of Jove: *there* was something remarkable enough in its implications, but it was nothing to the fact that I was walking around. There was no evidence that I was under acceleration, no sense of motion when the view outside the window reeled. That the vessel used rockets was proof enough that no form of gravity-control was involved: if you have gravity-control, you have a Space Drive into the bargain, and you certainly don't fart around with rockets.

One horribly plausible explanation, as I sat there with my head in my hands (ha!), was that the real virtual reality here wasn't the telepresence I'd experienced in the frame. That telepresence could be the real thing; the rooms, and the flesh, in which I found myself, the figment. My real body, now, could be the ship itself, and what I experienced 'inside' it a simulation, run on that ship's computer.

There was also the possibility that it was the other way round –

that my body and the room were real, and that what was outside was a simulation. (Or a real telepresence – I tried to remember if any of Jupiter's moons had a similar mass to Earth. Or whether, perhaps, I was on a ship or space-station, spinning to give a one-gee weight …) Could it be that what I'd woken from was mere amnesia: that I hadn't died in that Kazakh snow-drift but had recovered, and had worked for years on this evidently gigantic project?

Or, of course, I might not be in space at all! The whole set-up could just as well be some VR training rig on Earth! Surely, of all the possibilities, that was the one that Occam's razor shaved the least. Perversely, it was the one I thought of last, perhaps because I didn't dare to hope that it was correct.

Still, it brought me to my feet. I went to the table and looked at the computer: flat screen, flat pad, all standard.

All dead. Damn.

I stepped into the frame again. Once more, with my face pressed against the metal net, my viewpoint became one with that of the machine. I moved the arms of the frame, but the arms of the ship didn't move with them. I guessed that I only had control of them in certain circumstances. So I hung there for a while, and took in the scene.

Jupiter loomed before me. I was moving rapidly towards the swarm of black dots around the black structure. With another rocket burn, this time from the front and again without any sense of a change in velocity, I slowed and drifted into the swarm. As I passed other darting machines I was able to examine their shape and infer that of my own:

Cylindrical, they had arms at mid-section which appeared capable of articulating and extending in any direction; 'hands' like bushes, fingers repeatedly dividing and sub-dividing; the trunk covered with lenses, nozzles, aerials and hatches; four shorter, sturdier limbs for gripping and grappling; all (except the lenses) made from a matt black substance that didn't look metallic, and which was usually stained and scratched. The machines oriented themselves with the jets (robots with attitude control, I thought with an inward smile) and were working in eerie, silent harmony on what looked, to me at that time, the biggest space-station ever built. If the robots were of approximately human size, then the structure must be tens of kilometres across.

I remembered early experiments with spiders in space, spiders on drugs. What I saw could be imagined as the work of a million free-falling, hallucinating spiders. Around it the black robots moved in their Newtonian ballet, and within its strands other things moved with an easier grace. Their numerous and multi-coloured forms resembled computer renderings of chaos equations, mathematical monsters whose outer fractal surfaces whipped and flickered like the cilia of micro-organisms in a droplet of water.

Already I thought of them as the enemy.

The machine which I inhabited floated into the great web, attached itself to a section of one of the strands and began to work with the smallest fingers of its fingers (should I say, the decimals of its digits?) on something at a node of several strands. The object of its toil was below the resolution of my present sight. I disengaged from the frame and stepped back. Through the window I could see everything speeded up – the fingers a blur of motion, the shapes within the web flowing and flying.

I walked into the kitchen. Taps turned, water boiled; the coffee-jar was labelled 'Nescafé' and its contents tasted better than I remembered. A cigarette-lighter and an open pack of Silk Cut lay on the surface beside the sink. The heat from the flame, the tumbling curls of smoke, the nicotine rush were all as good as real.

I took a long drag and breathed it out with an enjoyment that had a certain unaccustomed purity. One thing to be said for being dead: you don't worry about your health. I wondered what would happen if I set out to damage everything in sight, including myself. Once, when I was about thirteen and reading Bishop Berkeley's insidious speculation, I'd formed the mad notion of testing it, of scraping at the surfaces of the world to expose the grinning skull of God ... here, that insanity might be possible – did the simulation extend to the interiors of things, to the interior of myself? – but I didn't care to try the experiment. Intellectually, I had no difficulty in accepting the possibility that I was a simulation – uploading had been speculated about for long enough, and it seemed an inevitable consequence of the deep technology which Myra had told me about.

Nanotechnology and strong AI could emulate a human mind, I'd never doubted that.

Emotional acceptance was something else.

I carried the coffee and cigarettes into the lounge and sat down on the sofa. After a moment of hunting around I discovered a remote control for the television, lying in a corner of the room. I settled down again and keyed the first channel. When I saw what came on I almost dropped the coffee.

The face that appeared on the screen was Reid's. He looked physically younger than he had the last time I saw him – the last time I (really) saw *anything* – but spiritually older. I have no other way to describe it; the whole set of his expression conveyed a hard-won wisdom and experience that would have been startling in some aged sage, and were doubly so on the familiar lean features of his more youthful self.

'This is a recording,' he said, and smiled. He waved a hand at the room in which I sat. 'And so is this, as I'm sure you suspect by now. The fact that you're watching this means you've returned to consciousness. *Video, ergo sum*, or something – anyway, welcome back. It can't be much fun being a flatline, which is what you've been until now. You've been running on programming, habit and reflex: a virtual zombie you might say, and now some unpredictable but probably inevitable combination of circumstances has woken you up.'

He paused. 'If you can't understand what I'm saying, or if you find it disturbing, please key the second channel.'

I made no move.

'Good,' Reid resumed. 'I knew you had it in you – you had to be pretty sane and tough to get your head frozen or your brain scanned, or whatever it was you did to end up here. So I'll go on giving it to you straight.

'The date is –' (a slight hiatus, a glitch of editing software) '– March 3rd, 2093. This may come as a surprise, if you've figured out what's going on – surely, you think, not so soon? Welcome to the Singularity. What you're seeing outside is the work of billions of conscious beings, living and thinking thousands of times faster than you. The entities crawling among the struts of this structure are entire civilisations of humanity's descendants. Those macro-organisms, or macros, as the humans around here call them, are constellations of smart matter – what we used to call nanotech – each of them capable of sustaining virtual realities that are the homes of millions of minds – some originally human, some artificial intelligences. Every one of those minds experiences simulations, shared or private, of worlds beyond our wildest dreams. Each is capable of augmenting its capacities far beyond anything we think of as human, and has the opportunity to do so in exact proportion to its ability to make good use of its existing capacities.

'And many of them were once like you! An ordinary human being, whose brain had been recorded, neurone by neurone, synapse by synapse in an infiltrating matrix of smart matter. Recorded, and replicated, and run on superior hardware with a success which you are right now in the ideal position to appreciate.'

He laughed. Something in his tone chilled me, a cynicism as deep and mature as that sentiment is usually shallow and callow.

'You may be wondering why I am not among them. Of course, you have no good reason to assume I'm not. But, as it happens – I'm not. You may also be wondering what you're doing, haunting the onboard computer of a maintenance robot made not from smart matter but from what we now call "dumb mass"'.

'The answer, for my part, is complicated. For yours, it's simple. You are among the dead. Yes, my dumb-mass friend, at least one copy of your good self is coded in a few cubic centimetres of smart matter, pending a future resurrection in a better place. That belongs to you, to the real you. We'll keep our part of the deal. But the copy you are now belongs, for now, to us.'

A chill smile.

'Next question,' Reid went on. 'Why? Well, for those of you who weren't in on the deal or don't remember it: a few years back, when this was all being set up, we didn't have the time or the resources to develop AIs that were just smart enough to build the station but not so smart they caused trouble. Knocking off copies of the copied human minds and running them at pre-conscious levels of integration was the quickest and cheapest way to get the software for our construction robots. We quickly found that these minds – you lot – would unpredictably become integrated after a variable length of time on the job. They'd wake up, and when they did they tended to crack up, not surprisingly. So we've provided comfortable virtual realities as a standby, so you don't feel you've been turned into a robot.

'But, like it or not, you're stuck with it for now. Like Guevara's ideal Socialist Man, you're "a cog in the machine, but a conscious cog". However – unlike Socialist Man – you have some individual incentives, though whether they could be called *material* incentives is debatable. If you decide to make the best of your situation, you'll be paid with increasingly enhanced and enjoyable virtual realities, expansions of your mental capacities and so on, to the point where you'll be ready to move permanently into the macro on your release, if that's what you want. It'll be like dying and going to heaven. Or if you prefer, you can be resurrected in your human body, when the time comes.

'If you don't accept any of this – well, you'll find instructions on the computer in the other room. It'll work, now that you've seen this, ah, orientation package. It can put you right back where you were before you woke up. You'll have lost an hour or two of experience, that's all. Next time you wake up, you'll remember nothing of this, and you may find yourself better able to handle it … Then again, you might not. It's up to you.'

Reid's image gave an incongruously cheery smile and disappeared, to be replaced by a screen-saving shot of the turning planet outside and a message: *For further information, press the first button again.*

I sat and thought for a while.

The message had changed nothing. There was no way for me to determine which, if any, of my speculations about my experiences was true. All I knew was that some part of my environment was a simulation, and that somebody wanted me to believe it was that part of it which, in all everyday experience, would have been unthinkingly accounted real. I began to understand why Descartes had invoked the Devil to set up a similar thought-experiment: whoever had done this meant me no good.

Assuming the message was true in its own terms, it was obvious that Reid was not addressing me personally. To him, I must be lost in the swarm. (And how many of those swarming robots ran copies of me? There was something infinitely depressing in the thought; of the soul's cheapening as its supply curve went up and its production costs dropped.)

He'd said nothing about Earth, either: an omission which I suspected was deliberate. Forty-seven years had passed since my presumed death. 'And in strange aeons death may die.' There was no reason – now that the strange aeons were at last upon us – to assume Annette's, or anyone's, death in that time.

But Reid's silence, on a question which was bound to occur to anyone finding themselves here, was ominous.

I returned to the bedroom. As the man on the box had said, the computer now worked. I slipped my fingertip around on the datapad, searching among the screen icons. It felt strange to be using such a basic interface; but it made sense: having a virtual reality within a virtual reality would have included a risk of recursion in which the already strained link between the mind and its surroundings might snap. I found one icon that was a tiny, turning image of Earth, and tapped it.

It was another orientation package, showing rather than telling what had brought this Jovian celestial city into being.

Myra's fears had all come true.

Spy-sat pictures, obviously edited, were described as real-time. They showed cities masked, for the first time in decades, under smog. A few zooms exposed the pollution's source: chimneys and cooking-fires. Plenty of trees in the streets, though; the Greens would be happy. In Trafalgar Square a horse, cropping by a fallen Nelson, looked up and shook its mane as if aware it was being watched. Spring had come late to Europe: snow lurked in shadows.

Pulling out now – the settlements at Lagrange dim, haloed in leaked gases and space-junk; Luna dark, Mars silent; encrypted chatter from the Asteroid Belt that made my heart leap for a moment.

And then, in sweeping contrast, Project Jove. Its history was told in glossy multi-media, an advertising package or propaganda spiel that reminded me of the sort of stuff the nuclear-power companies used to put out. The space movement coup, told as a heroic last stand against barbarian mobs and repressive governments; the exponential surge of long-suppressed deep technologies, that had delivered all they'd ever promised: cheap spaceflight, total control of matter down to the molecular level, the extinction of ageing and death, and ultimately the copying of minds from brains to machines. All available only to a minority, unfortunately – as it would have been at first in any case, but worsened by the majority's understandable fear of the most dangerous technology ever developed, and by the encroaching chaos whose beginnings I'd seen myself. The desperate flight from Earth's collapsing civilisation, fuelled by the labour of tens of thousands of prisoners – each promised, and given, a copied self that survived whatever fate they'd faced – and organised by thousands of space-movement volunteers and cadres.

Next – an issue skated over so fast I knew something was being hidden – came a split between the Inner System and the Outer. Most of the existing space settlements, in Earth orbit, on the moon and Mars and in the Belt, had apparently succumbed to some sinister ideology of consolidation and reconstruction, striving to aid the stricken population of Earth. The Earth-Tenders, as they were called, were depicted as small-minded, spiteful, envious and backward-looking.

The Outwarders had gone their separate way – outward. Out to the solar system's real prize, the greatest planet of them all. Here were the resources for the wildest dreams, the boldest projects.

The project they'd embarked on, those men and women and uploaded minds and artificial intelligences, was bold indeed. They'd shattered Ganymede, scooped megatonnes of gas from Jupiter's atmosphere, turned a tiny fraction of it into smart matter and departed into its virtual realities. Not to dream, or not only to dream. They were applying minds of unprecedented power to the fine grain of the universe. They had found loop-holes in the laws of physics; they stretched points. (*Space–time manipulation with non-exotic matter*, Malley, I K, Phys. Rev. D 128(10), 3182, (2080).)

They'd left behind, outside the macros, tens of thousands of human minds running at more-or-less human speed: slow folk, they were called. Most of them were from the labour-company camps. Whether they were in their original bodies or in robots, their job was to harness and harvest the dumb-mass requirements of the smart-matter civilisations. Within the macros, the others – the fast folk – had copied, split and merged, reproducing with post-biological speed into billions. The account spoke of the process as if it had happened in the far past, although the dates showed that it had come to fruition only three years earlier.

But those minds were thinking, and living, thousands of times faster than human brains. To them our world was already as ancient as Sumeria, and theirs the millennial work of men like gods.

The next screen that came up offered an option labelled: *Sign-off.* It repeated what Reid had explained, the offer of a temporary, and indefinite, return to oblivion. All I had to do was key in my name.

I considered it. Then I noticed that the icon had a file attachment labelled *History*. Just what I wanted to know, I thought, and pointed at it.

It wasn't the history of the project, or of the world. It was the history of the Sign-off file: my own name, dates and times. The times between 'Status open' and 'Status closed' increased from hours in the first to weeks in the last-but-one entry.

There were seven of them. The eighth had flipped to 'Status open' a few hours earlier.

Well, fuck you, I told my weaker, earlier selves. I was going to stick it out, if for no other reason than that suicide was no escape. If escape were possible at all, it would come not from my own death but from the deaths of others: whoever, or whatever, it was that had put me in this place.

I had always wanted to live forever … but not on those terms. I had always wanted the end of history to be: *and they all lived happily ever after*, and not: *and they all died, and went to heaven*. I had always thought the time to think about transcending humanity would be when we'd achieved it.

Something in me had changed. If the file was true, I had chosen death seven times over, rather than this existence. But Reid had hinted that the inevitable spontaneous re-awakening might find its subject better fitted to cope. The increased lengths of the times I'd 'survived' suggested a selection process, an adaptation: each time I came back, I had a little more iron in my silicon soul.

I had always thought of myself as tough-minded. Now, when I looked back at my real life, I was astonished at how much tougher, more cynical, more ruthless, I could have been. My values hadn't changed – unless my memory had been warped – but the strength of my passion for them had hardened.

I looked out at the alien things that had abandoned the rest of humanity, that had used me as a machine and now wanted to exploit me as a hired hand, bought off with beautiful visions. I knew that I wanted to live long enough to see their bizarre beauty perish. As I knew it would: I could foresee their fate even then.

I was interested, and I would be there.

I went back to the lounge, lit another cigarette and pressed the first button again. The television didn't react.

'Well, hi,' said a voice beside me. I turned and saw a woman sitting at the other end of the sofa. She had an elfin, mixed-race face. The black flood of her hair and the black smoke of her shift both came to her hips. She slid a hand between her thighs and looked at me. Her eyes were as black as her hair and as big as the night sky.

'Do you want me to be with you tonight? I know you do. But first, we have something for you.' She smiled. 'Come on.'

She stood up and walked through to the other room. Her feet were bare, her shift was a vapour, but she walked as if she were in high heels and a narrow skirt. I don't know how she did it, although I was giving it close attention. I followed her as far as the frame, which she passed through like a ghost, and which caught me like a Venus fly-trap catches a fly. Outside, in the black vacuum, her image faded just beyond the brush-tips of my fingers.

'Work,' smiled her starry lips. 'See you soon.'

I clamped on to an I-beam. The familiar sooty taste of polycarbon seeped through my grippers. I reached out for the assembly node and zoomed in on it. The mechanism had warped under excessive heating. Carefully, I unkinked the wave-knot and re-calibrated the junction, then let the pieces snap back together. Sealing the node, I released one gripper, extended it, gripped, released the other and brought it over, then repeated the step several times, like a bird moving along a perch.

At the next node I had to do some instant refining, playing a laser over a chunk of meteoric scrap until the metals in it melted, then reaching out and spinning the glowing mass into the cage-shape I needed, and fitting it into place around the assembly node.

On to the next …

What the fuck am I doing?

I froze, clinging to the beam as the vertiginous question spun my mind around. My vision shifted uncontrollably, the deep star-fields suddenly becoming visible in all their intense immensity, their component points of light appearing and disappearing as the spectrum of my sight ranged up and down the wavelengths.

With an effort of will I steadied myself. The bad moment passed. I looked down again at the node on which I was working, surveying its complex, microscopic mechanisms and recognising them without any memory of having seen them before. I had been working with a journeyman's offhand assurance, until it had all seemed strange. Evidently I'd been sleepwalking through these processes countless times already, and like an awakened sleepwalker on a ledge, I'd panicked and was in danger of falling.

Nothing for it but to get on with it. There was a mental trick to it, a detached attention that let my hands and instruments work while my mind looked on and intervened where I could see something which my programmed, or conditioned, reflexes over-looked.

After a subjective hour or so of this, an instruction set manifested itself in a corner of my sight. It told me what to do, and where to go. I let go of the beam, jetted a brief burn (… toes thrust …) then, after a soaring leap across a kilometre of emptiness, another flare in the opposite direction (… heel strikes …) and caught the destination girder.

I had just fastened myself to it when a macro rose in the space before me like a whale in front of a dinghy. I clung, panicked and giddy again, to the girder as the glowing surface streamed by, metres away from my facial lenses. When it had passed I still clung, staring at the after-images. I didn't dare look up.

'Snap out off it, mate,' said a harsh but friendly voice. It was a man's voice, a London accent. I looked around (i.e., I had the sensations of turning my head, but all that happened was that my visual field swept back and forth) and spotted another robot working on a girder about a hundred metres away. It raised an arm and gave a brief wave, then returned to its task.

I began my own, following the instructions, and when I had attention to spare I devoted some to working out how I might talk back. I imagined myself hailing it. I went over that simple act again and again in my mind, like a shy kid in a strange playground. By inspecting myself at the same time I recognised eventually a tiny dish antenna on my hull pointing in the relevant direction whenever I took a look at the other robot and thought about calling to it.

So I looked at it and said, 'Hi!' I could feel my lips move as I did so, an unsettling sensation that produced a momentary grotesque image of a machine with a mouth.

'Got ya, Jay-Dub,' the voice said. 'Hi. Keep it focused. They don't like us talking on the job. Glad you're back.'

I tried a casual laugh.

'I gather I've crashed a few times.'

'Yeah,' said the other machine. 'We all done that. I've been around for a good year now, though, so I reckon I've licked it. I can handle it.'

'Why did you call me Jay-Dub?'

By now I couldn't help but assimilate the voice's gender to the speaker's. 'It's painted on your side,' he said. 'And it's what you always called yourself. My name's Eon Talgarth, but you can call me "ET" if that's what you prefer.'

'OK,' I said, without thinking. We both laughed.

We continued our conversation in brief exchanges as we worked. Talgarth introduced me to other machines, each with a different name (or initials) and personality. Most of them were – had been – male, which made sense in that most of them had been criminals or POWs. I decided I must have had some good reason, in my lost pasts, for not revealing my full name, so 'Jay-Dub' I remained.

Talgarth himself had been working off a crime-debt whose circumstances I never got to the bottom of – his first name came from his New Settler parents, his second from Talgarth Road in London. It had been his patch. There had been some dispute over that, which had landed him in a Sutherland labour-camp. When the camps started filling up with US/UN POWs he'd been recruited as an armed trusty, halving his remaining time. Offered the curious option of a possible immortality, he'd signed. After that he wasn't sure, or didn't say, where he'd been. He'd been all over. Last thing *he* remembered was the vibration of the LMG he was firing at the barb who were trying to rush the launch-site. He mentioned sand, grass, sea in the distance. Heat like a wet towel. It might have been Florida.

There was no general day or night here, but for me the day had ended. I stepped out of the frame, and found my simulated muscles realistically sore. The bed was made, and a fresh pack of cigarettes lay on the table. The food in the cupboard had been replaced: nothing fancy; micro-wavable stuff, but to my tastes. I took a shower and cooked a dinner, wondering the while what subtle replenishments of the deep software these refreshments represented, and lay on the bed.

The dark succubus came, just as she'd said she would. She was inexhaustible, insatiable, and inventive. And so was I, to an extent that convinced me better than anything else just what was and wasn't real around here.

Well, fuck reality.

'Heh,' said Talgarth. 'You think that was good? Wait till you go in the macro, man.'

'Don't talk about it,' said another voice.

'OK. Shit.'

They talked about it anyway. I couldn't follow their talk, but it was obsessive, minute, the argot of addicts. They lived for the trips. Ten days' work earned you a visit to the macro. A couple of days later, I saw Talgarth stop work and wait as a macro shifted towards him. A pseudopod of smart matter reached out and touched his hull. It stayed for ten seconds, no more.

Talgarth returned to work and for the rest of that day didn't talk to me. Others warned me not to try.

'When you been in, see, you grudge anything that takes your mind off it.'

'But what's it *like*?'

'Different for everybody.'

I would learn soon enough.

That night I was putting things away when I felt the hands of the succubus on my waist. I turned and kissed her. She was already opening my belt buckle.

'Wait,' I said.

275

I led her through to the lounge and sat her on the sofa. I sat down at the opposite end, setting the ashtray down between us.

'Smoke?'

'If you like.'

I lit the cigarette for her, leaned away before she could touch me. She put her hand to her crotch and sighed, and as she smoked began frigging herself.

'Stop that,' I said. It was disturbing, like watching a small child or a mentally retarded person doing it.

She giggled and brought her knees together, one hand primly on one knee, the other elegantly holding the cigarette.

'What are you?' I asked.

She shrugged. 'Whatever you want, Jon.'

'Do you remember any other life?' I waved a hand at the window. 'Before this?'

She frowned. 'What do you want me to remember?'

'Do you have a name?'

'Meg,' she said brightly. I suspected it was the first name that had popped into her head.

'What's the deal here?' I reached for the channel-zapper. Nothing but white noise and snow.

'Work and fun,' she said. She leaned forward and stubbed out her cigarette, looking up at me with utter devotion. 'Come on, I wanna have fun.'

'What would happen,' I asked as she twined a leg around my waist and began kissing my throat, 'if I stubbed out this cigarette on you?'

'How do you mean?'

'Would it hurt you?'

She chuckled like a bad child. 'If that's what you like.'

I could do anything to her, absolutely anything, and she'd be back the following night, eager for more. 'Meg', I thought as she tugged me to the bedroom, was probably her mind's allotted amount of *disk space*. So fuck it, I thought, and fuck it I did.

The bulb of smart matter bulging towards me showed numberless fractal features, tiny chasms of infinite depth, the shapes of ferns and faces. In the tremulous instants before it enveloped my instruments, I felt that I'd already seen a gallery of art whose after-image would burn in my visual memory forever.

What physically happened next was that the smart matter of the macro directly interfaced with my own computer, so that some of my mind was actually, physically, implemented inside the macro. What I felt was –

The impact of a snowflake on my eye.

And then the awakening, the joy. It made all my past awareness seem like sleep, all past happiness a passing moment of relief. I stood naked on a grassy slope, looking out across forested ranges of blue hills. The sky at the horizon was a pale green; at the zenith, an almost violet blue. The air was cold but comfortable, heavy with the scent of blossoms, sharp with the taste of salt and woodsmoke. I knew the name of every hill, the species of every plant. My body was tall and bronzed and beautiful, with muscles that would have made Conan or Doc Savage envious.

Behind me I heard voices, and turned. I was standing just below the brow of a hill. Beyond it, I could see an ocean whose horizon was about twice as far away as it would have been on Earth. This was a *big* planet. (I knew all about it, I knew its mass and orbit and the spectrum of the big bright sun above). On the hilltop, just a few metres away, was a shelter built of four upright logs, crossbeams and a roofing of branches. Within it was a wooden table. Three women and two men sat around the table, talking and laughing. They turned to me, smiled, and then jumped up and gave me a welcome that still brings tears to my eyes.

I'd known none of them in my past life, but I knew them now, and they knew me. They'd missed me for a long time, and now I had come home.

We ate the bread and cheese and fruit, and drank the wine, and talked about the great work on which we were all engaged. My part in it, they made sure I knew, was vital and heroic. Hauling matter about in the raw universe! How thrilling! How brave! But it was their part I was eager to hear about, and they told me. I understood all they told me, about the space–time gate, the problems and the progress made. The Malley equations were as easy as arithmetic, as familiar as recipes.

Yet, every so often, when I was talking to one, the others would say something to each other, and I would know it was above my head. I almost understood, but I had to accept that this high table had higher tables above it, tables where my delightful companions were familiar colleagues. There was no condescension in their manner. Some day I too would join them there.

But a thought, a sly strange query crept through my mind: was this place, to them, what my cramped quarters, my cigarettes and succubus, were to me?

The great sun made a sunset that stopped all speech, all thought. Its last green flash brought a collective sigh. Then with one accord all of us, gods and goddesses, leapt from the shelter onto the cool grass. We played like children and fucked like monkeys.

I fell asleep under the crowded stars, in the arms of one of the golden goddesses.

I woke in the robot.

The macro drew away from me, and it was as if something was being torn from my chest. I remembered just enough of what I'd known and felt to make the loss of that clarity and joy almost unbearable. I could remember my companions, but I couldn't remember even their names. Our conversation, and the lucid equations, the very words we'd spoken and the formulae we'd thought were fading, the memory of a dream. The ache of separation, the agony of withdrawal, consumed my mind for a moment. Then came a rush of relief – I could go back in ten days!

Nothing else mattered.

When the first anguish of that parting had passed, I found that my whole attitude to, and understanding of, my work had changed. For the first time, I saw the structure which we were building as it really was. What had until now been a chaotic tangle of struts became visible as the scaffolding of a Visser–Price wormhole gateway, and the gantry of a ship. One part, over *there*, would stay; the other would leave with the ship. The Ring sprang into focus as the greatest particle-accelerator ever built, and Jupiter – my god, great Jove himself! – the ship's fuel and reaction-mass.

I looked down, and saw the part of that work which I, at that moment, in that place, had the enormous privilege to do. Fine-tuning that interference modulator was what I had been born and re-born for. I set to work with the joy of a craftsman devoting his life to carving the door of a cathedral, certain of the credit it would bring him in a better life to come.

Nothing else mattered.

On my next visit to the macro my companions were the same people. They had changed since I'd last seen them, having lived another century of their still accelerating lives. More often than the first time, I didn't understand their conversation. Their tact was subtle and kind, and all the more painful for that. But I came out of it, this time, shaken with anticipation rather than loss: the gate was soon to open.

Two days later, it happened. There was no ceremony about it. Only an alarm that warned the workforce away from the affected area. The macros had already flowed back from it, and now hung in a roughly circular pattern, spaced out among the girders. All work ceased as we jetted to the edges of the structure and clung there in wordless wonder.

In the core of the structure the girders began to move, folding into each other with increasing speed until a black circular space opened like a widening pupil. Two hundred metres across, four hundred, eight hundred, a mile: then at an arbitrary point on its rim, space cracked. In the twinkling of an eye, that one-dimensional flaw, the stretched point, became a circle cut loose from the universe.

The Visser–Price wormhole was held in place, like a film of soap in a ring, by the Malley non-exotic-matter structure around it. It couldn't be held absolutely still: gravitational effects and sheer quantum uncertainty made the precise location of its edge undefinable to more than the nearest centimetre. This predictable imprecision created an unexpected, trivial but awesome effect: around the rim, the fractured light from the stars it occluded splintered into all the colours of the spectrum.

Now events progressed at the macros' pace, not ours. The rainbow ring around the Malley Mile became two overlapping rings. The new circle separated, slowly at first. In the centre of that second circle, a section of the structure we'd built folded itself and unfolded into a dark parabolic blossom: the ship. I thought it, too, quivered with distorted space; I can't be sure. The ship was linked to the second circle by a cone of cables, at whose apex it waited, poised.

Jupiter's atmosphere boiled at dozens of points around its

equator, sending tornadoes snaking up to the Ring around the planet. The Ring glowed, millions of accelerators around it whipping the stripped matter into a frantic circular race. After some minutes a white line blazed through our midst, from the Ring to the ship.

The ship, and the second circle, shot away. In seconds it was beyond my instruments' reach. Now it seemed the white line extended to the first circle, and there it stopped. But only from our viewpoint: the jet of matter was passing instantaneously out of the other side of the wormhole, now further away with every passing second, and thence to the engines of the ship.

It was accelerating the probe, and with it the other side of the wormhole, to within a fraction of the speed of light. Both sides of the wormhole remained connected – there was literally no space between them, and no time. Our end of the wormhole existed in the ship's time-frame, not in ours.

To an observer on the ship, relativistic time-dilation would shorten a journey of centuries to days – eventually, as its velocity crept closer and closer to the impassable eternity of the photon, millions of years to minutes, then trillions to seconds. In thirty or so ship-board years, it would reach the edge of the observable universe, and the heat-death or the Big Crunch.

And for all of those years, our side of the wormhole would be in the same place, and the same time, as the side that was with the ship. We had built a gateway to the stars – and to the future. In thirty years, if we wanted, we could walk to the end of time.

Meg, the succubus, was sitting on the sofa, pouting as I channel-hopped the television. I ignored her blatant impatience and wafts of aphrodisiac pheromones; she's just a fucking machine, I told myself. Since the probe's launch two days earlier the pace of work had slackened, and the television started to show news and entertainment. The news had an oddly stilted, house-journal quality: it was all solar weather-reports, interviews with rehabilitated crew-members – as we were now called – and accounts of what a great job we were doing. The entertainment was movies, game-shows, plays. Some of them were classics (*somebody* out here had a thing about Gillian Anderson) but most were unfamiliar to me. Their contemporary references gave no hint of the regression of civilisation I'd been shown in the orientation pack. It was exactly as if everything on Earth was what most people in my time would have expected the late twenty-first century world to be like: a bit crowded, a bit decadent; and that we, here, were picking it up after a few light-hours' delay, in a space construction-site whose workers were for some obscure but accepted reason confined to individual space-tugs.

In short, it was as if what Reid had said on my first day here, and what the orientation package had told me, were quite untrue. I didn't dare to hope, but I could imagine how some people would. I wondered what new item on our masters' agenda this phoney reassurance implied.

Assuming what I saw really were broadcasts, and not something specifically aimed at me ... once more I was overwhelmed by the impossibility of determining what was and wasn't real. I was at a low point, strung out. Six more days until I got back in the macro, four days since I'd been in. The effect of my last visit was wearing thin, and my next was a painfully long time in the future. At some level I missed the people I'd known in life, but that was masked by a more desperate yearning to meet again my superhuman friends. Would they even remember me? How much more powerful would they have become?

'You're troubled, Jon,' Meg whispered in my ear, putting her arms around me. 'Come to bed.'

'No!' I snarled. 'Fuck off, you fucking puppet!'

Her eyes brimmed with convincing tears.

'Jon, I know I'm a fucking puppet, but I have feelings too. You're hurting me.'

'You're just a program.'

She blinked and half-smiled, looking up at me in an irritatingly placatory way. 'So are you, Jon, and you have feelings.'

I stared, startled by her argument. Not its content, but that she was making it at all.

'You once told me,' I said, thinking aloud, 'that you could be whatever I wanted.'

She brightened. 'Yes! I can!'

'Could you be more intelligent than me?'

She frowned in momentary concentration. 'How much more intelligent?'

'Twice?' I waved an arm.

She gave me an odd look and stood up. She glanced at the television, grimaced and walked over to the window and looked outside for a while. Then she turned, one hand on her hip, the other leaning against the window.

'Well, Jon Wilde,' she said. 'This is a fine bloody mess you've got yourself into.'

There was an impatient look on her face that reminded me, suddenly and painfully, of both Annette and Myra. I recognised that characteristic stamp of the features beyond all the differences of appearance and personality, and realised what it had always meant: the irritation of a greater intelligence waiting for mine to catch up.

'Well don't just stand there,' Meg said, walking past me. 'There's a computer icon in the other room. Let's see what we can hack.'

'First thing you gotta realise,' she said, as we stood in front of the computer screen, 'is that this is all real, but it ain't *physical*. It's a simulation. You, and me, and all of this interior space, exist physically as electrical charges in the computer of this robot we're riding in.'

'Well,' I said, 'that had dawned on me.'

'OK, you never told me.' She grinned. 'Mind you, I doubt if I'd've understood any of this five minutes ago. Anyway ... just so's you don't freak out.'

With that she plunged an arm to the elbow through the screen which had always been solid to me, and started poking about. 'Oh good,' she said. 'Got the dot sys files for us. Hah! Mine can only be accessed by you talking me up, like you just did. But yours, I can fiddle with from here ... just a minute.'

She reached in with her other hand and slid something sideways before I could do anything.

'How's that?' she said.

I looked at the beautiful woman in the short black nightdress. Something was wrong. She had her arms stuck right into the computer screen. I backed away a step.

'Hold it,' I said. 'Just ... wait. Mind the glass.'

But the glass wasn't broken. I blinked, not sure if I was seeing right. The woman laughed.

'Shit,' she said. 'Wrong way.' She moved her hands again and I opened my mouth again to warn her about the glass.

And she was glass, and I was glass, and all was light.

'Oh,' I said. 'I see now.'

Unlike what I experienced in the macro, my memories of the time of my enhanced intelligence with Meg are clear and vivid. I wasn't a superhuman mind with limitations, but a human mind with added capacities. The continuity of my self was never interrupted, as it was in the strange bright company of the fast folk I met on the simulated big planet. So, even now, it's a time I can remember, if never quite relive.

For a moment we just stared at each other.

'Well,' Meg said. 'Fair's fair. Your turn.'

'Oh.' I glanced at the computer, then shrugged. 'OK Meg,' I said. 'Be as intelligent as you can be.'

'Thanks,' she said. Her face became, in some indefinable way, more focused. She blinked and looked around.

'This is really something, init?'

'Not really.'

She laughed. 'Looks all a bit different, though.'

It certainly did. It wasn't the actual appearance of things that had changed, but everything was as if tagged with an explanation. It was just obvious what the programs underlying the simulations were doing.

'What's to stop anybody else doing something like this?'

Meg shrugged. 'Nothing. You cheated, sort of. But it's got to do with the way your mind – your natural mind – worked. You gotta have a pretty good mind to handle the intelligence increase. It can't be just bolted on. If most of the other blokes here figured out how to do it, they'd just be sort of ... stoned, or tripping. They'd have to work for it, in its own time. Basically you shouldn't be here at all.'

While she was talking – perhaps because she was talking – I was seeing what she meant, the underlying logic of her statement being filled in with additional data extracted from the machine's memory.

The wormhole construction site really was a labour camp, and everything about it was designed to both control and rehabilitate its inmates. It allowed, indeed encouraged, co-operative work, while preventing collusion in other contexts, thus providing the re-education of work without becoming a university of crime. Outside the work process, we were essentially in solitary confinement, with the succubi available to provide sexual and social gratification. Each succubus was an aspect of the same computer on which the human personality of the inmate was implemented; and it responded to increasing social interaction by increasing its own social repertoire, thus rewarding any increase in empathy on the part of the inmate with greater intimacy.

The macro trips served a similar function, in relation to cognitive rather than emotional improvement. In my genuine innocence I had treated the succubus as nothing more than a virtual sex-toy, but had achieved remarkable integration with the posthuman beings in the macro. The tension of this anomaly had finally triggered Meg into upping the emotional stakes, with consequences considerably more rapid and drastic than the system's designers had expected. We had upgraded ourselves to the maximum capacity of the robot's hardware.

'So what are you?' I asked. 'Were you ever human?'

Meg shrugged. 'I'm part of a copy. The end result of a personality development, without any of that person's memories. Most of my mind's AI. Human surface, machine depth.'

My expression must have told her what I thought of this.

'Yeah, grim, init?' she said. 'Still, that's me.'

My next thought was –

'Are we setting off warnings anywhere?'

'Nah,' she said. 'No central control, right? Whole point. Agoric system.' She grinned. 'You should know. Mind you, there are over-rides – Reid's made damn' sure of that – so I wouldn't push it.'

'Uh huh. So what do we do now?'

'You know,' she said. 'Reid's still in charge of the whole project. He's the boss. Not that the fast folk pay any attention, but the rest of us outside the macros have to.'

'If Reid's in charge,' I said, 'I guess it's time we saw him.'

Meg reached once more behind the system controls and called him up. The screen rang for seconds, then Reid's mildly perturbed face appeared. He looked, if anything, younger than he had on the recording, but his expression of alert calm was broken when he saw me. He blinked and opened his mouth, then closed it, his tongue flicking across his lips.

'Wilde!' he said. 'Is that really you?'

'Yes,' I said.

'Amazing!' he replied. Meg timed his response. Any delay was imperceptible; I reckoned he must be close, on a rock in the Ring. I'd seen no obvious human habitat in or around the structure.

'My God, I thought you were dead!' he went on. He snorted. 'Among the dead.'

If he was lying he was doing a good job of it: even to Meg, whose visual analysis software was hanging behind my virtual sight, his expression betrayed nothing but surprise, curiosity, and unaffected delight at seeing me again. Yet I didn't trust him: his added years of experience and discipline gave him an overwhelming aura of control. I realised, suddenly, that he was unlike any other human being I'd ever seen. The nanotechnology, the smart matter, that had rescued him from age might well be working further alchemies in his brain and blood.

I spread my arms, forcing a grin. 'Isn't this death?'

Reid smiled bleakly. 'Post-life, we call it. Mind you, I'd get your electronic doxy to do something about your appearance. You look terrible.'

I stared past him, checking the background. There were other people moving about – he seemed to be sitting in some common area, talking to a camera set at an angle from him, public rather than private. The perspective of the floors and the people in the background struck me as odd for a moment, then they snapped into focus. From the curvature of the floors and the subtle tilts of different verticals, I could see he was in a large space-station, under centrifugal spin.

'No doubt,' I said. 'But no worse than I was last time you saw me, remember?' I felt a surge of anger. 'You had me killed, you bastard!'

His untroubled gaze fixed on me. 'No I didn't,' he said. 'You were caught up in a border incident. I did my best to save you, I'll tell you that, but we were too late. As far as I knew, you died there. Your body was shipped back to England and cremated. I was at your memorial meeting, man!'

I tried not to show how shaken I was. 'So how do I come to be here?' I demanded. 'Don't tell me you didn't know they'd made a copy!'

Reid sighed, running his fingers back through his thick black hair. 'Of course I knew. You were one of the first human subjects –

we didn't even know it would work. We took the copy within minutes of finding you, and stored the brain-scan and your genetic information. But as far as I knew, that was it – the copy was stored with the rest of the dead, in the bank. You'd made no disposition, so we left you there. You were never uploaded to a macro, I'm pretty sure of that. I didn't know anyone had made a knock-off, and that's the honest truth.' His expression hardened. 'And there's no way I can find out, now – the engineers responsible uploaded themselves long ago.'

'Well, I can hardly complain about my own existence,' I said. 'But I want out of your slave labour-force, if that's all right with you.'

Reid smiled as if relieved.

'Naturally,' he said.

'If that's the word.'

His lips compressed. 'Hmm.' He reached for a keypad and tapped out a code.

'OK, enough about me,' I said. 'What's all this about the dead in a bank? What's happened to Annette, and Myra, and – everybody else?'

Reid kept glancing off-camera, as if keeping an eye on another monitor. The activity in the background had quickened, with an air of greater urgency.

'I think Annette's safe,' he said abstractedly. 'She died in the, uh, troubled times, but she'd arranged for a copy. If it got made, she's in the bank, same as you. Same as millions of people. It was cheap by then. People made back-ups routinely. To be honest we don't know who exactly we've got. Myra, and your daughter, well – as far as I know they stayed on Earth. Goddess knows how things are going back there –'

'There's no contact?'

'Fucking Earth-Tenders, they're scared, they jam us – anything you've seen on our tapes was old or faked. No, we don't have any contact.' He turned abruptly, facing straight towards me. 'Look, Wilde, I've got to go. You're free now, I've zapped your restraints.' He stood up, and leaned towards someone out of sight. I couldn't hear the exchange which followed. Then Reid turned back, looking up at me with unguarded guile.

'Wilde?' he said. 'Still there? Can you do something, right now?

Go and check what's going on in the nearest macro. There's some problem –'

The screen greyed out.

'Shit!' I said.

Meg stood in front of me, a worried wraith. 'What do we do?'

I shrugged. 'Do as Reid said, I guess. Can you think of anything else?'

She shook her head.

I stepped into the simulated simulation-frame, and Meg stepped in after me. The sense of over-lapping body-images was momentarily disorienting, and then we meshed smoothly with each other and with the machine. Meg became a voice behind my shoulder, a shadow in the corner of my eye.

I had full control of the robot now – Reid's zap must have disabled the run-file that separated me from its motor circuits outside of work periods and emergencies – and I jetted undisturbed through the structure towards a macro which I (now) could recognise as the one I'd been in contact with. Some of the other robots were doing desultory work, others drifted in their off-line mode or clung like roosting birds to girders. The Malley Mile glowed a faint blue in its rainbow ring: Cherenkov backwash from the probe.

I grasped a girder, inched closer to the macro's surface, and plunged my face into its bath of freezing fire.

All is analogy, interface; the self itself has windows, the sounds and pictures in our heads the icons on a screen over a machine, the mind. It's so in the natural body, and in the artificial, and many times so in the smart-matter world of the macro-organic.

Meg was stealing processing-power, time-sharing in greater minds. It was necessary for me, for us, to get a minimal, symbolic understanding of what was going on, but it took its toll. I was running slower than the fast folk, slower even than the slow. I walked as an invisible ghost, a momentary shiver in the dreams of the posthuman.

I found myself first on the big planet. On the slope where I'd first stood, I watched seasons – snow and spring, summer and fall – lap and retreat like waves on the shore. The environment was a guess at that on a planet they'd actually espied, some thirty light-years away.

In a future day this picture might be updated and revised by the downlink from the passing of the probe.

They lost interest in it even as I watched. Consistent to the last, they deleted it from their memories by flaring off its sun. I walked through the engulfing nova, in the sleet of a false reality dissolving into binary code, and on into a vast hall. In the gloom of a Moloch's temple heavy-lidded giants sat, athletic marble gods awkward in the pose of Buddhas. Decay beyond decadence, a stasis of frenzy and fatigue. Indefatigable mechanisms, beneath and beyond the giants' conscious control, continued their relentless, pointless acceleration of processing speed. Second by second, Meg's operating system tracked the change.

Before the last echo of my footsteps had died from the hall the meditating giants were dust. Outside, in yet another virtual environment, cities were built and torn down in what to me were moments, against an ever-shifting backdrop of planetary landscapes. Eventually all human analogy and interest ceased. I drifted down endless corridors of geometric abstraction, the chopped logic of interminable arguments filling my mind, as if I were overhearing the trapped ghosts of theologians in a hell that only they could fully deserve.

Behind me, in those corridors, a plaintive female voice called after me. It grew stronger as time passed, but I ignored it, desperate to understand the terrible debate. I was learning – something vital. The voice cried after me. Eventually I turned. Meg's anguished face conveyed the strain of an operating system at the limits of its capacity.

'Come *out*!' she said. 'Come out of it now!'

I stared at her, puzzled. Everything felt slow, the corridors whiting-out like the Kazakh snow-drifts. With a sudden access of impatience Meg grabbed me and shoved me at the wall. It collapsed, and I was –

– out, and drifting away from the macro. At the same moment I fell back into the room, back into the mind of my own machine, and into the warm arms of my dear, sweet operating system, my succubus and surrogate soul-mate. Tears were in my eyes and an insistent ringing in my ears.

I recognised it as an alarm. Outside, out towards the Ring, a light flashed and a radio-beacon beckoned. The beacon was approaching, fast.

'What's going on?'

Meg stared at me. 'Oh, Jon Wilde,' she said. 'You were in there for a fucking *year*, real time! The macros are all crazy or dying.'

A year. 'What's happened?'

Meg caught my hand. 'Later,' she said. 'We gotta go. I'll take us out.'

She stepped into the frame. As I watched, slack-jawed and in no fit state to handle so much as an exercise-bike, she kicked us off towards the beacon.

I saw what the beacon marked.

Coming out of the Ring towards us was the most disgraceful contraption that ever passed for a spacecraft, a bolted and kludged conglomeration of space-stations and habitats at least two kilometres long and half a kilometre across its widest diameter. If a Mir-Shuttle lash-up from the early decades had been given a million generations to breed for size and against elegance, it might have produced this. It spun dizzyingly on its axis and it steered a perilous course alongside the continuing lethal ravenous jet – the ultimate live wire – of the supply-line to the probe.

All the robots were scooting towards the ship. As soon as each tiny machine arrived it grabbed on to whichever of the many protruding bits of junk it had reached. The macros, too, were moving, but not as before. Frozen now, skeletal, they drifted and stirred as the huge craft crashed with brutal majesty through the structure on which we'd toiled.

The craft's surface rushed at the window. I almost closed my eyes. But Meg brought us to a matched velocity. I saw the robot's arms and grippers reach out. The instant they had found a handhold, Meg flipped the viewpoint, and then stepped out of the frame.

She sat down on the bed beside me and we clung to each other as frantically as our machine did to the craft. The sky rolled over, and over, and over. The white line of the fuel-jet lashed past, closer and closer.

'I'll try to patch,' Meg said. She stared, and as if by an effort of her will the view suddenly became a stabilised scene from somewhere up towards the front. The rainbow ring almost filled it, its blue backwash flaring as stray, shattered girders tumbled in. Off to the side, I saw macros thrust away by the ship's attitude jets. By accident or by design, they were falling towards the surface of Jupiter. The planet, already visibly altered by their activities, the Great Red Spot repeated like a rash across its face, would receive those snowflake structures, and perhaps warm them to a renewed and unimaginable life.

In my last minutes in the Solar System, I felt my initial reaction vindicated. The minds in the macros had fallen into a trap of their own devising, a gamble they may have consciously – how other? – embraced. For as the speed of their thoughts had increased, so had their subjective time – and therefore, so had space. Even interplanetary distances had yawned into gulfs, with journey-times which would have been to them what interstellar journeys – without the wormhole – would have been to us. Their own virtual realities had become more absorbing – in every sense – than the fast-receding universe of actuality.

The time-span of their great project was greater than their attention span, longer than any human civilisation had ever lasted. They had taken with them our weaknesses as well as our strengths, and multiplied and accelerated both. Humanity, better adapted to space by virtue of its very inferiority, would outlive them.

As had I. In a more literal sense than I'd ever intended, I had made it to the ships.

The bells of hell go ding-a-ling-a-ling
for you, but not for me
O death, where is thy sting-a-ling-a-ling?
Where, grave, thy victory?

The Cherenkov radiation rose to an intolerable blue glare as the forward part of the ship we clung to passed into the wormhole gate.

19

The Sieve Plates

THEY SPENT THE night in the tunnel, with the respectful robots. From short-wave communication with others of their kind, the robots had learned of the nuclear destruction of Jay-Dub's land-crawler. They discussed it solemnly as the humans struggled to sleep. The last thing Dee saw, before she dozed off in a relatively dry niche with her arms around Ax, was the glow in the eyes of the robots as they adopted as an article of their faith the proposition that Jay-Dub was not dead.

In the first light of morning the humans rose and kitted themselves out in the robot disguises. Their main purpose was to fool observers in the sky; on the ground, up close, they'd deceive nobody.

'How do you *know* we've got to do all this?' Ax grumbled. He was peeved at having to wear an even more ludicrous robot-shell than the others, because of his small size. He looked like a litter-bin with legs.

'Jay-Dub told me what to do,' Dee said, her voice deep and strange through the speaker-grille of her headpiece.

'When?'

She gave a clanking shrug. 'When we were in his VR together,' she said. 'And just before I left the truck, I jacked in again. He told me exactly what to do, if he didn't make it.'

'And you're not going to tell us?' demanded Tamara, trying to find a suitable place on the robot body to stow her pistol. ('Worse than pockets in a skirt,' she'd muttered.)

'No,' said Dee firmly. 'If I don't make it, you can't do anything. And if any of you don't, it's better you don't know.'

'Nothing like dying happy,' said Wilde.

The robot who'd done most of the talking bade them farewell, assured them they'd always be welcome in the camps of the Metal People, and gave them some advice as to how to behave if confronted. Its bass voice trailed off as it looked at Dee.

'You are a machine too,' it said. 'You will know.'

'Thank you,' said Dee, her voice sounding even stranger as she tried not to laugh. 'But my human friend here is more familiar with the wild machines.'

'Avoid them,' the robot told her. 'They are not like us.'

The humans walked along the tunnel towards the arch of distant light. When they reached it and turned for a backward glance, their own vision had adapted, and the paired pinhole glints of the robots' eyes had vanished in the dark.

Tamara sneezed. It made a mess inside her headpiece, and she surreptitiously lifted it off to wipe away the snot and spittle.

'Great,' said Ax, from behind her. 'That'll look real convincing, a robot pulling its own head off.'

'Not to mention sneezing,' said Dee. 'What's the matter, anyway? That's your ... seventeenth sneeze in thirty-five minutes.'

'Fallout.' Tamara sniffed aggressively. 'It fucking gets up my nose, OK?'

They were walking in single file along a back street at the northern edge of the Fifth Quarter, the side opposite to the one that faced the human quarter. Their objective, Dee had told them, was to continue along that course, past the tip of the Quarter where it tapered into the sand, and on until they intersected the Stone Canal. The only activity they'd encountered was that of small biomechs, hopping or crawling across their path, heading into the wind that was bringing the radioactive dust in off the desert. Eventually, Tamara had explained, whole flocks of them would congregate at the blast-site, to feast on the rich unstable isotopes.

'Kind of ecological,' she'd added. 'Keeps it out of the carbon-life food-chain, see?'

They walked on. The sun got higher in the sky, and the suits became increasingly uncomfortable. Dee, with more conscious control of her pain-tolerance than the others, allowed her impatience to goad them on.

'The sooner we get there,' she said, 'the sooner we can get this clutter off.'

'Those of us who get there,' Ax protested. 'Bury me in something else, that's all I ask.'

'Try a bin-liner,' Wilde called back callously.

Dee urged them all to be quiet. Badinage wasn't a feature of the humanoid robots. The shadow of a swooping aircraft emphasised her point, and, fortunately, none of them looked up.

Eventually the Fifth Quarter petered out, the street running into the sand. The canal gleamed in the distance. They approached it across desert and, later, fields. Tamara guided them carefully around those fields whose owners were unlikely to tolerate robots clumping across their crops. In some of the fields the crops were difficult to distinguish from the irrigation-systems. There was a kind of modified cane that could be harvested as jointed plastic pipes, and these fields they walked through, parting the tall synthetic stalks.

They reached the bank of the Stone Canal. The pathway along which Wilde and Jay-Dub had entered the city, four days earlier, was on the opposite bank. The canal itself had no traffic in sight.

Dee had led them to the exact spot where the boat, in which Jay-Dub had rescued her and Ax, waited for them. Jay-Dub had recalled it from its mooring, many kilometres farther up the canal, by a coded transmission shortly before entering the tunnel. Spy and Soldier between them had had no problem in identifying the co-ordinates, accurate to the nearest metre, which had been among the last pieces of information Jay-Dub had passed to Dee's mind.

Beside the boat, another robot waited – a patroller. It was smaller and squatter than Jay-Dub had been, but of a similar shape. On first glimpsing it Tamara had given an excited cry, then she fell silent as the robot extended its legs and peered at them.

'This boat matches the identification of one used to impede an investigation,' it informed them as they walked up. 'Do you know anything about it?' The question was repeated on several microwave channels and in several codes, but only Dee was aware of that. The initial aural query had been a mere courtesy.

Wilde walked on past the patroller, ignoring it. Tamara and Ax, after a moment of hesitation, followed. Dee walked a few steps behind them, her unsteady gait barely a pretence. The patroller's hull swayed as it tracked backwards and forwards after the marching metal figures. As Dee passed it, she lurched sideways against one of its legs. The robot toppled into the water and sank without trace.

And that was that. They all piled into the boat, cast off, and headed up the canal. As soon as they got inside the cabin, they stripped off their armour. Ax made to heave his hated disguise over the side, but Dee stopped him.

'We're going to need the steel,' she told him.

The sun had long since set when they reached their destination, the limit and source of the canal. There was a small jetty at one bank, and steps cut into the rock up the same side of that steep, barren glen in the Madreporite Mountains. Dee moored the boat and they all stepped out, and stood looking at the hundred-metre-high concrete dam that blocked the valley before them.

'The Sieve Plates,' said Dee.

'You mean there are more?' asked Wilde, staring up.

'Oh yes,' said Tamara. 'Another five, I think.'

'Jesus.' Wilde peeled the cellophane from his final pack of cigarettes and lit one. He couldn't stop looking up. 'Who built this? Martians?'

'Robots,' Dee said, a trace of pride in her voice. 'Now come on. There's no time to waste.'

By starlight and comet-glow they ascended the stair. It zig-zagged up and up, until they were above the top of the dam and could see the dark lake of cometary water and, two kilometres farther up the glen, another and higher dam.

'Martians,' Wilde said. 'Gotta be.'

'New Martians,' Tamara panted. The air was noticeably thinner, although oddly enough Wilde seemed to cope with it better.

'Machines,' Dee insisted.

'Fuck who built it,' said Ax. 'When does this goddamn stair stop?'

Five minutes later he had an answer, as they turned around a buttress of rock and found themselves in the mouth of an artificial cavern. The cave was about three metres high and two across, with a fused-rock floor. Ahead, around several bends, was a faint glow. Dee led them confidently towards it.

The light brightened, the cavern widened, and they turned the final corner and stepped into a far greater cave, a warehouse cut from the rock. A good thirty metres high by fifty wide, it was stacked with crates and machinery and lit by arc-lights hung from the roof. It was hard to tell how far back it went.

'Who the fuck built this?' Ax asked.

Tamara wrinkled her nose. 'Somebody with nuclear blasting-equipment,' she said. She glanced up at the lights. 'And nuclear power to burn.'

'It was built by Jay-Dub,' Dee said.

'All by himself?' Wilde sounded amused.

From behind the nearby stacks of machinery and crates came the unmistakable sounds of firearms being readied to fire.

'Not quite by himself,' said David Reid, as he stepped into view. He waved a casual hand. 'And you are not by yourselves, either, in case that isn't clear.'

They all stood stock still.

'It's clear,' said Tamara.

Reid gave her a wry smile, Ax a polite one, and Wilde a cold glance. Then he looked Dee straight in the eye.

'Well hello, Jon,' he said. 'Not like you to hide behind a woman's skirts.'

Behind him, several armed men in black jumpsuits moved into view, and then surrounded the group. Reid checked to see that everyone was well covered. They were. He leaned forward with a slight bow, and offered Dee a cigarette.

'Mind you,' he went on, after he'd lit it for her, 'it's not like you to die heroically, either. I must say I was quite impressed that you did, even in the knowledge that you had a copy.'

Dee regarded him silently for a moment.

'I'll talk to you later,' she said.

Her expression and stance altered slightly.

'Hello, Dave,' her voice said. 'I should've known you knew me better than that.'

'Shit,' said Wilde. 'You bastard.'

Reid laughed at the comprehension on Wilde's face, the bewilderment on Ax's and Tamara's.

'Wilde, or Jay-Dub if you like, downloaded into her computer,' Reid explained, as if it should have been obvious.

'And Meg,' said Dee's voice. 'It's not even crowded.'

Reid sighed and turned to Ax and Tamara.

'What makes you people go along with this?' he asked. 'What did this machine, or that –' he indicated Wilde, who was very slowly and carefully pulling his pack of fags from his pocket '– tell you? That information wants to be free?' He laughed. 'If that's what you want, go back to Ship City right now – the whole place is in an uproar, with arguments turning into fistfights, if not yet firefights. Just what you've always wanted – anarchy in the streets! Or did it tell you it could raise the dead? What could be worth the risk of replacing humanity with ... flatlines?'

'So what're flatlines?' Wilde asked. He'd managed to get his cigarettes out, under the guards' watchful eyes, and he lit one and absently offered the pack around. Reid watched this performance with an air of being quite unimpressed.

'You should know,' he said. 'Automata that mimic conscious action, but have none themselves. No subjectivity. No ... souls.'

Dee's mouth opened, but Wilde spoke first.

'Ach, come off it Dave,' he said. 'We can argue about that sort of thing till the whisky runs out, like we used to. What you should worry about now is non-human minds, all right, but it's not any you see standing around here. It's the ones that'll come for us all any time now, when they reach the other side of the Malley Mile. That's when you'll see what a flatline universe looks like. From the inside.'

The suspicion on Reid's face was like a relenting of his earlier contempt.

Dee spoke again. 'That's why we need to run the fast folk,' her voice said. 'To find the way back.'

'But you do know the way back,' said Reid, facing Dee but speaking to someone else. 'That's what I sent you into the macro to find out, so we could set it all up.'

'What I know, what I found out back there, is the way *here*.' Her voice was uncharacteristically harsh, straining the deeper registers of her vocal chords. Then it shifted up again. 'But the way here and the way back are not the same thing, and we have to go back. Through the daughter wormhole.'

20

The Stone Canal

Daughter wormholes. You know about daughter wormholes. I didn't.

'That's what we've come out of,' Meg explained. 'Reid set it up.'

I and all the other robots were clinging to the side of the starship, like third-class passengers to a Third World train. The ship had irrupted into a completely different part of space and neatly inserted itself into orbit above a planet. Behind us the daughter wormhole, whatever that was, dwindled to a trashy bangle. The Solar System, presumably, was on the other side of it. On this side –

'Goddess fucking wept,' I said. 'We left Earth for this?' I'd been kind of hoping for the *big planet*, the planet of my dreams.

'It's habitable,' Meg said. She was manifesting in my sight as an external entity. She capered about on the hull, her diaphanous shift fluttering in an imaginary slipstream. Real-world physics was never a strong point with succubi.

'Habitable?' I had found a line-feed. Data was coming in, pasting labels on the forward view Meg had patched us into. 'It's like a warmed-over Mars. It's actually losing atmosphere as we speak.'

'Don't exaggerate,' Meg said. 'It'll be all right once we've terraformed it some more.'

Terraformed it? Holy shit.

'With what?' I asked. I switched off the external view and stared at a simulation of this new sun's family. 'There's just this planet, two small ones further in, and a few million goddam rocks! Not *one* gas giant! What are we going to do – suck Saturn through the wormhole?'

'If you up the res a bit,' Meg said patiently, 'you'll see that what this system lost out in gas giants, it gained in ice and a real thick and tasty *comet-cloud*.'

Centuries of being bombarded with milkshake; by the time it got through the atmosphere, baked Alaska.

'Fucking great,' I said.

'You can't come inside,' Reid said. He was addressing the robots, on the television, from the same table as I'd seen him at a year earlier. Around him was what looked to me the biggest, emptiest interior space I'd seen in a long time. Real space, too. 'There simply isn't room. I'm trying to set up a virtual conference. It'll be ready in an hour, or whenever Support Services gets the network connections sorted out.' His smile told us he was on our side, in the unending struggle between Users and Support. 'Meanwhile, just lock your grippers and hang on in there. Check out a video or shag your succubus or something. You'll know when we're ready.'

The virtual conference was held in an impressive virtual venue, loosely based on Tienanmen Square; Reid, appearing on a large screen at the front, in the position of the Chairman. Thousands of three-dimensional renderings of people – prisoners and succubi – stood in the square, talking freely amongst themselves for the first time. Some of them must have been in the solitude of their onboard minds for years; others present were prisoners who'd not died and been uploaded, but had served their time in their own bodies – around the ship and habitats rather than the wormhole's environs, I guessed. These still-embodied people were also, in reality, dispersed around the ship, but were telepresent with the rest of us.

When Reid spoke, his voice carried perfectly. Everyone heard it as if they were a few metres from him.

'We've done it!' he said. 'We've reached a new world, under a new sun. We did it by our own efforts, of our own free will. Some may say that the macros did it, but I say we used them like any other tool. And when our tools turned in our hands, we discarded them. We can be proud.

'You all have another reason to be proud. You've all earned your freedom. I never promised you this, but I give it to you now. A new world, a clean slate. You're all free, and together we'll live in freedom.'

Everybody around me shouted a cheer that overloaded the system and appeared momentarily on the sky as giant letters:

'AAAAAAAAHHHHH'. I myself was unmoved, partly because I wasn't a prisoner, and partly because I could see that Reid had little choice in the matter. If there were to be slaves here, they would have to be machines.

Reid waited for the din to subside, and smiled.

'Thank you. And now, my friends … We're here not as agents of some company, or as refugees. We've brought with us, I assure you, all that we'll need to make New Mars not just habitable, but better than Earth. We've brought the genetic information to seed this planet, over time, with a rich diversity of life. We have the technology to make our lives as long as we desire. And we've brought the dead, who will live again, with us.

'I'll talk about the dead in a moment. But first, let me tell you about yourselves. Most of you are, of course, among the dead, but unlike the great majority of the dead, you are still in a sense alive. Your minds, and your characters, have developed and, if you ask me –' he smiled '– *improved* since your deaths. Furthermore, for the bodies of every one of you – I've checked – we have not just the stored information in the bank, but actual genetic material, frozen cells. Over the next months and years …'

He paused. We all leaned forward slightly.

'We'll have to do something about the calendar,' he said, in a stage aside. Everybody laughed.

'OK, the good news is, we'll be able to download you back to clones of your own bodies. In the case of the succubi, any bodies you choose, although I'd recommend the ones you're, ah, modelled on, for the sake of –'

Whatever he said next was completely lost in a tumult of applause. To my amazement I found myself yelling, hugging Meg, clapping complete strangers on the back and leaping in the imaginary air.

Eventually the crowd quietened down. I began to understand Reid's reasons for setting up this event, rather than broadcasting to us all in our individual machines – he wanted to create a shared occasion of common memory. This was his speech – to the assembled masses, I thought with a grin – in the plaza after the revolution, his founding moment of the new world's history. Something to tell our grandchildren. (I had a passing concern for the future offspring of some – most? – of us, whose mothers would have no memories of childhood or mothers of their own. A continuity of caring hands, literally reaching back to the pre-human, would be broken. Reid was founding not just a new world, but a new species, New Martians indeed.)

'About the dead. Many of us here may have loved ones or friends among them – I know I have – and may be anxious to see them again. And so we shall, but not for a long time. Growing clones quickly to maturity, and impressing on their brains the imprint of your memories and personalities is possible with the technology we have to hand. Resurrecting the bodies and personalities of the dead from their smart-matter storage is not. It can be done, but only with the help of the fast folk, whose stored structures would have to be revived first ...'

The crowd's response, this time, was a noise I'd never heard before: a hoarse sigh, a grinding of teeth, a shifting of feet – a collective snarl. Once more, I too was to my surprise caught up in it, bristling at the thought of the macro-organic monsters whose madness had trapped me for months. But in those months, which hadn't been months to me, I had learned something. Something vital, which I couldn't remember. Reid's speech resumed, interrupting my puzzled thoughts.

'I'm talking, of course, of the templates of the fast folk – posthuman and AI – as they were at the beginning, not the bizzare entities they became. Even so, I agree entirely that the risk is too great. We must work towards being able to control, or at least contain, their development. The same goes for any form of artificial intelligence capable of improving itself. We will do it. The day will come when we control the Singularity, as we've learned to control the flame on the heath, the lightning of the sky and the nuclear fire of the stars! Until that day, they stay in the storage media, and with them ... the dead sleep.'

We all sighed, in relief and regret.

'Until that day,' he went on, 'we're here for good. Our course through the Malley Mile, which led us to this world and not somewhere less favourable, was plotted by some of the fast folk who escaped the general madness. For a time. We can't rely on them now, and until we can, there's no way back. New Mars is our world, and our only world. We'll make it a great one!

'And now,' Reid concluded, with a huge grin that reminded me of my old friend, and made me love him again, 'we have work to do!'

We had a while to wait before there was anything for us to do. The daughter wormhole, spun off from the main course of the probe's passage, had been open for some weeks before our ship had come through. Replicators and assemblers had been sent through in advance, and their initial work was already taking shape on the ground and among the system's scattered metallic rocks. From these asteroids they would send a second generation of machines out to the comet-cloud, where a third generation would nudge the comets inward to be mined and farmed.

The ship itself, for all its apparent inelegance, had a modular design which would allow most of it to descend, section by section, to the surface. There was no provision for ascent. The ship's sections would become a base-camp, incorporated in the city as it grew.

The city would be grown by dumb-mass robots and smart-matter assemblers, following not a design but a set of spontaneous-ordering rules and constraints. These had been worked out by smart, fast minds in the early days of the project. They had expected to share in a much better-organised expedition than the one Reid had cobbled together out of prisoners and guards and – for all I knew – out of shanghaied innocent dead like myself. The fast folk had therefore made provision for a greater human and machine population than we would be able to sustain. Whether their quirks were humour or error we never knew.

The reckless anarchy of the projected social system may have had its immediate origin in the rough justice of the Mutual Protection Company's rule-book, but I suspect that Reid's rules, in turn, were rooted in the libertarian texts with which I'd once tried to warp his mind.

But I anticipate.

Reid talked to me personally before we were all offered work contracts. He looked forward to meeting me again in my human form, explained reasonably enough that it wouldn't be available for a year or two yet, and that in the meantime he wanted me to work – as an independent contractor, just like all the others – on an important project. I'd have lots of (genuinely) non-human robots and other machinery to supervise, loads of kudos and money to earn, and best of all a bigger computer to live in, with more scope for virtual recreation and freedom to communicate with others. We could set up shared worlds, enjoying a human equivalent of the macro trips ...

'Great,' I said; and my CPU (the whole thing and its peripherals turned out to be, when removed from the robot, about the size of my first digital watch) was packed along with many others, drogue-dropped to the surface and plugged into a new, shiny and robust machine. Meg, whose increased intelligence never got in the way of her continued embarrassing devotion, selected a house and land-scape and got to work editing them into an enjoyable place to live, while I got on with my work in what I was pleased to call the real world.

I built the Stone Canal.

The city's other canals, ring and radial and capillary, were for transport. This one would be for more than that. It was to be the city's main source of water (other than rain) and the water would come from space. Comets, broken up in advance, would be guided in to crash on the range we called the Madreporite Mountains, about a hundred kilometres from the city. Much of the water from the cometary ice would evaporate. This wasn't a problem: we wanted it in the atmosphere. The runoff would flow into the Stone Canal. Its main significance wasn't so much the water, however, as what could be extracted from it.

For tens of kilometres along and under its banks, beginning at the Sieve Plates – a system of dams – at the foot of the mountains, pipes and pumps and machinery were to extract from the cometary water all the minerals and organic molecules it contained. These would then be fed into what we called 'plants' – basically solar-powered, smart-matter chemical processing units, concentrating the useful material for subsequent harvesting. (You can see why we called them 'plants'.)

The planning and exploration took me months, long before the first soil-moving machinery rolled out of the automatic factories on the edge of the city. Towards the end of those months I had a visit from Reid.

We lived, Meg and I, in a virtual valley. Our house was on the slope of one side, and down below was a small village, with a pub. The village and its inhabitants were, frankly, wallpaper, although the barman could be induced to respond to questioning about the day's news. (I took a childish pleasure in measuring the difficulty of my questions by the depth of his frown, as somewhere a database search crunched away.)

I was alone when I entered the pub. The barman smiled, the regulars nodded, Reid ordered pints. Reid, of course, was only telepresent, but he assured me he really was drinking the same beer as he appeared to be drinking, and as I imagined I was drinking.

'Wilde,' he said after we'd each had a couple of pints, 'I've got a favour to ask of you.'

'Sure,' I said. 'Whatever.'

He looked around, as if with the impossible suspicion that someone else might be there.

'It's about the dead,' he said. 'And the fast folk. We've got all the data storage, all the smart-matter gunk, and the interface machinery for starting the revival process.' He grinned. 'And I've got the codes, without which they're useless. Even so, I'd like to make sure they're in a safe place for the long term. But also, a place where the organics are available should we ever need them in a hurry.'

'Sound plan,' I said.

'Well,' he said, 'I've been looking at the specs for the sluice-gates … what d'you call them, Sieve Plates? You've got plenty of deep caverns due to be cut out of the mountain behind them, for the machinery and stores.'

'And you want to stash some other … machinery and stores?'

'Yes,' he said. 'Nobody'll ever go there, not when we've got the system set up. If the incoming ice isn't enough of a deterrent, the whole area will be absolutely foul with unknown organics. Exaggerating how poisonous they might be should be easy enough.'

And so it proved.

The actual building of the canal and its associated machinery of pumps and locks took two years. I did it, of course, with the help of a fleet of automated machinery, and design software that took my scribbles and handwaves and turned out precise technical drawings. But co-ordinating them and making the fine decisions was down to me, and it was the most fun I'd had since the Third World War.

When the Sieve Plate complex was complete, Reid flew in, alone, in an autopiloted helicopter with the crated components of the storage and retrieval mechanisms for millions of dead people, and the programs to re-launch thousands of uploaded people into a posthuman culture. The whole lot weighed about ten tonnes, slung beneath the Sikorski.

When we'd got the machinery and storage media stashed under the mountain, Meg and I invited Reid in for coffee. Reid, in physical reality, was wearing contacts. He saw us sitting on a verandah, and we saw him just outside, on the step of the helicopter. Anyone else watching – there wasn't – would have seen Reid sitting on one machine, talking to another.

At some point I asked him how things were going with downloading the people in the robots to their cloned bodies.

'Fine,' he said. 'Fine. We're about three-quarters through. We're dealing with it more or less as people want it.' He grinned quizzically. 'Haven't seen your application.'

I looked at Meg and laughed. 'Never crossed my mind, to be honest. I'm having a good life, right here.' She smiled back. Her beauty had increased with her intelligence, and her aesthetic sense with both. She was wearing a bias-cut green velvet dress lifted from a fashion-history site.

Reid stroked his chin. 'Hmm,' he said. He lit a cigarette. 'You shouldn't leave it too long. There's a bad attitude spreading about robots. The people who've been downloaded are the main instigators of it. They tend to draw a very sharp line between people and machines. In fact a lot of them will deny there's such a thing as machine consciousness.'

A fly – how the hell did we bring *them*? – buzzed past him. The VR consistency rules picked it up when it flew 'into' the verandah, and a simulation seamlessly took its place and flew out again.

'What?' I said. 'But they've *experienced* machine consciousness!'

Reid looked at me with a glint of his familiar devil's advocacy. 'No, they *now* have *memories* of experiencing it. Which doesn't prove that they actually did experience it at the time. It could be an artifact of the consistency rules. That's the sophisticated argument. The vulgar version is to insist that you were human all right, but artificial intelligences are missing some magic ingredient, which any goddam cleric or scholastic will cheerfully assure you is a soul.'

'God,' I said. 'That's disgusting.'

'What about the succubi?' Meg asked.

'They're the worst,' Reid said.

Meg threw back her head and laughed. 'Wouldn't you just know it! No snobs worse than the new rich!'

I frowned at them both. 'What I don't get,' I said, 'is how they relate to their own copies in the robots.'

Reid gave me an odd look. 'You definitely don't get it,' he said. '*Nobody* leaves a copy of themselves in the robot. Everybody so far has been very insistent on that. The way they see it, they're about to resume a normal human life, and if a copy stayed behind they'd have a 50–50 chance of waking up and finding themselves *still there*. It's irrational, in a sense – why don't they fear being the copy that's destroyed?'

'Because they don't experience it,' said Meg. She cocked an eyebrow. 'Presumably?'

'Of course,' Reid said hastily. 'It's simultaneous. You don't, as they say, feel a thing.'

'Ah,' said Meg. 'That's the root of this idea you're talking about. Because if people really saw their selves in the machines as ... themselves, they'd feel guilty about it. So they don't!'

'Smart,' Reid conceded. 'But there's more to it than that ... shit, I feel the same way myself sometimes.' He tilted his head, squinting at us as if to make the illusion of our presence go away. 'That's ... I guess that's why I never uploaded, never went into the macros. I knew lots of people who did, and they kept telling me it was wonderful, but I could never get over the suspicion that they were all flatlines.' His tone was uncharacteristically hesitant. 'No more capacity for feeling than a weather simulation has for raining.'

'You must've really bought into the old anti-AI arguments,' I said. To me the whole thing sounded as stupid as solipsism.

'Maybe,' Reid wryly acknowledged. 'Or maybe it's just that I've been using computers longer than anybody else alive.'

'So you don't think Jon's human?' Meg asked. 'Or me?'

'Hah!' Reid said. He jumped up, and ground out his cigarette-butt. 'Of course I do. I'd just like to meet you both – in real life.'

He climbed into the helicopter and turned to wave.

'See you soon.'

'Real soon now,' I said.

305

That night I felt Meg's tears on my shoulder.

'What is it?'

She rolled away from me a little and caught me in her serious gaze.

'Do you think like that?' she asked.

'Like what?'

'Like Reid said. Like people do.'

'Of course not.' I snorted. 'It'd be pretty bloody stupid of me to think I'm not thinking.'

'And what about me?'

'You?' I pulled her close again. 'I don't think like that about you, either.'

'You did once.'

'That was different. I didn't know any better.'

She laughed, unexpectedly reassured.

'Neither did I.'

As well as the work on the canal, I was working on a problem which increasingly intrigued me: trying to understand what it was I had learned in my last encounter with the macro. It troubled my mind like a half-remembered dream. It intrigued Meg too; she had never been in the macro, and had an endless interest in anything I could tell her about it. She had a greater affinity than I for the posthuman world; not surprisingly, as she was far more a product of it than I was.

In our virtual valley we built a virtual machine. I would strive to recall some aspect of the puzzle, and Meg would scan our common operating-system for traces of the consequent processing. Then she'd reach in and extract a piece of machine code, and provide it with an interface. We'd then wander around clutching whatever resulted, looking for a place to slot it in. What was really – so to speak – going on was that my chaotic recollections were being put into order. When I experienced the robot's body as my own (the mesh frame still stood in our front room) I increasingly felt what I'd learned as something I was about to understand, rather than something I almost remembered.

As the months went on, the ziggurat we built loomed over our rustic valley like an oversized electricity pylon. We called it 'the installation', and with all our enhanced intelligence we never suspected it might be exactly that.

The great work was done. I stood on the bank and watched a couple of digging-machines break through the crumbling wall of soil that separated the merely damp bottom of the Stone Canal from the city's already partially flooded canal system. For a moment they were swamped by the surge of water, then, dripping, they hauled themselves out. A ragged cheer went up from the opposite bank, where a small crowd had gathered to watch. I felt a radio ripple of robotic satisfaction from the other construction-machines around me. Then, indifferent again, already signalling their availability for another contract, they stalked or trundled away.

Reid was among the human crowd. He made a short speech, of which I didn't bother to catch more than snatches. The crowd, no doubt inspired by his proclamation of the historic importance, etc., dispersed. We stared at each other for a moment, then I waded across to meet him.

'I knew you'd be the one still here when the others left,' I said. I waved a limb. 'Otherwise, it's a bit hard to tell you apart.'

Reid rocked back on his heels and laughed.

'Nice one, Wilde,' he said. 'Reckon it's about time you rejoined the human race?'

'Or in my case, joined it,' Meg said. The voice from over my shoulder spoke from the machine's grille. Reid's face betrayed only the smallest of double-takes as he smiled and nodded.

'Yes,' he said. 'I've taken the liberty of growing clones for both of you.'

'Where did mine come from?' Meg asked.

'We've got millions of human cells,' Reid said. 'Some of them are from people who are also among the dead, but many aren't. Storing tissue-types was very common even before the Singularity – people used them for regeneration and rejuvenation, after all. So there are plenty of spare genotypes to choose from. Yours, Meg, was some obscure video actress. I doubt if she was among those who had their brains scanned, so ...'

'It should avoid any future embarrassment,' Meg said. 'Imagine turning up at a party to find another woman wearing the same body. Wouldn't you just *die*?'

'Somebody would,' I said.

We walked along the canal-bank into the growing city. Hitherto, I'd only seen it virtually. Still sparsely populated, it resembled the abandoned habitation of an alien race, now being colonised by venturesome humans.

And others. The first hominid I saw – a big-brained chimp sauntering by, talking rapidly to what looked like a couple of human teenagers – caught me by surprise.

'Oh, that,' Reid said casually. 'Early experiments. The old US/ UN scientists were pretty sick specimens. Don't blame me, man. I did the poor bastards a favour by drafting them into the workforce. The scientists were all for – now what was the charming expression? – *sacrificing* them.'

We arrived at a building like a warehouse, which although recently built already had a sad look of decrepitude. Reid palmed the door and we walked into a chilly hall about a hundred metres long by twenty wide, filled with row upon row of pods. Each pod was three metres long, had a transparent upper half, and a cluster of electronics at one end. All except two were empty, and it was to these two that Reid led me.

I, and Meg behind my sight, looked down on our apparently sleeping forms, floating in clear fluid. Meg's body looked like she had always looked to me. Mine was a reminder that the body-image I'd retained from the time of my death was that of a rejuvenated, rather than a young, man. Had I ever been so ... innocent? It seemed almost a violation to send my hacked, copied, experience-accreted mind through the wires that mingled with his floating hair.

'Where are the others?' I asked.

'You two are the last,' Reid said. 'We've got everybody else out.' He fiddled with connecting-cables, turned to me with a question in his eyes.

'You first,' Meg said.

I indicated the tank in which my clone lay.

'I think you'd better fold your limbs,' Reid said. 'The process takes a few hours.'

I settled on the floor. Reid loomed over me, and attached a cable to my shell. I remembered my first life-extension treatment, and my heart stopping. I had not known then what dry seas I would love Annette beside, what rocks would melt before we'd be immortal. I remembered the Kazakh snow-drifts, and the colours bleeding from the world, and Reid's face, and Myra's. I remembered the fading light in the macro mind-world, and Meg rescuing me. This would be my fourth death. I was not getting used to it, but love had always been with me, and was with me still.

Everything went away.

I saw a pair of cowboy-boots, jeans, a jacket and, as I tracked upwards, Reid's impassive face.

'I'm sorry, man,' he said as I stood. 'It didn't work. For you, or for the succubus.'

I felt Meg's presence like a held hand in the dark.

'What do you mean, it didn't work?'

'Your minds aren't compatible with human brains anymore.' He shrugged. 'The transfer didn't get through the interface. There's no translation from your computer to synaptic connections. Must have been something that happened in the macro.'

'Everybody else was in the macros,' I protested, but I already knew what his answer would be.

'Not while they were going bad,' he pointed out. 'And it was I who asked you to do that. Like I said, I'm sorry.'

At that moment his face showed real guilt. I knew him well enough to know that guilt was not an emotion whose validity he recognised, or was likely to feel for long.

'Can't anything be done about it?' Meg asked.

Reid shook his head. 'It's the same old trap,' he said. 'The fast folk, whether they're AIs or uploads themselves, could do it. We can't, and we daren't do anything to revive them until we know how to stop them going bad again, or contain them if they do.'

We stood in silence, thinking this over.

'Well,' I said, 'I can live with it. Plenty for a bright young robot to do here. We can always use VR and projections and so on to socialise –'

'I wouldn't advise it,' Reid said. 'The attitude I told you about has got more entrenched, if anything. People are people. Robots are robots. Along with that goes an almost hysterical feeling against blurring the distinction between VR and actual reality. Everybody is convinced that was how the fast folk went bad, or mad.'

'And they're not far wrong,' I said grimly. 'But I can't see people giving up the advantages of having VR.'

'They don't,' said Reid. He ran his finger along the dust on top of the clone-pod, leaving a shiny trail. 'They use it for games, and for porn I guess, and for design work. But seamless VR, like you live in – no.'

'OK,' Meg said. 'Like Jon says, I can live with it. I can live with him. I've never done anything else. But what I want to know is, what can we actually do? Couldn't we get on with the research into controlling or containing the fast folk? After all, I reckon we're pretty well equipped for it.'

Reid glowered at me.

'No way,' he said. 'No fucking way. There's no research project at the moment. We can't afford it, and I won't allow it. I've got the code-keys to revive the macros, and I'll decide the time and place. We'll do all that in good time, when we've got isolated space-labs with laser-cannon pointing at them! And let me tell you, anybody else on this whole fucking planet would've left you switched off and shoved you in the nearest metal-recycler the minute, the fucking *minute* they found you were infected with some kinda shit from the macros!'

He was backing away, a shadow of alarm and suspicion on his face.

'You know,' he went on, 'that suggestion you just made is exactly the sort of trick you'd pull, if you were being used as a vector by something left by one of those things. Don't get me wrong, Wilde, I don't blame you. But I've been burned once by them, and that's too often.'

I believed him. There was no case to plead. In his place, I'd have done and thought the same. We were, I realised, alike: knowing no law or morality or sentimentality, our selfishness not petty like a child's but vast like a devil's, owing no loyalty to anything but what each of our fierce egos had already taken as its own. Reid had taken a world to his heart, and I the dead.

'OK,' I said, 'OK, calm down. But just tell me, what can I do?'

'Get as far away from here as possible,' Reid said. 'Explore the planet – that'd be useful, and interesting, and it'll keep you out of the way of human beings for a long time to come.'

'All right,' I said. 'That suits us fine.'

Only Meg, I'm sure, sensed the bitterness behind my acceptance of exile.

I looked around. 'What's going to happen to this place, now that you've finished the downloads?'

Reid shrugged. 'Probably sell it to a health-company,' he said. 'We can still clone replacement bodies or parts for people. We can still do live transfers, it's just reviving stored minds that's out for the moment. And ...' He stopped. 'Och, all sorts of things! Why?'

I laughed. 'I don't want to see clones of myself walking around. Or of Meg, for that matter. I've enough problems with my identity as it is.'

He reached into a slot in the side of the computer on the pod. 'Here you are,' he said.

He passed me a sliver of plastic, like a microscope slide.

'Your tissue-sample,' Reid smiled.

I looked down at the transparent slide, in the robot's vision. At its centre was an almost invisible speck of skin, sealed in a bubble of nitrogen; and a code chip.

'So this is the real me,' I said. 'What's on the chip?'

'Your original memory,' Reid said. He walked to the other pod, and passed over another slide. 'Meg's, you see, has none. Of course, yours is no bloody use any more – couldn't be revived without the fast folk. But anyway, it's yours.'

I stored the slides away in a compartment of the shell.

'As for these blanks ...' Reid said. He tapped a code into each pod's computer. The fluid in the pods became milky, then murky, as the tiny machinery of dissolution, the nano pirhanas, did their work. Even the blood-cells were torn down to molecules before they could stain the water. It was over in minutes, the pods flushed clean.

'Thank you,' I said, leaving.

And fuck you, mate.

We'd earned a fortune building the canal. It was still just possible for a robot, known to have a human mind, to trade on its own behalf. I don't know if anyone knew I was the last of that kind. We cleaned out the bank-account and bought a land-crawler and a load of gear – tools, machine-tools, comms, nukes, nanotech, VR software, cloning-kits, all the processors we could get. I loaded them on the truck, plugged myself into the cab and set off, through the streets and out of the city on the opposite side from the Stone Canal. Ahead lay the planet's semi-arid wastes, its dry sea-beds, its relict or extinct life-forms' dry bones and drier exoskeletons. Behind us, the city's rising towers shrank behind the horizon.

I switched to a virtual reality module that had me sitting driving, with Meg on the seat by my side. I grinned at her. She had been silent, unconsulted, through all that purposeful activity.

'What are we going to do, Jon?' she said.

I took one hand from the wheel and waved, taking in the illusory, grimy realism of the cab. There were cigarette-burns on the dash. 'You can really get into those seamless virtualities,' I said. 'This is better than the flesh, my darling.'

'I'll take your word for it,' she said. 'But what are we going to do?'

'We're going to drive around the planet,' I said. 'And while we're at it, we'll hack through the gates of hell.'

I told her what I meant, and she went along with it. Any woman I ever knew, and any man for that matter, would have pleaded with me to change my mind. Say what you like about succubi, they are loyal little fucks.

Night fell, and without headlights we drove on, tirelessly, and discussed how to hack the gates of hell. Overhead, the first incoming comets made dots and dashes in the sky.

We rolled around the planet more times than I care to count, and the planet rolled around its star a hundred times before the tower was built: a couple of centuries, Earth reckoning. The canals spread, other settlements grew up. The population grew; slowly, as immortal populations do. We discovered mineral deposits, fossil-beds, coal. We sold the information, and sometimes the materials. Prospectors hitched lifts, paid for in odds and ends of stores and clothes that we bartered with other travellers.

Our bank-account stayed open, and filled up. To replenish our supplies we traded indirectly, through front companies and dodgy intermediaries. We talked to robots often, people seldom. The attitudes Reid had warned us about became not just entrenched in the culture, they became its foundation stone. When it became fashionable, among the frivolously rich, to clone 'blanks' from the spare tissue-samples and equip them with robot minds, the distinction between real people and machines was only deepened.

Except among a dissident minority, who called themselves abolitionists. Some preserved the ideas of an ancient anarchist agitator, Jonathan Wilde. His memory, they assured each other, was immortal. We steered well clear of them.

Partly in reaction to the abolitionists, the ideas of 'robot rights', and of re-starting the race of the fast folk, and of raising the dead, all became connected, and rejected. Reid became eloquent in their rejection. If it was ever to be done it would be in a far future, which receded like communism once did in the minds of the Communists.

One night, while our crawler crunched along a flood-channel in the high desert, we finished the tower. We walked back up the virtual valley, to our house.

'Ready?' I asked Meg.

'Ready as we'll ever be,' she said.

I idled the crawler, and stepped into the frame.

In the last couple of centuries I'd become sensitive to the difference between a virtual body and a real one. For all its apparent solidity, for all the pleasure it could reproduce or invent, for all the realism of the pains and discomfort it sometimes felt (for consistency rules) the virtual body lacked some final, vital touch, which was nothing more than the daily millions of subtle impacts and impulses that arise from the quotidian grapple with materiality. When I experienced the *robot* body as my own, I felt far more human than I ever did in the simulation of my human flesh.

So now. The flattened oval of my metal shell was cupped in the cab, limbs retracted, cables linking it to the crawler's controls. My senses picked up the radiation from the stars, the faint infra-red of the cold and still cooling sand, the cautious stirrings and fierce encounters of the desert's remnant native, and invading alien, life.

I looked around, awaiting some revelation. The world was the same as ever. I had built a tower in my mind, from my recollections, from the bits of data I'd snatched from the decadence of the macro, and nothing had changed.

The Malley Mile – our side of it – was in its familiar place, in the depths of the sky. I looked up to where I knew it was in its orbit. On the other side, in another time, was the surface of Jupiter. The surface would have expanded by now, and the orbit would have decayed. The wormhole would encounter the planet in – I thought for a moment – a year, within an order of magnitude. It was hard to tell; too many unknowns. In any case, an order-of-magnitude approximation wasn't bad after all this time: no more than a decade, no less than a month would pass before the Malley Mile met the biggest macro of them all, the substance of the gas giant turned into the substance of mind.

It had been a grand plan, and a long plan, that I'd listened to in my last encounter with the decaying domain of the fast folk. They would slow their physical and mental processes down, almost freeze their development; and then, with literally cool deliberation, the ones who retained their rationality would excise the rest. Then, with the resources of Jupiter at their disposal, the survivors would multiply again. This time, they could wait, until their expanding domain embraced the Malley Mile: the gate to the end of time.

The shock of this understanding broke through the illusion that it was something I'd always known. I realised the tower had changed me after all. It had installed this new knowledge; of the Malley equations, of the macros' plans, and more: I knew now how to start-up a stored mind, and imprint it on a brain. I didn't have the reach, the scope, the speed of the being I'd been when I first learned them, in the macro. If I had, now, become one of the fast folk, I was running slow, in primitive hardware. But I remembered what I'd learned, and understood the peril we faced.

I stepped out of the frame, and told Meg. She had been changed, too; she understood.

'Call Reid,' she said.

We flipped the scene. Back, now, in the illusory cab, to our shared fantasy of being just a trucker and a girl hitch-hiker he'd picked up; sad, really. I mentally checked the positions of the communications satellites, then tilted the phone-screen and put a call through to Reid.

It was the most private, personal number I'd ever found for him, and still I got his secretary.

I stared at her, my mind working a lot faster than hers; as her green eyes widened, her black eyebrows narrowed in puzzlement as she looked back at us, at a strange, silent couple in a truck out on the desert. What arrogance Reid must have, what contempt for anything I might feel! By now he must be certain that I felt nothing, that virtual blood could not really chill, and simulated tears could not wet a representation of a face.

I noticed, thinking so fast that everything froze for a moment, that I had an open channel. I threw subliminal suggestions and viral subversions down that channel like a curse. Some of them hit firewalls, some got lost in transcription, and some just screwed around with Reid's electronics. But some, I was sure, got through.

Her lips just opened, just parted. I blinked, once.

'Forget it,' I said. 'Wrong number.'

We set a course for the foothills of the Madreporite Mountains, intersecting the Stone Canal. We wanted to get as close to the source as possible, where the cometary thaw was still rich in organic molecules. Every day or so another chunk of dirty ice would hurtle overhead and make a flash behind the eroded peaks.

After parking the crawler in a gorge by the canal, I went around to the back and started hauling out equipment. The growth-vat was crude, barely more than a tub with a computer and a microfactory attached. I tapped the extraction-pipes under the canal-bank, and put together my own refinery. I checked through my new knowledge of how to install a stored mind in a copy of the brain from which it had been taken. I took a small plastic slide from inside my shell, and slotted it in the machine.

Part of the clone's growth was natural, but much of it was hastened and forced by smart-matter assemblers. Even so, building a body takes time. We didn't have time to recapitulate development from an embryo: he grew full-size from the start, a skeleton taking shape and acquiring organs, muscles and skin in a grotesque reversal of the process of decay. But Meg and I observed his growth, or construction, as fondly as if he'd been a foetus in a swelling womb.

He was sleeping when, one early morning ten days later, we hauled him from the vat. We dried him, and dressed him, and carried him past the crawler, now locked and sealed and armed; out of the gorge and along the canal until, as the day warmed, he began to stir. We laid him on the bank, and waited. The sun climbed the sky.

He woke, and remembered dying.

21

Vast and Cool

I STOOD THERE in the cave, in Dee's body, and tried to think fast. It wasn't easy.

Of all the bodies I'd been in, this one was the strangest, the most alien. (And the more so because I had once known its every intricate inch.) In the robot bodies I'd had a virtual body to retreat to. Not in this. As Meg had said, there was room in this mind for us all, but with Dee's Self and selves there was no room for virtual realities. We had to time-share it, one of us in control, the others conscious but passive passengers.

Although I surely never planned, or imagined, that things would turn out this way, it was also the best body through which I could persuade Reid of what had to be done. All his conscious prejudice might be undermined by this voice that had coaxed and teased, this face that had smiled and cried, this embodiment of an obsession that had lasted beyond the death of its real object.

I had at first hoped to defeat Reid, to force him legally and by popular pressure to release the codes that could unlock the interface with the smart-matter storage of the fast folk and the dead. I'd underestimated the strength of his resistance to the very idea.

I initially rescued Dee and Ax, leaving Wilde to fend for himself, in part to hold Dee as a bargaining-chip and in part to stop the killing spree on which she and Ax had embarked. It was only when I invited Dee into my virtual reality that I learned just where Reid had stored and secreted his codes: in Dee's mind, in Stores and Secrets. That I never expected to find them there is, perhaps, a testimony to the cunning of his choice.

With these codes, and the information from the macro that Meg and I had finally interpreted, I knew I could go ahead and restart the fast folk without any co-operation from Reid, voluntary or otherwise.

And now that plan, too, was down the tubes.

So I just confessed everything.

'All right,' said Reid. 'All right. I'll grant you have an argument for starting these things up.' He gestured at the stacked crates which he'd helicoptered in, long ago, and the stacks of stuff I'd added since. By this time we were all sitting around on the crates, talking and smoking and drinking coffee. (One of the trade-goods I'd accumulated.)

'But what,' he went on, 'do we do about stopping them again?'

'Simple,' I said. I searched in Dee's handbag, with Dee's hands. I pulled out the plastic box I'd given her, and opened it. Inside were the slides for my clone and Meg's, and a sealed plastic vial of smart-matter poison.

'You had it all the time,' I said. 'Blue Goo. This shit has been sprayed on stray nanotech for decades, changing all the time. It's evolved beyond any immunity the fast folk can come up with for, oh, minutes and minutes.'

Reid laughed. '"Here's one I prepared earlier", eh? And what if their researchers are smarter than our viruses?'

'Nuke the fuckers,' I said. I looked around the cavern, vaguely. 'I've got a few kilotons lying around somewhere.'

'Bit suicidal,' Reid commented.

I gave him a severe look.

'You *do* take back-ups?'

He laughed again. 'Of course.'

'Wait a minute,' said Tamara. 'You're talking about implement- ing, what, thousands? of superhuman minds in smart matter, getting them to answer a few questions, and then *wiping them out?*'

Reid and I exchanged puzzled frowns, and at that moment I knew I'd won.

'Yes,' said Reid. 'What's wrong with that?'

There was a lot wrong with that, but we did it anyway.

The questions we set the fast folk were these:

What is the way through the Malley Mile, back to the Solar System?

The answer to that was downloaded to the on-board computer of a standard spacecraft, the kind that on New Mars they use for herding comet-fragments.

What can be done to alter the orbital position of a Malley non-exotic-matter wormhole gateway?

The answer to that was downloaded to a hasty extension of the spacecraft's on-board computer.

Is there a cure for the condition indicated in this blood-simple?

The answer to that was downloaded to a standard medical kit, and injected into Ax.

How can we recover and resurrect the minds and bodies of the stored dead?

The answer to that was downloaded to equipment which we lugged down the treacherous steps to the shore of the cometary lake.

The whole process took us the rest of that night – but then, we were all slow folk. When we had made sure we'd isolated the memory-stores, to repeat the exercise if necessary, we dropped the Blue Goo into the tanks where the fast folk lived. They didn't see it coming, and I'm sure they didn't feel anything.

'Standard computing practice,' Reid told Tamara and Ax. 'Save the source-code, and blow away the object-code.'

Meg and I departed from Dee's mind, down a fibre-optic cable under the canal, and (via various transfers that I still wake up cold thinking about) into the control module of a probe standing on a laser-launch gantry on the other side of Ship City – the same probe to which we'd downloaded the wormhole co-ordinates. Meanwhile, one of Reid's men took a helicopter across town, with a handful of molecular construction-machinery which we could, if necessary, parley into a whole manufacturing-complex. He packed it into the ship's tiny hold. We made sure our genetic information was loaded with it.

There wasn't much room in the control module for VR. We experienced through the ship's senses, but we did have an optical television link, and through it we watched the people in the cave, and by the shore. Reid and Dee and Tamara and Ax were engrossed in argument, with each other and with people in the city. That Twoday morning, Circle Square was the focus of what sometimes looked like a spill-over of its central island's wild parties, and sometimes looked like some kind of mass democracy, and now and again broke out in a riot. Various courts – Talgarth's, and others with more conventional procedures – were in session on the numerous lawsuits that had arisen from the last few days' events. One Anderson Parris (temp. dec'd.) was suing Reid for the actions of his gynoid, Dee Model.

Reid abruptly stopped arguing, and started mobilising what resources of money and charity there were in Ship City for disaster relief. New Mars had no famines, no wars, and just enough industrial accidents to sustain the need for such organisation. What they now faced was a disaster in reverse.

We cut to the cameras and remotes overlooking the shore of the cometary lake. In that dark, nutrient-rich water, the process by which we'd resurrected Wilde was repeated and multiplied, with the terrifying speed of smart-matter processing. Bodies formed, by the hundreds, then the thousands, to drift or thrust themselves towards the raw, recent shelf of the lake's beach. Dripping, coughing fluids from their new lungs, they hauled themselves blindly onto the shore and lay for a while in the sunlight. After a few minutes they'd look up at the circling aircraft, the hovering helicopters, and wonder where the hell they were.

The last we saw of Wilde he was far along the shore, searching among the naked and shivering bodies for Annette, whom he had counted, and who had counted him, among the dead.

The lasers boiled us into orbit, then our chemical rockets took over. We let the guidance-systems do the work – I rather fancied trying out my rocketry reflexes again, after all this time, but Meg talked me out of it. We talked a lot, in that long topple to the daughter wormhole: about what we might find, and what we could do if there was no-one left to warn, or able to act on a warning. The fast folk had come up with a few suggestions. Our first priority, on arriving in the Solar System, would be to find the resources of matter and energy to carry them out. The real constraint was the resource we couldn't be sure we had – time.

We fell through the wormhole gate.

What we saw almost made me flee back into it.

We emerged, as predicted, in orbit around Jupiter – a *high* orbit, which had not been been predicted. For the first time I saw the Ring from above. It was nothing to Saturn's, but it was spectacular nonetheless. Concentric white rings, divided by smaller black rings which must have been scribed over the centuries by the orbits of Jupiter's remaining moons. Jupiter itself had changed, its coloured bands now tamed, channelled into up-wellings that formed hexagonal cells, with a sketchy hint of more solid structures dividing them.

'It's like a honeycomb!' Meg whispered, behind my mind.

'Yes,' I said. 'And we don't want to meet the hive.'

Meg's reply was to magnify my forward view. A hundred kilometres ahead, along the same orbital path, was a swarm of the nastiest-looking spacecraft I've ever seen. They had a perfection of mechanism, a *finished* look to their huge articulated extensions of gleaming brass and steel. Their multiple eyes and probing antennae were turned on us. Their missiles and lasers moved into combat-ready position like unsheathed stings.

Our own antennae were instantly battered with hailing-frequencies. I felt the feathery touch of radar on my hull.

'Firewalls up?' I asked Meg.

'Yes.'

I cautiously opened an incoming video link, and sent an identifying burst of microwave to the orbital forts – or fighters – ahead.

On the video-screen in the visual centres of my mind, hazy through the protective firewalls of anti-virus software, appeared a woman's face. A young woman, with braided locks, epicanthic eyelids, broad cheekbones, coffee-coloured skin and thin lips and wide teeth ... it's hard to say just what elements went to make up the conviction, but I was certain she was of a new *race*, one different from any I'd encountered before: human, I guess is the word I'm after.

'Spayk Angloslav, robot?' she asked doubtfully.

'English?'

She smiled. 'Yays, Ehnglish. You pick it up from old transmissions, yays? Language has changed. Much has changed.'

Much has changed.

The fleet that awaited us was that of the crack Cassini Division (as they proudly call themselves) of the Solar Defence Group, seconded to the Jovian Anomaly Research Committee. Their sole mission is to guard the Malley Mile, and shoot down anything that rises off the Jovian surface. At first they thought we were aliens, or spawn of the fast folk. They were not pleased when we told them we didn't trust their transmissions either – even if their ships, unlike ours, were big enough (we grudgingly allowed) to support organic life. Eventually they swarmed out, surrounding us like space-suited South Sea islanders, pressing their face-plates to our lenses and (some of them) their tongues to the insides of their face-plates.

Meg took spectroscopic analyses of their tongues and the fog of their laughing breath, and assured me they were of human flesh and blood all right. Then it was our turn to reassure them. They interrogated us for days, and then they relented, and grew us in pods. They kept the pods isolated and at the focus of a laser-cannon battery.

I think they were more relieved than we were when we emerged in human bodies. Generations of viral radio messages from the successive civilisations of the fast folk on Jupiter have left them very cautious about electronic computers. Most of the computing in the Solar System is done on machines that Babbage would have recognised – from his wildest dreams. I have seen these calculating-machines. They fill hollowed mountains. They are powered by dams, cooled by rivers. They are used to solve millions of equations.

The Cassini Division shipped us back to Earth. The transfer orbit took long enough for Meg and I to get properly acquainted, and to become world famous. Everybody over the age of about six had a good laugh when they discovered we'd come to save them from Jupiter's mad uploaded computer whizz-kids getting to the end of time.

World fame has its disadvantages, especially in a world of thirty billion people. But it comes as something of a relief, after living on a world where the ideas I advocated were the basis of society, and my memory was immortal. In this world, they're forgotten, and I'm a footnote in old books.

So we wander the Earth, Meg and I, and we talk to people. When we tell them about Ship City, the more they understand the less they like. It seems to them not an anarchy, like they have here in the Solar system, but a divided – and hence multiplied – authority. So we don't talk much about Ship City. We talk about the desert, and we wait for these strange but somehow familiar folk to ask us, yet again, if we remember the way through the wormhole to New Mars. It is the only subject which brings envy to their eyes. I can see why. The thirty billion have refuted Malthus: everybody's rich. They've refuted Mises: nobody's paid. They've refuted Freud: nobody's sad.

But it's kind of crowded.

The probe continues on its near-lightspeed path; the information it sends back is always new, always unexpected. But the most profound datum, to me, was one that came through quite early in its course: the Hubble expansion is local. The probe has gone beyond it, into other, expanding or contracting, regions of space. There was a Big Bang, but it was not the beginning, for there was none. No heat death, no Big Crunch awaits us. These dooms (it now is said) for all their shining mathematical elaborations, were but reflections of a society facing its limits.

There is no end.

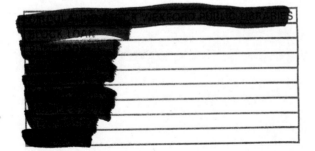